'A must-read for fans of Megan Abbott, and fans of TV shows like *Broadchurch*. Very highly recommended, this is an addictive, must-read. Excellent. I can't wait for Pinborough's next novel'

Civilian Reader

'*13 Minutes* is another fantastic demonstration of Sarah Pinborough's gifts for telling an enthralling tale. 9/10'

Sci-Fi Bulletin

'The ending was typically haunting and overall this was, well, just damn terrific. One of my favourites of the year'

Liz Loves Books

'For a wonderful, absorbing crime thriller set against the backdrop of teenage menace and melodrama, you need not look further'

Words and Wormholes

'This is an exceptional, contemporary, thought provoking thriller from an award-winning novelist'

Rising Shadow

'*13 Minutes* is a carefully crafted thriller which is utterly absorbing and makes you think twice about the teenagers in your life'

Books by Proxy

'Overall *13 Minutes* is an unmissable read for lovers of gritty, thrilling YA fiction'

Jess Loves Books

Also by Sarah Pinborough from Gollancz:

A Matter of Blood
The Shadow of the Soul
The Chosen Seed

Poison
Charm
Beauty

The Death House

As Sarah Silverwood:
The Double-Edged Sword
The Traitor's Gate
The London Stone

13 MINUTES

SARAH PINBOROUGH

First published in Great Britain in 2016 by Gollancz
an imprint of The Orion Publishing Group Ltd
Carmelite House, 50 Victoria Embankment
London EC4Y 0DZ

An Hachette UK Company

13

A CIP catalogue record for this book is
available from the British Library.

ISBN 978 0 575 09737 7

Printed in Great Britain by Clays Ltd, St Ives plc

www.sarahpinborough.com
www.orionbooks.co.uk
www.gollancz.co.uk

For Baria,
Gonzo to my Duke
and Pats/Eds to my Eds/Pats,
with much love.

Part One

One

Ophelia.

She was young. No more than eighteen. Probably less. Her hair could be blonde or brown, it was hard to tell, soaked wet in the gloom. She was wearing white, bright against the dark river, almost an accent to the fresh snow that lay heavy on the ground. Her pale face, blue lips slightly parted, was turned up to the inky sky. She was snagged on twigs as if the bent branches, bare of leaves and broken by winter, had grasped to save her, to keep her afloat.

His breath steamed a harsh mist.

He could hear his chest wheezing loud, although Biscuit's frantic barking, the alarm that had brought him from the path to the bank, seemed to be coming from somewhere far away. He couldn't move. It was five forty-five in the morning and there was a dead girl in the river.

I am a cliché, was his next coherent thought. *I am the early-morning dog-walker who finds a body.*

Biscuit ran in small darts up and down the dirty snow at the water's edge; furious, eager, disturbed by this change to their daily routine. By this *wrong*. The dog turned and whined at his owner, but still the man couldn't stop staring, fingers gripping the phone tucked deep in the pocket of his thick coat.

And then he saw it. Just the slightest twitch of her hand. Then, moments after, another.

He walked Biscuit early not out of necessity but because of the quiet. Because time moved more slowly in the hours before the world woke up. It was perfectly peaceful and sleep had never been his friend, anyway.

The later walk was for polite chats with other owners as the dogs raced through the woods and parkland. The mornings were his own. It was his routine, clockwork, never broken for the weather, only rarely for illness. Rise at five, even if he hadn't finished recording until two a.m. One coffee. Leave at five-twenty on the dot. This morning, however, they had been a rare five minutes late. Biscuit had hidden his collar, finally found under the sofa. Then across the meadow and past the meandering river, an hour or so in the woods, and after that he'd fetch the papers on the way home to read over breakfast. If they were ready, he'd have a warm croissant from the bakery, too. This time was sacred and belonged to only him and Biscuit; extra hours of precious life. Sometimes he called his little sister in New York – catching her before she went to sleep and checking that her world was still turning in the right direction – and they would have a bitter-sweet moment before the river of her own life reclaimed her and swept her away from him. Some mornings she surprised him by being the one to call, and those were the best.

The marbling hand twitched again and suddenly he felt the cold on his skin and his heart beating and could hear Biscuit's bark loud and clear and then the phone was at his ear and his voice added to the clamour. When he was done, he threw the phone down and pulled off his coat. The river would not claim this girl before her time.

*

The rest was a blur. The cold water on his legs that knocked the air from his lungs with the shock of it. Slipping. Almost submerged. Gasping. Numb fingers pulling her to the bank. The heaviness of her soaked clothes, the unexpected heaviness of his. Wrapping his coat around her limp body. The crispness of her soaked hair. No warm breath from her mouth. Talking to her through chattering teeth. Biscuit licking her frozen face. The sirens. The blanket wrapped round him. *Come with me, please, Mr McMahon, that's right, I'll help you. It's okay, we'll take it from here.* Pulled up onto legs that wouldn't quite work and led to the ambulance. But not before he saw the grim faces. The shake of a head. The defibrillator.

Clear!

The dreadful quiet as they worked. Him, the world, nature: all frozen. But not time. Time had ticked on. How many minutes? How long had they sat on the bank with her not breathing? How long before the ambulance arrived? Ten minutes? More? Less?

I've got a pulse! I've got a pulse!

And then his tears, hot and sudden, bursting up from deep inside.

Biscuit, beside him, pushed his stinking damp fur closer, paws scratching at his face, tongue on his cheeks, licking, snuffling and whining. He wrapped his arm around the dog, pulled him under the blanket and then looked up at the winter sky which was neither truly night nor morning and thought he'd never loved it more.

Two

Saturday, 09.03

Jenny

ur not picking up. Pick Up! OMFG.

09.08

Jenny

ur fone on silent? WAKE UP!

09.13

Jenny

I'm freaking out. My mum is crying. Think she's still drunk. Wants to go to the hospital. WTF??

09.15

Jenny

FUCKING PICK UP!!!!!
WTF is going on?

09.17

Hayley

Soz dad was in here!!! Woke me up. I'm fucking shaking. WTFWTFWTF??

Will call from shower. Delete txts.
Yesterdays 2. FUCK??

09.18
Jenny
K.

09.19
Hayley
DON'T SAY ANYTHING.

Three

'Rebecca!'

Her mum's voice, loud and demanding, was a thorn in the meat of Becca's brain, and she pulled the duvet over her head to block it out and sink back into her half-sleep. It was Saturday. It was too early. *Whatever* time it was, it was too early. It was also cold. Her toes felt like ice and a draught was creeping through the gaps between the covers. She hooked them closer with her foot, cocooning herself.

'Rebecca! Come down! It's important!'

She didn't move. Whatever it was, it could wait. Five more minutes at least. She breathed shallow, not wanting to come up for air. Her hair stank of smoke and her head ached slightly, a parting gift from last night's weed and tobacco. If it was before midday she was going to kill her mum. Saturdays were hers. That was their deal.

'Now! I mean it!'

She pushed the covers off and sat up, angry. What the hell was so pressing? She scanned her bleary memory. No late-night snacking so no pizza boxes or Coke cans abandoned in the kitchen. No TV left on. She'd double-bolted the door. All she'd done was come home, go quietly to her room and smoke one last joint through the window before passing out in front of some shit comedy on Netflix. She wasn't even home *late*. She glanced at the open window and sighed. *Good work, Bex. No wonder it's like Antarctica in here.* At least there was no trace of stale smoke in the air.

'Becca!' A pause. 'Please, darling!'

'Coming!' she shouted back, voice like gravel, head pounding with the effort. No more straight cigarettes, she thought, tugging on her joggers and pulling last night's sweatshirt over her head. Her chest felt like shit. Her room was ice-box cold and goosebumps shivered across her skin. Juice. She needed juice. And a cup of tea. And a bacon sandwich. Maybe going downstairs wasn't such a bad idea. At least it would be warm. But still, conversation with her mother first thing in the morning was not what she needed *ever*. She preferred to get up when they were all out. Have some quiet time that didn't require locking herself away in her room. Two more years and then she could escape to university. Out of this house, out of this suffocating town, and onward to freedom. London, maybe. A big city, definitely. Somewhere Aiden could come with her and work on his music career.

They would live like bohemians and eventually, one day, magazines would write stories about the successful couple who once lived on Ramen noodles in a run-down (but still cool) grimy flat somewhere while they followed their dreams. That's how it would be. But there were still two *long* years to get through before that would be anything more than a stoned fantasy.

She scraped her hair back into a semblance of a ponytail, sprayed it with deodorant and shuffled out of her sanctuary, grabbing her phone from the side of her bed. She pressed the home button for the time. Ten thirty-four.

Fourteen iMessages, six WhatsApps and two missed calls. She frowned, confused by the list of names appearing. She wasn't that popular. She never woke up to fourteen texts, unless they were from Aiden when he was high and horny. She scrolled through as she headed downstairs. Mainly group texts. That figured. She was a social add-on. She didn't let the tiny needles sting. Like she gave a shit.

U heard the news?

Seen about Tasha Howland?

Crazy shit on the news!
U gotta see!

By the time she'd read them all and reached the kitchen she was wide awake. Her mouth was dry.

Her mother was standing at the kitchen island watching the small TV in the corner – the one her dad had fought so hard to stop them getting – *too many TVs, too many computers, too many phones, everything's technology, nobody talks any more* – but had lost the battle, two to one. There was toast on a plate in front of her but she wasn't eating it. She didn't even look around, just stared, pale-faced, at the screen.

Becca's skin tingled, part apprehension, part strange thrill.

'What's happened to Tasha?' she asked. 'My phone's gone mad.'

Her mum turned then, wrapping herself around Becca's stiff frame, bathing her in the warm scent of foundation and citrus perfume. Even on a Saturday Julia Crisp made an effort. Her thin arms were all sinew and muscle beneath her cashmere sweater, and Becca instantly felt like the fat kid she'd once been all over again. *Like mother, like daughter* was not an adage that fitted them.

'It's terrible. She's in a coma. It's all over the news.' Her mother's hand stroked her back but Becca pulled away, pretending to get a better view of the TV. Her mum made her feel uncomfortable. The teenage years had drawn lines between them that neither knew how to cross.

'I'm sure she'll be fine, darling. I'm sure she will.'

'Was it a car accident?' *Natasha in a coma?* It couldn't be real. Shit like that didn't happen to girls like Natasha. It happened to girls like Becca.

She pulled up a stool and sat and watched, ignoring the buzz of her phone and her mother's bird-flutterings of care around her. Up onscreen Hayley and Jenny, red-eyed and yet still so perfect, hurried into the hospital, their parents clinging to them like dry autumn leaves to wool. The other two Barbies. Of course they were there. Rushing to their beloved leader's side.

'I know you two used to be close, darling, do you want to—'

'Shh.' She silenced her mother without even a glance as the reporter, nose red in the blistering cold, pushed back the hair blowing into her face and spoke into the microphone with that insincere sincerity only TV journalists had.

*

An hour later, Becca was standing on the small balcony at Aiden's flat, shivering alongside him as he sparked up a Marlboro Light. He held out the packet and she took one, her resolve of first thing gone. Fuck it. Anyway, it was too early for a joint, and even in the relaxed sloppy atmosphere of Aiden's mum's place, obvious drugs were a no-go. She might suspect he toked – she must be able to smell it coming out of his bedroom – but she was a long way from condoning it.

'They said she was dead for thirteen minutes.' Becca shuffled from foot to foot to ward off the icy air while they smoked. 'They're calling it a miracle that they revived her.'

'She's lucky it got so cold.' Aiden stared out over the snow that had fallen heavy since dawn. Becca thought he looked almost angelic against the white and grey that coated the world. Maybe not an angel as others thought of them, but her angel all the same. Pale face, sharp features, thick dark hair and those clear eyes that shone bright blue from under his long fringe. An angel or a vampire. Either way, she still sometimes had to pinch herself to believe he was hers.

'That's probably what saved her,' he said. 'The water would have been freezing – dropped her temperature so fast it put her heartbeat into some kind of survival mode.'

'How do you know this stuff?' Becca asked.

He grinned, sheepish. 'Saw it on some old underwater alien film.'

'It's weird, though, huh? To be dead and then not dead,' Becca said. 'Thirteen minutes is a long time.'

'Wonder if she saw anything. You know – bright lights, that sort of shit.'

'Knowing Natasha, even if she didn't she'll say she did when she wakes up.' It was a sharp comment but she couldn't help it. Her feelings about Natasha were a ball of wire she couldn't untangle. She missed her old childhood friend, but she didn't know the new *Barbie* Natasha. Her Natasha had braces and liked Chess Club. Her Natasha had been her Best

Friend Forever. Becca hadn't realised at the time that *forever* would only last until Natasha's tits grew and her braces came off and suddenly she was hot and Becca was a dumpy geek who got swiftly discarded.

'*If* she wakes up,' Aiden said, exhaling a long cloud of smoke. 'The news said she was unconscious. She might have brain damage or something.'

Becca tried to imagine that. She'd seen images of brain-damaged people on TV and they never looked quite the same as they did before. Natasha dying would at least be beautifully tragic. Natasha brain-damaged and hooked up to machines that let her shit and piss while she dribbled into soup for the rest of her life was horrifying.

'What was she doing out there, anyway?' Aiden asked. 'In the woods at night? You reckon someone took her?'

'Fucked if I know.' Becca shrugged. 'No one else seems to, either. Everyone's too busy being hysterical over it to say anything useful.' The hive, as she thought of their school sometimes, had been buzzing since the news broke. Texts, WhatsApp, Instagram pictures of Natasha's beautiful smiling face, tweets of everyone's shock and upset, the whole school proclaiming how much they loved her, as if somehow a part of what had happened to her could be theirs, too. #TashaForeva was probably trending by now. The hum from it was electric. It fizzed under her skin.

Becca had not uploaded any old photos to her Instagram account, or to her Facebook or Twitter. Partly, she'd not had time. More honestly, she didn't have that many followers, and, finally, because of the round of *Did you see what Becca Crisp posted? Clinging to the glory days!* texts behind her back that would no doubt follow.

And although she'd hated Tasha for a while, when she'd so unceremoniously dumped Becca and replaced her with Jenny, the new trio all Barbie-doll perfect, that shit had been a long time ago and there was nothing Tasha would hate more than for the world to be reminded of her bad hair and bad teeth of childhood. Even now, Becca wouldn't do that to her.

'There was that girl went missing over in Maypoole a couple of months ago,' Aiden said. 'Maybe it's the same guy.'

'She probably just ran away.' Becca threw the cigarette stub into the mug on the table to join the others rotting in the inch of thick brown water at the bottom. Her mouth was dry and her feet freezing. She sniffed.

'Shall we go inside? Watch a movie?'

Aiden looked at her, thoughtful, and the hairs on the back of her neck prickled slightly under his scrutiny. 'Don't you want to go to the hospital?' he said.

'Why?' She smarted suddenly. 'Do you? Feeling the need to check on the damsel in distress?'

He laughed at that, and then pulled her close. 'God, you're a dick. I asked her out *once*. Nearly two years ago. Before I had better taste.'

She breathed in the leather smell of his jacket. He was hers. She knew it. There was nothing worse than sounding needy; there was nothing worse than *being* needy. Why hadn't she kept her mouth shut?

'I know.' She exhaled hot air onto her own trapped face. He stepped away from her.

'*And* she was a complete bitch about it. I don't give a shit about Natasha Howland. But she was your best friend for years. You should go. For her parents if nothing else.'

It was almost exactly what her mother had said before Becca

had grabbed her coat and said she was going out. Somehow it sounded more reasonable coming from Aiden.

'Okay,' she said, eventually. Reluctantly. 'Okay, maybe we should go.' She looked up at him and kissed his cigarette-stale mouth with her own. 'But can we stop at McDonald's on the way? I'm starving.'

He grinned. 'That's why you're my girl. All class.' His phone buzzed and he checked it, frowning as he read the text. 'Man, that's weird.'

'What?'

'I've got to go to the hospital, too. But have to stop and pick up some stuff first. It's Jamie. He's there too.'

Four

It was odd seeing Natasha's mother, Alison Howland, so fragile and weepy, and somehow Becca found herself crying too, hot, wet sobs that sprang out of nowhere and hurt her chest. Gary Howland stood between them, one hand awkwardly on their backs, unsure of his place in this sea of feminine emotion. His jaw was tight and his eyes slightly too wide, but other than that and the stiffness in his spine, it was hard to tell if he was feeling anything at all. But then Becca had never really known him. He'd come in and out and gone to his office or the tennis club and smiled at them as they played while his mind was clearly elsewhere. Becca guessed that was how you became rich and successful. He wasn't one of those dads who got involved. Natasha was no doubt endlessly grateful for that.

'It's so kind of you to come, Rebecca,' Alison said, wiping away snotty tears. Always Rebecca with Mrs Howland, never Becca or Bex, just like Tasha was always Natasha. 'You're a good girl. You were a good friend to Natasha.' *Were*. Becca said nothing to that, just gave a vague nod. Alison was as aware as anyone that Becca was no longer part of the inner circle. The inner circle were standing to one side, their carefully made-up eyes delicately bleary, both checking their phones. Hayley and Jenny. Almost identical and yet so different.

Where Jenny was sensual soft and estate chic, Hayley was middle-class athletic. A hard body. She didn't climb trees any more, but when she abandoned her tomboy ways she hadn't given up sport. She was the fastest runner in the school. Never caught without lip gloss. And always with the shortest shorts no matter how many times she was told to change them. The two girls didn't look at Becca and she turned her attention back to Alison Howland.

'I just . . . I just wanted to show my support,' Becca said eventually. 'My mum sends her love, too.' That was middle-ground enough. 'I'm sure Tasha'll be fine. I'm sure of it.'

'I don't understand what she was doing there.' Alison's gaze had drifted somewhere past Becca, into her own personal nightmare, but her hands gripped Becca's like she was an anchor, the only thing stopping Alison from being dragged away completely. Her palms were dry and rough, as if all the moisture in her body had been cried out. 'I mean, why was she even there at that time? In this weather?' There was something in her tone, and the lack of response from Hayley, Jenny or Gary, that made Becca think these were questions Natasha's mother had asked aloud over and over during the past few hours.

Becca started to feel claustrophobic in the tight atmosphere of the small hospital relatives' room. The lights were suddenly too bright and the air too hot and thin. Her skin prickled with sweat under her heavy quilted coat. She didn't belong here.

Just when she thought she might have to break away from Alison Howland's grip and sit down for a moment, the door opened. Alison's head swivelled fast and then her shoulders drooped. It wasn't a doctor.

'Detective Inspector Bennett, is there anything—' Gary

started but the inspector shook her head.

'No,' she said. 'I'd just like to have a word with the girls.' DI Bennett had no make-up on and her hair was scraped back in a no-nonsense ponytail. She looked tired as she gave Alison a soft smile. 'See if we can piece together Natasha's movements. The doctors say you can go in and sit with her for a while if you'd like.'

'Thank you,' Gary said, one hand on his wife's elbow.

The DI held the door open and Natasha's parents hurried out, Alison in tears again. It was horrible, Becca concluded. Bright and clinical and real and yet not-real. Natasha was here somewhere fighting for her life. Natasha. Unbreakable, perfect Natasha.

'Shall I wait outside?' Becca asked.

'Are you a friend of Natasha's?'

Becca wasn't sure how to answer that honestly. 'Kind of. I used to be, anyway. We go to the same school but we haven't been close for a few years.' She glanced at the two blondes. 'Hayley and Jenny are her best friends.' Hayley dropped her eyes. Hayley who used to throw herself from tree branch to tree branch until Tasha and Becca were shrieking with fear and giggles that she might fall. Hayley who had faltered slightly when Natasha closed ranks against Becca. Sneaking round for tea once or twice, but then choosing her side and sticking to it. The winning side. The cool side. *Natasha's* side. Yeah, Hayley could go fuck herself.

The policewoman looked from the two Barbies to Becca and back again, mentally piecing the story together. It wasn't exactly unusual. Dull friend gets dumped for more popular, prettier friends. Given Inspector Bennett's scruffy appearance – *how old was she? Thirties? Less? Old, anyway* – maybe she'd been on the receiving end of similar treatment when she was at school.

'You may as well stay,' the woman said. 'This isn't a formal interview. And you might have a different perspective.'

Oh, yeah, Becca thought. *I bet I do.*

'What do you think happened?' Jenny asked.

'We're not sure. It might have just been an accident. A prank gone wrong.'

'Did someone hurt her?' Hayley's eyes were wide. 'Gary said you'd told them that she wasn't . . . no one had . . .'

'She wasn't raped, no.' Inspector Bennett's direct answer startled Becca away from her inner sneer at the way Hayley had said *Gary*. So faux-adult. She hadn't even thought about rape until now. Which was crazy because often it was all anyone *did* talk about, even if it was only an undercurrent. Don't drink too much because something could happen. Don't wear that, you'll send the wrong signals. Always walk home with a friend or get a taxi. Don't lead anyone on. Blah blah blah. At least since she'd been with Aiden her mother had stopped with those kind of comments. As if now that Becca had a boyfriend she had someone to protect her. She wondered if her mum realised how shitty that was.

'We need to figure out what Natasha was doing last night and during the early hours of this morning.' The policewoman sat down and, like sheep, the three girls followed suit. 'There's no blame here, no one's going to get in any trouble, but if she was attacked, then it's vital we have as much information as possible.'

'Is she hurt, then?' Becca asked. 'I mean, other than . . .' She trailed off. *Other than having been dead for thirteen minutes.*

'A few cuts and bruises, but they could have come from

being in the river. As I said, we really don't know if this was an accident or intentional, or an incident involving someone else.'

Intentional. The word, one that didn't quite fit, clunked around in Becca's brain trying to make sense of itself. Jenny, surprisingly, got there first, barking out a harsh laugh at odds with the solemnity of the room.

'You think Tash might have tried to kill herself?'

'We're exploring all avenues.'

'No,' Jenny said, shaking her head, adamant. Her hair wasn't quite as long or perfectly straight as Hayley's, and she tucked a stray curl behind one delicate pierced ear. The stud was cheap glass, not diamond. The Cinderella Barbie from the wrong side of town.

'No, Natasha wouldn't do that. And not *that* way. Not by throwing herself into a freezing river.'

'No,' Hayley added, as if the two nos weren't emphatic enough.

DI Bennett turned to Becca. She shrugged, hesitant. There was more going on for her here than just the police investigation. Becca had to choose her words carefully. She didn't want to piss the Barbies off or look as if she was sucking up to them. Especially not to Hayley. Hayley had been her friend – she knew how to get under Becca's skin in a way Jenny couldn't. Jenny was nothing. But whatever Becca said now might come back on her in bitchy subtweets and status updates and knowing looks. Words ran like strung barbed wire around the teenage community of this small town, ready to scratch and tear and snag you.

'I don't think so.' It was the truth. If Tasha was going to kill herself she would choose something far more romantic. And Natasha was not the killing-herself type. 'People bloat when they drown, don't they?' she said. 'If she hadn't been found quickly, she'd have looked like shit. She wouldn't have liked that.'

Hayley's face hardened. *Bitch. Fucking bitch.* Becca could see her thoughts loud and clear in the green flint of her glare. She stared back. So what? It was exactly what Jenny had meant. It was what Hayley had been thinking. Becca wanted to laugh at them. Even with their leader unconscious they couldn't bear a word spoken against her. They were pathetic.

'So, when did you last see Natasha?' Inspector Bennett didn't look at Becca for that one.

'At school,' Hayley said and Jenny nodded. 'We talked about meeting up tonight, maybe, but she had a family thing today – her gran's birthday or something – so it depended when that finished.'

'And you didn't text her or talk to her after that?' The inspector half-smiled. 'I thought you were all glued to your phones these days.'

It was disarming, but probing.

Jenny shook her head. 'No.'

'Did you two go out last night?'

More head-shakes. 'The weather was rubbish. And we both had homework.' Hayley was taking the lead – Natasha's deputy stepping up to the plate. 'Got to keep the parents happy sometimes.' She smiled, all cat angles in her face. 'And we both – and Natasha – had stuff to work on for the auditions for the school play. We're doing *The Crucible*. It should be amazing.'

'So you didn't hear from Natasha at all?'

'No.'

Becca, almost forgotten, noted the repeated question. 'Don't you have her phone?' she asked. 'Can't you tell who she spoke to?'

The policewoman looked her way, evaluating her. 'It's water-damaged – it was in her pocket. We're waiting for her phone records to come in.' She paused. 'I take it you didn't see her at all? Did you stay at home as well?'

Becca shook her head. The policewoman's tone was light but Becca could feel herself flushing at the question, as if maybe she was guilty, maybe she had pushed Natasha into the freezing water and left her there to die.

'I went to my boyfriend's house and then back home around midnight. He dropped me off and I went to bed. Ask him if you want – he's here somewhere. We had to bring Mr McMahon some clothes in.'

Her eyes narrowed. 'Jamie McMahon?'

Becca nodded. 'Aiden works with him. Plays some guitar and bass when Jamie's doing soundtracks.'

'Who?' Hayley asked. Becca felt a shiver of elation. She had something the Barbies didn't. An *involvement* with this they couldn't claim.

'The man who pulled Natasha out of the river,' Inspector Bennett said, without looking at Hayley. 'How does Mr McMahon know a schoolboy?'

'Aiden's not at school,' Becca said. 'He's nineteen. Mr McMahon was his private music teacher when he was a kid.'

'It's a small town, I guess,' the woman said, flashing that half-smile of hers again.

'Too small,' Becca said, trying to return one of her own. She felt uncomfortable again, which was just stupid. She hadn't done anything wrong.

'So Natasha was happy as far as you know?'

They all nodded.

'Does she have a boyfriend?'

'Nothing serious,' Hayley said. 'Boys like Natasha but there's no one she's really interested in. And no one was creeping her out or anything. She'd have said.'

'Does she sneak out of the house often?' She watched them all then, as if the other questions had merely been fluff to gently rest this one on. A pregnant pause followed as Hayley and Jenny considered how honest to be.

'Sometimes. Not often,' Hayley answered. 'Her parents are really lax, to be honest. They let her do pretty much what she wants, but if she did sneak out late, she'd go through her bedroom window and climb down the tree at the back. It still has a rope ladder on it from when she was a kid.'

'Her parents might want to consider taking that down,' Bennett said dryly.

She asked a few more questions, anodyne stuff about school and other friends who might be useful, and then, apparently satisfied, left.

Even though there was one less person in the room, it suddenly felt a lot smaller to Becca, just her and Hayley and Jenny, awkward in each other's company. Well, *she* felt awkward. It probably wasn't the same for the other two, their bodies turned towards each other slightly, squeezing Becca out, as if she was a stranger.

'Maybe we should bring some of her stuff,' Jenny said quietly, looking to Hayley for approval, her face tight, teeth nibbling at one perfectly painted fingernail. 'You know, music and shit from her bedroom. It might help wake her up.'

Hayley nodded. 'I'll ask Gary for the house keys. It'll be

good to get out of here for an hour or so – we must be starting to stink of disinfectant.'

'You should probably check with that detective first,' Becca said. 'She might not want anyone touching Tasha's things.'

Hayley glanced at Becca, irritated that she was still there. 'Your hair looks like it could use some medicated shampoo, Bex. You should ask one of the nurses for a bottle.'

'Maybe you should get something for your crabs,' Becca snapped back. The three girls stared at each other, contempt and a thousand social differences hanging in the air, no need for feigned politeness now the policewoman had gone.

'God, you're gross,' Jenny said.

'Just like her boyfriend.' Hayley didn't even look at Becca as she headed to the door. 'Barrel-scraping.'

'Just so long as they don't breed.'

Becca looked down at her phone and pretended to scroll through it until they were gone, her stomach twisting slightly. She hadn't cared what they thought of her for a long time – why should she start now? Pretentious, prissy bitches, that's all they were. So was Natasha. Why had she even come here? And where was Aiden? As if reading her mind, her phone pinged. *Taking Jamie home. Will come back for you. Hour maybe? Sorry x*

Fucking great. At least the Barbies were gone.

She flicked a quick *okay* back at Aiden, trying not to sound irritated even though she was, and then went in search of a drinks machine. Her mouth was still dry from last night and the waiting room was too warm.

*

She was scouring her coat pockets for change when Gary Howland found her.

'Rebecca. Let me. I was going to get a coffee anyway.'

'Thanks.' He looked tired and his sweater was crumpled, no doubt pulled on fast when his world collapsed early that morning. She felt sorry for him. The Howlands, from Natasha upwards, lived charmed lives from what Becca could see. Until this, anyway. It must have come as a shock.

'What do you want?' he asked.

'Diet Coke, please.'

He pressed the buttons and the bottle hit the tray loudly.

'Is Mrs Howland okay?' she asked. A stupid question but she didn't know what else to say. In all her years as Tasha's best friend, this was maybe the first time she'd ever been alone with Gary Howland. It was Alison who'd fed them and picked them up from school and brought them juice and biscuits. Gary was just a *dad*.

'She'll be fine when Natasha wakes up,' he said. The machine whirred as it filled a cup with watery coffee and powdered milk. The possibility that Natasha might not wake up was one her father was clearly not considering. 'But I don't think her crying by the bedside is helping Natasha.' He looked at Becca and for the first time she realised he was actually a pretty handsome man. Not grungy enough for her and obviously way too old, but good-looking anyway. Not in his uniform suit and tie he looked younger, somehow.

'Would you like me to go in and talk to her for a bit?' The words were out before she could stop herself, sucked from her brain in response to a sudden wave of pity for her ex-best friend's father. 'I've got some time.'

'Would you?' The gratitude that radiated from him landed

heavily on her shoulders and she cursed herself. She should have just texted her mum for a lift. She should have gone downstairs and waited for Aiden in the freezing cold. What the hell was she going to talk to Natasha *about*?

'Of course,' she said. 'I love Tasha, too.' Her face prickled with the lie.

Five

It's so cold, it's so cold I can't breathe and I panic hard in the water that's like shards of glass, and for the first time I think I might be in serious trouble. That I might end here. My white joggers and sweatshirt are so heavy in the freezing river. My lungs are raw and ice-scalded as I try to take shallow breaths, desperately keeping my chin above the water, but nothing is working, not my lungs, my limbs or my brain. The cold is overwhelming. It burns through my veins like fire. If I can just reach the branches I might be able to pull myself to the bank, if I can just stop myself from going under – and what time is it, what time is it – and oh fuck I can't feel my hands. The thin twigs are scalpels on my dying blue skin this is a terrible mistake and what the fuck time is it and . . .

. . . I suck in a deep breath, tearing pain through my lungs again, but the air is warm and sweet and there's no freezing water choking me.

'Natasha?'

'Oh my god, Natasha!'

'Tasha?'

'Get a doctor!'

My mother's face looms over me and my instinct is to swat her away. She's too close. I'm too confused. I'm still trying to breathe. My heart is racing. I don't know quite where I am. I blink and blink and blink. It's hot and bright and dry. Hayley and Jenny are in the room. I can hear their shrieks as a nurse pulls them back so she can get close to me.

I'm alive, I think, and then comes the flood of relief. *I'm alive. This is the hospital.*

I move my mouth but no words come out. My throat is dry and hoarse. There is a drip in my arm. How long have I been here? What day is it? My head throbs.

Too much activity around me. I try to turn my head sideways to look over to the door where more people are hurrying in. The bones and muscles in my neck scream at me. I see blonde hair spread over the pillow and it surprises my confused brain. My hair is dark. This is not my hair. No, my hair *was* dark. I dyed it to be like my friends. Blondes together. Interchangeable.

Everyone is talking, or so it seems. A stream of loud noise. I realise there's also familiar music playing, an iPod plugged into a speaker somewhere. Is it mine? Who brought it here? How long have I been here? Talking and noise. Talking and noise. It's all too much. Hard to focus. Suddenly I think of Becca.

'Was Becca here?' I ask. The voice, all sandpaper-rough, doesn't sound like mine. More like some possessed girl in a horror film. I guess it must shock everyone else, too, as silence answers my question. The room settles into some strange calm, blissfully quiet, as they all stare at me.

'Was Becca here?' I ask again.

'Yes,' my mother says. Her hand is tight around mine, papery dry and desperate. 'Yes, she came in yesterday and talked to you.'

'I thought so.' I smile and close my eyes.

Six

Excerpt of **CONSULTATION BETWEEN DR ANNABEL HARVEY AND PATIENT NATASHA HOWLAND, MONDAY 11/01, 09.00**

NATASHA: It feels weird. You'd feel weird, wouldn't you? I mean, to have been dead like that. I mean, I guess I must not have been properly dead, otherwise I wouldn't be here now.

(Small laugh)

But to think my heart wasn't beating for almost a quarter of a school lesson, when I think about it like that . . . yeah, it freaks me out. You know, if that guy walking his dog had been two or three minutes later or whatever, what would have happened then? It's all bad stuff to have in your head. But I feel fine now. I mean, it's not like I saw a tunnel or bright lights or any of that stuff. Nothing I can remember.

(Small laugh)

But then my memory isn't working right, is it?

DR HARVEY: How much anxiety is that causing you? The loss of memory?

NATASHA: I think that makes me feel stranger than the being-dead thing. I remember going for lunch on Thursday lunchtime. That's it. I don't remember what I did that evening. I don't remember any of Friday or Friday night. It's like that whole time just didn't happen. When I woke up last night, I had a vague memory of being in freezing water and panicking that I was dying. Apart from that, nothing.

DR HARVEY: The flash of memory you had about being in the water – how do you feel in it? Aside from the fear of the water. Are you aware of anyone else?

NATASHA: Like an attacker or something?

DR HARVEY: Try not to apply a label in your mind. Just think about the memory.

NATASHA: I remember being in the water and trying to reach the bank. I don't know if there was anyone else around. It's just a momentary memory . . . kind of like the end of a dream when you wake up. You know? Like you remember it, but it's just tiny images of something. I don't know if I'm remembering the memory or what I remember of the memory.

(Small laugh)

That sounds crazy but you know what I mean?

DR HARVEY: Why do you think you've lost those hours of your memory?

NATASHA: I don't know. We're just machines, aren't we? I was dead for thirteen minutes. That must mess up the wiring.

DR HARVEY: So there was nothing concerning you? That you remember?

NATASHA: You sound like DI Bennett. Same questions. Didn't she show you her report?

DR HARVEY: Yes, she did, but I'd rather hear it from you so I can make a better assessment of how to help you. I'm sorry if I'm making you repeat yourself.

(Pause)

NATASHA: I'm sorry. I know you're only trying to help. I'm just . . . Anyway, I was fine. Pissed off to be back at school after the holidays, but even that wasn't so bad, not really. It can be a drag being around my mum too long. She always wants to do stuff together, which is sort of sweet but she can be too much. I'm not a baby any more.

DR HARVEY: Is that why you sneaked out through the window?

NATASHA: I don't know if I did sneak out. I guess if my parents say I told them I was going to bed then I must have done.

DR HARVEY: The front door was locked and bolted on the inside.

NATASHA: Then I must have gone out through my window.

(Small laugh, nervous)

You know more about what I did than I do. I don't know why I went out. I wish I did, but I don't.

DR HARVEY: What about the text you received that night?

NATASHA: I don't know. I don't know the number. It's not answering when the police ring or text it, apparently. Goes straight to voicemail like it's switched off. I think that police detective said it was a pay-as-you-go phone. Most of my friends have contracts. Our parents pay for them. No one's had pay-as-you-go for ages.

DR HARVEY: Does it bother you?

NATASHA: Does what bother me?

DR HARVEY: That you don't know who sent the text. That the police don't know who sent it.

NATASHA: Should it bother me? I don't know. It's probably just some random guy I gave my number to when I was drunk.

DR HARVEY: Does that happen often?

NATASHA: Being drunk or giving my number away?

(Pause)

What's often, anyway? Sometimes I give my number out. Sometimes my friends do it as a joke.

DR HARVEY: The text told you to meet that night at three a.m., in the usual place. And then, in the middle of the night, you went out.

NATASHA: I know, but the two things might not have been related. I didn't answer the text, did I? Not according to what Inspector Bennett said. I bet that text wasn't even meant for me. Could have been a wrong number. How can I have a usual place with someone I don't know? I don't have 'usual places' with people I *do* know. Not even—

(Pause. Slight hiccup of hesitation)

Not even with my closest friends.

DR HARVEY: Are you all right? Did you remember something?

NATASHA: Yes. I mean yes I'm all right, no I didn't remember something. Sorry. Just tired.

(Shuffling in chair)

Look, I'm sure this will all come back to me and it'll be nothing. I was probably just stupid and went out because I was bored and fell in the river in the dark. Maybe that wrong-number text got in my subconscious and made me think about going out. We don't even know what time I left the house. Probably after the time in that text. I don't know. Maybe I'll remember, but right now I don't know.

DR HARVEY: I have something for you.

(A pause)

NATASHA: What's this for?

DR HARVEY: I want you to keep a diary. Your thoughts, feelings. Events. It can often help patients with memory problems. You don't have to show it to me.

NATASHA: Which means I don't have to write it. I just want to go home. I feel fine, honestly. This place stinks of disinfectant. It's going to take me three showers to get it off.

(Small laugh)

Still, better than freezing river water, I guess. Can I go home?

DR HARVEY: I'm afraid when you're released is not down to me, but I'm sure the doctors won't keep you longer than necessary.

NATASHA: I'll promise them I won't go out at night without swimming bands on in future. Just in case.

(Small laugh)

Extract from DI CAITLIN BENNETT'S CASE REPORT – MONDAY 11TH JANUARY

Natasha Howland has some bruises and cuts but there are no clear physical indications of an attack. Hospital psychologist Doctor Annabel Harvey believes that, despite the memory loss surrounding the accident, had Howard undergone a trauma such as an attack before falling, or being thrown, into the river, then PTSD would be evident in her reactions and behaviour. At present she appears calm and well.

Howland's phone records show no unusual activity before the incident apart from the receipt of a single text from an unknown number at 12.33 a.m.: *Meet tonight at 3am. The usual place.* Howland claims not to recognise the number and it is not in her contacts list. The text came from a PAYG phone sold by the One Cell Stop in Brackton Shopping Centre. It, and an identical phone, were bought for cash on October 14th. Security footage has been requested from the shopping centre and from One Cell Stop.

Howland suggests the text was a wrong number. I am concerned by her lack of response to it. When asked, more than twenty teenagers from her school say in that situation they would respond with, '*Who is this?*' Howland did not. Despite my concern over her lack of reply, this proves nothing; she may have chosen to ignore a text she did not recognise.

There was no indication of a struggle at the riverbank, or in the woods behind it, although the heavy snow that night and morning hindered the search. Until such time as Natasha Howland recovers her memory, there is little the police can do once further inquiries about the source of the text have been made through her friendship circle, and until CCTV footage has been recovered from the shopping centre.

At the present time there is no reason to consider this a criminal investigation.

Seven

On Monday, the hive was, as expected, buzzing, and Becca felt eyes turning her way as she moved between classes. Everyone knew she'd been at the hospital. They knew, thanks to a local newspaper photographer loitering outside, that Aiden worked for the man who'd pulled Natasha from the river. They knew that, long long ago, Becca and Natasha had once been friends and that Becca was the first person she mentioned when she woke up. It was all humming on the lines today.

Oh yeah, I think I remember that. Shit, Tasha had braces then, didn't she? Wasn't that Becca Crisp quite fat? Proper lard-arse?

Whispers. Mutters. Looks. She wished it would all stop. She didn't need it any more than Tasha did. Occasionally someone tried to talk to her but she just pushed past them. They could talk to the Barbies if they wanted news about Tasha. The Barbies *wanted* the attention.

Aside from seeing them surrounded by a throng of gossip-hungry wannabes in the common room at break, Becca had managed to avoid Hayley and Jenny for the first half of the day and was hoping to keep it up until the final bell rang and she could escape. It shouldn't be hard. She had double Art all afternoon, which neither of the other girls took.

'You okay?' Hannah asked. Hannah was kind of Becca's best mate these days, as much as anyone who wasn't Aiden could be, and they were sitting, as they did most cold days at lunchtime, on the radiator in the Science corridor sharing the dregs of a packet of crisps. Hannah hadn't mentioned the Tasha thing all day – not since Becca snapped on a text yesterday saying she really didn't want to talk about it – but it was still there between them, a darker knot in the grey cloud that hung over the whole school. In some ways, Becca wished Hannah *had* asked. It would have shown some fucking spine. Hannah was sweet and could be funny when she was relaxed, and she was great at listening when Becca was either gushing or raging about Aiden, but there was no denying she was a bit of a doormat. Becca was the one in charge of the friendship. Becca had other friends: Casey in Theatre Tech Club, Emily who she sat with in English, and of course Aiden. Sometimes it felt like Hannah only had Becca. Hannah never had other plans. Hannah was always available. Hannah was always happy to see Becca.

Becca was acutely aware that, basically, she was now best friends with the dull girl from school whose name no one would remember in five years' time. It was a massive fall from being Natasha Howland's forever friend. It bothered her more today than usual. Hannah didn't seem to notice, though.

'Yeah, I'm fine. I might go for a cigarette before Art. You coming?'

'No, I'll stay in the warm.' Hannah always said her mum would go ape if she came home stinking of fags, but Becca knew that deep down it was Hannah who hated the smell. If they were out somewhere, she always stood a couple of feet away when Becca smoked and her face didn't lie so well that

Becca couldn't see that she thought it was a bit disgusting. And she was right, it was. But it was also decadent and devil-may-care and she'd got used to it. She liked the feeling of the hot smoke deep in her lungs. A taste that carried in it a thousand 'fuck yous' to her mother and the hive.

'Cool,' she said, getting to her feet. 'I'll text you later. Have fun in Geography.'

'Oh yeah.' Hannah smiled and rolled her eyes. 'All the lolz.'

*

The bitter cold outside was sharp after being pressed cosily against the hot radiator, and Becca sniffed into the collar of her thick coat as she made her way around to the back of the Sports Hall. By the time she'd crept through the gap in the snowy hedge and into the small area of no-man's-land before the playing fields, her cigarette was already in her mouth and her hand was digging around in her cluttered pocket for her lighter. At least it had stopped snowing for now. Her feet were tingling and numbing in her wet Converse and the ground was slippery-damp under the smooth soles as she picked her way towards the corner of the wall. Her mum, as much as it hurt to admit it, had been right. They really weren't the right shoes for this weather.

'So I can't even smoke in peace.'

Becca looked up and her heart sank. So much for avoiding the Barbies for the rest of the day. Behind the slim Vogue cigarette, Hayley looked just as displeased to see her. She tilted her head back and blew out a stream of smoke as if she could blow Becca away with it.

'I didn't think running and smoking went well together.'

Hayley shrugged. 'They do if you run as well as me.'

Becca lit her own cigarette. Her heart was racing nervously and she wasn't sure why. It was only Hayley. She didn't give a shit about Hayley. 'Keeps you thin, I guess. I know how important that is to you.'

Hayley cast a perfectly made-up eye over Becca. 'It wasn't me who used to be fat.' She leaned back against the wall, her blonde hair floating out over her furred hood as she smoked, cool and casual. She was beautiful, Becca had to admit. Maybe even more beautiful than Natasha. Striking, her mum would call it. Elegant. Even last term, when she'd fallen down some stairs and had to wear a support on her arm for weeks until nearly Christmas, she'd made it look stylish. Becca tried to picture Hayley halfway up a tree, but instead only remembered how close they'd been back then. Suddenly she felt too tired to trade spiteful digs. What was the point? As soon as Natasha was better and out of hospital, Becca would be forgotten and they'd slink back to their opposite ends of the social spectrum.

'You okay?' she said eventually, hating how Hannah-like it made her sound. Submissive. Meek. A doormat.

'Like you care?' Hayley countered.

Becca wasn't sure she did, she just wanted to say something to fill the awkward silence. She drew hard on her cigarette, willing it to burn down more quickly. 'I was only asking. No need to be a bitch.'

Hayley glanced down at her boots. Uggs, of course. Becca could see the tag across the heel. Jenny's style might be fake – Jenny's mum, a single parent, had no money – but Hayley must have been wearing two hundred quid on her feet. She scuffed snow from the heel of one onto the toe of the other, dirtying it, as if flipping the finger to the cost. Becca could see where the damp was soaking through the outside. Despite the

Uggs' cost, Hayley's feet were probably as cold as her own.

'You heard from Tasha?' Hayley asked, her eyes down. The words were snowflake-light, but Becca tensed.

'Should I have?'

'I'm only asking, Bex.' Hayley mimicked Becca's own response, but she sounded tired, the polish her smoking and make-up and designer clothes gave her slipping for a moment. 'Whatever.'

'No,' Becca said. 'I haven't.' She paused, her cigarette almost in her mouth, and looked at Hayley, the reason behind her question clicking into place. 'Why? Haven't you?'

Hayley shrugged, non-committal, but the answer was there. A fat no. 'I'm just worried about her, you know.'

'Can't you call her?'

'Her phone's wrecked. I tried her home number. Alison said she'd given Tasha her iPhone and got herself a cheap one that just does texts and calls. She said at last she had a phone she understands how to use.' She half-smiled. 'You know what she's like with technology.' Becca didn't, really. The last time she'd been hanging around in the Howland home, phones and computers weren't important. Building dens and playing pirates had taken up most of their time. 'Anyway, I called it then sent a text but she hasn't replied,' Hayley finished.

'Maybe she's not feeling great. She might still be sedated.' Becca wasn't sure why she was trying to make Hayley feel better. Natasha was the one in hospital, after all. What did it matter if she hadn't texted the Barbies for a day? How needy were they? She took a long pull on her cigarette as Hayley ground hers out and kicked it under the snow. She was down to the filter but didn't want the awkwardness of heading back to school with Hayley.

'Yeah, that's probably it.' Hayley pushed away from the wall. 'She's probably not allowed to text much in there. Me and Jenny will go and see her tonight.'

'Cool.' Becca didn't know what to say, the sting of that old rejection still needling her skin as Hayley brushed past and ducked elegantly through the bushes. She disappeared without so much as a glance back.

Bitch, Becca thought. *Fucking bitch.* She stamped on her cigarette with more force than was required.

*

After the calming influence of double Art with Miss Borders and her hippie relaxed atmosphere, school was finally done and she headed through the throng of shrieking kids racing for buses and cars and the school gates in general, then forced her way to the sixth form locker corridor. She frowned to see the small crowd gathered there. It was rare. Required presence in the school building was more relaxed in the final two years, and if there was no assembly or tutor meetings last thing then no one cared if they slipped out early. The same applied to coming in late. Normally by the end of the day there were only a few stragglers at the lockers; most of them left their bags in the common room if they didn't take them to lessons.

'Ah, Rebecca!' A male voice called from somewhere within the slowly fracturing throng, which was breaking up into small, splintered swarms of the hive's whole. She looked up, catching glimpses of the caller through the gaps. Light brown hair. A friendly smile. Creases in his face that would one day be proper wrinkles but for now were just enough to make him interesting. Older. Hot.

'Mr Jones,' she said, raising a hand in a half-hello. Suddenly she understood the crowd. Mr Jones was the Head of Drama and today should have been auditions for the school play. He wormed his way through a gaggle of girls trying to get his attention to reach her. 'Glad to have caught you,' he said. Becca thought that up here, in the corridor, he was the caught one, a dolphin in a tuna net. She wondered if he could feel it – all the *heat* coming from the sixteen- and seventeen-year-old girls around him. The way they glowed at him.

'Are you going to do the set this year?' he asked. 'Would be great if you could. You're the best. And now you're sixth form, you could run it. What do you say?'

Behind him, she could see Hayley and Jenny. She ignored them.

'I thought the auditions were today?' she said, not answering his question. 'You cancelled them?'

'I didn't cancel,' he said, one hand tucked into his jeans pocket. 'Just moved them until Friday. Jenny asked if it could wait until Natasha was out of hospital because she really wanted to audition. Couldn't really say no to that and a few days' delay won't matter.'

'If she's back by Friday.' Her eyes kept flitting to Hayley and Jenny beyond his shoulder. Why didn't they just leave? Were they loitering to flirt with Mr Jones? Probably. So tragic.

'Oh, she will be,' he said. 'I rang the hospital to ask how she's doing – apparently they're going to send her home in the morning. She's a very lucky girl.'

'She was dead for thirteen minutes,' Becca said. 'How freaky is that?'

'That's the kind of thing you shouldn't think about.' His brown eyes were kind. 'Trust me, if you think about those things you'll go a bit crazy. She's going to be okay and that's what actually matters.' Becca smiled. She couldn't help herself. She didn't like Mr Jones like *that*, like all the other girls seemed to, but she did like him.

'So,' he said, holding out a battered copy of the play, 'can I rely on you to make us all look brilliant, Lieutenant? Now that I'm promoting you to colonel?' She stared at the book, and then at the disappearing blonde heads of the Barbies and their minions who'd given up waiting for him and were no doubt going to loiter outside his office instead, and then raised her hand in a weary salute. 'Oh, go on then, sir.'

'Excellent!' He grinned and winked at her. 'I feel better already. Take a look and see what you think. Draw up a couple of sketches then we'll meet and go through it. Doesn't have to be anything clever. Striking and stark could work.'

'This had better look good on my Uni forms,' she said.

'You'd do it anyway.' Mr Jones squeezed her arm. 'I know you.'

'Whatever.' She rolled her eyes, in part to disguise the blush that rose from nowhere to appal her with its existence, and then went to her locker.

'Come to the auditions on Friday,' he called out, walking away. 'Help me manage the fragile egos!'

She snorted a laugh at that. Mr Jones wasn't fooled by the Barbies, either. He might humour their flirting with him a bit but that was all. Her phone buzzed. Hannah.

You going home? Or fancy Starbucks hot chocolate?

She'd hoped it was Aiden but he was shit at texting unless he actually had something to say. She probably wouldn't speak to him until that night, and wouldn't see him till tomorrow, and then only for a couple of hours. That was the only fucker about having a boyfriend who wasn't at school. You couldn't even pretend you were studying together.

Meet you at the gates in 5.

A hot chocolate with Hannah might be a good way to end the day.

Eight

Taken from DI CAITLIN BENNETT'S FILES: EXTRACT FROM NATASHA HOWLAND'S NOTEBOOK

I'd been looking at all the local newspapers, laid out over my bed, when Hayley and Jenny turned up. It's been so strange to read it all, in sensational black and white. To see my own face staring out at me. My mother must have given them that picture (absolutely not one I'd have chosen). Taken some time last year at a family lunch. I look chubby in it. Then there's a photo of where I was pulled out of the river, and an awkward picture of the man who saved me, Jamie McMahon, so clearly caught unawares by the cameras when leaving his house. He used to be a solicitor in London before switching careers, according to one of the papers. Why the hell would you live in London and then move here? *Hero dog-walker*, they're calling him. *Reclusive musician saves 'dead' teenager.* How many other people have had their deaths recorded in inverted commas? He hasn't said much, the usual *anyone would have done the same thing* stuff that people always say. We all know most people wouldn't. He said he was late that morning and was just grateful he wasn't any later.

You're grateful? is what I thought as I stared at his grainy face. *How do you think I feel?* I closed the papers. It was the third time I'd pored over them, reading and rereading the details. I wondered what that said about me. I wondered what Dr Harvey and her blank eyes would make of that. *Like I'm ever going to let her read this stupid notebook!*

I'm twitchy and bored being stuck in bed and I want some fresh air. My bruises hurt and my muscles ache most of the time. It's like I've been running cross-country or something. I've been running a lot recently and my jogs have become something more. Something stronger. I'll never be as leopard-quick as Hayley but I'm faster and firmer than I was. The thought makes me stare through the glass at nothing. I just want to go home.

It's only about five o'clock but it's pitch dark outside already. An empty, cold dark. No one usually closes the curtains for ages and I don't mind. The room's high up. No one can see in. I quite like being able to look at that darkness, even though it reminds me of that *other* darkness, the one inside the freezing cold. The one that took my breath and my heartbeat. If I stare into the night for long enough I can defy the fear. It can't touch me anymore.

Hayley and Jenny were both smiling when they came in, but it instantly felt awkward, like we were suddenly strangers. Maybe it's the hospital. These kind of places can do that to people.

Anyway, it felt weird, and they looked so uncomfortable in the doorway, but I smiled at them (because, to be honest, I'm so bored of my family visiting and even though it was odd at first, they are a million times more fun than my gran) and pulled at my blonde hair, so much like theirs now. The mood softened after we hugged and they'd squealed their happiness at my continuing survival, and saw I was pleased to see them. They stripped off their coats and scarfs and I could almost feel them relaxing in the overheated room. Normality again.

Jenny's mum has saved all the newspapers. Jenny told me while rolling her pretty doe eyes after seeing them on my bed. Apparently she's put them in a scrapbook, like she did with Jenny's baby pictures. It's like everyone want a piece of the excitement of me nearly dying. It made me smile, though. Jenny's mum is from a different planet. She's poor, at least in comparison with mine and Hayley's comfortable middle-class wealth, and too often drunk. She's trailer trash or Essex scum and Jenny tries so hard to metaphorically wash it off. But sometimes you can still smell it on her. That slight *Eau de Desperation.* It's a mean thought, I know, but it's true.

'Am I supposed to look at them in the future and think, "Aww . . . remember that time Tasha nearly drowned? How sweet?" She's barking,' Jenny said.

I almost pointed out the technical error in her statement. I *did* drown. There wasn't anything *nearly* about it.

Then it was Hayley's turn. She didn't look at me. She was nonchalant when she said, 'I texted you,' folding up the papers and tucking her perfect hair behind her ear. She was so nonchalant that I knew it hurt that I hadn't texted back. *I'm still their leader. Even after everything. Maybe more so now.*

'My gran was here and I had my phone on silent,' I told her, which was a blatant lie. 'They don't really like us using our phones in the rooms.' Which *is* true, but the nurses let me off because they feel sorry for me.

They sat close together on the end of my bed, my two

best friends. Watching me. Wanting to ask me questions. Not knowing how to.

'So,' Hayley said as Jenny pulled some chocolate and crisps out of her bag, 'do you remember anything yet?'

I don't. I shook my head. It's so weird. I remember nothing from Thursday lunchtime to waking up here. I shrugged at them and for a moment Hayley didn't say a word. She just studied me, then she smiled a little. That enigmatic smile of hers. I used to always know what was going on in Hayley's head, but these days I'm not so sure.

Jenny was still focused on the contents of her disorganised bag, her face hidden from me until she finally, with a grin, produced three Crunchie Bars. My favourite chocolate.

I took them but just put them on the side. Every calorie counts, as my mum always says, and all I've done is lie in bed for days. 'I'll be fine,' I said to them. 'I'm sure it'll all come back at some point.' We talked about it a bit then, what I'd done in that time. Went to school, went home, then the mysterious going out again. Until the actually-falling-in-the-river bit, it all sounds so dull.

'We were all so scared for you,' Jenny gushed, before saying how everyone at school was talking about me, like I wouldn't know that already. She gets that from her mother, that sudden blurting. Her words come out in clumps. No real control, and just a rush of feelings wrapped in words. Her face was flushed while she talked, her eyes darting around the room. It was like she was nervous of me but I think maybe it's just that she doesn't know how to behave after something like this. Maybe she's trying too hard to be normal. Hayley cut her off in the end, otherwise I think she'd have been going on about school all night.

'That policewoman actually thought you might have tried to kill yourself.' Hayley grinned when she said it. 'I mean, fucking what?'

It made me laugh a bit, too. I told them about Dr Harvey and how I have to go to all these follow-up counselling sessions, and rolled my eyes and laughed at how bland and dull and boring she is. (She really is.) I didn't tell them about this note-book, though. About how I'm supposed to write everything down. Firstly, it's private and I'm only doing it because I'm so bored, and secondly, I don't want them thinking I'm putting everything we say and do in here and that someone else might want to read it. (That's *not* going to happen! Dr Harvey can keep her head out of my head.) I don't want them worrying about that.

'Are you okay, though?' Hayley asked.

The question was heavier than it needed to be and their smiles were suddenly gone. I could see beneath their veneer for a moment – because veneer is what we three do *so* well – to the worry underneath. We were in different territory – un-charted waters. I nearly died. I *did* die and I don't remember why. It changes everything.

I said, 'Yeah.' My voice isn't quite such a growl any more but I still sound as if I've had the worst tonsillitis ever. I said I just wanted to get out of here and Hayley said she didn't blame me because the whole place smells like old people.

It does and we all laughed at that – Hayley's not often funny, but when she is it's dry and on the money – and the weird ten-sion faded. Things have changed but our old camaraderie is like me: it doesn't die easily.

Jenny gave me a copy of *The Crucible* from her bag. She'd had to get it from Mr Jones. She admitted she'd looked for my copy when they found my iPod and other stuff to bring me but couldn't find it. She flushed slightly as she said that. I wondered how much rummaging through my stuff they really did. *How many drawers did you two check out? All of them? The boxes under my bed?*

The copy she handed me was battered and worn but I liked the feel of the paper. Apparently the auditions are on Friday now. They made Mr Jones put them back so I could take part. 'You'll make a great Abigail,' Jenny said. Jenny was really thinking that *she'd* make a great Abigail but she'll never say it. She wouldn't before and she definitely won't now. Even if she was offered the part I bet she'd persuade Mr Jones to give it to me. Jenny is such a *pleaser*. Most of the time, anyway. And the thing is, she probably will get offered it. I'm good – I'm way better than Mr Jones gives me credit for – but Jenny shines on a stage. She doesn't realise it, though. Not properly. She is sort of sweet at heart, I guess. In her own way. We may be quite different, we three best friends, but we all love Drama, in life and on stage. We all love the school plays. It's where we rule.

'Maybe he'll give James Ensor the part of John Proctor,' Hayley joked. We laughed at that. I went on two dates with James in the summer after drunkenly kissing him at a party. The hottest boy in school, or so they say. I thought he had a tongue like a wet fish and clumsy hands that shook too much. It was never going any further and James has mooned around after me ever since. I've never told Hayley or Jenny – even we have our secrets – but I don't really understand the sex thing. I giggle and squeal along but I must be the only girl in school who pretends things have gone further than they really have. The idea of it leaves me cold. Maybe I belong in that river in some ways. Maybe I should be Elizabeth Proctor, not Abigail.

But that wouldn't be very *Barbie*-like of me, as they call us at school, and I *am* the Barbies.

I said that maybe Mr Jones would play the role himself and that I couldn't imagine a teenager taking it on, not even James. It needs rough skin and hands. I looked at my friends then. They were both thinking the same – an unbidden thought of Mr Jones naked and doing *it*, passion made somehow more powerful by the unlawfulness. Abigail and John Proctor all mixed up with the whole school's crush on the Drama teacher. I could almost feel the temperature rising in the room.

'But I hope not,' I said, in the end. 'That would be weird. And a bit disgusting. I mean, fucking someone that age. Even just acting it.' I made a vom face. 'Creepy.' They made suitably appalled sounds – of course they did – but they looked guilty. (Sometimes they are so predictable.) I felt a strange warmth for them, though. Maybe I shouldn't play with them so much.

'What about that person who texted you?' It was Jenny this time, bringing the conversation back to my story – my *event* – to pick over the bones of it. 'The policewoman asked us about the number but we didn't know it.' She was trying to sound casual but I didn't buy it. I told her I didn't know it either and that it must have just been a wrong number and nothing to do with what happened to me.

'She asked Becca, too,' Hayley said. She was flicking through the pages of the play but her eyes looked up from the shield of her poker-straight hair and I noticed how perfectly arched her eyebrows were. I need to get mine done again. 'Like Becca would know.'

'She was here.' I said it quietly. 'She read to me when I was unconscious.'

'Could you hear her?' Jenny asked. She doesn't care about Becca. She doesn't share the betrayal Hayley and I do. She was never Becca's friend. 'That would be weird.'

'I don't know,' I told her. I say: 'Maybe a little bit like in a dream.' I don't even know if that's true, but it's what they wanted to hear.

'What about . . .' Jenny leaned in '. . . when you were . . . you know . . .'

'Dead?' I finished.

Hayley was grossed out by that. Hayley hates death. We all do now we're realising it will happen to us one day – although I may have reached that moment somewhat faster than my friends. We hate it and are fascinated by it, but Hayley has a real terror of it. She's really grasped it, I think. Under her perfection she's well aware of the fragility of her flesh. I've seen her worry over a freckle when she thinks no one is looking. Did someone in her family die when she was young? I don't remember. Maybe. Perhaps it was something she didn't talk about, but which stopped her swinging in trees and climbing walls and scaffolding – something more than just the advent of her boobs.

'Well, it's true.' I smiled, but all I could think about was the blackness and the overwhelming enormity of my fear in that memory of trying to reach the branches. Like the darkness was waiting for me. Like it was laughing at me. It makes my breath catch a bit in my throat. Not that I can let it show. I want to get out of here in the next few days. I have to. I must stay *normal*. I told them I can't remember anything. Judging from Hayley's face, I don't know if that was a good thing or a bad one for her many fears. Maybe she wanted stories of bright lights and tunnels and angels.

When the nurse came to say that Hayley's mother had arrived to take them home, I wondered for a minute how she knew which of my friends was which and then remembered that they spent the weekend crying around my bed. It's strange to have been here but not here for that. It still makes me shiver, despite the warmth. It was like they'd attended my wake and I was some kind of vampire risen from the dead.

My friends squealed their disappointment but the nurse told them I needed to rest (I'm so bored of resting) and looked at me with such warmth it was as if she loved me. She must be a good nurse. 'They'll be round with your dinner soon,' she told me and then spied the crisps and chocolate. 'If you still have room after all that.' She's a large woman, comfortable with her fat. I doubt she's ever eaten just one piece of chocolate from a bar and thrown the rest away. Did she ever feel the pressure of perfection? Yes, I wanted to eat chocolate. Someone like her would eat it without a second thought. I almost envied that.

Hayley and Jenny hugged me and we three became a tangle of hair and coats and hot breath. Lean arms were the tightest on me and I knew that was Hayley. When they pulled away, we were all damp with condensation.

'Text us,' Hayley said. She looked sad. She paused for a moment. And then she said, 'We do love you, Tasha. You scared the shit out of us.'

Jenny nodded. 'Hurry back to school. We miss you.'

It's only been one day. I wonder quite how much they could have missed me when no doubt all they'd done was talk about me the whole time. I know it's a bitter thought. I should be happy we're friends again. It's what I want, after all. Things have been a bit *creased* between us recently.

'I've missed you, too,' I said. The past tense slipped out but they didn't notice it. I *have* missed them, in my own way. They've been my best friends.

Maybe things will be different now.

Nine

18.20
Jenny
That was 2 weird. Don't u think?

18.21
Hayley
U really txting me from the back seat? ;-)

18.22
Jenny
Want 2 talk about it. Grrrr to ur mum. And what is this shit music?

18.23
Hayley
90s crap.

18.24
Hayley
Yeah it was weird. She really doesn't remember.

18.24
Jenny
U think she will? Im scared.

18.24
Hayley
Me 2. I'll call you l8r.

18.25
Jenny
I wish she'd died.

18.25
Hayley
DELETE! We'll be ok.

18.25
Jenny
Delete thread or just that?

18.26
Hayley
Thread.

18.26
Jenny
This shit is so crazy.

18.26
Hayley
Don't worry. Now delete.

Ten

Aiden rolled joints faster and smoother than anyone Becca knew. His joints, Becca concluded as she sucked in deep and watched the paper burn orange-red, small grass seeds popping inside, were goddamn awesome. Three, five or seven Rizlas, they were always even, a perfect balance of weed and tobacco, and you never had to tug too hard nor did you ever get a mouthful of shit because the roach and paper were too loose.

She giggled and coughed as the buzz hit, warming her face which still stung from the cold outside even though the room was roasting. Aiden's mum did not skimp on the heating. And long may she live for that alone. That and the pizza she'd bought for them.

'Good shit?' Aiden said.

Becca was lying in the crook of his arm looking up at the ceiling. 'Good shit,' she said and grinned. 'Now feed me pizza.'

He dragged a heavy slice out of the box, holding it over her head. She reached up for it and he held it just out of her reach.

'Swap.'

She waved the joint at him and then hauled herself up, letting her head fuzz, smiling at him as she took a huge bite of the

Hawaiian, cheese stretching out in a long thread until it broke and landed wetly on her chin.

'Sexy.'

She shrugged. 'I'm not a Barbie. What do I care?'

'A Barbie?' Aiden blew a lungful of sweet smoke into her face, and she breathed it in while pulling away the offending food.

'You know, like Natasha and her gang. They never eat. They probably *purge*. How fucking tragic.'

'I think you're an amnesiac bulimic,' Aiden said, thoughtfully. He grinned. 'You binge and then forget to throw up afterwards.'

'Arsehole!' The word had less potency spluttered around a mouthful of pineapple and cheese. She finished the slice and then took the joint back from him.

'Anyway, why are you even talking about them? You never do. Why do you care? Natasha's fine. All this shit will blow over.'

'I know,' she said. 'I guess it's just brought it all back. What bitches they were to me.' *More than that*, she wanted to say. *It's brought back how much I wanted to keep them. How I would have let them be bitches to me forever if I could have stayed in the circle. I was such a loser.* Some humiliations, however, you had to keep to yourself if you wanted to keep your boyfriend. No one needed to know what a twat she could be, least of all Aiden.

'Jamie went up to see her,' Aiden said, 'but she was too tired, apparently. I think it made him feel like a bit of an idiot. He doesn't do people at the best of times.' She offered him the joint back but he shook his head. 'You finish that. I've got to play guitar in a bit.'

It was the only thing that irritated Becca about Aiden working with Jamie McMahon – they recorded at night from seven or eight through to midnight, or even later if they were close to a deadline. It meant that sometimes she barely saw Aiden at all for days, whereas if they worked during the day like normal people his evenings would be free.

'I'd want to see him if he'd saved me,' Aiden continued. 'To say thank you if nothing else.'

'She didn't text Hayley back, either. Maybe she's not as well as they think. When I was reading to her in the hospital she was so still. It was hard to believe she wasn't dying. Or dead or whatever. Maybe you can't just bounce back from that stuff?' Why was she suddenly defending Natasha? How hard did old habits die?

'Still odd. And very Natasha not to give a shit that he'd gone all that way to see her. She could have managed five minutes.'

'True,' Becca said. 'Her mum rang mine. Apparently she doesn't remember very much. Like, nothing from that whole day.'

'All the more reason you'd think she'd want to see him.'

'Yeah, but this is Tasha. I'm not sure hospital-bed hellos would be her thing.'

Aiden looked quizzical.

'No make-up. No hair straighteners. No padded bra.'

'Oh, meow.' Aiden laughed, pulling her up to him. 'You can be such a bitch.' His tone was light, though, and he had one hand in her hair as he leaned in to kiss her. She loved the way he kissed. Gentle, sweet exploration. It was even better when they were stoned – which was most of the time they were together, if she was honest. The tingle in her tongue ran through to the buzz in her veins and it was only ever a moment or two until her whole body was throbbing. She'd never get tired of Aiden. Never. Natasha had been stupid to turn him down.

She had Natasha's cast-off. She tried not to think about that. Aiden loved *her*, Becca. He would never have loved Natasha, not like this. Not in this soulmate way. But it still bothered her that he'd *wanted* Tasha. That he'd thought she was beautiful. She *was* beautiful. That made it worse. But even if they had dated it wouldn't have lasted. He would have found Rebecca eventually. Once Tasha's gold-plated shine had worn away to show the cheap metal underneath, he'd have seen that Becca was his diamond. Of course he would.

'What?' he asked, pulling away from her as if he could feel the distraction in her kiss. His eyes were hazy red and his smile soft.

'Nothing,' she said. 'Nothing at all.' They only had half an hour or so before he'd have to drop her home and then head off to work on whatever soundtrack Mr McMahon was composing for the rest of the night. She didn't want to spend it thinking about Natasha Howland. Natasha Howland was part of her history. She could stay there. Even if Tasha came crawling back to her – which she never would – Becca would have nothing to do with her. If it had been Becca out by the river, she wasn't even sure she'd have pulled her ex-best friend out. So much for forever. The only thing that lasted forever was death. The thought made her insides cool a little. Death and her love for Aiden. She wrapped her arms around his neck more tightly. This was *forever*. She was sure of that.

Eleven

From the *Brackston Herald*, Wednesday 13 January

Although it is still a mystery how sixteen-year-old Natasha Howland (pictured left with her mother) came to be found in the local river on Saturday morning, the police are not currently considering foul play.

According to hospital sources, Miss Howland, a sixth form student at Brackston Community school, has made a good recovery after being pulled from the water and was released from hospital this morning. Feared dead on discovery, her resuscitation has been hailed as miraculous by both doctors and her family. She still has no memory of the events of that night. Although this story has a happy ending, it would appear the beginning is destined to remain a mystery. Both the Howland family and police are appealing for anyone who might have seen Natasha on the night of Friday, 8th January, to come forward.

Twelve

Taken from **DI CAITLIN BENNETT'S FILES: EXTRACT FROM NATASHA HOWLAND'S NOTEBOOK**

My mum took me shopping. Of course she did. What she lacks in interpersonal skills, she makes up for with cash. I guess in some ways it's a good trade, and it's not as if my dad doesn't earn enough to keep us in the *manner to which we have become accustomed*. I hate that phrase. My mum uses it all the time and tries to make it sound like a joke, but it isn't, really. It's more of a threat. A reminder of what makes her marriage tick.

She loves my dad, I'm sure of it, but only as long as he keeps providing. She stays pretty and trim for him, goes to the gym and has facials, but all of it has a price tag. Not that he minds. He likes buying her things. Even the things she never uses – her untouched-for-months MacBook Air – the same as mine, *matching gifts – how sweet*; her iPad mini, the only thing she sometimes uses, her Kindle and the various other electronic devices he thinks will make her life easier. They gather dust around the house. Unless I use them, of course.

All my mother really wants is for him to continue paying off her credit card every month when she's spent hundreds on shoes and lunches and 'wine with the girls'. And of course he does. Because that's how they show their love. But it's their life, not mine. I'm just another accessory. If this madness makes them happy then who am I to point it out? Especially with the allowance I get every month. And the freedom. It all works in my favour.

We came back from the hospital as a family, but as soon as we were through the front door and it was clear I wasn't an invalid, Dad didn't know what to do with himself. He headed off to work in his study so we could have some *mother-daughter time*. I don't know how my mother felt about it, but it made me groan inside. I just wanted to chill out in my room. Do what I needed to do. Think about things. Maybe read the play before the audition. Prepare to go back to school. Go shopping on my own. I checked my various social media accounts on my phone as she made tea and cut us slices of chocolate cake – a sliver for her, a wedge for me – but the well-wishing was getting boring. Since it became clear I wasn't going to follow through on my half-promise of death, a lot of the outpouring of love had dropped off. The drama was over. We'll see about that when I get back to school. I have to laugh at myself a bit for that – the vanity of it all.

Once we'd drunk our tea and eaten the pieces of too-sweet cake, Mum declared that she'd have to skip dinner to make up for it, even though she's as thin as a twig. It made me think I should skip dinner, too, as I'd eaten the Crunchies as well, and that irritated me. I don't need to lose weight. I know my figure is good. So is hers. I was half-tempted to tell her that the skinny look doesn't necessarily work on an ageing woman, but why spoil the moment?

I wonder if she was lean and toned like me when she was younger. Her skin is different from mine. It almost hangs from her in places. Mine is firm, welded to the flesh and bone underneath, one smooth, strong machine. Her body is starting to show its different parts. The droop of her breasts. The sagging skin at her elbows. I've never noticed them before, those whispers of physical mortality. I think I've become slightly obsessed by death over the past two days. I guess that's to be expected.

My bedroom looks a little odd to me now. In it for the first time, once I'd fled the calorie conversation, I stared at the window – firmly shut – and out at the tree and rope ladder beyond. There was a lot of snow. I wouldn't have wanted to scramble down there in this weather, strong body or not.

I sat on my bed, idly flicking through *The Crucible*, and wondered how long it would take. (She's nothing if not predictable, my mother. But then, most people are.) As it turned out, about twenty minutes. I had my bag ready and my shoes on when she knocked on the door to suggest we go shopping. 'I could treat you to something nice?' she said, like that would sort out my near-death. 'A new coat, maybe, for this terrible weather?'

I'm not short of coats as my walk-in wardrobe will attest, but you can never have too many clothes. I smiled at her. I could have a worse mother in many ways, that's for sure.

*

I wore a hat with my hair tucked in, just in case anyone recognised me – it's not like I'm a celebrity or something, but there were reporters and photographers outside the hospital this morning and I bet I look shit in their pictures. They want me to do a photo and piece with Jamie McMahon. Maybe I will. I can't decide if I want to speak to him or not. I turned him away at the hospital, but perhaps it could be interesting. I feel like I know him already. Maybe I should see him. I'll think about it later. It's not urgent.

We cruised around the shops, which were quiet in the foul midweek weather, and after an hour or so – however long it took to buy three tops, a skirt, a coat and a pair of skinny jeans – I mentioned that I'd like to get Hayley and Jennifer presents of friendship bracelets or something, so they'd know how much it mattered to me that they were there. I looked down at my snowy boots and tried not to blush. I didn't want to sound needy or too grateful they were at my bedside. 'It was strange being in hospital,' I explained. 'It made me realise how fragile everything is.' It's true. The idea that I was nearly dead – *for-good dead*, not just thirteen-minutes dead – still makes me tremble.

'Then let's do that,' my mother said, smiling. 'But make it a celebration of your friendships rather than a fear of loss.'

Sometimes she's overly sentimental, but maybe she had a point. I smiled, too. I had to, really. I needed her credit card to pay for everything.

'What about Rebecca?' she asked, almost tentatively, after we'd picked out the delicate charm bracelets, each with a silver heart attached that read *Forever Friends*. Maybe they're a bit childish – okay, a lot childish – but they're certainly not tacky. Not at the price tag they came with.

I had to think for a moment. Becca. Of course. Not a bracelet, though. That would be ridiculous, given everything, but I did have another idea.

*

When we got home, there was a phone call from the drably serious police inspector, Bennett, checking that everything was all right and I was home safely. She told my parents that they weren't taking the investigation any further at the moment but to call her immediately should I remember anything. She said it all to my father, as if I was from some far-off distant land and didn't speak English – or, worse than that, as if I was five years old.

I mean, what if my dad was the one who pushed me in the river? What if *that*, Mrs Clever Police Inspector? I can hardly ask him for your number so I can call and say, *Hey, guess what I remembered?* It's bad enough not remembering without people thinking that it's suddenly made me stupid.

When the call was done, my dad asked if I wanted take-away for dinner. We rarely have take-away. Mum's proud of her homemaking skills, even though she's so embarrassed about being a housewife that we have a cleaner who comes twice a week and does the ironing. Amongst her friends, choosing not to work is a status symbol, but I sometimes think that so much wine at lunchtime doesn't indicate a fulfilled life. She had a job a long time ago, before I was born. It's how she met dad. Anyway, the long and short of it is that mum is an excellent cook and takes pride in serving up a healthy but tasty meal every evening. It's the one thing I *try* to be here for, because it makes life easier if I am. My parents don't seem to know where I am from one minute to the next but they do like us to sit down as a family once a day, even if my mum's just nibbling on a salad pretending to eat. I usually manage about fifteen minutes with them, and they usually find that acceptable.

Appearances. It's all appearances. I thought about the cake at lunchtime. I thought about all the extra calories. Fuck it, I concluded. I nearly died. 'Chinese would be nice,' I said.

'Chinese it is,' My dad said. 'Whatever my princess wants.' He took his coffee and headed back to the study.

It was gone two o'clock by then. I needed to get going. I had things to do. 'I want to drop these presents off,' I said. 'Make it a surprise when they come home from school.'

Mum made some feeble effort to say she'd drive me but I cut her off.

'I'll be fine. I promise.' I was firm. Like my skin. And I knew she wouldn't argue with me. She never really does. And to be fair, apart from this one near-death incident, considering I've been able to do pretty much whatever I want since I was about six, we've had a clear run. No issues or terrifying accidents. Except for the thing with the class hamster in year one, and what happened with Becca's stupid party dress when we were six, but those were forgotten fast enough. People forgive children. They were good lessons, well learned.

I promised I'd be back in an hour or so. *I won't stay out. I'm still quite tired.* That last was a lie. I wasn't tired. If anything, I felt invigorated.

My mother agreed. I put on my new coat, though, to please her. In the main I'm a good daughter. At least, I try to be. And it's a great coat – red. It goes well with my blonde hair and will work with my dark hair when I change it back. Even though I like that we all look the same now, I miss being a brunette. I miss being *the* brunette.

I hurried, the air cold with the threat of impending snow, striding along the street, confident over the icy slush. It's the best way. Those who are too careful are always the ones who slip. You have to be bold. Working from my furthest friend back, I started at Jenny's.

I had to suffer Jenny's mum's suffocating embrace on the

doorstep and then asked if I could leave a gift for Jenny on her bed. Liz's eyes were watering and her make-up was so heavy her tears were black. She was crying cheap mascara.

'Oh, sweetheart, that's so lovely. They've been really worried about you, both of them. You know, I don't think she's slept at all since we heard. She doesn't know I know. I understand how you girls need your space, but I've heard her on the phone in the middle of the night. Heard her get up for a drink. It must have showed at school because one of her teachers even called to check on her. And of course whenever she could be, she was at the hospital with you and Hayley.' She stroked my hair. 'Like sisters you three, aren't you? Twins.'

I wanted to point out her mathematical failings but instead murmured a *yes* and fled up the stairs, already unzipping my handbag. My mum was probably starting her first glass of the day, but Liz must have been nearly through a bottle already. I don't know how Jenny copes.

I did what I'd come to do – left the gift-wrapped box and small card on her pillow and enjoyed a moment of satisfaction before heading back down. Liz hadn't followed me up. Our bedrooms are our sanctuaries, and Jenny is capable of a major tantrum if her mum messes with her stuff. Liz is only allowed in to leave Jenny's clean laundry on her bed. Jenny likes to put it away herself. I hugged Liz again on my way out and then headed to Hayley's. I counted the turns on the streets between them. *Thirteen.* I pushed the number from my head.

It was easier at Hayley's. Hayley's mum is more like mine – she cares, but it's a reserved love. She shed a few tears at seeing me healthy on the doorstep but they didn't streak coal down her cheeks. In her face I mainly saw relief that it was me and not Hayley who'd nearly died in the river. She looked at me with my blonde hair and I watched her thinking how easily it could have been her beautiful daughter instead. I saw guilt at the thought there, too, and then relief that it all turned out okay in the end. I read faces well.

Her hug was looser than Liz's and after she ushered me to the stairs, she waited at the bottom until I returned. She didn't touch my hair. She didn't gush over me. I was in and out in five minutes.

It was weirder at Becca's house. By the time I got there, my face was flushed from the cold and my nose was starting to run. I hadn't counted the turns. I didn't want another thirteen. I rang the doorbell and my heart clattered in my chest with sudden, unexpected nerves. I hadn't been there for a long time. Years.

Julia Crisp's mouth fell into a surprised 'O' when she saw me and then reshaped into a warm smile. I saw her take in the coat, the neat, sleek hair, the all-round girl-next-door gorgeousness of me. I saw her wonder how Becca would look if we were still friends. Would she be so grungy? Would she be less moody?

To be honest, I don't know if Becca is moody or not. At school she always looks moody with her black T-shirts, spiky belts and pale make-up. Almost goth but not quite. Rocker, I guess. Whatever it is, it isn't the prettiest Becca could be and Julia knows it.

They've had the kitchen redone since I was last there and redecorated the hallways. I don't know why it was a shock to see the house looking different. I can't have been inside for four years, maybe more. I shuffled from foot to foot as she asked me if I wanted a drink or something to eat and politely declined. I didn't ask to leave the present in Becca's room – that would have been weird, and unnecessary – so instead I held it out. I felt awkward and I blushed.

'It's just a . . . well, a kind of thank you, I guess. You know, for coming to the hospital. She didn't have to. And for reading to me and everything.'

As she took the box, she was smiling so hard I thought her face would split right open. 'Oh, Natasha – how thoughtful. I'm sure she'll love it. You two always did like to play chess.'

It wasn't a cheap set – hand-carved soapstone pieces. Just over a hundred pounds. I wonder how I'm supposed to learn the value of anything when my mum spends that much on my friends for tokens of thanks.

We had enjoyed chess, and Becca was very good at it. Not as good as me, though.

'It's a shame you two didn't keep Chess Club up,' she said. 'Becca still plays against her dad sometimes.' She shrugged. 'I guess chess just isn't cool for teenagers.'

I shrugged back. She was right. Chess Club is a no-no. Not even I could maintain any level of cool and still play. Not that I'd want to. I've *seen* the losers who go. I doubt even Becca would go these days, and she's taken to hanging around with Hannah Alderton, which is pretty much scraping the bottom of the social barrel.

Although I'd never tell anyone, I sometimes play on my phone, on one of those apps that pits you against the computer. I'm still really good, too. But it's not the same as when me and Bex used to play. Standing there in her kitchen, I had a pang of missing her. A sharp one. How strange is that?

*

By the time I got home, I *was* exhausted. Dog-tired. Eyelids drooping. Too much fresh air, Mum declared, and sent me off to bed until dinnertime. If I wanted to be ready to go back to school on Friday then I needed to rest. She was probably right.

The sheets were fresh and I relished the smell. There was safety and childhood trapped in the weave. It was nearly four o'clock and the sky was midnight-blue already, on the cusp of darkness. Curled up on my side, I looked out at it. The blue was beautiful but the blackness filled me with dread. I closed my eyes. That blackness was worse – it was within me. It was in my head. It was eating me. *Thirteen turns in the road. Thirteen minutes dead.* I gasped for breath and sat up. I had to get control of myself.

I'm fine. I know I am.

I turned the bedside lamp on and took three deep breaths. I am not weak. I *survived*. It was just darkness. It wasn't death. Still, I left the lamp on and lay back down. When I closed my eyes again, the world behind them was a reddy-orange that made me think of autumn. I could cope with that.

The darkness still came, though, of course it did. It grabbed me as my breathing slowed and my mind emptied. It pulled me down. I was tangled in branches. Undercurrents and drag. There was a void beneath me. Pitch-black. Hungry. The world dissolved – no ice, no cold, no twigs tearing into my frozen skin. Just the darkness.

And there was something waiting in it.

Thirteen

'He remembers me,' she said, as Biscuit jumped at her and then crouched down to play, tail dusting the carpet madly, and then jumped again.

'He must do,' Jamie agreed, although Biscuit was like this with everyone, stranger or otherwise. He was crazy and over-friendly and greedy, a mad ball of stinking fur who would never be fully trainable. Right now, maybe Biscuit was the only one who didn't feel awkward in his sitting room. Jamie certainly did and Natasha's mother had perched on the very edge of the sofa, hands clasped in her lap, one wary eye on the dog. Alison Howland looked like a cat person, if she liked animals at all.

'I've made some tea.' Aiden shuffled in with the tray. He put it down on the coffee table, the brim-full milk jug spilling slightly. There was a plate of chocolate digestives, too, left-overs from their munchie sessions in the studio upstairs.

'Hey, Aiden,' Natasha said, flashing the dark-haired boy a perfect smile. 'How are you? I barely recognised you.'

'I'm good.' He shrugged, his eyes sliding away from her and over to Jamie. 'Anyway, I'm going to finish laying that track upstairs. I want to get that second guitar line right.'

'Thanks.' Jamie wished he could join him.

'I hope we haven't disturbed your work.' Alison was already pouring tea, and Jamie had a moment of wondering how she could look so uncomfortable and yet have that confidence in a stranger's home. Contradictions. Like her daughter.

'No, it's fine. My hours are pretty irregular.' Unlike Aiden, Jamie could barely take his eyes from Natasha. It wasn't anything sexual – although she was a very pretty girl and in that perfect bloom of youth women go through – it was that she looked so alive. So healthy. It was Thursday and when he'd seen her less than a week ago she was cold and blue and not breathing. There'd been pictures in the papers since, of course, but they were from *before*. She was different then. Brown hair, for a start.

She looked at him, quizzical, and he flushed. 'Sorry, it's just strange – and great, obviously – but the last time I saw you, I thought you were dead. It's a little like seeing a ghost.'

'I'm very much alive.' She smiled, blushing slightly. 'Thanks to you.' Her teeth were perfectly even and white. He hadn't noticed that when he'd pulled her from the water. Her mouth had been open and all he'd seen was the terrible blue of her lips. Now those same lips were tinted with a pale pink gloss. Make-up but not quite. Adult but not quite. 'Although that would have been different if you'd been later on your walk.' Her tone was light as she took a mug of tea from her mother, but her face was shielded by her blonde hair and he felt a sudden moment of irrational guilt.

'Trust me, I've thought that, too,' he said. He leaned down and tickled the small dog's ears. A wet tongue snaffled at his fingers. 'Blame Biscuit. He hid his collar.'

'I read about it,' Natasha said. 'But he also found me in

the river, so I'll forgive him.' Neither of the women had taken a digestive and the dog was starting to drool. Jamie picked up the plate and held it out, but both Howlands shook their heads.

'We have dinner waiting at home,' Alison said with a smile. She was trim and good-looking, an older version of the daughter. Jamie figured there weren't a lot of cakes or treats on her daily intake.

'Then I'll put them out of the way,' he said. 'Biscuit has no self-control with food. He'd have one off the plate in no time – I named him well. It's probably a good thing I don't have children. I'm not so great at instilling rules.'

'I just wanted to apologise for not seeing you at the hospital,' Natasha cut in. She was petting Biscuit, although Jamie noticed she was careful not to get his fur on her clothes. He didn't blame her. Smelling of damp dog wasn't good at any age, but definitely not hot for teenagers. 'It probably felt quite rude of me,' she finished.

Jamie shook his head. 'No, of course not.' That wasn't entirely truthful. Being turned away had made him feel like an idiot, especially with the reporters outside demanding to know how she was.

'I asked them to tell you I was resting, but that wasn't entirely true.' Her wide eyes, fixed on him, were full of apology and a need for understanding. 'I just wasn't ready to . . . well, to face you yet. That probably sounds odd. It was like if I saw you, then I had to admit it really happened. And I keep thinking I'm okay with it all and then odd things – like seeing you – come along and I weird-out a bit.'

'I get that,' he said. 'And it's fine, honestly. All that matters is that you're better.'

'She still can't remember what happened, though,' Alison said, leaning in. 'Nothing. I wish she could. I mean, thank god she wasn't physically attacked in any way, but I still wish we knew why she was out there.'

'Mother!' Natasha rolled her eyes, embarrassed. 'It's not Mr McMahon's problem.'

'I wish I could help you,' Jamie said, 'but all I saw was a girl in the river. No one else. No sign of anyone else, either.' He'd trawled through his memory over and over, worrying he'd missed something that morning. He was sure he hadn't, but all his focus – what little remained through the shock – had been on Natasha, and once he'd gone into the water, too, his senses were fucked.

'Ignore her. Please,' Natasha said. The teenager was clearly embarrassed, but Jamie was surprised by how she spoke about her mother, as if the woman wasn't even there, as if their roles as parent and child were reversed. He was even more surprised that she got away with it. Alison didn't say a word, but instead gave an apologetic shrug. Maybe she was too relieved to have her daughter home in one piece to tell her off, but there was something *ingrained* in it. Natasha had said it so easily. 'We know that if you remembered anything you'd have told the police,' Natasha finished. 'And I'm sure my memory will come back when it's ready and it will be all my fault, just a stupid accident.'

She sipped her tea. From upstairs in the attic studio came the sound of guitar-playing. Aiden couldn't have closed the door properly.

Biscuit, hearing the noise and always looking for distraction, padded out of the room.

'So much for my charm,' Natasha said.

'He likes it in the studio. It's always warmest up there in the evening.'

'You work at night?' Natasha's eyes widened momentarily. 'Till late?'

'Sometimes. When I'm in the middle of a project.'

She looked stunned. 'Wow. How come you always walk your dog so early, then? Is it before you go to bed?'

'Occasionally yes, but I've never been a great sleeper. I don't normally sleep more than four hours. And I find it's good to tire Biscuit out early because otherwise he drives me crazy.'

'I'm not sleeping so brilliantly, either,' she said, softly, a small cloud on the perfection of her youth, but it lifted, her thoughts returning to the dog. 'He's so sweet, though.' She waggled a finger at Jamie. 'But don't let him hide his collar again! A girl's life might depend on it.'

Jamie laughed with her, glad she could make fun of it. It lightened his irrational guilt. She was fine. It had all turned out okay. Natasha got to her feet and her mother followed suit.

'Well, we should leave you to it, but I just wanted to put your mind at rest about the photo thing the paper wanted to do? I've said no. I know you're a private person – the papers have harped on about that – and to be honest, I just want to go back to school and get life back to normal. I bet you do, too.'

Jamie couldn't help feeling a wave of relief. 'Yes. I'd have done it if you asked, but it's not really my thing. If I wanted attention I'd be in a band, not working on soundtracks.'

'I figured.' She reached up on tiptoes and brushed her lips against his cheek. 'Thank you again.'

He saw them out, Biscuit darting around his feet, having flown down the stairs when he heard them moving, and then, leaving the tray where it was, took his tea up to the studio.

'They gone?' Aiden asked.

He nodded.

'She seems like a nice kid.'

Aiden shrugged. 'Yeah, she probably does.'

Jamie almost asked what he meant, but left it alone when he saw that Aiden's face had dropped, hidden behind his hair. Sometimes Jamie forgot that Aiden wasn't long out of school himself. The same school Natasha went to. Maybe they had some history. It wasn't his business to pry, though. Instead, he sat at the desk and studied the various computer screens. 'Right,' he said. 'Let's get this into the mix. And close that door. I could hear you downstairs.'

Biscuit whirled in and thumped into his basket, the door closed and, unheard by the outside world, Aiden started to play.

Fourteen

Becca really hadn't known how to feel about the chess set. The way her mum's eyes sparkled when she handed it over made her instantly want to hate it. It was as if her mum was saying, *Look! Look! You can be a Barbie, too, if you just make yourself prettier. You could be the daughter I've always wanted. You could be the girl they fish out of the river rather than one on the sidelines.*

But it *was* beautiful, each piece so delicately carved and yet solid in her hand. She liked the size and weight of them. At school they'd always played with small sets and somehow they never felt right to Becca. Each move in chess was important. These pieces reflected that.

'Beautiful, aren't they?' her dad said as they set the board up on a small coffee table. She had to agree. They were.

There was a fizz in the pit of her stomach and she realised, partly in horror, that what she felt was excitement. Maybe Natasha was going to be her friend again. Maybe they'd play chess in the long winter nights like they used to, cross-legged on the floor and munching junk food. It was a stupid thought. They were too old for that shit. Life was too busy. Still, there was a little spark of firefly light buzzing around inside that she couldn't spit out.

You're not a Barbie, a voice from the shadows inside her whispered. *Remember that. Remember how they treated you.* But still, as she wrote out the thank-you card her mum said she'd drop round the next day, Becca was almost looking forward to Natasha coming back to school.

That feeling lasted until about 9.05 on Thursday when, while she was unloading her scarf and gloves into her locker, the hive buzz reached her. *Oh my god, did you see Hayley's and Jenny's bracelets? Aren't they beautiful?* It was another couple of hours before she saw them herself – at break time. She didn't exactly see them, just the flash of silver accompanied by the jangle of charms and coos of *Oh, that's so lovely, Forever Friends. So sweet! God, you must be so happy she's okay. You three are so close . . .*

Becca zoned it all out after that. *Forever Friends* on their charm bracelets. Maybe Natasha actually meant it with those two. She bit her tongue and turned away rather than spitting out that Natasha had once been her *best friend forever* and look how well *that* turned out. She didn't want anyone to see she cared. She didn't care. Why should she? It was a long time ago. The chess set seemed clunky and stupid now, though. She sure as shit had no intention of using it.

She snapped at Hannah throughout lunch and then blamed an imaginary period for it when she saw her friend trying to hide her upset. At the end of the day, when the relief of the final bell came at three-fifteen, she went straight to Aiden's and got massively stoned before having giggly, drowsy sex, trying to keep quiet while his mum cooked tea in the next room. It wasn't great sex – she wasn't sure she knew what *great sex* was yet – but it was warm and close and she enjoyed the sound of his breath getting faster and faster in her ear. It was like she was making him lose control. *Her.* Becca. Not a Barbie. Just a grungy girl. That made her hotter than any of the rest of it.

When they were done, he had to go back to Mr McMahon's to work, even though he'd been there all day, but he drove her home first, the freezing cold air straightening her out a little before she had to deal with her own stiff parents.

'So, Tasha will be at school tomorrow, then,' he said as the car pulled up.

She nodded.

'At least everything can get back to normal now.'

'Yeah,' she said, staring through the windscreen at the snow and ice and clear, dark sky. The glass had barely defrosted on their short trip to her house and ice still cracked the surface where the heaters didn't touch it properly, framing her view. She wondered how it must have felt to plunge into black freezing water. Like tumbling out into space, your breath slowly being sucked from you. For the first time, she properly wondered what had actually happened to Tasha that night. The police didn't seem bothered – she hadn't seen that DI Bennett again – but at the same time, it was still a mystery. Natasha. Always the centre of attention. 'Yeah, I guess that's what matters.'

She thought about smashing the chess set.

*

'*Hey.*'

Becca had not been looking forward to the auditions and almost didn't go, only Mr Jones had bumped into her in the corridor at lunchtime, grinning and waving a schedule under her nose and that had been that. Why shouldn't she go, anyway? She actually liked working on the set and the lighting and making sure everything went smoothly, and this year she'd get to run it. Mr Jones was right. Those things could make or break a show.

Friday of week one in the school's two-week timetable was her best day. A double free in the morning meant she got a lie-in, and then she had a free lesson in the afternoon, too. Not having really given the play any thought, she used this to find a quiet corner by a radiator and skimmed through the text, jotting down ideas for how the stark and powerful piece could be presented. Something simple was right. Maybe stick to black and white to fit thematically and match the costume of the Puritans.

She had to admit, it was a great play. Shakespeare left her cold – it was too much hard work trying to dig through the poetry for the meaning – but Miller's tale of hysteria, lies and truth sang to her. It was so full of emotions. Nothing to do with the romantic love they all chased, but about dark, consuming passions, and parts of the story made her almost hold her breath. The honest, hurt wife's lie to try and save her husband. The protecting of reputations and all that was bound up in them. She saw herself as Elizabeth, no shining Abigail or timid Mary Warren or any of the others out dancing to Tituba's spell. Those were the Barbies. It was going to be challenging to get right, but Mr Jones had picked the ideal play for that bunch of spiteful bitches.

For a while she'd actually started to feel enthusiastic about it, but then the final bell rang and her nerves jangled again. If Hannah – her trusty assistant – hadn't met her to go to the theatre together, she might have bailed. Made an excuse to miss this, if nothing else. Given her slack timetable, she hadn't seen Natasha all day and she and Hannah had spent lunch curled up by the Science corridor radiators, hiding, although neither of them would say so. The hive was too noisy and alive, and there was a swarm around Natasha, Hayley and Jenny today. Becca could survive without seeing them until all the fuss died down.

She arrived at the auditions early, knowing the others would be at their lockers or having a quick cigarette before turning up. The Barbies would saunter in ten minutes late to make an entrance anyway. Mr Jones was already there and she took her seat next to him, facing out from the front. It should have made her feel powerful. It didn't. It just made her feel exposed. She kept her head down, rustling through papers but not really seeing them, and when Hannah came over to talk about the new lighting rig, she snapped that it could wait until later. People had started to arrive, Year Elevens upwards, the occasional Year Ten, the talented *leads-in-waiting* as Mr Jones called them, all casual nonchalance, as if it didn't matter who got the parts.

Becca *felt* the Barbies' arrival before she heard it. A surge of energy through the chilly room. It didn't matter. She didn't care. She hadn't cared for a long time.

So why was she feeling so weird now?

'Hey. Bex.'

She looked up, and there was Natasha. Glowing with life. Whole. Well.

'Hi,' Becca said. Her neck was blotching with patches of sudden heat, she was sure of it. 'Glad you're okay. Thanks for the chess set.' The words came out in a rushed mumble.

'I'm so glad you like it!' Tasha grinned. 'My mum got Hayley and Jenny bracelets, but I thought you'd prefer the chess set. Not sure charm bracelets are really your thing.'

For a moment, Becca's blood rose thinking it was a dig, calling her a butch fat dyke or something, but there was nothing nasty in Natasha's tone, and from the corner of her eye Becca saw the Barbies watching. She glanced their way. The small posse of girls deciding which chairs to take were staring over with disdain and disbelief and a touch of horror. Whatever this was, it wasn't a wind-up. *My mum got Hayley and Jenny bracelets.* Natasha hadn't chosen them herself.

'Anyway, I'd better find a seat. Just wanted to say thanks for coming to the hospital and everything.'

'It's fine.'

Mr Jones clapped his hands to get their attention.

'Oh,' Natasha said hurriedly, leaning forward. 'There's a party tonight if you want to come? I have to go to my stupid counselling session after this, but it won't start till nine or ten anyway. At Mark Pritchard's house.' She turned Becca's notebook round and scribbled down an address and a phone number, and tore the strip off, handing it over. 'That's where the party is and that's my number until the police give my phone back. They won't let me get a new sim yet. Fuck knows why.' She pulled a face about the delay. 'Be great if you could come, though.'

Becca took the strip and nodded, not sure what to say, but was saved by Mr Jones launching into his pre-audition pep talk. Tasha hurried to her seat and as Becca watched her go, she caught Hayley's eye. A cool, cold, appraising stare. Becca matched it. *Bring it, bitch.*

'What was all that about?' Hannah whispered, pulling up a chair just slightly behind Becca's. 'You okay?'

'Yeah. Just a party. Tonight.'

'She invited you?' Hannah sounded incredulous and Becca

wanted to turn around and slap her hard in the face. What the fuck did Hannah know, anyway? She'd never had many friends. Never a friend like Natasha was to her when they were kids. Maybe nearly dying had made Tasha remember that.

'Yeah.'

A long pause. Pete Cramer and Jenny were reading first. They were good, but Becca couldn't concentrate. That short conversation was more than she and Tash had spoken in at least three years. Why did she feel excited? What was this? Was she now going to jump just because Natasha asked her to? No way. Why should she? She looked at Hayley and Jenny, all smug and perfect. It would really piss them off if Natasha started talking to Becca again. They wouldn't know what to do.

'I probably won't go,' she said, feeling the weight of Hannah's anxious gaze. 'I told Aiden I'd see him tonight.' She didn't look at Hannah as she whispered it. It was a lie. She probably *would* go, but she didn't want to take Hannah. If she went, she'd go on her own. Maybe it would be shit and they'd be bitches, and if so she didn't want Hannah's sympathy. Also – and the thought was like an oil slick of guilt – if she took Hannah, then they really would be laughed at and end up sitting in a corner for the whole night wishing they were somewhere else. Becca wasn't cool but she had her own thing going on. Hannah was just empty space in the social construct of the hive.

'Be careful,' Hannah said. 'You know what they're like.'

Becca wasn't sure if Hannah sounded disapproving or hurt. Probably both. She sounded *victim*.

'Like I said, I probably won't go.' The paper was getting

sweaty scrunched in her hand and she tucked it into her pocket.

Natasha was reading with James Ensor, who was in line for the role of John Proctor. Tasha wanted to be Abigail, that was clear. She was pretty good, too – not as good as Jenny, but good – and she'd obviously practised the scenes she thought might come up. When she finished, the rest of the gathering gave her a round of applause, and she blushed and smiled. They hadn't clapped for each other.

'They're applauding her just for being alive,' Hannah muttered. 'Like that was anything more than chance or fate.'

Becca said nothing. Hannah was right, of course. But it was more than that. They were clapping because they wanted her approval. She was special now. They all wanted to be her friend, even more than they had before.

*

'You're still coming over tomorrow, aren't you?' Hannah said as they headed for the gates once the auditions were done. Natasha hadn't spoken to Becca again, but she did flash her a smile and mouth, *See you tonight*, over her shoulder as she left, flanked by the Barbies.

'Tomorrow?' She frowned. 'What's happening tomorrow?'

'My mum's birthday.' Hannah looked hurt, all sad, myopic eyes in her pasty face which had never quite got past the teenage-spot stage, the occasional outbreaks on her chin leaving pink scars that never had time to heal before the next wave. 'Going out for lunch?'

'Sorry, yes.' Becca said. Of course she remembered. It had just slipped for a moment. 'Yeah, I'll be there.' Hannah beamed then and Becca suddenly felt a wave of affection for her. Hannah was her friend. She needed to remember that. Just because she didn't shine like Natasha, and just because Becca sometimes got frustrated by her lack of spine, that didn't mean she wasn't a nice person. She was. And clever. And a good listener.

Maybe she wouldn't go to the party after all. Maybe she'd just go home and watch a movie.

Maybe.

Fifteen

Excerpt of CONSULTATION BETWEEN DR ANNABEL HARVEY AND PATIENT NATASHA HOWLAND, FRIDAY 15/01, 18.30

NATASHA: What were you expecting? That somehow just being at school and home again would make everything come rushing back?

DR HARVEY: I had no expectations. Is that what you were expecting?

NATASHA: God, you really *are* a shrink.

(Giggle then pause).

I think maybe my mum was. I think she wants to know how I ended up in the river more than I do.

DR HARVEY: Don't you want to know?

NATASHA: No. Do you think that's weird? No, don't answer. You're only going to say 'But do *you* think that's weird?' Maybe it is a bit weird. But I feel okay. I wasn't beaten up or raped or anything. The police aren't bothered any more. And I mean, I could go crazy wondering about it, couldn't I?

DR HARVEY: How was school today?

NATASHA: Fine. You know, everyone was looking at me

but I can cope with that. We had the play auditions. That was good. Hayley and Jenny – they're my best friends, I guess – they're sticking to me like glue, which is also nice. I guess.

DR HARVEY: You don't sound convinced.

NATASHA: No, it's good. They're great. They're protecting me from everyone who wants to ask questions. Which is kind of funny. Like *they* don't have questions.

DR HARVEY: What kind of questions?

NATASHA: Mainly what was it like.

(Pause)

The whole being dead thing.

DR HARVEY: What do you tell them?

NATASHA: What can I tell them? I don't remember anything. They're expecting me to say something about white lights and tunnels, I think.

(Pause)

I invited Becca to the party.

DR HARVEY: Party?

NATASHA: There's one tonight. In my honour for still being alive. I invited Becca. I don't even really know why.

DR HARVEY: Should you be going to a party so soon?

NATASHA: Ha. You're more parental than my parents.

DR HARVEY: They don't mind you going?

NATASHA: Oh, I'm sure they do. They won't say so, though.

DR HARVEY: Becca sounds significant to you.

NATASHA: She used to be my best friend. A long time ago. I've just found myself thinking about her more since all this happened. It used to be me and her, then it was me, her and Hayley. Then it became me, Hayley and Jenny.

DR HARVEY: Did you have an argument?

NATASHA: No. Not really. Just, well . . . things change at school and stuff, don't they?
Different things become important. Who you hang around with. That stuff.

DR HARVEY: But you've asked her to the party.

NATASHA: Yes. She probably won't come, though.

DR HARVEY: So Becca was your first best friend? How old were you when you met?

NATASHA: Maybe seven? I'm not sure. I feel like I've known her for ever.

DR HARVEY: Perhaps she's your security.

NATASHA: What?

DR HARVEY: There is always a child in all of us. You're sixteen. You're almost grown up. But this incident, the trauma you've just been through, might make you want the security of your childhood. Perhaps your parents don't fully provide that. Perhaps you're looking to Becca for it?

NATASHA: (Laughs)
I think you're thinking too much about it.
(Pause)
Although I'm not sleeping well.

DR HARVEY: Why is that?

NATASHA: I don't know.

DR HARVEY: What's preventing you from sleeping?

NATASHA: Nothing. I'm in my room. Everything's the same.

DR HARVEY: Perhaps you're not the same.

NATASHA: (Quiet)
It's the dark. I'm afraid of the dark.

DR HARVEY: What frightens you about it?
NATASHA: (Long pause. Shuffling. A cough)
I think there's something in it. Something bad.

Sixteen

Becca didn't dress up – not like the others would, anyway, just an off-one-shoulder black T over her jeans – but she put her full warpaint on, dark kohl shading all round her eyes tapering to Cleopatra points. She thought it made her look fierce. She *was* fierce. Though right until the moment she came to a stop outside the house that throbbed with music in the night, she hadn't been sure she'd actually go.

She'd told her mum that she was meeting a couple of other girls from school and that she might stay over, appeasing her clucking worry with *Of course I'll text when we're home* and then she texted Aiden and asked if he'd be around to pick her up at about one, maybe earlier, and that she had an all-night pass. That part had made her smile through her nerves.

Mark Pritchard wasn't as wealthy as Natasha but his house was big, with two downstairs living rooms, a large kitchen and a den at the back before the garden. At first, coming in from the cold, and with her stomach suddenly in knots of nerves, Becca felt almost disorientated. People were flashes of coloured clothes, milling everywhere. Faces she recognised but didn't really know. A couple of boys who'd left the year before. Music thumped from the front room through the fabric of the building. She was never going to find Tasha here. Coming was the stupidest thing she'd ever done, she decided. Were they all going to laugh at her?

All. *Get over it*, she thought. *Who is all? Just the Barbies. You're not Hannah. No one else sniggers at you. You're invisible but you're not a joke.* But maybe the Barbies were all that mattered. And if the Barbies did something to humiliate her here in front of all their peers then she *would* become a joke. Another Hannah. Maybe she should just text Aiden now. Maybe she should just—

'Bex!'

She looked up. A hand waved from the kitchen and then Natasha was worming her way through the people talking and drinking in the corridor and grabbing her. 'Isn't it great? Mark's mum even left a load of food and booze. Come on!' There was no going back now.

She took her coat off in the kitchen, nodding hellos at people and keeping a wary eye out for Hayley and Jenny as Natasha made them both strong vodka and cranberry drinks.

'Cheers!' They clinked plastic glasses. 'Here's to being alive.'

As she drank – too fast, needing the hit for confidence – Becca thought Tasha had never looked better than she did now, so soon after being nearly dead. Her skin glowed even under the bronzer she'd dusted herself with, glittering like stardust over her bare arms and neck. She was slim and perfect in her skinny jeans and silver strappy sequinned top. She made Becca feel like a rugby player. She looked down at her comfy Doc Martens and then at Natasha's four-inch cream stiletto heels. Had they really been best friends? How? How much could two people change?

'So glad you could come.' Close in, Natasha smelled of

perfume and bubblegum. Becca no doubt reeked of cigarettes. 'You can save me from Mark. He's starting to piss me off. How many times do I have to say no? And don't you think it's strange to want to go out with a girl *more* just because she drowned? He should go out with Hayley. She really fancies him.'

'Where is Hayley?' She tried to keep her voice light but her eyes scanned the party-goers warily.

'Oh, she and Jenny have gone to get some fun. They'll be back in a minute. Come on, let's dance.'

Becca had never felt less like dancing, so she necked the vodka and poured herself one so strong the cranberry was barely a pink trace through it before following Tasha towards the music. So far, the 'dancing' was just five or six girls swaying in time to the beat while laughing and talking, and they flung their arms round Tasha's neck and made space for her. Then one of them, Vicki Springer, who'd been at the auditions, did the same to Becca.

'Becca! If you know who Mr Jones is casting, then feel free to share! Or better still, if you can find out which one of us he'd fuck, I'll pay to know!' Her eyes were glazed drunk. She must have arrived at the party early. 'He's totally up for it. You can tell. The way he is around us – he's gagging to get into a teenager.'

'Maybe he'd let us share him,' Jodie added. They all squealed and with booze buzzing her brain, Becca laughed along, agreeing how hot Mr Jones was and how they'd all like to bone him even though she didn't think that at all and she couldn't imagine cheating on Aiden with anyone. They fluttered around her wanting details about him as if Becca had a special 'in' by doing the stage sets. Maybe she did, but maybe that was because she was the only one *not* trying to get into his trousers.

It was still funny, though, she thought, her eyes darting about the room. All the boys were dicking around loudly but secretly watching the girls dance, and all the girls were thinking about fucking someone so much older than them. Her head spun slightly and she laughed for no reason, swaying along with the rest of the pack. She was a stoner, not a drinker, and the vodka was going straight to her head. She was in the hive. She was part of the buzz. That made her laugh a bit more.

Mark appeared from nowhere and grabbed at Natasha. She started to shake him off, but he leaned closer and whispered something in her ear. She nodded and then took Becca's hand. 'Come on. They're back.' It felt strange having Tasha's warm, slim fingers wrapped around hers. She felt ten years old again, off on an adventure with her *best friend forever*. It was like a weird dream where the past had melted into the present, making everything surreal. She felt both at home and out of place. The latter took over as the door to the den closed behind her, cramming her in with the Barbies and some of the boys.

'So,' Hayley said to Becca as Jenny collected money from the seven or so teenagers gathered. 'You in? If so, we'll need some cash. Jenny's saving for Uni. No freebies.' Her eyes were fixed on Becca.

'Like Jenny's getting into any Uni.' Mark snickered. 'Little Miss Maths Retake.'

'I've paid for a gram,' Natasha said, 'so Becca can have some of mine if she wants. Don't be such a bitch.' It was said light-heartedly but Becca was sure she saw Hayley flinch a little. 'The same goes for you, Mark. Jenny's cleverer than you think.'

Hayley hadn't taken her cool eyes from Becca throughout the conversation, although at this her gaze flicked over to Jenny and then Natasha and then landed back on Becca.

'Do you want some or not?' she asked.

'What is it? Mandy or coke?' Becca asked.

'Mandy,' Jenny said, tucking the wedge of notes into her wallet. 'Top shit. It will blow your cares away.' She took out a packet of Rizlas and passed them to the boys, who had already started undoing their wrap. 'Bomb it, don't snort it, though. Better buzz. Lasts longer, too. And you won't spend the next half an hour thinking your nose is on fire.'

'Staying friends with that dealer your mum dated is the best thing you ever did,' Hayley said drily.

As the boys began tipping the glittering white powder carefully onto the cigarette papers, Becca looked down at their own wrap on the coffee table, the weight of the Barbies' eyes on her. 'Sure. Why not?'

Natasha let out a small whoop. 'Let's get this party started.'

'Are you sure you should?' Becca asked, immediately hating herself for sounding so sensible. 'You know, after everything.'

'I'm physically fine,' Natasha said.

'Yeah, you are.' Mark winked, tossed the bomb of paper containing the drugs into his mouth and swallowed it down with some beer.

Natasha glanced at Becca and rolled her eyes. Hayley's perfect jaw tightened slightly. Jenny glanced from one friend to the other as she sorted the drugs. Was this a rift in the Barbie camp? Becca wondered. Over an idiot like Mark Pritchard?

'Here you go,' Jenny said, four twists of Rizla sitting on her palm. 'They're all the same so take your pick.'

Becca took a deep breath as they waited. So it was going

to be her first. What was this, some kind of test? Of course it was. Everything in the hive was a test. She picked up one of the bombs. How bad could it be? Not as bad as looking like a twat in front of the school cool gang. She put it in her mouth, wondering if there was a way she could tuck it into her cheek or something and not actually swallow it. There wasn't. *Fuck it*, she thought. *Here we go.* She lifted her glass and took a long drink, washing the makeshift pill down.

She stared defiantly at Hayley. 'Let's get this party started.'

*

By midnight, she was flying. It had started slowly. As the paper dissolved in her stomach and the drug began to hit her bloodstream, there was a tingle and then a sudden surge of heat and brightness. Her heart beat faster. For a nanosecond, Becca thought, *I'm not sure I like this*, and then that was carried away on a wave of bliss. The music pumped through her, each beat making her throb with pleasure. Natasha was dancing but Becca was content just to watch everyone. This wasn't her scene. She was happy to be invisible.

In the kitchen she grabbed another vodka. Hayley and Jenny were deep in conversation in the corner of the room, blonde heads bent towards each other. They looked over at Becca and even through the haze of the drug's buzz she could see their dislike. Was it dislike? Wariness? Something. She grinned at them like an idiot, unable to stop herself, as they came over to her. If only they could be friends. If only they could—

'What do you want, Becca?' Hayley said quietly.

'What has she said to you?' Jenny joined in. She chewed her

bottom lip as they waited for Becca's response. Becca grinned some more. At least, she thought it was a grin. Her jaw had clenched, so she could have been gurning like a loon at them for all she knew.

'You guys are so beautiful,' she said. 'I mean, really. Even without all the fake shit like make-up and stuff. You really are.'

'Are you taking the piss?' Hayley said.

Becca frowned. Hayley's eyes were sharp. So were Jenny's. How come they weren't off their tits like she was?

'What's going on?' she asked. 'What's the matter with you two?'

They looked at each other, a silent glance of perfect communication.

'Don't worry about it.' Jenny pulled Hayley away, leaving Becca alone. Barbies. She would never understand them. Suddenly she missed Aiden. Not so much missed as wanted to see him desperately. To wrap herself around him and trap them in their world of two forever. She loved him. She loved him so so much. They were soulmates. Meant to be. Hayley and Jenny could look down on her as much as they liked. She had Aiden. No one else mattered. Not even Natasha.

She pulled out her phone and sent him a text with slightly sweaty fingers to see if he was nearly done working, and then grabbed her coat and went out into the cold night for a cigarette, leaving the front door on the snib so she could get back in.

The drug had made her hot and the crisp air was refreshing. She sat on the step and sucked in the smoke, eyes on the stars above. The night was clear and by morning the slush and snow would have frozen into treacherous ice. She could still hear the thump of music and noise from inside, but it felt a world away from the quiet of the night. All the other smokers were in the back garden with easy access to the kitchen and drinks, and Becca thought this moment could sum up her entire school experience. Always just on the outside of everything.

She smiled. It didn't bother her. She loved them all right now, anyway. All their attempts to be cool and fit in and be perfect. They were the same really. They were her peers, her classmates, and she loved them.

Her phone buzzed. Aiden. He'd pick her up in ten minutes. Her smile stretched to a grin and her joy at the thought of seeing him sent another rush of drugged pleasure through her, making her shiver. Whatever it was, it was good shit. All the mellow of being stoned but with a clarity of perception. A pureness of emotion. So much warmth. She liked it. Maybe Aiden could score them some and they could do it together. And then they could *do it* together. She giggled aloud at her own joke.

'What's so funny?'

Becca turned to see Natasha pulling the door to behind her.

'Nothing. Just thinking silly thoughts.'

'Good shit, isn't it?' Tasha said, sitting beside Becca on the step. Her pupils were dark and wide, black holes eating up the universe of her irises.

'Yeah.' Becca held out her cigarettes and Tasha shook her head. Despite having just put one out, Becca lit a second. The smoke felt good. It enhanced her rush. 'You do it a lot?'

'No. Just felt like letting go tonight.'

'Don't blame you.'

'How come you're out here?'

'Waiting for Aiden,' she answered. It wasn't why she'd come out into the quiet, but it would do as an explanation.

'Going already?'

'Yeah, I've got shit to do tomorrow. Thanks for asking me, though – it's been fun.' She paused. 'Even if Hayley and Jenny didn't want me here.'

Natasha's face darkened and she let out a long breath, mist in the night. 'They can be strange, but they've been nice over the past few days, like guard dogs around me – normal again.'

'How do you mean?' Becca watched her. 'You guys not been getting on?'

Natasha shrugged. 'I'm not really sure. It's just been odd.' She squeezed Becca's arm. 'But everything that's happened has made me look at things differently. I guess it's why I wanted your friendship back. I just . . . It's hard to explain. I thought of you when I woke up and knew I needed to make amends for being such a bitch.'

'Don't worry about it,' Becca said. She actually meant it, too. Maybe it was the mandy, maybe it was that Tasha had nearly died, or maybe it was just too much water under the bridge. 'We've grown up very different. We were probably always destined to go our separate ways. And you and Hayley and Jenny, well, you know. You were always going to be close.'

Natasha shrugged and looked down at her shoes. 'I suppose so. But we all change. Sometimes I think . . . I don't know. They . . .'

A car turned into the road and crawled towards them, the driver trying to spot the house numbers in the dark.

'That's Aiden.' Becca got to her feet. But then she frowned and turned back. 'They what?'

'Oh, nothing. I'm just being stupid. I'm drunk. High. I'd better go back inside, anyway.' She held out her hand and Becca pulled her up. 'My adoring fans will wonder where I've got to. Well, Mark will, anyway.' She pulled a vom face and they both grinned. 'I've left him with Hayley. Maybe she'll make a move and save me.'

'He's not so bad,' Becca said. 'You're too hard on him.' Aiden pulled up to the kerb and flashed his headlights. Becca waved and then turned to hug Tasha.

'Thanks again.'

'Enjoy the rest of your night,' Tasha said with a wink. She looked towards the car. 'I saw Aiden yesterday. He's so different now. Like, all grown-up. What's the score with you two? Is it a proper love thing?'

Becca nodded. 'Yeah. Yeah, it really is.'

Tasha grinned. 'Cool. Go fuck his brains out.'

As they both giggled, Tasha leaned past Becca and waved.

'Laters,' Becca said and darted down the path.

'Laters!' Tasha called after her.

*

Aiden's car was melted-chocolate hot as Becca slid across the passenger seat to kiss him. She held his face with her cold hands and pushed her tongue into his mouth, the warm, wet sensation making her rush all over again. Drugs were awesome. Maybe they were *bad* but they were pretty fucking awesome, too.

'Slow down, you nympho,' he said, laughing and pushing her off him. 'Let's get away from here first.'

Becca slumped back against her seat, grinning, then took the half-smoked joint from the ashtray between them and lit it.

'Good party?'

'It was pretty cool.' The weed and mandy made for a good combination. Street lights swirled in the darkness, tracing across her vision as the car moved away.

Aiden glanced at her. 'You and Natasha looked pretty cosy.'

She shrugged. What was it to him? She frowned, distracted for a moment from the pleasantness of the thrills in her body and the streaking lights outside.

'You never said you'd seen Natasha.'

'She and her mum came to Jamie's house. I didn't see them, really – took them some drinks and then fucked off back to the studio.'

Becca stared out at the night. Even with the mellow love drug in her system she felt a pang of jealousy. *He liked Natasha first.* She'd come after. She was second prize.

Aiden reached over and poked her playfully in the side, making her cough out a lungful of scented smoke. 'Don't go getting weird on me over this. I have no interest in shallow little Natasha.'

'She's not so bad,' Becca said.

'Give her time to get back to normal.' He took the stub of the joint from her and finished it, throwing the roach out into the night. 'Then you'll change your mind.'

'I think it's Hayley and Jenny,' she said. 'I think they've changed her.'

'Or she changed them.'

Becca said nothing. She didn't really want to defend Tasha too much in case Aiden suddenly fell in love with her all over again. She almost laughed at her own exaggeration. He'd never been in love with Tasha – he'd hardly known her, just asked her out once a long time ago. *Get some perspective, Crisp*, she told herself. *And calm the fuck down.* But Natasha was hot, there was no doubt about it. And perhaps Aiden sometimes thought of that hotness when he was sliding between Becca's legs.

'Maybe,' she said, twisting sideways so she could look at him and pulling her knees up under her chin as best she could within the constraints of her seat belt. She didn't want to think about Natasha. They were being friendly again. She mustn't let her own paranoia fuck that up. 'Who cares, anyway.'

'Exactly.'

'You are so beautiful,' she said, the words surging up from her heart and out through her mouth. 'You really really are. I mean, so handsome. Like a painting.' She giggled at herself and Aiden joined in.

'I love you so much,' she said. 'I really do. You're amazing.'

He studied her for a second and then she saw the realisation dawn on him. 'Your eyes are fucked,' he said. 'What are you on?'

'Nothing really. Just a bit of Mandy.'

'Who gave you that?'

'Jenny had some. I didn't buy it – Tasha offered me a bomb. Rude not to take it.' She suddenly felt slightly defensive, like she was in a conversation with her parents.

'Got any left?' he asked, eventually.

She shook her head. 'It wasn't mine.' He was so handsome and he was hers. She wanted to suffocate in him. 'Is your mum out tonight?' she asked.

'I don't know. Maybe. She didn't tell me her plans. Why?'

She stretched like a cat, her legs falling open slightly and her top riding up against her bare stomach. 'I want to make some noise,' she purred. She felt sexy. She felt alive. She saw the dip in his throat as Aiden swallowed hard. It made her feel powerful. He wanted *her*. Not Tasha. Only her. Her hand reached over to his thigh and, watching him, her fingers traced and teased until they brushed over the crotch of his jeans. He pressed her hand down onto the hardness there.

They didn't make it to his flat. Instead, they pulled into the car park by the woods and killed the lights. Within seconds, she'd kicked her jeans off and straddled him, pushing him far inside her, grinding on him like she couldn't get enough. And she couldn't. For the first time sex was something for her, not just some mystery for him, and as he pushed her T-shirt and bra up, his eyes glazed and breath heavy, she slid one hand down to touch herself as she fucked him.

'Jesus, Becca,' he said, and the helpless need in his voice intensified her own lust. She was lost in the sensation, and as she rode him and worked herself, feeling him getting harder as he fought to control the urge to come, she moaned load and hard and adult. Finally, she collapsed on his shoulder and it was his turn to cry out, all the need, all the anger and lust and love pounding into her with his last few thrusts.

When satiated sanity returned, they smiled and giggled at each other as Becca pulled on her jeans, her legs suddenly cold without the car engine and heater running. Aiden rolled another joint and they shared it in a comfortable silence, both staring out at the night and basking in their afterglow. Becca, although no longer rushing, was still too high to feel awkward or embarrassed about their sex, as she usually did if she thought about actually letting go and doing what made her feel good. Tonight was like the first time all over again. Except this time she felt like an actual *woman*, not a girl.

As they passed the joint between them, Aiden looked at her, almost in awe, and she was hit by the thought that there was nothing dirty in enjoying her body or his, and that he might actually like it if she did just do whatever she wanted. There was nothing to be ashamed of. It wouldn't stop him loving her. Judging by how he was looking at her right now, it might just make him love her more.

Sex was weird. Or maybe it wasn't so much that sex was weird, it was just that it was like drugs. All the way through growing up, people tell you how you shouldn't do it. Then you do it and it feels great. Why didn't they ever tell you that bit? And at least sex wasn't illegal. But why make you feel so guilty about something you're actually allowed to do by sixteen? Not that age had stopped plenty at school. Jenny for one. Everyone knew that Jenny fucked around. Even Becca's mum knew. When they'd bumped into Jenny clothes shopping with her mum, after the polite hellos and quick escapes, Becca's mum had glanced back at the rack they'd been browsing and quietly sneered, *Like mother, like daughter.* She might as well have spat *sluts* at them. It was all in the look. Maybe her mum was jealous. Maybe her dad didn't cut it in the bedroom department. That was a thought and an image she *really* didn't want to linger on – there weren't enough drugs in the world to make her want to think about her parents fucking – so she turned on the radio and let the music distract her.

When they'd finished the spliff, Aiden drove them home, Becca's head on his shoulder even though it meant her midriff was uncomfortable with the stretch. She didn't care. She loved him. She loved touching him.

It was gone two a.m. when they crawled, naked, into his cold bed, huddling together under the duvet until their feet thawed, and as their shivering subsided, they did it again. It was quieter this time. Gentle. *Lovemaking*, Becca thought, even though the word made her cringe. But that's what it was.

Seventeen

Taken from **DI CAITLIN BENNETT'S FILES: EXTRACT FROM NATASHA HOWLAND'S NOTEBOOK**

I let Mark Pritchard snog me. I could see Hayley watching when he did it and I stared right back at her, as if I was victorious. I *was* victorious. She was like an ice queen, as if she was the one who'd frozen to death and come back to life. Perhaps Hayley has grown prettier than me, but she doesn't have what I have. She doesn't have my *mystique*. Not now. She doesn't have Mark Pritchard chasing her like I do.

I met her eyes as he pushed me up against the wall. He was trying be all manly but just made himself seem too eager, and he hurt my spine against the dado rail. Despite that, it didn't even feel like he was there. Not really. It was all about me and Hayley. Our gazes were locked as he wormed his way between my lips, pushing his thick tongue against mine. She tried to smile but her neck was going blotchy like I'd almost drawn blood.

I pretended I'd done it because I was off my face, the same reason I gave for coming back home rather than staying over at hers with Jenny, but that wasn't the truth. I don't know what the truth is. I didn't want to snog Mark. I just know it felt good to see Hayley beaten. Cool, calm Hayley. The running star. The girl with the perfect abs. The girl who was my second and is now becoming something of her own. Sometimes I think they're strangers. We're all strangers. Circling each other.

I see the same thing with my mum and her 'ladies' lunch' group. They laugh and joke and say how much they love each other, but as true as that might be, they still watch each other for weakness. For chinks in the armour. I don't think boys are the same. Boys are dogs. Women are like cats. Individuals by nature. We are not pack animals. And now that we three, we inseparable, admired rulers of the school roost, are almost women, maybe that's starting to show.

Hayley didn't shout at me or snap or anything. She pretended it was totally cool. She said she didn't even really like him and I could have him. I laughed at that. I don't want Mark Pritchard. He's a dick. I think most of the boys at school are dicks. I think maybe it was worse for Hayley that I said I didn't want him. It was mean. True, but mean. I just wanted her to know that I *could* have him. That he preferred me.

Jenny isn't so good at hiding her feelings. She's our sheep, after all. A sweet, funny, sexy sheep. Sometimes I'm not sure if she even has a mind of her own, or just some mash-up of mine and Hayley's. She kept looking at me, confused. Half-going to say something and then stopping herself. When I said I was heading home rather than coming to Hayley's, neither of them really argued. They looked relieved. Maybe they were. They're whispering together again, like they did before my accident sometimes. They think I don't see, but I do. Maybe that's why

I snogged Mark. Maybe I needed to remind them who's in charge.

I still wish I'd gone to Hayley's, even though it's better that I didn't. Not while I was still high.

If I'd gone to Hayley's, I might not have dreamed. I thought getting high would save me from the fear of that darkness. I thought it would protect me from the nightmares. But it didn't. After I finally fell asleep, I woke so drenched in sweat that I thought I was back in the river, trapped there forever.

I can't remember the whole dream. Only fragments. I was in the terrible, endless darkness. It swallowed me up. I was alone. It was beyond cold. I couldn't breathe. I wasn't supposed to be there. It was wrong. I tried to propel myself upwards, swimming breaststroke, but I didn't move. I don't think I moved, anyway. It was hard to tell. There was no sense of anything around me. No water. No current sucking at my feet. I was just suspended in the void.

And then someone whispered my name.

I froze, hanging in the nothing, unable to see. They whispered it again. A voice I knew I *should* know. Closer. And then I was screaming silently into the dark.

Eighteen

The Barbies would probably die if they were seen anywhere as tacky as Frankie & Benny's, but Becca, still a bit wired and on a major comedown, was glad of the starchy, fattening food by the time two o'clock came around.

Still, she thought as she drained another Diet Coke and wished her mouth would feel less dry, it was a bit lame to take your best friend out on your mum's birthday lunch. Parents' birthday meals were a drag at the best of times – not something you'd want to put someone else through. But then not everyone got on with her family in the way Hannah did. Becca looked at them, all smiling and happy to be with each other. Maybe that's what came of being the absolutely least cool kid in school – you got to stay friends with your parents.

'And you're doing all the stage set and design, Hannah says?' Hannah's mum, Amanda, said. 'That's quite a responsibility.'

'She did it last year, too,' Hannah cut in, as if Becca needed the support, as if Amanda with her doughy body and slack bosom was anything other than fully supportive at all times. 'And it was amazing. Really was.' Hannah grinned over at her, and for an instant Becca could see her as a mum, a skinnier version of Amanda, but filled with that same yearning to live through someone else rather than risk living for herself.

'Katie Groud did most of it last year, but she's at Uni now.'

'I'm sure it will still be brilliant.' Amanda looked from Becca to Hannah and back again. 'With you two working on it, I can't see how it couldn't be.' Her eyes and smile were so full of warmth Becca almost blushed. Hannah was clever and had got all A*s in her exams and would go off to Oxford or something, no doubt, but sometimes Becca thought that she was Hannah's greatest school achievement in her parents' eyes. If Hannah had a friend like Becca then she couldn't be doing too badly. She wasn't one of those girls with no friends who got bullied online and hanged themselves.

Becca wished she could tell Amanda that she didn't have to worry. Hannah hadn't even been bullied when they were young. Hannah was too bland, too invisible for that. Always had been, always would be. While they were at school, at least. People couldn't be *bothered* to bully Hannah. Becca bit into her burger, the juice running down her chin, and her stomach growled. How had she ended up Hannah's best friend? Wrong place at the wrong time, probably. Paired up in Science just as Natasha had dumped her. And here she now was, in Frankie & Benny's for Hannah's mum's birthday like they were kids. It was depressing, even if she felt bad for thinking that way.

'And how's that boyfriend of yours?' Amanda asked. 'Does he have any nice friends for Hannah?'

'Mum, please!' Hannah's pasty skin flushed. 'Dad, tell her.'

'Don't embarrass her, Amanda,' Mr Alderton muttered from behind a fistful of sticky ribs.

'What? I was just asking a question.'

'He's fine.' Becca swallowed her burger and spoke through meaty teeth, eager to answer and stop Amanda going further. She wasn't backward in coming forward, and while Hannah was a shy virgin, Amanda had no such reserve. 'But I'm not sure his friends would really be Hannah's type.'

She caught the sideways glance from Hannah, a defensive pre-empting of hurt, unsure if this was a little dig or not. 'Hannah needs someone brainier.' Becca smiled. 'She's too clever for most of the boys Aiden knows. Hannah needs, like, a doctor or something.'

'You're right there.' Amanda nodded approvingly. 'She's academic. She needs someone who can match that.'

'Come to the loo with me,' Hannah said, tugging on Becca's sleeve. 'Let's have a moment's sanity.'

'I thought it was just a stereotype that women went to the toilet in pairs,' Mr Alderton said. 'What can you two have to gossip about when out for lunch with just us?'

Amanda slapped him playfully on the arm with her napkin. 'They're teenagers. They've always got something to gossip about, isn't that right?' She winked at the girls and they dutifully smiled back, sliding quickly out from the booth.

It's a sitcom, Becca thought. *Hannah's living in a sitcom without much intentional com.* She suddenly felt sorry for her. It must be hard being liked by your parents all the time. Having to be nice to each other constantly. She couldn't remember ever seeing Hannah just grunt a moody hello at Amanda when they got in from school. Not once. There was always a smile and a quick chat about the day as they grabbed drinks and snacks. Very different from her home where just a slightly odd look from her mother could send Becca into a full teenage flounce to her room.

'Sorry about that,' Hannah said as the door to the ladies' swung closed behind them. 'I'm sure she's getting worse.'

'She's still better than my mum,' Becca said, although she

wasn't actually sure she'd ever want to swap.

There was a moment of quiet as they went into cubicles side by side and willed their bladders to work knowing other people could hear them.

'Did you stay at Aiden's last night?' Hannah asked through the thin wall. 'You look tired. Your eyes are a bit stoned still.'

'Yeah,' Becca said, and then flushed. Hannah emerged at the same time and they went to the sinks. Becca kept her head down as she focused on washing her hands. 'I went to the party for a bit.'

'Natasha's one?' Hannah stared at her.

'I didn't stay long. Just thought I should show up, you know. She *did* invite me and everything.' She felt uncomfortable. She'd considered not telling Hannah she'd been to the party, but that would have been stupid. Hannah would've heard at school. And really, why should she lie? It wasn't like she'd done anything bad. Hannah wouldn't have wanted to go anyway. It was just a party. No big deal.

'Sure,' Hannah said. She paused, though, as if she hadn't quite said everything.

'What?'

'Just be careful.'

'How do you mean?'

'You know. It's *Natasha*. Be careful. I don't trust her. She can be mean. Amongst other things.'

'You don't know her,' Becca snapped. *Maybe she can be mean to you*, she wanted to say but bit it back, because yes, Natasha and the Barbies had sneered at Hannah over the years, but they'd also sneered at Becca. Hannah knew that. Becca knew that. 'Look,' she said, calmer, 'I'm not planning on getting all close with her again. Those days are done. She asked me and in the end I thought it was polite to go. That's it. I mean, she nearly *died* and we still don't know how she ended up there.'

Hannah shrugged. 'I just worry about you.'

'Now you sound like *my* mother.' Becca rolled her eyes and then squeezed Hannah's arm. 'Come on – I really need one of those huge chocolate sundaes that make you want to puke by the time you've finished them.'

They were giggling when they got back to the table and Amanda's approving smile. That was when Becca noticed the text message on her phone.

> Want 2 come over l8r? Bout
> 4/5? Let me know. Tash.

Her heart thumped. What was going on with Tash and the other Barbies? Why would she want Becca there and not Hayley or Jenny? Or would they be there, too? Why was Tasha being friendly again?

Sure, she sent back. *See you then.*

'Aiden?' Hannah said. '*Does he looove you? He want to kiiisss you?*'

Becca smiled. 'Something like that, you dick.' It wasn't even a proper lie. She hadn't lied. She hadn't said if it was or wasn't Aiden. It didn't matter anyway. They were allowed other friends. Well, Hannah would be if she ever made any.

Still, she only ate half her ice cream when it came, and as they walked out into the cold and the other girl linked arms with her, Becca couldn't help but feel she was somehow betraying Hannah. Maybe she wouldn't go to Tasha's. Maybe she'd text again and say she couldn't make it after all.

*

It was weird being back in Tasha's house. Alison pulled out the leftovers of some huge chocolate cake and said how *urban* Becca's look was as she cut them big slices despite Becca saying she honestly couldn't eat any, which appeared to win her more approval from Alison Howland. They sat at the kitchen table with her for a few awkward minutes of polite conversation until Becca, her shyness making her clumsy, nearly spilled her Coke all over a pile of neatly stacked magazines balanced on top of a slim Airbook.

'Don't worry, don't worry,' Alison said as Becca grabbed a cloth to mop up the spillage she hadn't quite prevented before catching her glass. 'I never use the thing. All that's damp is a corner of some celebrity's face.' She held up the wet magazine. 'See?'

'We're going upstairs now, anyway,' Tasha said. 'Come on, Bex.' She left her plate of barely touched cake behind and Becca did the same.

'Nice to see you again, Mrs Howland.'

'You, too, Rebecca.' The older woman squeezed her arm. 'And thank you. For being there. It really helped.'

'No problem.' Becca's face flushed hard. Adults being grateful to teenagers was weird. And a little bit scary. Like they were all becoming equals and there was no safety left in the world. Their childhoods were over. They were in a waiting room at the cusp of adulthood. No-man's-land, neither one thing nor the other. Sometimes it was brilliant. Sometimes it totally sucked.

*

Natasha's room had changed. Gone were the boy-band posters and pink walls, now replaced with a pale yellow, stylish mirrors and a dressing table. One wall had a photo collage on it and Becca glanced over it. It was mainly Barbie selfies. And mainly from a year or two ago, pre-Instagram. Their lives were all online now. It was a bigger admiring audience that way, and the Barbies definitely needed an audience.

'If you want to smoke, go ahead.' Natasha locked her bedroom door and then opened the window.

'Your parents let you have a lock on your door? They are so not normal.'

'Girl needs her privacy. I'm past the age when I'll risk my dad walking in and seeing my boobs. Or worse.'

'Gross, Tasha. Most dads just knock.'

'You know my parents – they like an easy life. I wanted a lock. I got one.'

They swung one leg each over the old windowsill and sat half-in and half-out of Natasha's room, cold air one side, central heating warm on the other. They had done this many times in the long-ago past, but right now Becca felt like Alice in Wonderland after she'd drunk or eaten whatever it was that made her grow. The windowsill looked so much smaller. The last time Becca had sat like this, she didn't need to hunch and her hanging leg hadn't felt the drag of gravity. She lifted it and let it rest on a branch of the old tree whose limbs had carried Natasha out into the night and to the river. It was an easy reach.

She wasn't as comfortable with heights as Tasha and Hayley were, but she'd have no problem getting to the ladder and climbing down from here to the garden. The branches were thick and even, solid, and Becca could see where Tasha had broken smaller ones off lower down to make easy footholds. The snow outside was finally melting and the tree was clear of it, just as it would have been that night.

'You still don't remember anything?' Becca asked, before quickly adding, 'Sorry, you must be so tired of that question. I figure you don't.'

Tasha shook her head. 'Nothing. Nothing real. Sometimes I dream stuff, but it's more about being afraid and in the water than anything else. Thinking something's in there with me, something I can't quite see.'

'Maybe that's your memory trying to come back.' Becca blew out a long stream of smoke. 'Something just out of reach?'

'You sound like the shrink.' Tasha glanced back into the bedroom. 'She makes me write a diary. Stuff I'm doing and thinking. I wasn't going to do it, but . . . you know. Maybe it helps.' She shrugged, looking almost embarrassed. It was strange seeing Tasha so unconfident and Becca's heart thawed a little. She glanced at the notebook, and the pen sitting on top of it, by her friend's bed. It must be so strange, not knowing how it happened.

'I hope to shit you didn't put the drugs stuff in there,' she said with a grin.

'No! I thought I'd make some stuff up, just in case she ever asks to read it. In case you were wondering, I'm currently having a three-way with Mr Jones and Mr Garrick from English.'

'Once again: gross.' Becca said.

'Well, we can't all be loved-up like you.'

'How come you don't have a boyfriend? Don't you want one?' The afternoon sun was setting, painting the horizon a burning envious orange under the cold, darkening blue. Becca stared at it, suddenly worried that Tasha was going to declare she'd made a terrible mistake and had been in love with Aiden all along and was hoping she could just take him now and they could all still be friends.

'I don't think I do,' Tasha said, quietly. 'I just don't get what all the fuss is about. I can't tell Hayles or Jen that, of course. They wouldn't get it. Jenny fucks like a rabbit – practically everything you've heard about her is true and then some – and Hayley would tit-fuck Mark Pritchard *and* his dad if it would get him to go out with her. But I don't really see what the point of a boyfriend is.'

The words were harsh and crude, rougher coming from Tasha. She wasn't like that. Although, Becca had to admit, she didn't really know what she was like any more.

'You guys okay?' She studied Tasha. One of the slim girl's knees was under her chin, the other still dangling over the ledge. She was hunched up. Thoughtful. Her face tight and eyes dark. Still beautiful, though.

'I think so.'

'It's just, last night you were going to say something about them and then you stopped.' She stubbed out her cigarette butt on the underside of the ledge and then pulled her leg inside to go and flush it down the toilet. She envied Tasha in so many ways. A lock on the door *and* her own en-suite bathroom. No shouting through the door for privacy. No hurrying along the landing in just a towel. She wondered if she'd ever stop envying Natasha Howland or if this was her life's fate.

'Things have been a bit weird,' Tasha said eventually. Becca sat on the bed. 'I don't know, it was just different. Before my accident.'

'Different how?'

'It's hard to say. As if they don't like me so much any more.'

Becca couldn't picture it. Natasha *was* the Barbies. Jenny and Hayley were just satellites.

'Maybe three *is* a crowd,' Tasha finished.

Becca bit her tongue to stop a barbed remark about being left on the sidelines, kicked out like some rejected runt of a litter, any one of a million metaphors that still didn't quite cut it, to express how much it had hurt. Tasha had said sorry. And it was a long time ago. They'd all changed. Grown up, for better or for worse.

'But they seem fine now. More than fine, actually. Constantly texting and checking on me. Wanting to come over. I had to tell them I've got a hospital thing this afternoon just to shut them up for a while.'

'At least they care.'

'Something like that, I guess. Hey,' Tasha said suddenly, 'you want a game of chess?'

'What, now?' Becca asked.

'Why not? Let's start now and text our next moves as and when. You can set it up at home on the board I got you, so it matches mine.'

'Sure. Okay, then.' Becca's face brightened with undisguised joy. The clock was rolling backwards to happier times. 'You'll win, though.'

'Maybe.' Tasha's eyes shone, already competitive. 'It can be our secret, anyway.'

Becca nodded. Of course it would be a secret. Natasha Howland playing chess with Rebecca Crisp again would be gossip of the wrong kind. She wondered when, if ever, these things would stop being important.

They were interrupted half an hour later by Natasha's dad knocking on the door.

'Quick! Pack your tits away,' Tasha said, groping her own chest and sending Becca into giggles. 'Dad alert.' The start of the game had been slow, interspersed with chat about school and declarations of how bad they were both going to be at chess after such a long time away from it – even though Becca suspected that Tasha, too, had played occasionally since the Chess Club days.

'I brought you these,' Gary said. He stood in the doorway holding two cans of Coke which Tasha took. He peered into the room, slightly surprised. His hair was gelled and tousled, straight from the tennis club changing room, Becca imagined. A waft of citrus aftershave hit air still laden with the remnants of cigarette smoke. If Gary noticed it, he didn't say. He stared at Becca for a moment, though, and then gave a hurried smile. 'Sorry, I heard voices and thought it was Hayley.'

'No, just me.'

'Good to see you. Anyway, I'll leave you to it. Remember you need an early night, T-Bird. Still the doctor's orders.'

'Yes, Dad.' Tasha was already shutting him out.

'He still calls you T-Bird?' Becca said, laughing.

'It was funny when I was nine,' Tasha said. 'I've had to shout at him to stop him using it in public.' She frowned a little, irritated, and Becca was surprised. Maybe cute family nicknames didn't sit so well when you were a Barbie. She checked her watch. It was still early, but she was tired from lack of sleep and the drugs of the night before, and if she didn't get her shit together she'd be screwed for tomorrow and her mum wanted them all to go out for Sunday lunch. She needed her eight hours. Where possible, she gave herself ten.

'I'm going to head home,' she said. 'I'll text you my next move when my brain is working better. I'm still fucked from last night.'

'Uh-huh.' Tasha raised an eyebrow, wry.

'Not like that. Well, maybe a bit like that.' She grinned. Talking about sex, or at least *around* sex, with Tasha made her feel more sophisticated. Things *had* changed since they fell out. Becca might not be a Barbie but she had a boyfriend who'd left school already and they had sex. So what if it was someone Tasha once turned down?

'Anyway,' she said as they headed downstairs, 'thanks for asking me round.'

'It was great to see you.' Tasha squeezed her arm. 'I mean it. And I'm . . . you know . . .' She flushed and hesitated, her gaze dropping to the ground. 'Sorry again. For everything.'

'Forget about it,' Becca said. 'I mean it.' In that moment, she did. All the pain and tears and rejection didn't matter. At least temporarily.

Something sizzled in the kitchen and Becca's eyes stung with fried onions. Whatever Alison was cooking as the two girls headed to the door for their goodbyes, it smelled good. Even after her huge lunch, Becca's stomach still rumbled.

'Thanks for having me, Mrs Howland.'

'Any time, Becca.'

'Oh, one more thing,' Tasha said, softly, as they stood on the doorstep, the damp air making them both shiver. 'Don't say anything about this, will you? You know, at school.'

'Sure.' Becca felt a stab of hurt and it must have showed.

'It's not about you – I only want to cover my back with Hayley and Jen. I can't be arsed with all the drama. I just didn't want to see them today – they won't get that.'

Becca smiled. 'It's fine. I won't say anything.' It suited her, too. This way, Hannah wouldn't find out, either. Not that Becca needed to keep secrets from Hannah, but she definitely wouldn't *approve* of this. Not after what she'd said in the restaurant toilets. And more than that, she'd be really hurt that Becca lied. For a second, she had a pang of guilt. But from here on Tasha's doorstep, Hannah felt a long way away.

'See you Monday,' Tasha said.

'Yay, English mock results.'

'Oh, crap. But also maybe casting for the play.'

'True. Good luck.' It didn't really matter to Becca who got what part. She was in charge backstage. That was her world.

Tasha pulled her in to hug goodbye, Becca feeling awkward in the tight embrace. Then the door closed and she started her walk home. All she wanted was to curl up in bed and go to sleep. But she'd set the chessboard up first. She lit a cigarette. They'd opened into the Ruy Lopez game – no real surprise there. It gave nothing away. Maybe she'd bring her second knight out. Her brain was too tired to think the game through right now. Playing against Natasha was not like playing against her dad. He was impulsive and never thought more than one move ahead. That wasn't really chess, as far as Becca could see. She inhaled hard. God, she was a nerd. No wonder Tasha wanted to keep it all secret. Even so, she smiled. She couldn't help it. It was nice to have her friend back.

Nineteen

18.03
Jenny
Pick up!

18.04
Hayley
Cant. In car with dad. Getting takeaway.

18.05
Jenny
She lied. She didnt go to hospital.
Why?

18.07
Hayley
What? U sure?
How do u know?

18.09
Jenny
Went past her house on my bike.

Lights were on so I hung around a bit across the road. Saw Becca Crisp coming out. They even hugged goodbye. ???

18.10
Hayley
What??

18.12
Jenny
Why would she ignore us like that? Im scared. U think she remembers?

18.14
Jenny
U there?

18.15
Hayley
I'm thinking.

18.16
Jenny
If she remembers why hasnt she said anything? Should we talk to him? Tell him? I think we should.

18.18
Hayley
No! He'll freak. Maybe she doesnt

remember but
kinda knows we fought.
Just keep being normal.

18.20
Jenny
Im freaking out.

18.22
Hayley
Maybe she just wanted to hang out with Becca. Didnt want to say. Knows it would piss me off. Maybe wants to know about auditions? Thinks Bex will know parts?

18.23
Jenny
If she remembers maybe she told Becca? I feel sick.

18.24
Hayley
She wouldnt. Not her style. I'll call when home.
Delete delete delete!

18.25
Jenny
I know!!

18.26

Jenny

;-)

Twenty

Taken from DI CAITLIN BENNETT'S FILES:
EXTRACT FROM NATASHA HOWLAND'S
NOTEBOOK

After Becca went, while I waited for Mum to call me down for tea, I couldn't help thinking about sex. Even Becca was having sex. It was strange to contemplate.

When Mark Pritchard was shoving his tongue into my mouth I could feel his dick pressing through his jeans. He ground it against me like I was supposed to be impressed. Maybe I am supposed to be impressed.

I've seen one before. Hard and naked. A dick, prick, cock, penis, whatever you want to call it. All the words make me cringe a bit. It was last year with Alfie Jonas at a party before the Year Thirteens left. I laughed first. I couldn't help it. It looked so odd, jutting out from the tangle of hair at his crotch, this strange, pale column of skin and veins. A drop of fluid erupted from the hole at the top, within the circle fold, sitting waiting for me to touch it. He looked so hurt when I giggled and I pretended it was because his trousers and pants were halfway down his thighs, but it was actually at how pathetic it was. How this *thing* caused so much fuss. I had liked Alfie a bit before this. His kisses were soft. They weren't invasive.

It was weird. He was staring at me like an eager puppy and I didn't know what to do. I touched it. The skin was softer than I expected, the hardness all within. He wrapped his hand around mine and made me grip it as he moved my palm like a puppet's, up and down, the looser skin moving with us.

Then it was over pretty quickly, thankfully – just a groan and a damp sticky patch on my hand. I never saw him again. Not like that, anyway.

Becca does that – and more – with Aiden. I don't know why she would. Lanky Aiden with his greebo hair over most of his face. Aiden who can never look me in the eye properly. Aiden who tripped over while asking me out and just sat on the ground staring up at me while I laughed. He looked so broken and that made me laugh even more, even though it was terrible and hurtful. I couldn't help it. And then Hayley and Jenny were laughing, too, and everyone was looking at him like he was some spastic special.

And now Becca's in love with him. He's not quite such a geeky loser as he was in school, but he's not exactly a catch now, either. I think he'd still dump her to fuck me if I'd let him. I can't imagine them fucking. She probably even puts his thing in her mouth.

Sex is ugly in my head. It shouldn't be, I know. But it is. Maybe I'll never do it. I think sometimes power comes from *not* doing it. I can feel it from the boys who look at me. They want it so badly. But really, how good can it be? No different with me than with any other girl. But they want me because they can't have me. Look at Jenny. She has no power. She gives it away. She says she loves it but I'm not so sure she always does. She's damaged by it, exactly like her mum. I can feel that, too. I think I feel it more since my accident, which is weird. She believes it's all she has and she just wants to be loved. How terrible is that? She does *that* for 'love'. I don't think I want to be loved that much.

And yet they're all so proud of it. Becca and Jenny and even Hayley, who I don't think has fucked anyone yet, but she's definitely given a hand-job. Proud of the sticky, grunting mess. Like it's a secret. Maybe that's what sex gives people. Secrets.

But I already have my secrets. I don't need sex for that.

Part Two

Twenty-One

Extract from *The Times*, Monday 18th January

> A body found last night in the River Ribble, between Maypoole and Brackston in Lancashire, has been identified as that of the missing 19-year-old Nicola Munroe, who disappeared from her home in Maypoole more than two months ago.

Extract from the *Maypoole Gazette*, Monday 18th January

The parents of Nicola Munroe have formally identified their daughter's body after it was found in the Ribble on Sunday night. Sources state that identification was made by Miss Munroe's clothing and confirmed by dental records after two months in the water and severe decomposition left the young woman unrecognisable. Nicola's father, Gerard Munroe, released a statement asking that his family be allowed to grieve in private. The Munroes may intend to make a complaint about the police's failure to dredge the river during the initial search for their daughter. Nicola Munroe was taking a gap year before starting a Music Technology degree at Leeds University. She had recently returned from a trip to Thailand teaching English as a foreign language and was working part-time in the Nag and Pineapple in Chester Street.

Extract from the *Brackston Herald*, Tuesday 19th January

The cause of Nicola Munroe's death, whose body was found in the river at Brackston on Sunday night, remains a mystery as police refuse to release any details. It is still unclear if Miss Munroe's body was moved by currents to the location where it was found, or whether it had lain there for the past two months. The proximity of her body to the location where local teenager Natasha Howland was saved has raised questions from the local community about a link between these two cases. Miss Howland, who was rescued by local musician Jamie McMahon while walking his dog, was clinically dead for thirteen minutes before paramedics revived her, and has returned to studying for her A Levels at Brackston Community College. She has no memory of the day leading up to the incident. Her family have declined to comment.

Twenty-Two

It was last lesson on Wednesday afternoon and it was fair to say that no one, not even Jenny, who oddly loved English and was good at it, was paying attention much in Mr Garrick's English class. As the afternoon slunk into darkness on the other side of the window, Emily was texting her boyfriend under the table and Becca was doodling designs for the stage. Mr Garrick had been late, slamming the door shut and muttering about exam papers and how it only used to be once a year and other stuff of absolutely no interest to them, before smiling his somewhat awkward smile and reaching for *The Whitsun Weddings*.

Becca had hoped he was off sick and they'd be sent to the sixth form study area with some 'work'. But no. Mr Garrick was the Exams Officer as well as their English teacher and he spent a lot of time bundling up coursework and sorting out resits and papers.

As the hour finally drew to a close, the in-seat shuffling was becoming more pronounced. It was a big class for sixth form, about twenty of them, and at least that meant you could hide a little. Plus Mr Garrick wasn't stupid. He knew last lesson of the day wasn't the time to get the best work out of anyone. If there'd been a video he could show them, he would have.

Becca wondered if she might persuade him to let them watch *The Crucible*. Maybe he would. He could be pretty cool like that. He was cool like Mr Jones and maybe a couple of years older, but there was something about him that was kind. Sweet. Like the classic bumbling professor only slightly better-looking. Yeah, maybe she'd ask, she thought idly. Even those not in the play wouldn't mind. It would beat these boring poems, anyway.

She thought about Tasha. Becca had kept their secret about Sunday and fully expected to be ignored back at school but that hadn't been the case. They weren't really hanging out but there were a few 'hellos' and waves in the corridors. Hannah noticed. She was a little bit rabbit-in-the-headlights about it, especially yesterday when Becca had lunch with Tasha to talk about the play. She'd looked hurt and Becca had pretended not to notice as she breezed off.

They'd had the cast meeting on Monday – the list went up on the board at lunchtime to many squeals of delight – and as she'd predicted, the Barbies had done well. Tasha was the gorgeous, vital but vengeful Abigail, Jenny the somewhat skittish Mary Warren and Hayley had claimed the cool, calm Elizabeth Proctor. Becca didn't feel bitter about any of it, partly because being *on* the stage had never appealed to her and partly because it was a strong cast. She'd watched Hayley and Jenny preen around Tasha when she got Abigail, as if she was by far the superior actress, but Becca knew that although she was good and *would* be good in it, Jenny was better, and she was pretty sure the Barbies knew that, too. But Jenny had to resit her Maths GCSE to get it up to a C and Mr Jones didn't want to overload her. It was a good call, Becca thought. Plus, Mary Warren was a tricky part, harder than Abigail in a lot of ways.

'This lesson is never going to end,' Emily muttered, still holding her phone behind her open poetry book, fingers flying across the screen. Becca muttered agreement but she was distracted, studying Hayley and Jenny in front. The two Barbies were passing a scribbled-on piece of paper between them, back and forth in some conversation. They were right under Mr Garrick's nose, too. Maybe he just chose to ignore them. Maybe he couldn't be bothered with this lesson, either.

Becca doodled some more. It was the first full read-through after school and she wanted to check the lighting rigs and stuff with Casey while she could. Casey had royally fucked up her exams and it was unlikely – despite Theatre Tech being one of her subjects – she could be full on with the play. Performances, yes, but rehearsals and prep, no. So it looked like Becca would only have Hannah to help, and Hannah was great when under direction but not exactly confident enough to be a self-starter. Becca hadn't seen Tasha all day, and if she didn't show up, Becca would probably have to read in for her as well and miss her technical-stuff time.

'Thank fuck,' Emily groaned as the bell finally rang. She and Becca were on their feet before it had even finished, Emily heading to the door with her bag already over her shoulder. 'See you tomorrow, bitch.'

'Back at ya, ho,' Becca answered. She glanced at Hayley and Jenny, who were still packing up. *Fuck it*, she thought. Why should she be nervous of talking to them?

'Hey,' she said, loitering close to their table. 'Where's Tasha today?'

Hayley looked at her with disdain. 'Why do you care?'

'Hayley, can I have a word?' Mr Garrick sounded nervous,

cutting into the strained atmosphere between the three girls. Becca didn't blame him.

'Sure.' Hayley looked at Jenny. 'I'll catch you up.'

'Goodbye, Mr Garrick,' Jenny said with a smile, and Becca muttered the same. Jenny pushed past her but Becca stayed close, waiting until they were out in the corridor and the two Barbies separated before she spoke again.

'I just want to know whether it's worth having the read-through today or not. If she's not in school I'll tell Mr Jones.'

'*I'll* tell Mr Jones,' Jenny said. 'What are you, like a nanny?' She stared at Becca, her chest heaving for a few seconds before more words blurted out of her. 'I don't know what you think's going on with you and Tasha but she dumped you before. Remember? She'll do it again.'

'What's this?' Becca snapped back. '*She's my friend so she can't be yours?*' The last sentence came out in a sing-song whine and Jenny's pretty, seductive face looked like it had been slapped. 'Anyway, she was my friend first,' Becca finished, knowing how childish she sounded. But it was true. She probably knew Tasha better than either of them except maybe Hayley. Who the fuck was Jenny, anyway? Some dumb council estate slut who just rocked up at school and happened to have the right look? She could fuck off.

'Yes, she was,' Jenny said, stepping in closer so her rosebud lips, slightly glossed, were only inches from Becca's face. 'So what? She telling you all her secrets now? Like what, Becca? What's Tasha told you?'

There was an edge of desperation in her voice and her eyes were wide and watery, gleaming with tears but still angry. Her pupils were full, Becca noticed as they faced each other in the corridor. Was Jenny high? In school? On what? Her eyes dropped immediately to Jenny's nose. She had too much fire to be stoned.

'Are you on something?' she asked. 'What is wrong with you?'

'Oh, fuck off, Becca,' Jenny said, suddenly slumping a little. 'Just *fuck off*.'

'Rebecca?'

She turned, and for a moment couldn't place the woman calling her name. Familiar but not someone she knew. Someone she'd met, though. Someone—

'Detective Inspector Bennett. We met at the hospital,' the woman said. She glanced from girl to girl as Hayley joined them from Mr Garrick's classroom. 'Everything okay?'

'Yeah,' Becca said. 'We're fine.' Jenny nodded in reluctant agreement and that was enough for Bennett. She didn't care about their squabbles.

'I'd like to talk to you,' the policewoman continued. For a moment, Becca presumed she meant the Barbies, but it was her name the woman had called and it was her she was looking at. Becca suddenly felt cold.

'What about?' What could a policewoman need to talk to her for? Jenny and Hayley moved away but not so far that they couldn't listen in. Her panic must have showed because the DI smiled.

'Don't worry. It's just some routine questions. Nothing to look so nervous about.'

'Has Natasha been with you?' Hayley asked. 'Is this about her accident?'

So they hadn't known where Tasha was today, either, Becca realised. Pair of sneaky bitches. What was it with the constant putting her down? Why couldn't they have just said?

'Natasha's gone to see her psychologist. She'll be home soon,' Bennett said, ignoring Hayley's question. 'It's routine,' she continued to Becca. 'Let's go to the Head Teacher's office. I'll get someone to drop you home when we're done.'

'But we have play rehearsals,' Becca said, feebly. There was something in the stern kindness of the woman's face that terrified her. She didn't want to go with her.

'Rehearsals have been cancelled.'

Twenty-Three

Excerpt of **CONSULTATION BETWEEN DR ANNABEL HARVEY AND PATIENT NATASHA HOWLAND, WEDNESDAY 20/01, 16.30**

NATASHA: There are thirteen leaves on your potted plant. Did you know that?

(Pause)

Well, there are. Look. Count them.

DR HARVEY: Is that important?

NATASHA: Thirteens. I keep seeing them. It's like the number stands out to me. Thirteen peas left on my dad's plate. Thirteen raindrops on the window. Thirteen people on the top deck of the bus. That number is everywhere.

DR HARVEY: Why is that?

NATASHA: (Laughing)

Seriously? Like you need to ask?

DR HARVEY: You know that's approximate, don't you? They can't be sure exactly how long you were in that condition for. It might have been fourteen minutes, it could have been twelve.

NATASHA: But it was thirteen. I just wish it would leave me alone.

DR HARVEY: Are you still having bad dreams?

NATASHA: (Long pause)

I wonder if she drowned there.

DR HARVEY: Who?

NATASHA: That girl from Maypoole. Nicola whatever.

DR HARVEY: Nicola Munroe.

NATASHA: Yeah, her. They think her death and mine might be linked.

DR HARVEY: What do you think?

NATASHA: I don't remember anything.

(Shuffles in chair)

DR HARVEY: Is something bothering you?

NATASHA: Even before the DI, Caitlin, came to talk to me, I was thinking about her. Since I saw it on the news. You know, about her being found in the river near me. It made me feel sick. I swallowed water she'd rotted in. She died there. I died there.

DR HARVEY: You didn't die. You should try not to see it that way.

NATASHA: Easy for you to say. My heart stopped just like hers. I wasn't breathing just like her. Maybe she's the one in my dreams. In the darkness.

DR HARVEY: Nicola's body was only discovered on Sunday night – you were having these nightmares before that.

NATASHA: Maybe she's mad I didn't die properly. Jealous.

DR HARVEY: Nicola Munroe was dead long before you went in the river. She was not capable of any emotion. Perhaps you have survivor guilt. You lived and she died. Did you know Nicola Munroe?

NATASHA: No.

DR HARVEY: Then you can't make assumptions about any

feelings she might have. Even if she was capable of feeling now, surely it would be more natural for her to be pleased that one of you made it out of the water alive?

NATASHA: (Laughter)

DR HARVEY: Why is that amusing?

NATASHA: Do you know anything about teenage girls?

(Pause. Sniffing)

(Quieter)

I don't think it's got anything to do with him. I really don't. Even if I can't remember, I'm sure I would feel something, you know? When I saw him.

Extract from DI CAITLIN BENNETT'S CASE REPORT: 20TH JANUARY (COPY ALSO IN CASE FILE NICOLA MUNROE)

Given the extreme decomposition of Nicola Munroe's body, it is still unknown whether she was drugged or under the influence of alcohol prior to her death. Samples have been sent for further testing. It is also unknown whether she was alive or dead when she went into the water. Beyond the comparable location of her body, it is difficult to draw comparisons with Natasha Howland's case; however, there are the following similarities:

1) Both women went into the water fully clothed, although Munroe wore several more layers than Howland, including a heavy coat and boots.
2) Both women were in possession of their mobile phones.

3) Neither woman shows any obvious signs of attack or rape – although in Munroe's case, given the condition of the body, the medical examiner is unable to state for certain.
4) Both women were white, middle class and mid- to late-teens.
5) Both women were blonde.
6) Both women knew Aiden Kennedy.

Extract from DI BENNETT'S NOTES (UNOFFICIAL RECORD) IN INTERVIEW WITH NATASHA HOWLAND AND REBECCA CRISP 20/01. 14.00/15.45 RESPECTIVELY. BOTH GIRLS AGREED THAT THE HEAD TEACHER, CHRISTINE SALISBURY, WOULD STAND AS RESPONSIBLE ADULT:

Natasha Howland

Howland clearly unsettled by discovery of Munroe's body so close to the site of her own incident. Referred more than once to them both being in the water at the same time. Less collected than on previous conversations. I asked her routine questions. Brought up Aiden Kennedy. Both women were acquaintances of Kennedy.

Howland has seen Aiden Kennedy twice since her accident: once at Jamie McMahon's house when she and her mother went to thank him, then again when he picked Rebecca up from a party Friday night/Saturday morning held at student Mark Pritchard's house. Confused by my questioning. Surprised to hear Aiden's name mentioned. Has had nothing to do with him since he asked her out nearly two years ago. Embarrassed by this. Says she laughed at him. (Interesting.) His behaviour at McMahon's was the same as normal towards her – says AK never looks her in the eye. (Shy? Guilt? Obsession?) Says to her knowledge his relationship with Rebecca Crisp is both serious and sexual, and that Crisp sems happy. She asks why we're interested in Aiden. What he has to do with anything. Genuine surprise. No memory prompt. On completion of interview sent her to meet the doctor again. Need her memory back. Frustrating!

Rebecca Crisp

Smart kid under the shell. Asks why talking to her not the other two girls. Teen dynamics interesting. Ask her about the night of the incident. She repeats she was with Aiden until he dropped her home at midnight. Did she speak to him later? She responds as per previous statement that she fell asleep watching TV on her computer. Asked where he went after that, she states home. Clear on questioning that she can't be sure he did, but that's what he said. Defensive here – realisation of something? Shaky. Angry. Scared. Says to check with Aiden's mother. Then asks if we have already. Mention AK asking NH out on a date. How does he talk about her? Crisp outburst. Teary. They don't talk about her. It was a long time ago. (Jealous? NH makes her feel insecure? *Does* he talk about NH?) Takes a moment to calm. Crisp confirms their relationship is sexual. Nothing abnormal. (She's uncomfortable here. Not cocky. Maybe not giving everything sexually he wants? AK frustrated? Needs the fantasy of others?) Does AK see other girls? Has he ever cheated? Anger at this. No, they are in love. (Bless her!) Leave a moment. Write notes. She asks why I'm asking so many questions about AK. Defensive. (nervous?) I ask if she knew that Aiden knew Nicola Munroe, the Maypoole girl . . .

Twenty-Four

'What is she talking about?' Becca knew she was shouting. She couldn't help it. Her whole body had been shaking since the policewoman let her go. 'Why didn't you answer my calls?' She wanted to throw up now they were face to face. She'd run from school to his flat and then to Mr McMahon's house and her anger hadn't faded. Here he was. Shaken, pale and beautiful. He tried to hold her but she pulled away. She was too angry. Too angry and upset and suddenly terrified.

'I don't have my phone. They took it. I went and bought another one as soon as they let me go.' He pulled a cheap handset from his pocket. 'But I don't have your number in it. I came here to see if it was on any of Jamie's phone bills. I use his landline sometimes – you know how shit the reception is in this house.'

'Why don't we all calm down?' Mr McMahon – *Jamie* – stood in the corner of the sitting room, awkward in his own home. His dog sat at his feet, whining occasionally, upset. 'Whatever it is, it's a misunderstanding.'

'She says you *knew* her!' Becca almost spat the words at Aiden and then, much to her own shame, burst into tears. Strong hands were on her shoulders, bigger than Aiden's, and then she was being led to a sofa. She sank into it, heavy, the fight going out of her.

'Hey.' Jamie crouched beside her and handed her a tissue from his pocket. 'It's crumpled but it's clean.'

'Thank you,' she mumbled, hating herself for being so weak. 'I'm sorry.'

'It's okay.' His voice was soft. Kind. She wanted to cry all over again. Her world had been, if not pulled out from under her, then very severely shaken. 'But you know that this will just be nothing, right?'

Becca looked up at her boyfriend, who immediately rushed over and sat down. He smelled clean. Shampoo and soap and the unique scent of him underneath it all. She loved him so much she would break from it. Even now.

'They said that Nicola Munroe had her phone contacts backed up on her MacBook.' His voice was shaky. 'My number was on there.' The world shimmered around Becca a little, light refracting sharply from the edges of the coffee table as she stared at it, unable to look at him.

'How?' Becca asked. 'How did she have your number?'

'I'm not sure.' Aiden shrugged helplessly and it made her want to hug him and punch him all at once. 'I had hers, too. She was a muso. I go to gigs and people know I do some pro stuff. I guess we must have swapped numbers at something.'

'Why didn't you *say* anything?' Swapped numbers. The words carried weight. It was something they giggled over in the girls' changing rooms at school, or on the bus, or in McDonald's. Swapped numbers. Private messaged. DM'd. All those things were the prelude to the first kiss. *Everyone* knew that.

'Never occurred to me. When I get my phone back you can

look through it. I have a lot of numbers. I didn't realise I had hers. I was probably stoned when she gave it to me. You know, one of those in-the-bar-post-gig things.'

She didn't know, not really, but she nodded anyway. Sometimes the three years between them felt non-existent and at others they were a lifetime.

'You've got to believe me, Becca.' He grabbed her free hand. His palm was sweaty. 'You have to. Why would I have anything to do with this? Or with Natasha?'

'So you never asked Nicola out?' She hated the doubt and suspicion in her own voice, and Aiden recoiled, his beautiful blue eyes, *eyes she could drown in*, wounded and hurt.

'No. No, I didn't. Jesus fuck, Bex, what are you suggesting? That if I ask a girl out and she says no, I just lob her in the river and let her die?'

She stared at him. She felt stupid. And yet not stupid. The worm of bitter insecurity was growing in her gut. 'No, of course not. I just . . . I just don't understand.'

'Why are they asking you about this now?' Jamie said. 'Nicola Munroe went missing months ago. Surely they checked her phone records and contacts then?'

'They did, but I wasn't important to that investigation. Not until her body showed up so close to where you found Tasha. Then they must have passed it all over to that Bennett policewoman and she recognised my name. She spoke to me when I picked you up from the hospital.'

'She spoke to me there, too,' Becca said. She felt tired. Hugely, massively tired. 'I'm sorry,' she said. 'I'm sorry. I'm just scared.' The tears started again. 'She asked me all these questions about you and me, and then about you and Tasha, and then when she mentioned Nicola I guess I just totally lost it.' She wrapped her arms around his neck, sobbing freely, wetting his skin with hot tears and snot.

'It's okay. It's okay.' He held her tight. '*You* know I didn't do anything, and *I* know I didn't do anything, so that's it. It's just a coincidence. And not even a big one. It's not like we live in the middle of some huge city. If you think about it, it's not exactly totally random that I had the number of some girl my own age who went to all the local gigs.' He pushed her gently away. 'Just fucking bad luck.' He smiled. 'You're freaking out more than my mum did. I think you're freaking out more than *I* did.'

'I'm calming down now. It was just a shock.'

'You're telling me.'

'Did they speak to you, too?' she asked Jamie.

'Yep,' he said. 'Not a lot I could say. Just that Aiden is perfectly normal – whatever that means – and happy with you and had never mentioned either of the girls to me. More importantly, I told them he knows I walk Biscuit early every morning so he'd have to be pretty stupid to push Natasha in the river knowing I'd be coming along at any second.'

This practical logic calmed her more than any of Aiden's heartfelt protestations had. Aiden wasn't dumb. Even if he was some crazy woman-attacker – and she felt even more like a lunatic hearing the words like that in her head – he wouldn't risk getting caught like that.

'They have to follow up these leads,' Jamie said. 'It's their job.'

Becca knew he was making sense. She took a deep breath. Bennett was just dotting i's and crossing t's as her dad would say. Of course she had to follow up on Aiden. She wouldn't be doing her job if she didn't. Suddenly she felt stupid for rushing there. Or at least rushing there so full of high drama.

'Were you guys working?' she asked. 'I'll go. I'm sorry. I need to be less of an idiot.'

She wanted some fresh air. She needed to get a grip on herself. She'd acted like some hysterical bitch. And what had freaked her out so much? Was it that the DI made Aiden sound suspicious, or was it that he had the dead girl's number and never told her? She really hoped it was the first but she wasn't entirely sure. She knew her insecurities could turn her into some kind of jealous mental. She constantly thought that Aiden was going to fall in love with someone else. Some sophisticated muso girl. She tried to control it, or at least not let it show.

'Yeah, we were,' Aiden said. 'I figure carry on as normal. And you're not an idiot. But give me your number again now and I'll call before you go to bed.' She took the cheap handset from him and typed it into the contacts with her name, and then sent herself a text so she'd have his new number, too.

He walked her to the door and she felt almost as awkward as they had in the early days, when there was all this emotion and attraction between them but neither had the guts to actually talk about it.

'Sorry I was a dick,' she said, eventually.

'You weren't a dick. Sorry the police thought I might be a psycho maniac.'

She laughed, and then so did he, and the tension between them slipped away as they kissed their goodbyes. He was just Aiden. Warm and handsome and chilled. So what if he had some muso chick's number in his phone? He wasn't a kid. It didn't *mean* anything.

'I'll call you later,' he said. 'I love you.'

'I love you, too.'

The door closed and she took a deep breath of damp air. It was crazy to think that Aiden could have anything to do with what happened to Tasha. She was with him that night. He'd been relaxed and happy. They both had. And pretty off their heads. He'd been in no state to throw anyone in a river.

Her phone buzzed as she headed down the gravel drive to the cut-through path leading to the main road. It was Hannah, checking up on her since rehearsals were cancelled. Wanting to know where she vanished to, and if she was okay. It was so Hannah. Never brave enough to be pissed off. If it was the other way around, Becca's text would have been more *Where the fuck are you??* She typed back a quick reply saying she'd call her later and shoved her hands in her pockets to keep them warm. The snow had melted but it was still cold, especially so close to the river.

She'd just reached the short, narrow path when she caught sight of something in the gloom. A glint of metal through branches. Someone was parked in the lane. Someone was watching Jamie McMahon's house. Her stomach dropped. It was DI Bennett, or one of her lackeys, keeping their eye on Aiden. The cold suddenly forgotten, she started to text him but then stopped. Why worry him? Let them watch, she thought angrily. They wouldn't see anything. Aiden was innocent. *Fuck you, Detective Inspector Bennett*, she thought. *Fuck. You.*

Twenty-Five

Taken from **DI CAITLIN BENNETT'S FILES: EXTRACT FROM NATASHA HOWLAND'S NOTEBOOK**

So, finally I have a clue *and* an ally in figuring out what really happened that night. I'm feeling a bit better already. It's been a long day but I want to write it all down before I (try to) sleep.

I had an itch in my head that bugged me all last night so that even when I woke up (silently gasping for air in the way that's become normal since I got home) it was the first thing I thought about. Not the whispering voice in the void in my dreams. Not the thirteens I see everywhere. (Thirteen hairs in my hairbrush yesterday. Thirteen exactly. I pulled them out carefully and counted. I laid them on my dressing table. Thirteen dead minutes, thirteen dead hairs. Go figure.) And not Nicola Munroe and her bloated corpse. In some ways I guess this thing just out of reach was a gift. But it felt like a scab, itching at me and driving me mad. They think Aiden has something to do with all this. It's almost comical. He didn't kill Nicola Munroe and he sure as shit didn't throw me in the river. I knew this. I knew it in the itching of something in my head. Not my memory – it's still not coming back – but something else. Something I *should* have grasped but was just out of reach.

It was only half-past four when I woke up this morning, but I dragged my jogging gear from the bottom of the wardrobe. I dressed in the dark, got everything ready and then climbed through my window and down the tree, letting myself out of the side gate, like I must have done that night. I fell into a steady pace and let my mind relax. It's strange how much I've come to enjoy running. I've missed it over the past week or so and my legs were happy to stretch out and shake away the tightness of inactivity. I've grown strong. I liked the feel of my muscles and sinews working together as my feet pounded confidently along the paths in the darkness. Within minutes I was no longer cold. My face was flushed. I wasn't breathing that hard, though. I know my rhythm. I wonder what Hayley would make of it if she saw me. Natasha, the runner. We all have our secrets.

It was dark and nearly all the town was asleep. I was off the main road for most of my run and it was eerily silent, just the *whump* of my trainers and the steady pants of my breathing. I went down by the river and through the woods. I should have been afraid, out there alone in the darkness and so close to the river, but I wasn't. I was exhilarated. As I headed home just after five, I felt good. Proud of myself. I could even ignore that I'd been counting my paces in my head and restarted every time I hit thirteen.

The day passed in a haze. I was *there* at school – I huddled with Hayles and Jen and told them about the police and how they thought maybe what happened to me and Nicola Munroe's death were connected – but I wasn't really there. They asked why the police wanted to talk to Becca and I shrugged. I didn't tell them about Aiden. And although they nodded, I saw them glance at each other and the scab in my head itched some more, and I wondered what they were hiding. Was there something they weren't telling me? They suffocated me throughout the day with their adoration and by the time we got to the read-through after last period, I could barely breathe. I felt like I was in the river again.

I smiled at Becca. She looked tired. I wondered if she'd been awake while I was out this morning. She smiled back and I could see her relief that we were still okay. Beside her, Hannah watched me the way a mouse might a cat. I didn't even look at her. She's a nothing, really. Maybe Becca thought I was going to ignore her after the Aiden thing. She thought wrong. I wondered about texting her my next chess move when they were reading bits that I'm not in. Thinking about texts made the scabs itch again. I looked at Hayley and Jenny. The scab in my head came loose and I knew what was bugging me: the wrong-number text message.

That's when I knew I had to talk to Becca.

*

She didn't want to come out, of course. She wanted to go and see her boyfriend. She kept asking what the fuck we were doing out there – how was it going to help Aiden? But I needed her and she never could refuse me. She was still grumpy, though, I could tell, despite being relieved I'd kept to myself the fact that the police questioned us about Aiden. She was cold and miserable and I hadn't explained myself very well, but I needed her to come with me. To see it with me, if there was anything to see at all.

We had torches, huge dad-type square ones from my garage,

not the type your mum keeps under the sink. I'd told my mum I was at Becca's. She'd told hers she was at mine. Neither would be happy if they knew we were out in the woods in the dark. In fact, they'd both be hysterical.

'It's about the text. The one I had that night,' I'd tried to explain, ducking under branches. The paths were slippery with mud from the thawed snow. Our torches shone wide streaks of white light ahead of us, as if we were walking beneath dual moons.

'What about it?' she asked.

'I don't know the number – it could have been from anyone – but it said to meet in *the usual place*.'

'And?' She swore under her breath behind me as a twig snagged her.

I pressed on, still trying to explain. I'd told the police it didn't mean anything to me, which is true. It didn't. But then I started thinking that it didn't mean anything because I didn't recognise the number. If I ignored the number, then maybe it might mean something. I'd timed the trip and conversation pretty perfectly for dramatic effect. I pushed back the last branch and stepped into the circular clearing – mine, Hayley and Jenny's secret meeting place.

Becca's eyes went really wide at the thought we met out here.

And we had sometimes. Not for ages, but it was always our place for avoiding everyone. Somewhere to get high. Play some music. Dick around.

I could see it hurt Becca. She thinks she should have been part of that. 'It's how we would say it sometimes, if we were on the phone or whatever. "*Usual place?*" or "*Our place?*" – pretty much like in that text.'

'But why didn't you answer it?' Becca asked. 'And why would either of them use a different phone?' They were good questions. I don't know the answers. Becca lit a cigarette, inhaling hard.

'I don't know.' I said it slowly. 'But thinking about it kept me awake. I've been thinking about it all day and I just had a feeling – maybe it's my memory coming back to me? Maybe we came here that Friday night? I mean, can they really prove their alibis? They say they were at home, but then so was I supposed to be. And in my dreams I'm in this terrible dark and I hear this girl whispering my name and I can't move. Maybe it's not a fear of the water. Maybe it's something to do with them.'

The way Becca stared at me, I couldn't decide if she thought I was crazy or not. I was babbling like an idiot, that's for sure. I needed to find proof. Proper evidence to convince her. I swung my torch across the ground, heading towards the fallen log. 'It's been itching at my head all day and I finally thought of coming out here to have a look. I needed you with me – I didn't want to come alone. See if we can find something, or not. To stop me feeling like I'm going crazy.' I could see Becca was touched that I'd thought of her. But who else was I going to ask? Who could I trust like I trusted her?

Becca moved her torch beam across the clearing, eyes focused. I did the same, both of us quiet in the search.

'Look.' Becca had crouched and was staring at something. I added my torchlight to hers so it was almost too bright to look. And then I saw them, too. Filthy and falling apart after being covered in snow but I knew what they were. What they meant.

She said it first: 'Vogue cigarette butts,' she said. She was grasping one. *Hayley.*

I tried to talk/think it through. 'They can't be that old. She's only been smoking them a little while. Since she fell and had that wrist support a few months ago. She switched to them then – I remember because Jenny copied the *Vogue* writing onto her cast thing. But we haven't been out here in ages. Probably not since February last year. '

Becca looked at me thoughtfully. 'Maybe you haven't, but they might have? You said they've been acting weird. A bit secretive? Maybe they were coming here without you.'

I'd wondered that, too. Becca has always been cleverer than she gives herself credit for. That's why she's good at chess. She looks at all the possible moves and remembers those that went before. I swung the torch away, light skimming across the ground towards a tree, and something shone gold and silver in the light. Easier to spot than the cigarette butt. An empty Crunchie wrapper. I had to say it out loud to Becca: 'I must have been here – Crunchies are my chocolate fix this year.' Becca got up and carefully trod across the small clearing. She didn't touch the wrapper. 'Jenny's always on a diet and Hayley only eats chocolate when she's training for a race.' I was thinking out loud, too.

'And you honestly don't remember anything?'

I shook my head, feeling completely weirded out. It was getting colder now night had fallen and in the torchlight we must have looked like characters in some found-footage horror movie. 'I know Hayley and Jenny have been different recently, like they're keeping something from me, but they wouldn't *hurt me*, would they?' I stared at Bex, wanting confirmation, but she didn't give me any. Instead she looked behind the tree, and then scanned her torch up and down the bark. Her face was tight, serious. Pale – and not just from the cold.

'I mean, it's crazy,' I said. Suddenly I wanted a cigarette even though I've never inhaled in my life, apart from once when I was thirteen and it made my head spin so badly I thought I was going to puke. It was all becoming too real. '*This* is crazy. What am I even thinking? They're my best friends.'

'Look at this,' Becca said. 'Around the back of the tree.'

I went to where she was pointing and saw a piece of frayed rope, green tent rope, maybe, on the mossy earth, almost lost against the background.

'Maybe they tied you to the tree,' Becca said. 'Holy shit. I mean, Jesus fuck, Tasha, could they do that? *Would* they do that?' We were silent for a few moments, only our ragged breathing breaking the silence in the woods. Both of our hearts were racing, though, with the thought of it.

'*Why* would they do that?' I asked. She didn't answer. Her body had tensed, alert and aware. Focused. She suggested we scour the clearing, look for anything odd, and I did as I was told, bending over and searching for any clue as to what happened here. My nose ran and I sniffed hard, heard Becca doing the same, both of us hunched over the muddy ground.

'But why would they tie me up?' I had to ask after a few minutes' silence. 'And why let me go if they did?

Becca was still looking at the tree. 'Maybe you got yourself free and ran away? Maybe it was a joke that went too far? Maybe you fell in the river after you'd run away?'

I stared at her. 'But we're talking about *Hayley*. Hayley and Jenny.'

She was all tough sympathy as she ran through it: 'We still don't know what happened here, but I do know this – the text said to come to the usual place. This is *it* and it looks like you've all been here – recently, too. And if you *were* all here and you were just pissing around –' she paused to emphasise what was coming next, words I didn't want to hear her say '– then why haven't they said anything? *Why didn't they say anything when you were found?*'

'I don't know,' I muttered, stamping my feet to ward off the cold.

'You brought me here,' Becca pointed out. 'There must be part of you that thinks they're involved somehow.'

'But what about Nicola Munroe?'

'What about her?' Becca straightened up, thinking it through again. 'She was found in the river. That's not proof that what happened to you is linked; she might have gone in the river up by Maypoole and washed down here. Aiden is the only other connection at the moment, and he didn't even really know her, and he didn't do anything wrong.' It was sweet to see the defiant lift of Becca's chin as she said that. She doesn't have to convince me, though. I believe her. I know Aiden's innocent. 'And it's not like he's been stalking you or anything, has he?' she finished.

She tried to make the question sound like a confident statement but I heard the insecurity in it – her need for some reassurance.

'Of course not. I'd kind of forgotten all about him.' I chose my words so carefully. Even if I really don't get it, he's Becca's whole world. I don't want to upset her or alienate her. I need her.

'So what happened to her and what happened to you are probably entirely separate events,' Becca concluded, glancing around her again. 'Maybe you should call that Bennett woman. Tell her about this.' She looked at me. 'I can't do it

– she'll think I'm just trying to get Aiden out of trouble.' *She needs me, too*, I realised.

'But what does any of this prove?' I shrugged, helplessly. 'Nothing. Just that at some point recently we were all here. Or they could claim they were here without me and one of them ate the chocolate. Or that someone entirely not them just happened to be dog-walking through the woods. There's nothing here to prove we were here *that* night.' She knew I was right. This was flimsy at best. And they're my friends. I don't want to go to the police and accuse them of something without being sure. I mean, shit . . . what if this is just my head being mental? They've probably done nothing.

Becca pocketed the stub of her own cigarette – no doubt not wanting to *contaminate the scene* – and then lit another. Her eyes were narrow. She was thinking hard.

'We need to draw them out,' she said. 'Test them.'

My face prickled with the cold and the start of the buzz of excitement.

'Pretend you're beginning to remember,' Becca said, her face alive with the hatching of a plan. 'Nothing solid – just say you're getting vague images you don't understand. Be a bit cautious with them. That kind of thing.'

'What then?' I knew where she was going but I wanted to hear her say it.

'See how they react. What they *do*.' She was shivering now and we started to walk back, quiet in single file through the trees to the narrow path I know so well, and then out to the river and onto the main road. When we could walk comfortably side by side, I slipped my arm through hers, like she was my boyfriend or something. It'd been a long time since we last walked like that. It was comforting. I've missed Becca and it surprised me to realise that.

'I'll text you to come and have lunch with us tomorrow,' I said. 'I'll do it then. That way we can both see how they react.'

Becca didn't ask to bring Hannah along, which was a relief. I really don't want to be seen having lunch with Hannah. It shouldn't matter, but it does. Poor Hannah, she's so easily dumped.

But Becca was still talking, working it out. 'Something happened in that time you don't remember,' she said. 'It must have. Something that led to you meeting them in the middle of the night and then ending up nearly dead.' She was speaking quietly, as if it was too horrible to say aloud.

But what could have happened? Mum says I was at home in my room on Thursday night and Friday was school as normal. From what everyone else tells me, it was a perfectly ordinary day.

'From the outside, maybe,' Becca observed. 'But, like, who really knows? My mum doesn't know what I do. If she was asked what I did last Friday, her answer wouldn't involve drugs and fucking my boyfriend's brains out.'

'What if they don't do anything? What if they're pleased for me?' I said.

'Then you can go back to being Barbies together and—' It stopped me cold and I stared at her for a long moment.

'*Barbies?*' I said. 'Even you call us that?'

Her arm stiffened right up in mine. 'Sometimes. It's just a name. I'm the one who first said it about you guys. Years ago.' She paused. 'It wasn't meant as a compliment at the time.'

'No shit.' It was my turn to take a moment. 'Barbies,' I said again. 'You came up with that. Man, you bitch.' I could almost feel the heat coming from the painful blush on Becca's face, and suddenly I was laughing. I was laughing so hard I had to stop walking. Becca looked at me like I was crazy and then she was laughing, too, until we were both wheezing for breath and crying between fits of uncontrollable giggles. Barbies. It was her insult that we took and *owned*. We were proud of being called that, my posse of three. The Barbies. I saw us as Bex saw us. Empty, plastic, beautiful people. I was still proud of it. I can't help it. I *am* the Barbies.

Eventually we stopped laughing and the cold gripped us again. I wiped the last tears from my aching face and said, 'Okay. Let's plan this. Properly.' And as we talked, the laughter drained away with the seriousness of why we were doing it.

We will lead the horses to water and see if they drink. I like plans. I like details. I'm not a *wing it* girl. But we both play chess. If anyone can set a good trap, we can.

Twenty-Six

Aiden was hunched over his phone as Jamie put their coffees down, and at first he presumed the teenager was locked in conversation with his girlfriend, but there were no beeps or buzzes. Curious, and under the guise of reaching for another amp lead, he leaned across the desk where Aiden was sitting. The kid barely noticed. His shoulders were hunched and tight – too tight to make anything he'd played thus far in this session usable – and he was absently chewing his bottom lip. The phone was open on a Google search pane: *Brackston CCTV streets*.

'Coffee's there,' Jamie said. Why would the kid want to know where the street cameras were? And why look so worried? Was this to do with the police? Surely he'd *want* the police to know where he'd been? Maybe that was it. Maybe he wanted to make sure they could track his movements after he dropped Becca off that night. That must be it.

'Come on,' he said. 'Have a smoke and then let's try and get this track right or we may as well call it a day.'

'Sure. Cool.' Still distracted, Aiden reluctantly put his phone down and went over to the balcony. He was never overly talkative, but normally the two of them shared a relaxed quiet, not this tense, stilted atmosphere. Aiden was physically present, but mentally somewhere else entirely.

Jamie snatched a quick look at the screen before it went blank. From what he could glean in that moment or two, his back blocking Aiden's view of him in case he turned around, there was nothing for the boy to worry about. Brackston wasn't short of speed cameras or CCTV around the main roads. If the police checked, he'd be fine.

This would all blow over, he was sure of it. Biscuit thumped his tail in his basket as if he was agreeing with his master's thoughts. *Yeah*, Jamie thought. *It will all be nothing*. But he hoped it turned out that way before this work needed to be delivered. Having to use another guitarist at this stage would be a pain in the arse.

Twenty-Seven

It was a really clever plan, Becca thought, as she tried to look casual and relaxed in the Barbie corner of the sixth form common room, even if she said so herself. She sipped her cappuccino, harvested from the Starbucks around the corner in the first five minutes of lunch, but didn't eat anything. She was tentative with her drink, too. She didn't have coffee that often and it tended to make her jittery and queasy, but that's what Tasha was drinking and she'd found herself ordering it too.

'Just relax,' Tasha said, sitting opposite. 'They'll be here.'

'Yeah, I know,' Becca said. 'I just hate the waiting.' That was kind of true. She was also a bit worried – she couldn't help it – that Hannah was going to come in and see her all cosy with Tasha and know that she hadn't been invited. Again. There were only so many times Becca could blame ditching Hannah for Tasha on the play, especially as Hannah was also involved with that. This time she hadn't even made an excuse, just chickened out and not answered Hannah's text about lunch. Becca's last lesson had been Art so she hoped Hannah would go and look for her there. Sometimes she stayed longer to finish up. God, this was ridiculous. Why was she even worried? It wasn't like Hannah was her boyfriend or anything, so why was she feeling guilty about not having lunch with her a couple of times?

'Here they come,' Tasha muttered quietly, her head bent over her salad.

'Hey,' Jenny said, sitting down. 'What's going on?' Her voice was light, but Becca noticed her eyes, a little bloodshot, darting between Becca and Tasha. 'You didn't answer our texts.'

'I thought I'd have lunch with Becca, that's all,' Tasha said. She toyed with her salad, her shoulders hunched over a little. She looked uncomfortable. Becca thought she was doing brilliantly. But then, Tasha *was* the actress of the two of them. Becca stayed quiet and sipped her bitter coffee as Hayley took the last chair. 'Lucky you, Bex,' she said dryly. 'An audience with the queen. First lunch together in how many years?'

Jenny flashed Hayley a hard look across the table. Hard or panicked? Becca couldn't decide. Either way there was a reprimand in it.

'I don't mind,' Jenny said. 'We've never really got to know each other.' She smiled at Becca. A half-hearted, lopsided affair that somehow still managed to look pretty and endearing. Becca wondered how often she practised it. 'Hayley doesn't mean anything. She loves to play being a bitch for show.'

Becca thought of the cigarette butts out in the woods, the Crunchie wrapper, the frayed piece of cut rope. *How much is just for show?* she wondered as she tried to smile back.

'Look, if it's a problem, I can go,' she said.

'No,' Natasha said, suddenly and almost fearfully. 'Don't.'

'Are you all right?' Hayley frowned. 'You're being weird.'

Natasha glanced up then, at her *Forever Friends*, evaluating them almost warily. Nervous. She looked down and picked at the skin around her fingernails. 'I think I'm starting to remember some things. You know. From before my accident.'

Becca felt it then. A tension as both Hayley and Jenny froze in their seats. A still uprightness that had no place in the energetic gesticulating babble of the school. All of that was shut out for now. The four of them were in a bubble of something else. Something not quite tangible. Becca thought that even if metaphorical pistols hadn't been drawn, there was definitely a sense of hands hovering over guns.

'Wow,' Hayley said, after too long a moment. 'That's great.' She didn't look at Becca, her eyes focused on Natasha. She swallowed. Becca almost missed the telltale movement of her throat, but it was there. Nerves? Fear? Or just a natural reaction to the news?

'Anything you can tell the police?' Hayley added.

'Not yet.' Tasha pushed her salad away. 'It's just more flashes. Images. Nothing I'm ready to share. Not till I figure out what it means. If it means anything at all.'

Jenny had begun tugging at a strand of hair, twirling and twisting it around her fingers. In another situation it might have looked sexy or flirtatious, but Becca thought she just looked scared. A rabbit in the headlights of her friends' exchange.

'Well, if you want to talk it through,' Hayley said, 'let us know. We can always come round to yours one evening, if you like.'

'That would be great,' Jenny said, jittery, over-excited. 'My mum has a new boyfriend. They spend every night drinking and shagging.' She pulled a face. 'It's disgusting. The *noises* they make. Save me.'

'Feels weird not having been round to yours since the thing happened.' Hayley was the queen of cool, but the edge in her voice was clear. She was feeling excluded. Now she looked at

Becca, almost accusatory. What did they know? Becca wondered. What do they suspect? Or were her own suspicions making her see guilt where there wasn't any?

'Yeah, maybe.' Tasha was non-committal. 'I don't know. Things just feel weird.' She looked up. 'I feel like I need my own space. I don't know why.' She hesitated before the next words and the other three girls automatically leaned in slightly. 'This might sound stupid,' Tasha continued, 'but did we argue that day? Why do I have the feeling we did?'

'If you need your own space then why is Becca here?' Hayley said.

Jenny laughed. An almost hysterical titter. 'Why would we fight?'

'No,' Hayley said. 'No, we didn't argue.' She paused. 'Maybe you should chill. Don't force anything. Your brain might just be making shit up trying to fill the space. You know, that false-memory stuff.'

'Yeah,' Tasha said. 'I guess so.'

'Maybe you should try not thinking about it at all,' Hayley added.

You'd like that, Becca thought, *wouldn't you? If she never remembered?*

'I've got to go,' Jenny said, suddenly rising to her feet. 'I have to see Mr Garrick about my Maths exam. I've been carrying my mum's cheque for the resit around for days. If I don't give it to him it'll end up bouncing – again – and she'll kill me.'

'You have to do that now?' Hayley said.

Jenny didn't answer, just darted off, tossing her mane of hair to one side so the strap of her bag didn't catch it. She wiggled as she went, apparently nonchalantly unaware of it, her body soft but tight. It wasn't only the boys who watched her go – the girls did, too, and in their faces Becca could see their longing to be able to pull off the effortless gorgeousness that oozed from Jenny. The longing to have that Barbie magic.

'This is like old times,' Hayley said, looking from Becca to Tasha. 'Except Becca's half the size she used to be.'

'Ha fucking ha,' Becca said. 'And you've got half the personality you used to have.'

'It was a compliment,' Hayley snapped. 'Jesus, I don't remember you being so touchy.'

Becca's phone buzzed. Hannah. *Where are you? I'm by the radiator. Same old!*

'Speaking of personality,' Hayley said.

It stung. Becca couldn't help it. The implication of social retardation was clear in Hayley's disdain.

'Don't be a bitch,' Tasha snapped, and Hayley's eyes widened.

'Seriously? Like you haven't said worse?'

'I've got to go,' Becca said. Her heart was still racing from the cat-and-mouse game she and Tasha were playing, but she didn't want to sit there while Hayley recounted all the bitchy things they'd said about her friend and left all the silences where they'd said bitchy things about her. And as much as Becca was starting to feel some shame about hanging around with Hannah, she *was* her friend. Also, maybe Tasha would learn more if she was alone with Hayley. She and Jenny were hiding something, that was for sure. But what? Could they really have pushed Tasha in the water? As much as she was starting to believe it – had definitely believed it last night out in the woods – it was a surreal idea when they were all sitting in the bright lights and normality of the common room.

'I'll text you later,' she said to Tasha, enjoying the clearly irked look on Hayley's face. 'Don't forget the rehearsal after school.'

'*We* won't,' Hayley sniped.

Becca left them alone, but cast a quick glance back when she reached the common room door. Neither of the girls was speaking. Hayley's face was tense. Thoughtful. Becca gave Tasha a conspiratorial grin and was sure she got a quick dropped-lid wink in return.

Sorry got caught up with something, she texted Hannah. *Lost track of time. Need loo!*

See u there.

Of course she would. Becca sighed internally. There was never an *ok see you later can't be arsed to move* with Hannah. Hannah was *always* there for her.

*

There was only one cubicle occupied in the girls' toilets and in the quiet Becca heard a snort coming from inside it, something being sucked up into a nostril, followed by two or three short sniffs. Then the door opened. It was Jenny. As she recoiled slightly, her hand flew instinctively to wipe her face, but not before Becca saw the flash of white powder.

'What?' She glared at Becca, twitching and defensive. 'What are you staring at?'

'There's still powder around your nose.' Becca didn't know what else to say. She was stunned. A cigarette out the back of the school was one thing, but snorting coke or whatever else at lunchtime was a whole different world.

'What the actual fuck, Jenny?' she blurted out. 'I mean, what is that shit?'

'Oh, fuck off,' Jenny said, her eyes suddenly filling with

tears. 'What the fuck do you know about anything? You don't understand.'

'What don't I understand?'

Jenny hiccoughed then, somewhere between a sob and a laugh. 'The joke is even if I told you, you still wouldn't understand.'

Becca's heart raced, her pulse thumping in her ears. Was this it? Was this Jenny almost confessing? She thought of Lady Macbeth in their Year Ten English Literature play, driven to madness by guilt. Was Jenny getting high in an attempt to keep it together?

'Try me.'

'Yeah, right. Because you're my friend, aren't you? I see the way you look at me. Like I'm trash.' She pushed past Becca to get to the sink. 'You worry about your own shit, Bex. I don't know what your game is, but I don't need your pity.'

The door opened behind them and Hannah bustled in, clutching a thick ring-binder to her flat chest, a flustered flurry of normality.

'Hey, there you are,' she said. 'God, I am so not up for Geography next. I'm sure he's trying to bore us to death. Why is everything so much harder at A Level? Looking forward to the rehearsal later, though. I've had a few ideas about the set, wanted to run them by you—' She stopped her rushed speaking and her eyes darted from Becca to Jenny and back again. Prey not hunter. 'Everything okay?'

'We're good,' Becca said, voice hard.

Hannah looked at Jenny. 'You sure, Jen? You look upset.'

'I'm fine,' Jenny said, either regaining some control or whatever she'd snorted in the toilet was kicking in and giving her confidence. She smiled at Hannah. 'Thanks.'

'All right, as long as you're okay.'

Becca wondered why Hannah was even the slighted bit concerned. When had the Barbies ever been on her radar? They lived in different worlds and Hannah was just a bug under their shoes. Surely she must know that?

Jenny nodded. 'Yeah, it's nothing. See you at rehearsals.' She pushed past Becca as if she wasn't there, and then she was gone.

'What was all that about?' Hannah asked.

'I don't know. She was like that when I came in.'

'Well, you could have been nicer to her. Poor thing.'

'What do you mean, *poor thing*?' The idea that Hannah, a damp dishrag of a girl, could feel sorry for someone as glorious as Jenny was beyond Becca's comprehension. And Jenny would be mortified if she knew. Becca thought she might add it to her arsenal in case she needed it. It would make Jenny crumple. Jenny who might have done something to hurt Tasha, who might even have tried to kill her, being pitied by Hannah Alderton.

'I just feel a bit sorry for her, that's all,' Hannah said. 'She's had a shitty time of it. Her dad wasn't very nice at all, from what my mum says.'

'What would your mum know about it?'

'She used to work at the doctor's surgery down by the Gleberow Estate. She'd see them coming in. Jenny and her mum. Before Jenny's dad ran off. She heard stories from the doctors.'

'Like what?' Becca was intrigued.

'Like the sort of thing I promised never to repeat.'

'Not even to me? Oh, come on.' Hannah was so middle-aged. Who kept stuff like that secret? They were best friends, weren't they? She felt a stab of shame at that thought. Becca hadn't been acting much like a best friend recently and Hannah was many things, but she wasn't dumb. She knew.

'Even to you. She really shouldn't have told me in the first place.' Hannah locked herself in a cubicle, ending the conversation. 'But enough to know that Jenny's turned out pretty well, all things considered.'

'Suit yourself,' Becca muttered, irritated.

'And if you must know, she's the nicest of the lot of them as far as I'm concerned. She seems quite kind to me. Gentle, underneath it all.'

Becca wondered how much time Hannah had spent studying Jenny. Had she been aching with envy and creating this little fantasy about who the soft beauty really was? What a load of bullshit. She'd expected more of Hannah.

'What were you doing at lunch, anyway?' Hannah asked as they emerged for the afternoon's lessons.

'Oh, nothing, really,' Becca said, keeping her eyes on the scuffed lino of the school corridor. 'I got trapped talking to Tasha and couldn't get away. She bought me a Starbucks and there was a queue, so it took longer to get back to school than I expected.' She tried not to think about how easily the lie came. *What was I doing at lunchtime? Oh, just the usual. You know, trying to figure out if a couple of girls nearly killed their friend the other week. Same old.*

'I figured it must be something like that,' Hannah said, quietly. 'You two are getting pretty matey again. I still think you should be wary of her. She can be mean. I was in Year One with her. Even then, she was a bully. Let me tell you what happened with the class ham—'

'What are you, my bodyguard?' Becca snapped, cutting her

off. 'And maybe she's just growing up. She's not been mean to me recently. She bought me an expensive chess set as a thank you for visiting her. What am I supposed to do? Ignore her?' She realised how defensive she sounded and tried to rein it in. 'Anyway, I wouldn't put it quite like that – *matey*. She's just being normal. Does it matter?'

'No,' Hannah said, her chin lifting defiantly. 'I suppose it doesn't.' They reached the fork in their journeys. 'I'll see you at rehearsals,' she finished, and without even looking at Becca, she strode away. For a moment, Becca felt stung – *who was Hannah to get shitty with her?* – and then remembered how many times she'd wished Hannah would grow a backbone. She couldn't have it both ways. Hannah was a bit protective, that was all, and Becca had bitten her head off for it. *And you lied*, she added. *You lied to your friend for a girl who dumped you on your arse*. She turned back around to call after her, but Hannah had caught up with a girl Becca didn't recognise and they were already heads together and talking. She watched as Hannah laughed at something the girl said. That stung, too. Maybe Hannah did have some other friends after all. Becca wasn't quite sure how she felt about that.

Stop being such a bitch, she told herself as she headed to Theatre Tech. Y*ou're in danger of becoming like the Barbies.* The Barbies. Whatever the fuck they were.

Twenty-Eight

14.10
Hayley
Why did you fuck off like that? Leave me there?

14.11
Jenny
Felt sick. Tasha's remembering!!!
Saw Becca in the bathroom. She's a bitch. I bet she knows!:-(

14.12
Hayley
Don't think so. She'd have said something???
Don't know what Tasha remembers anyway.
If anything. Didn't say much when alone.
Just looked at me funny.

14.12

Jenny

She said we'd had a fight! She remembers that! I want to be sick. Feel like I can't breathe.

14.13

Hayley

Don't think she really remembers. She'd say.

14.13

Jenny

How do u know? U always think u know everything.

14.13

Hayley

I don't! Just trying to be calm.

14.14

Jenny

Seriously thinking of running away. Never stopping.

14.15

Hayley

You've got no money.
You think he'd give you money???
You don't want to go.

14.15
Jenny
I can't think straight.

14.16
Hayley
That's cos you're never straight! (;-)) Maybe I'll be nicer to Becca? Used to be friends. See if I can figure out if she knows whatever Tasha knows? Don't get why they're so friendly again.

14.16
Jenny
She's gonna remember everything soon:-((

14.16
Hayley
She doesn't yet. Time to figure something out.

14.16
Jenny
I just want to get off my face. Forget all about it.

14.17
Hayley
:-((

14.17

Jenny

Sorry I'm snappy. Don't mean it.

Just scared.

14.17

Hayley

I know. Xx BFF. Ha! ;-)

14.18

Jenny

BFF ;-) now delete. (Beat ya!)

Twenty-Nine

Taken from **DI CAITLIN BENNETT'S FILES: EXTRACT FROM NATASHA HOWLAND'S NOTEBOOK**

As it turned out, we didn't do much reading at the rehearsal. Mr Jones told us it's a character play at heart. These people were real. John Proctor died because he couldn't give up his reputation. He couldn't confess to something he hadn't done to save himself because of what his name meant to him.

I think John Proctor should have thought about that before he stuck his dick into a teenage servant girl.

Mr Jones paced up and down as he spoke and all the other girls were rapt, mouths half-open – subconsciously ready for his cock or something (god, I'm getting cruder since I died), gazing at him like he was some Hollywood heart-throb. Even the boys were hooked. Mr Jones has what they want. All that confidence. That *ease*. The play is sexually charged and the room was humming with it. Sometimes I think schools are filled with more sexual tension than any other place. Even I feel it sometimes. Like there in the theatre.

Mr Jones gave us group exercises to do, and of course I was to lead my dancing girls. The girls Abigail Williams takes out into the woods to cast a spell on poor Elizabeth Proctor. As we started to mull over how to improvise what they did, I wondered at the irony of it all and wanted to say, *Oh, the subtext!* to Jenny as she came over, as nervous and mousy as her character Mary Warren, hands twitching by her sides and her eyes downcast even though we weren't acting yet, but I doubt Jenny knows what subtext is. I thought of that clearing in the woods – our clearing. The cigarette butts. The Crunchie wrapper. While I chatted to Maisie and Ella (Ruth Putnam and Mercy Lewis – both *gushing* at me and Jenny as if by getting these parts they were almost Barbies themselves), I bet Jenny was thinking about it, too. Her eyes were red-rimmed. Tears? Lack of sleep? Drugs? Knowing Jenny – and I know Jenny – it's probably drugs, but maybe it was all three. Maybe I dream of the darkness and she dreams of the woods.

I looked around for Hayley – *count thirteen slim panels of wood on the wall as my eyes go by* – she's over on the other side of the room working with James Ensor. They had to improvise the unwritten scene of Elizabeth discovering Proctor's affair with Abigail – *moi*. She looked up as if she could feel me staring at her, although I wondered if she'd been glancing my way often, and gave me a hesitant smile. Just for shits and giggles, I didn't return it. She paled. Even from so far away I could see it.

They're *my* Barbies. I'm in control. Still.

Becca was at a table out of the way, sketching plans on a large sheet of paper. Hannah wasn't with her. She was in the back somewhere sorting through the costume cupboard and taking stock of the staging and panels. I heard her telling Becca that's what she was going to do, anyway. I wondered if they'd argued. Hannah was trying to be tough but I know hurt feelings when I see them.

Becca's eyes darted upwards, no doubt to the curtains and the rigging and wondering what she can do with them. She's actually quite creative in a very logistical way, and our theatre can cope with that. This is a Performing Arts school so the Music and Drama departments had a big influx of money. Local am-dram groups (and how tragic is that? Sad old wrecks of people clinging to dreams long gone) use the facilities for their summer shows when the school is shut.

When we had a break, while the others huddled together, I went and joined her. I said it looked good, although I wasn't really sure what I was looking at. She was sketching in charcoal and it was a bit like seeing a designer's drawing of a dress and trying to picture the real thing.

'I'm thinking of doing it in the round,' she said, 'with the audience on all sides. Then the main cast could be constantly onstage, observing from the sides when they're not in a scene.'

'That's really cool,' I said, and I meant it, too. It's clever. It feeds into the theme of a community that's always watching each other.

She smiled. 'Of course, Mr Jones still has to approve it.'

'What's that?'

We both looked up to see Hayley. Her tone was curious, though, rather than snipey.

'That bit, there,' she said, stepping a little forward and pointing at a sketch in one corner of the stage.

Becca explained, patiently, that it was the lighting rig. She darted a glance at me, a nod to our secret alliance. 'It will need re-rigging for the square set-up. Shouldn't be a problem – Casey can do it, she's great with heights. And we can leave that first line of lights as they are – the Head might want to do something in here between now and the show.'

Becca was on a roll, at ease with her own subject, but I could see Hayley was at a loss. She's not really logistical. It was just scribbling on paper to her.

'I was going to have a quick smoke?' she said. 'You want to come?' She didn't look at me, but bright pink spots appeared high on her cheeks.

'Sure,' Becca said, after a minute. 'Why not?'

She was good. She didn't even glance back as they sauntered off. I looked over at Jenny. She'd locked eyes momentarily with Hayley.

Everything was in the subtext, there in the noise of the theatre. The secrets hummed inside us.

What web are you weaving? I wondered as I looked from one of my perfect *Forever Friends* to the other. Jenny, nervous Jenny, rabbit-in-the-headlights, looked my way. I dropped my head to examine Becca's drawings again.

'They're good, aren't they?' It was a voice like a leaking tap, wet and irritating. Hannah. I didn't answer, just looked at her with disdain, let out a lazy sigh of a laugh and walked away. Hannah got her bag and left after that. I saw her texting someone. Probably telling Becca she was going. She was mad at me, but underneath it she was still Becca's lapdog. She's always been like that. Even since nursery. I remember her wetting her pants three times. She'd been *that* girl.

*

Finally rehearsals were done and our improvisations applauded. There was an excitement in the air, as if we all knew this play could be something special if we got it right. We had to be a team, Mr Jones said, but what he really meant is that we're like a cheerleading pyramid. Those at the bottom must support those of us at the top.

Once everyone had taken their turn to drink a private mouthful from the well of Mr Jones and he'd left the theatre, the group fractured. Jenny muttered something about lockers and disappeared towards the main school building, and me, Hayley and Becca wandered outside, our casual strolls belying our internal tensions.

Becca was in the middle, a dark thorn between white roses, as we went out into the crisp night. It was gone half-five but it was still busy. Ours was not the only after-school activity and boys in dirty football kits climbed into the back of waiting 4x4s or headed off, laughing and jeering at each other, to the parade of shops where they would no doubt wolf down bags of greasy chips.

My stomach rumbled. How wonderful to be a boy, to be able to eat like that. For eating like that to be a badge of pride rather than a crime.

Someone called, 'Natasha! Hayley!' and a hand waved, and I frowned. I couldn't make out the figure, only an outline against the glare of the headlights. A shape in the darkness. I wondered if it would whisper my name next. I didn't count the line of cars. I knew it would be thirteen.

'Is that your dad?' Becca said. It was. Of course it was. I felt such a flood of relief and then silly for my momentary panic. I had nothing to panic about. (If Dr Harvey ever does read this, she's really going to think I'm bonkers and will lock me up. I'd rather burn it first.)

Then Hayley asked, happy, 'What's he doing here?' I think maybe she has a little crush on my dad, gross as that sounds.

We finally reached him, Hayley first, then me and then Becca, the awkward tag-along. He must have finished early so come by to give us a lift. We three came down the last few steps to the road to find him smiling. Pleased with his surprise.

'I could have walked, Dad.' I sounded bored. His smile didn't falter, though. He was determined to feel good about this.

'Well, I'm here now. And it's cold,' he said. 'Hayley – you can come for dinner if you want. There's always enough to feed an army.' He finally saw Becca, the afterthought, who half-waved and then went back to texting. Hannah, no doubt. Making their peace once my dad's surprise to see her reminded Becca she wasn't a Barbie. Whatever she is, she's not one of us.

'I'm quite tired, actually,' I said. 'And I've got some work to do.' I smiled at Hayley as if butter wouldn't melt and she instantly said it was cool, although I know she was smarting with disappointment.

'Do you want a lift? I can drop Tasha then drop you after? It's only an extra five minutes.' It dawned on me, in a horrific moment, that maybe my dad fancied Hayley a little bit, too, and I could sense her hesitancy. It was cold and the buses are crap during rush hour. I gave her no hint which way to go, my face impassive.

'No, it's okay, Gary,' she said eventually, coming up with an excuse about meeting Jenny. The second she did, I offered Becca a lift – sticking the knife in and twisting it a little.

'No,' she said. 'It's fine. Honestly.'

I didn't argue. I actually wanted some quiet time in the car anyway, and it's not as if me and Bex could talk about anything that mattered in front of my dad. He'd think we were crazy. What the hell does he know about anything, anyway? They think they understand us, but they don't. We're still children to them.

I hoped Becca wasn't seeing Aiden this evening. Maybe he'd be too busy worrying about being arrested to want to meet up. Maybe he'd even been arrested. No. He can't have. I'd know – they'd have told me. I am the golden thirteen-minutes-dead girl. It irritates me that he comes first with Becca all the time, though. I mean, *Aiden*? I just don't get it. This is important. This really is life or death. This is me.

*

They're wriggling like maggots on fish hooks, my best friends. That's what I thought when I finished talking to Becca. I lay on my bed and tapped the phone against the duvet as I considered it all, my eyes wandering absently over the chessboard. Becca is good at reporting back. She gives pretty much every word – she knows what to remember. No vague, *Well, they kind of said this*. Or, *It was something like that*. The details matter and Becca knows it.

She said that when they went for a smoke, Hayley was curious. That's no surprise. Wanted to know what I could remember. Becca said she had no idea. Hayley was doing her best to be nice to her, though. Edgy. Nervous. Apologising for being a bitch and reminiscing about the old days. Saying we should all hang out more. Becca played along – just enough but not too much. Nice but slightly wary. She asked Hayley if we'd really had an argument and Hayley denied it again but Becca said she was tense. Wouldn't look her in the eye. So Becca changed the subject. Didn't want to push too hard.

It's interesting that their first move is to try and make friends with Becca, maybe thinking Becca will be so grateful she'll tell them whatever it is I've 'remembered' (as if). It's so transparent. Surely they must see that? But I guess they don't have a choice. Maybe they're desperate already, seeing the battle lines I'm drawing. My stomach tightens thinking about it. Everything is unsettled.

I checked Facebook on my phone. Neither of them were online and they hadn't updated their pages. That's weird, especially for Hayley. We like to collect our *likes*. Compare numbers. I know she loves it when she gets more than me. As if she can rival me.

I keep checking my notifications. My update when I got home, about loving the play and the people in it, already had more than forty likes and twenty comments, and the girls I'd name-checked had shared the post full of excitement that I'd mentioned them. I didn't read the comments. Since my accident it's become Facebook law to like whatever I say. It pretty much was before, to be honest. I've sent Bex an 'add friend' request. I should have done it already but some things can't be rushed. This is the right time. We have secrets together now. We should at least be Facebook friends.

I looked up Aiden's page, too, on a whim. It's not public so I couldn't really see anything except his profile picture, which was him playing guitar onstage in some dingy club somewhere, his hair sweaty over his face (*oh god of course it's all the wannabe rock star pose clichés and oh god I'm such a bitch*) and his cover photo's some band I've never heard of and never want to hear of, but it does say he's in a relationship with Rebecca 'Bex' Crisp and that he's a *full-time musician.* I remembered his face as I laughed at him on the ground and my fingers flew over the small keyboard. I hit 'add friend' and then I hit 'message'.

Hey, I just wanted to say hi and I don't think you had anything to do with what happened to me. Just so you know. Tasha xo.

My stomach fluttered when I sent it and I still worry that maybe I shouldn't have messaged, especially since the police have been interested in him, but it's done now. I did one more scan for Hayley and Jenny online but they were still silent.

When I glanced back at the chessboard, I could suddenly see my next move. Becca has taken a knight and two pawns, but we'd both played aggressively and she wasn't without losses of her own. Suddenly I knew how to force her queen out of safety and take one of her bishops. I texted her the move.

And I sent Jenny a text to shake her up a bit and make them sweat over the weekend.

What did you do, Jen?
I know you and Hayley did something.

The phone buzzed at once but it was just Becca.

Good move! Cow!

It was, I decided, when I got no answer from Jenny. It *was* a good move. Were they in a panicked phone call now? What would they be saying? I imagined them wriggling on hooks again and slowly, in my head, they morphed into maggots, blind and stupid and desperate to be free.

*

I was still thinking of maggots when I went to bed. I didn't want to be, but I was. I imagined them bubbling out of Nicola Munroe's distorted, blue corpse. I imagined her loose skin sliding off her as they pulled her from the river, and maybe maggots or something wriggling free into the freezing water. It made me itch all over. I took deep breaths and tried to think of other things. The play. The uneven ground of my friendships. The clearing. I wished I could put my trainers on and go out for a run and not think about any of it, but then I'd have to explain my secret jogging and my muddy, sweaty clothes, and neither my mum nor my dad would understand my need for *privacy please*.

I turned the light off when I had to, after shouting my obligatory goodnight down the stairs and locking myself in so Mum couldn't invade my space by checking on me. They used to get it, my need for space, but since the accident she's become quite clingy. She touches my hair, like she used to when I was small, and when she lets her guard down – or maybe it's when she's had too much wine – I see all that fear in her eyes. The fear of what might have happened, what nearly had. I feel sorry for her, but I can't help her. *I* survived it. *I'm* the one who was dead for thirteen minutes. If I can get over it, she can.

Dr Harvey suggested Nytol might help me sleep after I turned down proper sleeping pills. I didn't want anything too strong. Nothing that could drown me in sleep. I have to stay in control. I'm not sure if they work or not but I took them anyway. I think maybe they do a little bit. I know my breathing slowed, even as I fought the encroaching darkness, me and my head full of maggots clinging to the driftwood of consciousness.

Eventually, though, the endless black claimed me. Perhaps part of me wants to go into the void. Terrified as I am, I'm also fascinated by it. It was cold. Vast. I heard the whispers again.

This time I listened.

When I woke up I didn't remember what I heard, but I know, as I write this, that I was afraid. I am still afraid.

Thirty

10.14

Jenny

That's what she just texted me. She knows. The fucking skank bitch remembers! I hate her. I fucking hate her.

10.16

Hayley

Doesn't say she actually remembers? Not properly.

10.17

Jenny

This is Tasha. Who the fuck knows? She must remember something! This is such a fuck up.

10.17

Hayley

She's testing us. I don't think she remembers. Not properly.

10.18
Jenny
Stop saying that! How do u know? I'm so over this. I can't take the fucking stress of pretending all the time. She's going to remember soon. What are we going to do then??

10.19
Hayley
I'll think of something.

10.19
Jenny
U need to think faster.

10.20
Jenny
And dont tell me to delete. Sick of that shit too:-(

10.21
Hayley
U will tho?

10.22
Jenny
Yes.

10.22
Jenny
I wish she was dead. She should be dead.

10.23
Hayley
Yeah, she should. :-(. I'll think of something.

Thirty-One

Extract from the *Maypoole Gazette*, Saturday 23rd January

The police have still not released an official cause of death in the case of local teenager Nicola Munroe, whose body was found in the river between Maypoole and Brackston last Sunday. Their press officer confirmed that they are following up fresh leads in the case but declined to comment on any links between Miss Munroe's death and the near-fatal drowning of teenager Natasha Howland.

The Nag and Pineapple pub, where Nicola worked prior to her death, is holding a fundraiser from 2 p.m. next Saturday to help the Munroe family with funeral costs.

Extract from the *Brackston Sunday Herald,* Sunday 24th January

Insider sources at Kilmourn Central Police Station have confirmed that detectives are investigating a person of interest in relation to both the death of 19-year-old Nicola Munroe, whose body was recovered last week from the River Ribble, and the attack on 16-year-old Natasha Howland, which left the Brackston Community School student technically dead for 13 minutes.

Officers are believed to have questioned a 19-year-old Brackston man who knew both victims, but no arrests have been made at this time. The man, a musician, is a former Brackston Community School student and is currently in a relationship with a sixth form pupil there.

Thirty-Two

They were starting early. It was midday, so early for Jamie, anyway. Aiden was smoking a cigarette at the back door – Jamie was pretty sure he'd smoked at least one joint already – and a pot of coffee was brewing when the quiet peace of the countryside was broken by tyres on the gravel. They barely had time to exchange a glance, Jamie's confused and Aiden's scared, when the doorbell rang.

'I'll get it.'

Jamie saw the badge first because she held it up to his face. Official. Officious. He smiled. He couldn't help himself. She wasn't at all who he was expecting, and the first time he'd seen her he'd thought she was actually very pretty under that fierce outer shell. Or maybe because of it. 'You don't need to show me that, DI Bennett. Did our time in hospital together mean nothing to you?' He wasn't a natural flirt and as he said it, he knew this wasn't the moment for flirting, either. Even to his own ears his words sounded, at best, sleazy, and he cringed.

'Is Aiden Kennedy here?' she asked, as if he hadn't even spoken.

'Yes.' Jamie's smile collapsed as the initial surprise of seeing her vanished. Context was suddenly everything. 'But surely you're done with him now?'

'May we come in?' she asked, not answering his question, and he gave a small nod.

She pushed past, a move she managed without actually touching him but which still made him feel as if he'd been shoved aside, and a uniformed constable followed in her wake, nodding a semi-apology to him. They headed to the kitchen. Bennett didn't rush. Her stride was purposeful, not urgent. Aiden hadn't moved.

'We'd like you to come with us to the station, Mr Kennedy,' Caitlin Bennett said. 'We have some more questions for you.'

'Can't you just ask them here?' Jamie said. In the kitchen doorway, Aiden's tall, lanky frame looked as if someone had just removed a section of his spine. He'd slumped over a little, his shoulders curving in as if he wanted to curl up into a ball. Maybe he did.

'We need you to come to the station,' she said, ignoring Jamie. 'There's some new evidence we'd like to talk to you about.'

Evidence. Jamie stared at Aiden. The Google search on street cameras. The dark shadows under his eyes. His snappiness. Ignoring Becca's calls after his initial rush to reassure her. *Oh, Aiden*, he thought. *What have you done?*

'Are you arresting me?' Aiden asked, crushing out his cigarette. His voice was hollow. Resigned.

'No. But this would be easier at the station.'

He nodded.

He'd been expecting this, Jamie realised. Maybe not right now but at some point. But whatever they'd found, Aiden was no killer. He was sure of that.

'Do you want me there with you?' Jamie asked. 'I can follow behind in my car.'

Aiden nodded again.

'We will provide a duty solicitor to sit in on the interview if Mr Kennedy so wishes.'

'I *am* a solicitor,' Jamie took a little pleasure in the reminder. 'I was, anyway. For today I can be one again.'

'Then it's up to Mr Kennedy,' Caitlin said, dryly. What did Caitlin Bennett see when she looked at Aiden, Jamie wondered. She probably saw a surly, guilty teenager. A stoned loner who listened to hard rock and heavy metal. The kind of kid who had deeply hidden emotional issues that could erupt in unexpected violence. From the outside, maybe that's what most people would see. But Jamie knew that wasn't Aiden. He was a sweet kid. Shy. Sensitive. A great musician. Not a loner, just selective and private in his life.

'I want Jamie with me,' Aiden said quietly.

'Okay, mate.' Jamie squeezed his arm. 'I'm with you.' He met DI Bennett's eyes and this time he didn't smile at her. Right now, she might not be the enemy, but she was definitely wrong about Aiden. 'Let's go,' he said. 'Get this cleared up once and for all.'

Thirty-Three

Becca had hoped to hide in the theatre alone at lunchtime, working. She wasn't in the mood for company and didn't even care about the psycho Barbies. She'd barely eaten for two days and had a huge row with her mum on Sunday night when she wouldn't accept that Becca just wanted to be left alone. *Have you had a fight with Aiden?* She'd slammed her door on that. *Or is it about Natasha?* The extra concern in that last question sent Becca over the edge. The words *just fuck off* had definitely been used as her face burned, and then she'd had to listen to all the shouting downstairs as her mum and dad disagreed about how to handle it. Her dad was particularly loud about just wanting some peace.

She'll come downstairs when she's hungry.

That's not the bloody point, Jim, and you know it!

She had stuck her headphones on and drowned them out while trying Aiden's number again. He didn't answer. Again. Eventually he texted back, just as she was about to puke with worry, saying he'd been sick all weekend and then sleeping all day. He'd call her tomorrow. She almost sniped back that he could have said so on Saturday because then she could have gone out with Hannah or done *something*, but realised how tragic that made her sound. How tragic she was – sitting in her room waiting for him to call. At least Tasha hadn't been around to witness her distracted mood and hurt. Tasha would have made her talk about it, and then Tasha would have thought she was a total wet blanket. Thankfully, Tasha was away with her family for her gran's delayed birthday. Aiden aside, that was a relief, too. They'd texted a bit, but it wasn't about the Barbies so much, just comedy about relatives, Becca's next chess move, dull shit. She was quite glad they'd left it alone. It gave her some breathing space in her head. She couldn't think about the shit with Hayley and Jenny as well as Aiden ignoring her.

Monday had been difficult. At school she felt pulled in all directions. Hayley and Tasha were both texting her between lessons, and every time her phone buzzed, her heart leapt at the thought it would be Aiden. She didn't mind Tasha so much, but it was hard to keep her pretence up with Hayley, especially as she was being more like the old Hayley. She had to be careful not to get drawn in. Hayley and Jenny were grade-A bitches and Becca needed to remember that.

She'd had lunch with Hannah – the only person she could offload with about Aiden. And that had been fine, but the others kept texting her and Hannah had done the shitty passive-aggressive thing of saying, *You're popular today. Back in with your old crowd, then?* All the time with that needy *don't hurt me* look on her face. But what was Becca supposed to do? Not answer? She almost told Hannah what was going on just to shut her up, but she couldn't betray Tasha's confidence like that. Not to Hannah. And it was their secret for now. Theirs alone. At least until they could actually *prove* something.

Aiden had eventually called her, just after school finished, and claimed he was still sick. To be fair, he didn't sound great

– he sounded exhausted and low and quiet – but she still felt hurt that he wanted to be on his own. When he had the flu, they'd stayed curled up on his bed and watched movies all day while he worked his way through three toilet rolls blowing his nose. The pangs of insecurity and self-doubt crept up from whatever hidden pit inside her they called home and she instantly felt sick again.

She still felt sick now, Tuesday lunchtime, and was desperately trying to throw herself into preparations for the afternoon's rehearsal rather than thinking about her shitty boyfriend or listening to the equally shitty voice in her head telling her *he didn't love her any more. He was mad she'd got mad at him. She'd basically accused him of murder so how he was supposed to still love her? No way, José. You're out of luck, chubby little Rebecca Crisp.*

She swallowed it all down and gritted her teeth. He was just sick. That was all. She tried not to think about the fact that his phone was now switched off and had been since about 11.30. His phone was never switched off. *Avoiding. He's avoiding you.*

Mr Jones had thought her ideas for lighting and staging sounded pretty cool but before committing and planning his direction around them, he wanted to try one scene out in the round. She'd hoped to do it on her own or with Casey, but Casey was in a coursework catch-up class and Hannah had insisted on coming to help instead. They'd only run masking tape down one edge of what would be the performance area when all the Barbies turned up, Tasha first, then Jenny and Hayley.

Hannah pretended not to really care but Becca noticed the sudden clumsiness in her movements. They unsettled Hannah.

They made her remember her position in the hive. Girls like them were – Becca was sure – the reason Hannah had never opened an Instagram or a Twitter account. She was on Facebook, but Hannah's *mum* was on her friends list and she only had thirty-something friends, if that.

'This is going to be so cool,' Tasha said, standing close to Becca and looking at her planning drawings and then down at the lines they were marking out, bringing what would become the stage to life little by little. 'You're so clever, Bex.'

Becca saw Hayley awkwardly trying to join in, as if she were part of this moment, too. She wasn't, though. She was an intruder. A threat. *Now you know how it feels, bitch*, Becca thought. *Now* you're *on the outside*. And whatever Hayley had done to Tasha, Becca was determined to find out. If they were right and some argument between the Barbies had caused Tasha's accident, then it was Hayley's fault that Becca and Aiden had fallen out, too.

'Any more memories surface over the weekend, Tash?' Becca asked sweetly. 'Maybe they'll all come back in a rush now you've started getting flashes.'

'I hope so,' Tasha said. 'I'm considering hypnosis. Try to drag it all up that way.'

'Cool,' Hayley muttered. She barely looked at Tasha. 'Although I've heard that shit can fuck with your head. You might be better just waiting.'

'You think?' Tasha said. 'Maybe you're right. Or maybe you just don't want me to remember whatever it is we fought about. Is that it?'

'I told you,' Hayley snapped. 'We didn't have a fight.' Her eyes darted from Tasha to Becca, looking for some solidarity there. Becca just stared at her, she hoped with a *who are you kidding, you stupid slut?* look.

'Fuck, you've got paranoid, Tasha,' Hayley finished. She tried to smile again. It was weird seeing ice-cool Hayley so unsettled. She was a shit liar, that was clear. Something had definitely happened during the time Tasha couldn't remember. And judging from Hayley's face it was nothing good. It was useful evidence, though. Even if a look wasn't something they could go to the police with, it *was* something. 'But maybe you *should* do that hypnosis. Then we can get back to being normal again,' Hayley concluded, trying to make it sound light-hearted and failing miserably.

'Just chill out,' Becca said. 'It's probably nothing, right?' This was her role, the one she and Tasha had decided she should play. Partially backing Tasha up but not cutting Hayley out entirely. To look like maybe, just maybe, she might be someone Hayley could confide in if she started to crack.

'Hey, Hannah,' Jenny called from where she was standing over by the stacked chairs. 'Want to go through my lines with me?'

'Sure,' Hannah answered, meek and mild and obedient.

Becca had totally forgotten Hannah was even there. While she and Hayley and Tasha were having their little stand-off, Hannah had quietly finished marking out the corners of the stage area and running tape between them to outline the whole area. It wasn't as neat as she'd wanted but Becca bit her tongue rather than saying anything. It was a two-person job and Hannah had done it by herself. 'I'm finished here,' Hannah said, and she flashed a look at Becca, not a fiery one – Hannah could never manage fiery – but one full of reproach and hurt. *Always with the hurt*, Becca thought. *It's only been five minutes.* Fuck, Hannah needed to grow the fuck up.

If Hayley was doing her best to be friendly, Jenny didn't have it in her. Or wasn't capable of it. She couldn't be standing further away from them if she tried, and every so often she sniffed and rubbed the back of her hand against her nose. She might have started the day wearing foundation but it was long gone now – around her nostrils, anyway. They looked red at the edges, almost scabby, like she had a cold, and her golden hair, Jenny's pride and joy, was pulled up in a loose bun. She didn't look so sexy today. She looked twitchy. Too much powder in the toilets, probably. Becca wondered if she should shift her focus to Jenny. Jenny looked ready to burst with whatever was eating her up. She sure as shit couldn't look at Tasha.

She pulled out her phone, absently checking once more to see if Aiden had texted – he hadn't – and swore when she saw the time. Nearly half of lunchtime had gone already. She needed to focus if she didn't want to fuck up later. She looked up at the lighting rig and then at the stage area in the centre of the hall. The way she saw it, the main action would be happening there – Elizabeth, Proctor and Mary Warren, and the heated exchange when Mary returned from the courthouse. Abigail wasn't actually in the scene but Becca thought Natasha could stand just beyond one corner of the central square – technically offstage and in the aisle. Then, at the point when Elizabeth Proctor realised she'd been accused, the moving rig above would tilt down, pooling Abigail in light and making her visible – but as if she were watching from the shadows, standing under a streetlamp.

If it worked, it would be awesome. But if it didn't, on their one try this evening, then Mr Jones wouldn't include it in his directing plans. She might not want to shag him like everyone else seemed to, but she did want to impress him. She wanted to feel she had some creative input into the show rather than being the workhorse behind the curtains.

She moved to the spot where Tasha would stand and checked the position of the rig. Her heart sank.

'Oh, for fuck's sake.'

Both Hayley and Tasha looked up from studying their parts. 'What is it?' Tasha said.

'The moving light – the one that needs to be above you, right here – Casey's positioned it in the wrong place. We should have marked out the stage first. Fuck it.' She'd been too distracted, that was the problem. Aiden not answering his phone, the Barbies' craziness, Hannah, everything. God. 'It's only a foot or two out, but that's enough to wreck the effect. It has to be right above you.'

Hayley looked over at the ladder leaning against the wall. 'Well, can't you just move it?'

'I'm shit with heights,' Becca said. She stared up balefully for a long moment.

'I'll do it,' Hayley said, eventually.

'Really? That would be so great!' For a moment, in her wave of relief, Becca almost forgot her mistrust of Hayley and the fact that no one was supposed to touch the lights without having done the lighting course. But it wasn't like Hayley was doing it without Becca watching, and it wasn't exactly a difficult job. A Year Seven could do it. 'It's really easy,' she said. 'Just loosen the clamp bolts on the moving light and slide it along till I tell you to stop, then tighten them up again. And you'll have to take the safety chain off and loop it through again once it's moved. The caretaker's tools are over there – we got the tape from him. There might be a spanner to help tighten them up.'

'No probs,' Hayley said, already prepping the ladder. 'You want to test it out now, too?'

'No – I can't get into the control booth until after school. I just want it all in place.'

Natasha and Becca steadied the ladder even though it was quite stable, and Hayley climbed. She didn't look down once, and at the top she rested one knee on the small silver ledge and started loosening the light with both hands.

'Okay, where to? Put Natasha wherever she needs to be.'

Becca did as she was told, directing Natasha to stand just beyond one of the corner stage markings, and Hayley took the last step onto the very top of the ladder and leaned out, the chain rattling as she unlooped it and rested it on the ladder while she moved the light. She looked totally at ease, but Becca's stomach tightened watching her.

'Be careful!' It was strange seeing Hayley up there. A flashback to the girl who'd climbed trees.

'Stop worrying!'

'Whatever you do,' Natasha said, 'don't drop that light. It looks heavy.'

'Just all stand back,' Hayley answered, her voice quiet as she concentrated on pushing the light along, using the secure metal poles of the rig for balance, and then finally relocked the safety chain. 'Okay, we're done.' She rested her hands on her hips, balancing so easily, fifteen feet or more from the ground. '*Voilà*.'

'Thanks, Hayles,' Becca said when the agile girl was back on the ground. From where Becca was standing, the light looked fine. She felt so awkward. *Why don't you just tell us what happened, Hayley? Then all this shit can stop.*

'Why don't you mind your own fucking business!'

Jenny's voice cut through them all, so uncontrolled and filled with rage that Becca almost jumped.

'I only asked if you were ill.' Hannah looked and sounded shell-shocked. She'd taken three steps back. 'That was all. I was concerned.'

'I don't *need* your fucking concern!' Jenny threw her copy of the play into her bag. 'There's nothing wrong with me.'

'That's okay, then.' Hannah was holding her hands up as if Jenny had pulled a gun on her.

'Hey,' Becca said. 'What's going on?'

Jenny's head whipped around and all her attention was suddenly focused on Becca. Rage burned in her bloodshot eyes. 'What do you care? You're pathetic. You think we can't see how happy you are that Tasha's being all nice to you again? Like you don't even care about all the shit things she's said about you, all the times she's laughed at you?'

'Shut up, Jenny,' Hayley muttered. She might as well have stayed silent for all Jenny heard her. She was on a roll and wasn't stopping.

'How fucking tragic is that? And you think you know her cos *you were friends first*? How retarded are you? You think people stay the same? Are you the same as you were then, Becca? Maybe you're still fat on the inside, cos that's the only way you'd be stupid and needy enough to forget everything that's ever happened.'

Becca couldn't speak. She knew she was just standing there with her mouth open and her face burning, but she couldn't get her brain or tongue to function. Every word was a blow.

'And you're such a bitch,' Jenny said, more softly this time, as if she didn't have the energy to maintain the fire. 'You're a total bitch to Hannah.'

'I am not!' Becca said, her voice a little shrill.

'Yes, you are.' She looked at Hannah then and spoke more softly still. 'Hannah, you deserve a better friend than one who dumps you every time she's summoned by the Queen Bitch.'

'What's your problem, Jenny?' Natasha said. 'What did I ever do to you? Nothing!' She was breathing fast, almost panting, and Becca knew how she felt. Her own heart was racing with the awfulness of confrontation, all the girls standing within the marked stage engaged in a heated performance of their own. 'Why are you two being so weird?'

Jenny laughed. 'It's not us avoiding you, Tasha.'

'I am not avoiding you!'

'Let's go, Jen.' Hayley had reached Jenny's side and grabbed her arm, but Jenny shook her off. Hayley tried another tack: 'Come outside while I have a cigarette.'

'Stop telling me what to do! I'm fine!' She looked back at Natasha. 'And if you're not avoiding us, why did you say you had a hospital visit the Saturday before last when you didn't? I *saw* Becca coming out of your house. Why couldn't you just say you didn't want to see us?'

Hannah looked at Becca. 'That was my mum's birthday. I thought you were seeing Aiden after? You said that text was from him?'

'I didn't say that, exactly,' Becca said, suddenly aware that her self-justifying *it's not quite a lie* at the time now felt very hollow. Why had they come in here at lunchtime? Why hadn't she just got on with this shit by herself? Even if the light was in the wrong place, that would have been better than this awfulness. 'You just assumed it was and I didn't want to say it was Tasha in case it upset you.' It sounded so lame. It *was* lame.

'See?' Jenny said.

For a moment, everything was still, the five girls locked in a silent showdown, emotional wounds leaking into the air and making it heavy. And then, very carefully, Hannah picked up her bag.

'Hannah . . .' Becca started, but her friend turned away and started walking to the doors. God, she felt like shit. God, she *was* a shit. Aiden had gone off her and now Hannah hated her. *Well done, Bex*, she thought. *Queen of the fuck-ups. And it's all your own fault for being such a bitch*.

Jenny looked as if she was going to say more, and then the bell rang and broke the moment. Becca could have fallen to her knees in relief. The end of lunch.

Jenny and Hayley left without another word, Hayley sending one long, cool, unreadable look back at them before she followed the dishevelled Jenny out.

'What the fuck is wrong with Jenny?' Tasha said. 'Guilt? About whatever we fought over? About what happened that night? She's off her face, that's for sure.'

'Yeah, probably.' Becca was only half-listening. She'd text Hannah from English. She'd explain. She'd be a better friend. She'd tell her about all the shit with the Barbies and why she'd been so distant. She'd tell her about Aiden knowing Nicola Munroe. She'd tell her everything she should have told her best mate already.

Her thoughts were desperate, she knew, and probably too little too late. She'd seen Hannah's face. It was hurt but also angry. No one liked to be pitied – Becca knew that from personal experience – and no one liked to be lied to out of pity. She'd done both.

'Don't worry,' Tasha said. 'She'll come round.'

'I know.' Becca tried to smile but she felt sick. She didn't know at all. She wasn't relishing the idea of English with Hayley and Jenny now, either. She just wanted some breathing space. And for Aiden to text her the fuck back.

'Oh, fuck it all,' she said suddenly. 'The caretaker's tools.'

'Don't stress it,' Tasha said, grabbing the box. 'I've got a free – I'll take them back.' She suddenly wrapped her other arm around Becca and squeezed her close. Her hair was soft and smelled of apple.

'I don't know what I'd do without you, Bex,' she said. 'I really don't. Thanks for being my friend again. Those two are both weirding me out.' She pulled back. 'Now get your shit together and I'll see you later.'

As she left, Becca felt her stomach untangle slightly. Hannah would get over it. She'd have to. Maybe she and Tasha would even become friends. Tasha *needed* Becca. She could trust Becca. Once Becca explained, once they'd figured out what actually happened that night and what Hayley and Jenny had done, then Hannah would understand why Becca had been weird. She'd have to, otherwise she'd be a pretty shit human being, and she wasn't. And if she didn't understand, then maybe it was time they stopped being friends. Like Jenny said: people change.

Thirty-Four

It was a small room with a standard-issue desk, Jamie and Aiden on one side, Caitlin Bennett and her sergeant on the other. The walls were blue but there was nothing vivid in the colour. A dead blue. Drained of life. Dulled into despair. It still somehow managed to clash with the green industrial carpet and black plastic chairs. Combined with the sickly yellow strip lights and lack of windows, the effect was mildly claustrophobic. Jamie suspected that was intentional. A clunky tape-recording machine sat on the shelf and was rolling, though it wasn't getting much from Aiden to save for later. He'd been mostly silent through the opening questions other than acknowledging who he was.

He was scared, Jamie could see it even if Caitlin Bennett couldn't. Or maybe Bennett had seen too many scared young men sitting in interview and didn't have time to be sympathetic. Plus fear and guilt weren't mutually exclusive – maybe guilty people were more scared than the innocent. Still, looking at Aiden it would be easy to mistake that fear for surly arrogance. He'd pushed his chair back slightly and his long legs were stretched out in front of him, one foot over the other. His arms were folded across his chest and dark hair hung over his eyes, slicing across the sharp blue of his irises as he scowled at the cheap Formica tabletop. He hadn't touched his tea and a brown film had formed on the surface as it cooled.

'Your version of events presents a problem for me, Aiden,' she said coolly. 'You said you dropped Rebecca Crisp at her house at midnight and then went straight home in the early morning of Saturday ninth January. Why would you say that?'

Jamie looked at the kid, who still refused to lift his eyes. 'Whatever's going on, just tell her the truth, mate,' he said. 'If you haven't done anything wrong then there's no point in lying.' He wondered if he was being naïve. Criminal law hadn't been his speciality, but there were plenty of cases of the police charging the wrong man. Or at least arresting them and letting the media wreck their lives before fresh evidence proved their innocence.

Bennett had a brown folder in front of her – an ominous item that clearly held some truth in it that Aiden wasn't sharing. Why had he clammed up like this? Surely he knew it couldn't do him any good? *Unless maybe he's guilty*, a small serpent voice said quietly in the back of Jamie's mind. *Unless maybe that.* He crushed it.

'Mr Kennedy refuses to acknowledge the question.' She opened the folder and carefully took out two grainy printed photographs. There were time stamps at the bottom of each but from where he was sitting Jamie couldn't read them. He saw Aiden swallow hard, though. That wasn't a good sign. His own heart was starting to race and he wasn't even the one under suspicion.

'Since you are, by your silence, sticking to your previous story, let me show you what CCTV cameras picked up that night. For the benefit of the tape I'm now showing Aiden Kennedy stills taken from those cameras.'

A slight shuffle in the seat beside him. Jamie remembered Aiden's phone search again. *Oh god, what did he do?*

'Your car was caught by a camera on Elmore Road. For clarity, that's the main road that runs parallel to the river, the park and the woods. The footage shows your car on Elmore Road in the early hours of Saturday 9th of January. Here –' she pushed the first picture across '– it can be seen turning from Elmore Road into the visitors' car park for the woods. The time stamp at the bottom of this picture shows that was at twelve thirty-seven a.m. After you'd taken Rebecca home. When you told us you were going straight home. You didn't leave the car park until . . .' She passed Aiden the second picture, where a car could be seen turning into the road again. 'Five forty-five a.m.'

Jamie's breath caught and suddenly, despite the dry too-hot warmth of the room, he felt cold. He felt caught in a magician's trick. *While you were over here concentrating on saving a dying girl, over HERE –* voilà*! – your young friend was making his getaway!* His memory of defending Aiden to Becca by saying he wouldn't be so stupid as to lie to the police was turning to ash.

'I didn't leave my car the whole time,' Aiden said quietly. He glanced at Jamie and then sat up and leaned his elbows on the table. 'If there's a camera in the car park you'll see that.'

'But there isn't, Aiden. So I'd have to take your word for that.' Bennett's eyes didn't leave Aiden's. Jamie might as well not have been there. 'And as you've already proved, your word is not something I can trust.'

There was a long moment of silence as Aiden grew more tense and Caitlin Bennett leaned back in her chair and folded her arms as if she had all the time in the world to break the boy.

'I didn't hurt anyone,' Aiden said eventually. 'I sat in my car, smoked some weed and fell asleep. I didn't see any other cars or anyone or anything that would be of any use to you, so I didn't see the point of telling you I'd been there. And I didn't want to own up to possession of cannabis.' He looked up at her then, all earnest blue eyes. 'I mean, would *you* tell you any of that?'

Aiden's surliness had evaporated. Jamie kept staring at the photos. They were gritty and real and they made his stomach turn. They looked like pictures of some wrongdoing, sneakily taken in the middle of the night.

'The same way you didn't tell us you knew Nicola Munroe?'

'That was different! I didn't remember that I'd met her! I couldn't tell you something I didn't remember!'

Another long pause.

'Look,' Aiden said, 'I haven't done anything wrong. But I do know Tasha – well, I used to – and I asked her out once when I was at school and she was epically shit about it – which I presume you already know. And I figured if I told you I'd smoked some weed and fallen asleep in the car park then none of it would have looked good for me. So I didn't tell you, and when you asked about the Nicola thing, I didn't know how to tell the truth.'

'I can almost understand that. Almost,' she stressed. 'But what I don't understand . . .'

She paused again and Jamie couldn't help but be impressed. She was one step ahead of Aiden all the way. She was tying him up in knots.

'What I don't understand,' she continued, 'is why you lied to Becca. You told her you were going straight home and the following day you didn't say anything different. I would have thought – if you were innocent – the first thing you'd do was tell her you'd been there. Shock reaction. The need to share. Your "*holy shit*" moment when Natasha was found so close to where you'd been. But you didn't tell her. You didn't tell anyone. Why not?'

Aiden was chewing his bottom lip, his eyes darting left and right at nothing in particular, but Jamie knew the signs that he was thinking hard. Looking for a way out of something. Suddenly it struck Jamie. It was so obvious. And it wasn't murder or attempted murder, that was for sure.

'You weren't alone, were you, Aiden?' he said. The boy looked up.

'I'll ask the questions, Mr McMahon.' Caitlin tried to interrupt but Jamie wasn't going to stop. He knew why Aiden had lied.

'Did you have another girl in the car with you, mate?'

Aiden's shoulders slumped and suddenly Jamie's question had the policewoman's attention.

'Was there someone else in the car with you?' she asked.

Aiden stayed quiet for a moment longer before finally starting to speak.

'Becca can get so jealous. She's insecure, you know? If I'd told her, she wouldn't have understood. She'd have thought it was something more. You saw how she can get.' He glanced up at Bennett. 'Like she did when you told her Nicola Munroe had my number in her phone. She thinks every girl is a threat or something. So I don't always tell her if I hang out with other girls. It's easier that way.'

'So who was the girl?'

'Her name's Emma. She works in the bar on Queen Street. JoJo's. It doesn't shut till one a.m. and sometimes I go in there after finishing at Jamie's. We got talking one night and kind of became friends. She's pretty cool. Into the same sort of shit as me.'

'And she was with you in the car park that night, after you dropped Rebecca off?'

'I planned to go home. That was true. But I wasn't tired and it can get cramped in my mum's place so I thought I'd just stop in and say hi. It was quiet for a Friday so her boss said she could go early. The rest you've got on the pictures. We went back to my car, we smoked, we talked shit and fell asleep.'

'Does this Emma have a surname?'

'I don't know it.'

A knock on the door interrupted them and a uniformed officer came in. 'A word, ma'am?' Bennett nodded and suspended the inteview before stopping the tape before getting to her feet.

'Hasn't that answered all your questions?' Jamie said as she turned to leave. 'Can't we go now?'

'We're still doing tests on Mr Kennedy's car. And until we've confirmed his story I wouldn't look so pleased with yourself, Mr McMahon. One girl is dead and another, as you know better than most, is very lucky to be alive.'

He smarted at that. She was right. And she was just doing her job. If he and Aiden had to sit here for a few more hours, it wouldn't hurt them. His work deadlines, maybe, but that was it. And once Aiden was in the clear, they'd race through to the end anyway.

As she closed the door, the room slipped into the awkward silence of a doctor's waiting room. How long were they going to be here? After a few minutes, Jamie felt his bladder twitching. Aiden might not have touched his tea, but Jamie had drunk two cups.

'Could I . . . perhaps?' He looked at the po-faced sergeant, who was clearly bored babysitting them from the other side of the table, and pointed at the door. The sergeant had the air of a man who knew he could be in here for some time until someone remembered they were there. 'Bathroom?' Jamie finished. He held up a his empty teacup and felt immediately stupid, like he was being an Englishman abroad and trying to make himself understood to a scathing Spanish waiter.

The sergeant nodded. 'Two doors down on your left.'

Jamie had expected an escort, but he wasn't the suspect. And as they were down in the basement of the building, there probably wasn't much trouble he could get into on this floor. He nodded his thanks and left.

He hadn't expected Bennett to still be in the corridor. She was standing near the toilets with her back to him, focused on watching some colour footage on an iPad with the policeman who'd interrupted them. He took a couple of steps closer.

'And he's not on here at all that day?'

'No, ma'am.'

'Wait,' she said. 'I know that coat. I've seen that coat somewhere.'

'So have I,' the policeman said. 'Sandra on the front desk has one like it.'

'That's not where I saw it.'

'Where, then?'

'We need to go,' she said. 'First, we need to see Sandra.'

She turned around and almost walked straight into Jamie.

'Sorry,' he said and pointed towards the toilet entrance which she was currently blocking. 'I was going in there.'

She pushed past him and he watched her go, small and curvy but with absolute drive. He'd never met a woman like her. Not that it mattered, given the situation. He had no chance, he decided. Her contempt for him was absolutely clear.

Thirty-Five

Becca, Hayley and Jenny were called out of English before the lesson had even really started, and now they sat in a row in the Head's office staring at DI Bennett, who was leaning against the back of a chair in front of them and watching them silently. Ms Salisbury was behind her desk shuffling papers around, but Becca was pretty sure she wasn't doing any actual work. How could she be? Becca's palms were sweating. What were they doing here? What did Bennett want?

'Are we waiting for Tasha?' Hayley asked when the silence became unbearable, only the tick of the Head's old carriage clock carrying over Jenny's twitches and foot-tapping.

'She's on a free,' Becca muttered.

'I don't need to speak to Natasha,' DI Bennett said and moved away towards the window as if looking out at something. A coat that had been hidden from view by her body was folded over the back of the chair. Silver-grey and shiny with a hood trimmed in red fur.

'What are you doing with my coat?' Jenny asked, frowning.

Bennett turned, and Becca, her heart thumping, thought she looked like a cat who'd just spotted a mouse in the middle of a kitchen floor with nowhere to hide. Behind her cool exterior there was a hint of excitement.

'That's not yours,' Hayley said. 'Yours has that cigarette burn on the sleeve.'

'You were wearing your coat in the hospital, when I met you?' Bennett asked.

'I think so,' Jenny said. 'Probably. I wear it a lot.'

'Thank you.' Bennett smiled. Becca couldn't see anything reassuring in her expression. 'I couldn't remember which of you it was.'

'Do we all look the same to you?' Hayley said, with a hint of contempt that Becca knew was aimed at her. She definitely didn't look the same as the gorgeous blondes, but it still surprised her that she'd speak like that to the policewoman. If Jenny was nervous and twitchy, Hayley was the opposite. Bennett did a good line in impenetrable, but Hayley was the ice queen. She sounded bored and was looking at Bennett as if the DI was just an inconvenience. Becca's heart thumped and she hunched over slightly, trying to make herself invisible. Forgettable. Something was going on here, something to do with Jenny, and she didn't want to be sent away before she found out what it was.

'A blonde girl wearing a coat matching this one was caught on CCTV footage taken in the One Cell shop in Brackston Shopping Centre on 14th October last year.'

'So?' Jenny wiped her nose. Her foot tapped on the floor. Becca watched Bennett taking it all in. Logging it.

'Were you in the shop that afternoon?'

Jenny laughed and tugged at a strand of her hair. 'I don't know. How am I supposed to remember a random day in October?'

'Try.'

'No,' Jenny said, after a moment. 'No, I wasn't.'

'You suddenly sound very sure.'

'I got my iPhone in the summer, so why would I go into a phone shop in October?'

'Loads of girls have that coat,' Hayley said. 'Loads of *women* have that coat.' A small smirk formed on her face and it didn't take a genius to read its meaning. An elegant *fuck you and swivel* to the detective.

'What does it matter, anyway?' Jenny said. She looked slightly teary. Maybe she was starting to come down from whatever she'd been snorting all day. 'I need to get back to English. Mr Garrick is waiting for us. We've got exams.'

Becca suddenly couldn't breathe. A phone shop. The text Tasha got. An unknown number. Meet in the *usual place*. That's what Bennett was needling Jenny about. She thought Jenny had bought that pay-as-you-go phone. Why didn't she come out and say it? Why was she just standing there, looking thoughtful? Becca was building up the courage to say something, to point out the links, when the detective spoke again.

'You can go back to your lessons now,' she said. 'Thank you for your help.'

Becca was stunned. That was it? She had to find Tasha. She had to tell her. Hayley sauntered to the door, Jenny in her wake, and Becca hurried behind them.

'One moment, Rebecca.'

She turned. 'Yes?' As the two Barbies scurried off, heads together, Becca almost blurted everything out. But then she bit down on it. She needed to talk to Tasha first and she didn't want to say anything in front of Ms Salisbury. The Head Teacher would tell her she was being ridiculous. She'd say anything if it meant the school would stop being the focus of unwanted attention.

'If you've been trying to reach Aiden Kennedy today, then you should know he's at the station helping us with our inquiries.'

Helping us with our inquiries. She knew what that meant. That meant they thought he'd done something. Something bad.

'Have you arrested him?' she asked, her mouth drying.

'No. He'll be released later. I just thought you'd want to know.'

Oh, you're all heart. She bit her tongue from asking more questions. Was that what Bennett wanted? Was she trying to lure Becca into confessing something, too? Did she think Becca and Aiden had conspired together?

'Thanks.' She forced the word out and left.

In the cool corridor, Becca's face was hot, her breathing rapid. She had no intention of going straight back to English. Bennett clearly still thought Aiden was somehow involved and she needed to prove her wrong.

She ran across the quad to the sixth form common room, cold air burning her lungs. Her heart had lifted a little, though, she couldn't help it. Aiden hadn't gone off her. He wasn't ignoring her. He just couldn't answer her texts. A second thought followed which made her want to cringe with embarrassment. Shit, when he *did* turn his phone on again he was going to get *all* her messages and texts, and there were a lot of them. Some were properly passive-aggressive, too. Why wasn't there some fucking app that would let you recall unseen texts? Why hadn't someone Kickstarted that? Why did she have to be such an idiot? Aiden *loved* her. Why couldn't she believe that?

She pushed it all away in her head. When she cleared Aiden's name, he'd forgive her for all her shit. She wouldn't look so needy and insecure then. But first she had to find Tasha. Any suspicions still on Aiden would be blown out of the water if she and Tasha took what they suspected to Bennett. The phone shop CCTV footage combined with the evidence in the clearing would surely exonerate him. She took the stairs two at a time and arrived in the common room sweaty and panting. Smoking and running might work for Hayley but they weren't a good mix for her.

Natasha was at her usual place in the corner and she looked up, confused. 'I thought you were supposed to be in Eng—'

'Listen.' Becca cut her off. 'That Detective Bennett was here. I think she thought Jenny bought the phone that texted you. Something to do with her coat, and someone in the shop that day looking like her. Only I think she believed Jenny when she said she wasn't there because she stopped asking questions and now she's leaving.'

She was talking too fast, that was clear from Tasha's face.

'Slow down,' Tasha said. 'Bennett thinks Jenny's the one who sent that text?' Colour was draining from her almond-perfect complexion. The truth of their suspicions was suddenly sinking in.

'Yes.' Becca nodded. 'But we have to tell her the rest of it. Come on, Tasha, we have to tell her. You've got her number, right? Call her. Like *now*.'

Tasha seemed to shrink into her chair. 'I can't,' she said. 'It'll sound so stupid. What will my mum say? What will *they* say?'

'Who gives a shit what *they* say?' This wasn't the reaction Becca expected at all.

'Maybe we should forget about it, Becca. Maybe it's all

just crap. I mean, we don't *know* anything, not really.' Her eyes glanced up to Becca's face and then lowered back to the carpet. 'I don't know, Bex, perhaps I'm just being stupid. What if they're right and I'm making connections that aren't there?'

'Like the way Jenny was at lunchtime? Like Hayley calling you paranoid every time you say you've remembered something?' Becca was almost shouting with frustration and Tasha flinched. 'Jenny's off her tits at school. She's scared. And look at Hayley all trying to be Miss Nice-As-Pie. Why would she be like that? Why would she be like that with *me*?'

'I know.' Tasha leaned over, hugging her stomach as if she suddenly had bad period pains. 'But I keep thinking about it. What if it's something else? What if we're wrong? What if by accusing them, whoever actually did it gets away with it?'

'But we're *not* wrong! You *know* that. What are you afraid of?'

'Say I talk to Bennett. What if they find out? What if she doesn't believe me? What will they do *then*?'

Becca suddenly got it. It wasn't that Tasha had changed her mind about anything. She was just afraid. Pure and simple. Frustrated as she was, Becca could understand it. Tasha had died in that freezing water. Tasha was the one who was lucky to be resuscitated. And it was Tasha who was faced with the truth that maybe her two best friends had something to do with it.

'They already think you're getting your memory back so staying silent isn't going to keep you safe. Not if they're the ones who pushed you into the river.'

'It could have been an accident,' Tasha said slowly. 'Maybe we did argue. They were doing something mean, maybe that's all true. But maybe I got away, like you said, and fell in the river? So it might not be anything as major as we think? Shouldn't we try and find out for definite first? I mean, *why* would they do it? *Why?*'

Becca wanted to scream. Tasha was blowing so hot and cold about this when *she* was the one who'd started it!

'I get that you're shitting yourself about this, Tasha, I do. But the police have got Aiden and this could clear him,' she said and turned for the door. 'If you're not going to talk to her, then I will.'

*

'Wait!'

DI Bennett was about to get into her car when Becca ran into the car park from the back of the school. She was still warm from her last sprint and her face was burning pink when she came to a halt. Bennet had a mouthful of flapjack and was carrying a sandwich from the canteen, the silver coat stuffed awkwardly under one arm as she ate, and Becca felt a surge of relief. She was sure she'd have missed her.

Bennett swallowed and wiped sticky oat flakes from the corners of her mouth. She looked slightly awkward about having got her lunch from the school canteen and Becca almost warmed to her. A large flapjack and a BLT, and eating the flapjack first. DI Bennett would never have made a good Barbie.

'Look, if this is about Aiden –' Bennett opened the car door and dropped the coat onto the passenger seat '– I can't tell you any more right now. But—'

'No, no, it's not about him,' Becca said, breathless. 'It's about Jenny and Hayley.' She waited until she had the woman's full attention. 'You think Jenny bought the phone that texted Tash that night, don't you?'

Bennett studied her. She didn't take another bite of her flapjack. 'No,' she said. 'Actually, I don't.'

'But that coat – you said—'

'I know what I said. But that coat comes from Primark – Hayley was right, there are hundreds of them. This one belongs to someone at the station. And the footage we have simply shows a blonde girl wearing that coat in the shop. Not at the counter. Not with anything in her hand. There's no CCTV footage from that area.'

'Well, can't you get it?' Becca said. 'I mean—'

'Have you been in the One Cell Stop? To any of their shops?' Bennett said, calm. Becca shook her head. This wasn't what she'd expected.

'They're cheap for a reason. They skimp on everything. They've got a shit security camera set-up, for one thing. Now look, I know you want to—'

'But there's more,' Becca blurted, just wanting her to shut up and listen. 'You don't know everything. That text said to go to *the usual place*, right? That's what they call a clearing out in the woods, their *usual place*. Tasha hasn't been there for months, as far as she knows, but the other night we found stuff that shows they've all been there recently – her, too! And there was some cut rope. Only she doesn't remember it so it must be from that night.'

'Slow down,' Bennett said. 'Where is this place?'

'I can show you later.' Becca couldn't slow down. It was rushing out of her, all of it, like a tidal wave. 'There's more, too. Tasha said they've been acting weird with her for a while, like maybe they didn't want to be her friend any more – right up until her accident. And now all they care about is if she remembers anything. You need to search their stuff, their homes and their lockers. Because if they've got that phone or anything else that proves they did something to Tash, then after today they're going to get rid of it and then you'll never know!'

Bennett was looking at her with something close to pity. 'Friends have spats,' she said, and Becca felt her hope crumble with that word. *Spats*. What did Bennett think they were, ten years old? 'Don't tell me you've not fallen out with anyone recently. People do it all the time. It doesn't mean they go around pushing each other into freezing rivers. Don't let your imagination run away with you.'

'Or you could just *listen to me*,' Becca snapped, hoping to sound in control but knowing she sounded both desperate *and* like she was stamping her feet. 'We told Hayley that Tasha was starting to remember and now they're both freaking out. Did you look at Jenny? She's off her face on something and she's cracking up.' Her hands waved madly as she ranted, as if they could add weight to her words. 'And Hayley's all over me wanting to know if Tasha's told me anything or if she's remembered any more. It's all shit like that. I'm telling you, if you don't search their stuff today, then as soon as rehearsals are done and they go home, anything they've got will be gone. Jenny might be a mess, but Hayley's fucking nails.'

'All right,' Bennett said. 'So where's Natasha, then? If she thinks the same then why isn't she here?'

It was Becca's turn to give Bennett a withering glare. 'Why do you think? Because she's afraid!'

Caitlin Bennett stared at her, then took another small bite of the flapjack and chewed on it. 'Go back inside,' she said, when she'd swallowed. 'You'll freeze out here without a coat.'

Becca searched her face for a flicker of hope but there was nothing. *Shitting hell*. She let out a grunt of frustration, turned around and stomped back into the school. *The woman is a fucking idiot*, she thought. *She's too focused on accusing Aiden to see the truth*. Fuck DI Bennett. And fuck Natasha. If Becca had to prove it by herself, then she would. She'd find a way.

Thirty-Six

With Aiden's interview suspended, Jamie had gone to the small café of a nearby supermarket to grab a coffee and return some some work calls. He was about to head back and see what was going on when the police rang him to say Aiden was being released without charge. He was on the steps outside waiting when Jamie got there, hunched over in the cold and dragging hard on a cigarette. He did manage a smile, though.

'They spoke to Emma. She said she was with me. Plus she said she was too cold to really sleep and was pissed off she was stuck, so spent most of the time just dozing after I passed out. No way I could have got out of the car without her knowing.'

Jamie grinned. 'So that's that, then.'

'Fucking hope so.'

'How did Bennett take the news? Disappointed?' He couldn't help but ask. He hoped the DI was above pinning it all on one person until she could make it stick, just because she'd decided it fit. She'd been warm and kind when she'd spoken to him in the hospital. So different from the cool, closed woman he'd seen today. That was the job, he guessed, but he wondered if he'd met the real Caitlin Bennett at all. Who was she when she got home and relaxed? Cat person? Dog person? *Married* person?

'Didn't see her again,' Aiden said. 'Don't think she came back. Some uniformed bloke came in and told the sergeant, who then told me and said I could go.'

'You want to get a beer?' Jamie asked. The day was screwed anyway, they might as well write it off and start again tomorrow. 'You look like you might need one.'

'Fuck, yes. But not anywhere within sight of this place.'

'Deal.'

They parked and walked in an amiable quiet while Aiden smoked, lighting a second cigarette from his first.

'They didn't let you out for a smoke?'

'I didn't want to ask.'

'So,' Jamie said, as they stopped outside the King's Arms, 'what are you going to tell Becca? The truth?'

Aiden shrugged and shuffled his feet. 'Dunno. She's been calling and texting all day. I might just say I've been working and had my phone switched off?'

'Why lie again? You're worried about this Emma girl?'

'It's complicated.'

'Something going on there?' Jamie was suddenly reminded of how young Aiden was. Nineteen, with a sixteen-year-old girlfriend. However grown-up she was, that might as well be ten years between them.

Aiden shook his head. 'Not really. A snog once, but that was ages ago. It's not like that with Emma.'

Something in his body language was saying otherwise, but however attracted Aiden might be to this Emma, Jamie didn't think he'd done any more than kiss her. He had no reason to lie to Jamie.

'She's just different from Bex, you know? Becca's so insecure all the time. Emma's laid back. Older. Knows her shit.'

'Well, if you're just friends, why don't you tell Becca about her?' *Oh, poor Becca*, Jamie thought. *This boy is going to hurt your heart.*

'She wouldn't get it.' He threw the cigarette butt down and trod on it. 'I care about her and everything but it's all too much sometimes. I just want to chill and have fun and play music.'

'It's your call,' Jamie said, pulling the pub door open, 'but if I was you I'd tell her. Maybe not the kissing bit, but that this girl is your friend and you got stoned with her that night. The truth has a habit of coming out. What if Bennett talks to her? What if the press get hold of it? They knew about the police talking to you. And if Becca's pissed off, she's pissed off. You haven't done anything wrong. You can't live in each other's pockets.'

'I don't know, man,' Aiden said, following him into the warmth and letting the door swing shut behind them. Despite having just been released from the police, Jamie thought he had the air of a condemned man. That was women for you. Aiden was learning that fast. 'I'm not sure the truth is worth the hassle.'

'I hope you didn't use that line on Bennett,' Jamie said and signalled the barman.

Aiden laughed. 'I reckon you set me up just to spend some time with her,' Aiden said.

It was Jamie's turn to look awkward and embarrassed. So it was that obvious. Great. If Aiden, stoned most of the time and preoccupied by his own situation, had noticed, then there was no way that Caitlin Bennett hadn't. He groaned inside. Today was just getting better and better.

Thirty-Seven

Taken from **DI CAITLIN BENNETT'S FILES: EXTRACT FROM NATASHA HOWLAND'S NOTEBOOK**

I don't even know how to start writing this. I guess from where Becca whirlwinded at me in the common room. I don't even know if I *should* write this. But better out of my head and on the paper. I can close the book, then. End this journal that no one will ever read. It's purpose is done. It's not even this stupid diary that made me remember, is it? Eat that, Dr Harvey.

The fractures between us have proved to be fault lines we can't repair and today has become a hellish nightmare. All that hate I never realised was there. And now this terrible thing has happened. I can't quite comprehend it.

I sat in the sixth form common room for a full ten minutes after the bell before I moved, and even then my legs felt heavy as I walked to the theatre. I didn't care about the play. My world was spiralling out of control. I tasted cold, dirty water in my mouth. I remembered the fear. I wondered if Becca hated me for my reluctance to tell the police. I just wanted to go home and sleep and never leave the house again. We didn't need the play. Everyone was already pretending to be someone else. *Jenny sent the text.*

The first thing I heard when I put my bag down was the bickering. It's always a couple of degrees colder in the theatre than the rest of the school, and that chill went well with the sheet-ice atmosphere between us. Mr Jones was enthusiastically talking James Ensor, Hayley and Jenny through the scene they were about to read. I didn't listen in but caught snippets of what he was saying anyway.

. . . it's a difficult scene filled with undercurrents of emotion. Betrayal. Hurt. Fear.

No shit, Mr Jones, I wanted to say. *Welcome to our world.* Hayley looked over and smiled at me. I tried to smile back. Jenny looked at the ground. Her foot tapped and I thought maybe she was high again. I felt so distant from them all. Like I wasn't really there. Like maybe I *did* die in that river and I was just a ghost.

'For fuck's sake, Hannah.' Becca's voice cut through my strange reverie. They were standing at Mr Jones's director's table where all his bits of paper and coffee were. Becca was wrangling a key from a heavy school key ring. 'Stop being so moody. Why is it such a big deal, anyway? What are we? Twelve?'

'I just don't get why you lied to me, that's all.' Hannah was doing her best to hold her own, but she was no match for Becca. Not behind that desk. Not in school. All she was really doing was clinging to the driftwood of the wreck of their friendship and hoping Becca would pull her into the lifeboat. But Becca had me again now. Why would she want Hannah?

'Maybe if you weren't so needy all the time I wouldn't have had to lie,' Becca muttered. I felt that sting and it wasn't even aimed at me. Hannah was saved from responding by Becca turning and walking away to the lighting booth, leaving Hannah's face a cracked portrait of hurt.

'Come for a smoke with me before we start,' Hayley said to Jenny. They were speaking quietly but I'd moved closer, pretending to study the play. There's nothing in this scene for me, though. I just stand in the shadows and wait to be lit up.

'Fuck off,' Jenny mumbled. 'Leave me alone. I don't want to talk to you any more.'

'Jen—'

'I said fuck off.' It was a hiss, but one that was desperate to be a tearful scream.

'Okay, everyone!' Mr Jones clapped his hands together. 'Let's get started.'

Hayley's smoke was going to have to wait until later.

My stomach cramped and I sat down on a chair away from the action. James Ensor came over to dump his jumper. He grinned at me and said something, but I didn't hear it. *Jenny bought the phone.* I think I smiled back. Maybe I didn't.

'As we talked about. And remember – power plays, fear, passion – it's all here.' Mr Jones took his seat. 'Tasha, I want them to go through it first then we'll set you up for Becca's lighting test, okay?'

I nodded through my gloom, feeling an odd relief that I wasn't a ghost after all.

They started and even I was drawn in somewhat. Hayley had all the cool required for Elizabeth Proctor and James had that *thing* that made all the girls rage about him. But Jenny . . . Jenny was always the revelation. Even there, mildly off her face and distracted, she shone on stage. She lost herself in

Mary Warren. She *was* Mary Warren. I am rarely jealous, but I was jealous of how good Jenny was. I wondered if she had any idea how talented she was, really. Mr Jones did. He positively glowed when he watched her. Jenny and men. Bees and honey. But we'll come to that.

'Great,' he said as they reached the end of the scene. 'That's really great. Let's do it again. Give it all you've got.'

Even though my skin was starting to feel hot and I was trying not to think about coats and texts and icy water, I found myself watching. Mary Warren would not be the cowed little servant girl any more. Abigail's court – *my* court – had given her power.

'*Aye, but then Judge Hathorne said, "Recite for us your commandments!"*' Jenny owned the stage with her wild eyes and unstable passion. '*And of all the ten she could not say a single one. She never knew no commandments, and they had her in a flat lie!*'

'*And so condemned her?*'

'*Why, they must when she condemned herself.*'

'*But the proof, the proof!*'

James Ensor was good. The rational character. The earthy man who saw it all for what it was because he knew his own part in it. Jenny's stage confidence was making them all stronger. Even Hayley, standing between them, was fully in character.

'Okay.' Mr Jones was on his feet again. 'Brilliant work. Jenny, you're perfect already. Now let's move Tasha in position for this lighting test and see if we're going to do the play this way.' He said. 'Becca's getting an assistant director credit if this works.'

'I'm seeing her here.' Becca was out of the booth and

standing beyond the marked corner of the stage, looking up to check that the light was actually in place. 'And the cast on benches between their scenes around here and here – almost like a gallery in a trial – then it'll be easy for her, and anyone else, to get to this spot. We can just seat the people we need at the ends.'

Mr Jones looked impressed and Becca was clearly happy that he was. It was so crazy and my stomach lurched again. We are so resilient. It's not just our bodies that are strong. A couple of hours earlier, Becca was screeching at me about the police, and now she was totally focused on getting this right. I wondered what she was thinking. I wondered what she'd said to Bennett, if she found her. My face burned.

'Great. Tasha?' Mr Jones said.

I couldn't. I shook my head. 'I feel sick. Dizzy.' My legs wouldn't work and there was a humming inside my skull. I didn't want to be near the stage. Near them. I willed myself to calm down, but the more I tried, the hotter my face felt. Thinking about it now makes me feel sick again. What might have happened. What did happen. Relief and a terrible guilt all mixed up together. *It should have been me.*

Mr Jones frowned and they gathered around me, which didn't help. I needed air. I needed them to ignore me. I tried to apologise between deep, shaky breaths. My face was clammy.

'You have to do it,' Hayley said. 'You've only got to stand there for a few minutes so Mr Jones can see.' She was irritated with me, it was so clear. She thought I was pretending. Attention-seeking.

'Do you want to go and have a lie-down, or get a glass of water, maybe?' Mr Jones said. 'Or call your mum to pick you up?' All adults treat me with kid gloves. They don't bounce back from things like the young do. They're not hardy like we are.

'I'll be all right in a minute,' I said, although I wasn't remotely sure I would. 'Just suddenly felt sick. Light-headed. If I can have a little while to catch my breath . . . I don't know what's wrong with me. I'll be better in a minute.'

Hayley tutted, sucking air between her teeth. 'It'll only take two minutes.' She looked at Mr Jones. 'Just tell her to get up and do it.'

'I'll do it.' A meek voice cut in and everyone turned to look. It was Hannah, with her new-found backbone. 'I'm about Tasha's height. It doesn't have to be her.'

'But surely,' Hayley said, 'part of it has to be the expression – the moment of victory on her face when Mary Warren says I've been accused of witchcraft. That's what makes it so powerful, not just the lighting.'

'That's true,' Mr Jones said, 'but I'm not going to be responsible for Tasha fainting or something, and, to be honest, I'd expect more sympathy from you, Hayley. You're supposed to be best friends. What's wrong with you all today?'

Our broken landscape hadn't gone unnoticed.

He turned around and smiled at Hannah. 'That would be great.'

'But I think—'

'Enough, Hayley! Let's just do it.'

Cowed by Mr Jones, Hayley stared at me for a long moment and then went back to the stage. Mr Jones turned to check Becca was at the lighting panel and she gave him a thumbs-up.

And so they began, the scene unfolding, but this time getting further into it. I knew the line was coming: *I saved her life today.* The moment when Abigail/Me/Hannah would steal the scene from Jenny as the light rose, but still I found I was caught up in the drama. They were that good.

The crescendo built, Proctor moving in on Mary Warren in frustration at her tales from the court, threatening to beat her, and then—

'*I saved her life today!*' Jenny, cowering, pointed at Hayley.

The light shifted. A figure emerged. Hannah doing her best to look manipulative. Triumphant.

And then it all changed. I felt underwater again. I stared. We all stared. Hayley said her next line and then everything stopped. Long seconds of *wrong*.

Becca had been right. It looked amazing. For a second. Maybe two. Then the light changed again. Into a momentary falling star. A hollow thud. An empty sound as it landed, heavy, on Hannah's head. Not a big enough sound to warrant the effect. She let out a surprised *oh* before she crumpled. An instant of confusion, not even enough time to raise her hand to her skull, to feel the pain, before her face was empty and her legs gave way.

She was gone. I could tell. I saw the switching-off in her eyes. *Is that all it is? Is that all it takes?* I was stuck in my chair. I think my mouth was half-open.

No one was moving apart from Mr Jones. He was on his knees, his hands over Hannah, unsure what to do. I think he was shouting, but all I could hear was the river in my ears. Jenny had her hand over her mouth. Becca rushed out of the booth and then stopped near Mr Jones. She stared. I knew why she was staring. Why we were all staring. It wasn't the small pool of blood under Hannah's head. It was her eyes. They were open. And they were empty.

Hannah has left the building, I wanted to say, in that way my mum does sometimes, and then I wanted to giggle so badly, to laugh out loud, and I didn't know why and I'm not even sure I should write it down, but it's how I felt. I was on the verge when the doors swung open.

They strode in without seeing her, at first. The Head Teacher, DI Bennett and another man and woman who must have been police, too. They walked straight past me. Bennett held a piece of paper in her hand. It had been crumpled and then smoothed back out. A receipt. It was level with my eyes when they come to a halt. I could read *The One Cell Stop* at the top.

Suddenly there was movement everywhere but I was in a bubble. It was all distilling. Everything. I gasped. My mouth moved but I couldn't get the words out. I found myself standing. I gulped like a fish torn from water until eventually they burst out of me. I was loud even in there, amidst the crying and the shouting and the man and woman taking Hayley's and Jenny's arms. My own words were sharp in my ears, making my eardrums ache.

'I remember,' I said, too loud. 'I remember!'

Part Three

Thirty-Eight

Excerpt of **CONSULTATION BETWEEN DR ANNABEL HARVEY AND PATIENT REBECCA CRISP, FRIDAY 29/01, 09.30**

REBECCA: The doctor gave me sleeping pills but I don't want to take them.
DR HARVEY: Why not?
REBECCA: Just don't want to.
DR HARVEY: Are you afraid to sleep?
REBECCA: No.
DR HARVEY: Then you should take them. You look tired.
REBECCA: (Pause)
I was a bitch to her. Right before. For a few days before. But in rehearsal I was mean. I really snapped at her, you know. I called her needy. I hurt her feelings. I know I did.
DR HARVEY: You didn't know what was going to happen.
REBECCA: Doesn't make it any better. It's still in my head. It still happened. I'm still the one who was in the control booth. I moved the slider to tilt the light.
(Pause)
I should have moved it myself. Technically, I killed her. That sound when it hit her head—

(Breath hitching)

DR HARVEY: You didn't sabotage the light so it would fall. You didn't kill her. You're a victim here, too. You have to reframe the way you think about Hannah's death.

REBECCA: (Long pause)

(Quiet)

When Tasha went in the river, I remember thinking that stuff like that didn't happen to girls like her. They happened to girls like me. But I was wrong. I think they do sometimes happen to girls like Tasha, the bright, brilliant ones. Or they happen to girls like Hannah. The nobodies. The ones desperate to be liked.

DR HARVEY: Is that how you saw Hannah? A nobody?

REBECCA: It's how everyone saw Hannah. That light was meant to fall on Tasha but it killed Hannah instead. I think that's what I don't get the most. So Hayley and Jenny wanted Tasha to stay quiet. To not remember. They wanted her gone. Dead. Whatever. But when Hannah said she'd stand in Tasha's place, why did they let her? I mean, that's, like, psycho behaviour, to just let someone else be hurt or die instead. Did they really think that little of her? Why not come up with some excuse to move her?

DR HARVEY: Perhaps they couldn't think of one.

(Pause)

REBECCA: Hayley tried, I think, to make us wait for Natasha, but not hard enough. They didn't *stop* it. They let her die. They let me kill her.

DR HARVEY: You didn't kill her.

REBECCA: I controlled the light. And I'd been a bitch to her. Such a bitch.

DR HARVEY: Why was that? Had she upset you?

REBECCA: (Half-laugh. Weepy)

No. Hannah doesn't – *didn't* – really do upsetting people. She was just . . . Hannah. And I was distracted. I had Tasha again.

(Pause)

I was embarrassed by Hannah. I didn't want Tasha to judge me by her. She was a nobody. You must remember this kind of shit from when you were at school.

DR HARVEY: Yes, just about.

REBECCA: Which kind of girl were you?

DR HARVEY: I suppose I was something like you. In the middle somewhere.

REBECCA: You're Natasha's doctor, too, aren't you?

DR HARVEY: Yes, I am.

REBECCA: Will you be Hayley and Jenny's doctor as well?

(Pause)

I haven't spoken to Tasha yet.

DR HARVEY: Don't you want to talk to her?

REBECCA: I don't want to talk to anyone – including you. And the police keep coming and asking questions I can't answer. I told Bennett everything I knew in the car park. Must be harder for Tasha. Remembering everything suddenly like that on top of what happened to Hannah. And getting her head around Hayley and Jenny.

DR HARVEY: Are you getting your head around it?

REBECCA: I don't know. We suspected them of something but it felt like a game to me. I don't think I really *believed* it. Not like this. Like now. It's too much.

(Pause)

I used to be friends with Hayley. I *liked* her. Back then, anyway.

DR HARVEY: Murderers have friends. And families. They can be very likeable. What Hayley did or didn't do doesn't make her evil. Evil doesn't exist.

REBECCA: I don't think Hannah's mum would agree.

(Pause)

Me and Tasha, we wound them up. We pretended she was starting to remember stuff. You know, from that night and the day before. If we hadn't done that then Hannah would probably still be alive. It will come out in the papers eventually. Or at court. Hannah's mum will know we were meddling and she'll blame me, too.

DR HARVEY: You're not guilty of anything. Hannah's mother is grieving – as are you. You need to stop blaming yourself.

REBECCA: It must be so weird for Tasha. She must feel so lucky in some ways and like shit in others. If it wasn't Hannah it would have been her. Must be driving her crazy.

(Pause)

Will you sign me off for when school opens again next week? I don't want to go back.

DR HARVEY: You don't want to go back next week, or you don't want to go back ever?

REBECCA: What do you think?

(Pause)

I wish all the newspaper people would go away. I feel like I can't breathe for them. It's going to be hard enough with everyone looking at me, anyway. The girl who pushed the button. The girl who didn't check her own rig. I don't need them saying it, too. Maybe it will be better after Hannah's

funeral. Maybe everything will go back to normal then.
(Pause)
Except nothing's ever going to be normal again, is it?

Thirty-Nine

Extract from *The Times*, Monday 1st February:

Two 16-year-old girls, who cannot be named for legal reasons, have been remanded in police custody and charged with one count of murder and one count of intent to cause grievous bodily harm. Brackston Community School reopens today after the death of sixth form student Hannah Alderton last Tuesday and the Head Teacher has asked that the press respect the privacy of students and staff at this difficult time. A teacher from the school has also been arrested and charged with sexual activity with a minor while holding a position of trust.

Brackston Community School received an Outstanding grade in its recent Ofsted evaluation but local parents have now expressed concerns about the levels of bullying in the school. There is a divide between those from the wealthier areas of this quiet suburban town and those who come from the Gleberow Estate, which has a high level of unemployment and long-term benefits claimants. It is believed that one of the two girls charged with the murder of Hannah Alderton lived with her mother on the Estate.

Extract from the *Brackston Herald*, Monday 1st February:

After the dramatic and tragic events at Brackston Community School last week, police have confirmed that they no longer believe the death of Maypoole teenager Nicola Monroe to be linked with the near-death of Natasha Howland last month. Charges of murder and attempted grievous bodily harm are being brought against two local teenage girls. The girls, who can't be named for legal reasons, are both 16 years old and were present when Hannah Alderton died last Tuesday. A teacher from Brackston Community School has also been arrested on charges of sexual activity with a minor while holding a position of trust. Police have yet to confirm whether this is a separate incident, or in some way linked to events at the school last week.

Extract from *The Sun*, Monday 1st February:

Sex, drugs and murder in a middle-class school. Is Brackston becoming a byword for Broken Britain?

. . . although the two girls cannot be named, neighbours and parents have described them as best friends with one of their victims. The mother of a sixth form pupil told us, 'Those three were always together. It's such a shock because they seemed the perfect friends. My daughter heard rumours that they took drugs quite regularly and liked to party. One of the girls comes from the Gleberow Estate. It's a bit rough up there. Not like the area where Natasha Howland lives. Maybe there was jealousy? But it's frightening that this can happen in a school like Brackston. As for the teacher – well, there's so many cases like that in the paper now, aren't there? How are they getting to teach in schools? Where are the checks on them?'

Although the member of staff arrested cannot be named, sources claim that a male member of the English department has been suspended and will not be returning to work when the school reopens today.

Forty

Extract from DI BENNETT'S NOTES (UNOFFICIAL RECORD), TUESDAY 2ND FEBRUARY, USED IN A REPORT TO THE COMMISSIONER

Hayley Gallagher remains silent. Pale. Shaken. Can't make that one out. Even her mother can't get her to talk.

Jenny Coles also quiet now after her initial hysteria but she remains withdrawn. Closed in. She needs a mental health evaluation.

Once presented with the list of evidence against her:

– CCTV footage of Jenny in the phone shop
– The receipt for the two pay-as-you-go phones in her locker
– The discovery of the phones hidden in the girls' bedrooms
– The nature of the texts on those phones, which stop on the night of the incident with Natasha

and when informed that English teacher Peter Garrick had confessed to several instances of sexual activity with Jenny (and confirmed the location of their meeting on the night Natasha Howland now remembers seeing them), her hysteria quietened. All she's said since is, 'Hayley said she'd think of something.'

Although not specific, I believe this is an implication of Hayley's guilt in tampering with the stage light at the school, and an attempt by Jenny to distance herself from that. Hayley has not responded to the accusation. She still refuses to speak.

Between the phones, the fact that Hayley sabotaged the theatre light thinking that Natasha would be beneath it, the evidence found in the clearing (the cigarette butts, Dalmane sleeping pill capsule cases – which match the pills Jenny's mum uses – the piece of rope) and Garrick's confession of a secret sexual relationship with Jenny in which Hayley was complicit, along with Natasha's statement and her diary entries in the notebook Dr Harvey gave her – now in evidence – we have enough to press charges even without confessions. Hayley can be charged with murder and attempted grievous bodily harm and Jenny with accessory to murder and attempted grievous bodily harm. We also have their primary mobile phones and are in the process of retrieving deleted texts from them.

There's no evidence to suggest Peter Garrick knew anything about the attack on Natasha Howland or was in any way involved beyond his relationship with Jenny, the discovery of which was a catalyst for the attack on Natasha. He is clearly shocked that the girls went so far and is distraught. He claims he was in love with Jenny and intended to leave his wife. He had already handed in his resignation and was leaving the school at the end of the summer term, once he had fulfilled his obligations to his exam students and his role as exam officer. The CPS will pursue the charges against him, but had he known of Jenny and Hayley's intention to harm Natasha, I believe he would have stopped them or called the police regardless of the outcome for himself.

He has been released on bail and is at his home. His wife and two children, who knew nothing of his affair, are now staying with his mother-in-law in Manchester.

Hannah Alderton's body has been released to her family and her funeral arranged for Friday. They have asked the police not to attend, other than to keep the press as far back as possible.

Neither Rebecca Crisp nor Natasha Howland have returned to school yet. Both plan to return after the funeral. Rebecca is understandably traumatised after the death of Hannah Alderton and has been going to counselling with Dr Harvey. Natasha Howland is suffering from survivor's guilt, knowing she should have been beneath the stage light. Dr Harvey is confident, however, that neither girl will suffer any lasting problems and that the process of the trials and giving evidence – which will no doubt be harrowing – will probably give them closure.

Natasha was very reluctant to hand over the notebook Dr Harvey gave her – which is not surprising given the detailed content including evidence of drug-taking and her private thoughts on sex, friends and family. However, her written account does fully support Rebecca Crisp's statement.

Forty-One

It was the night before the funeral and Becca's nerves were tangled. She was wired even though she hadn't touched so much as a puff of a joint since Hannah's death. Some days she wasn't sure she ever would again, and on others she just wanted to get shit-faced. She'd waited till it was dark before leaving and didn't call ahead. She hadn't called anyone in days. Someone had leaked her mobile number to the press and now her iPhone locked out all calls apart from her parents' or Aiden's. Not that she needed her mum's number to come through to know it was her calling. Unless she was with the police or that head-doctor woman, she'd barely been out of her mum's sight.

Aiden had come over to the house, but even he didn't know quite how to handle the situation. It wasn't just that Hannah was dead, which was a head-fuck on its own, but that Becca had controlled the light. How were they supposed to talk about that? She'd wanted to, but he was awkward and unresponsive, even though he hugged her and told her it would all be okay. He was stoned, which hadn't helped. She *needed* him – how could he not see that? But the easy way they'd had with each other appeared to have vanished.

But she had to talk to someone. So here she was.

'She's in her room,' Alison Howland said, squeezing Becca's arm. 'Go on up. I'm sure she'll be pleased to see you. Tomorrow will be hard for both of you.' She wasn't slurring but her words ran together a little too quickly and Becca saw the wine bottle sitting on the kitchen island. It was open and two-thirds empty. Becca couldn't blame her. Tasha had very nearly died. Twice. She'd be surprised if the Howlands ever let their daughter out of the house again. 'Do you want anything to drink? Something to eat?'

Becca shook her head and escaped the warmth of the kitchen, taking the stairs two at a time. She was tired of the claustrophobic care of adults. They wanted to make everything better. They couldn't.

Tasha's door wasn't locked and she opened it quietly, suddenly nervous. It was stupid because there was nothing to be nervous about, but without her phone and having stayed away from all social media it was like coming out of a bubble. She was used to knowing how people were feeling, what they were doing, with the click of a button. Not any more.

'Hey,' she said. 'I just thought I'd . . .' She shrugged. 'You know . . . with tomorrow.'

Tasha looked up. She was sitting on her bed, an old shoebox beside her, and had been examining the contents.

'Come in,' Tasha said, finally, making space on the bed for Becca to sit down. 'It's good to see you. I feel like I haven't seen anyone but Bennett and my parents for my whole life.'

'I know what you mean. It's like we're the ones in prison.'

'You okay?' Tasha asked.

Becca nodded but focused on the contents of the box. She wasn't ready to talk about how she felt. 'What *is* this shit?' she asked. There were old badges, tickets from gigs, loops of hair, a pressed flower, all kinds of crap.

'Oh, just stuff. I like to keep things from good times.' She held out the purple dried flower. 'This is from the first day we found the clearing and made it our secret place. I saw it on the way home. Thought it was beautiful, sitting alone in all the green.'

Picking through the items, Becca saw something familiar. 'Is that my old Livestrong bracelet?'

Tasha pulled it out of the box. 'Yep! From when we were in Year Six and we did that challenge. Well, you did it – I never finished. You gave it to me, remember?'

Becca smiled and nodded, her heart almost melting with the resurfacing memory. This box wasn't just for Barbies. She was in here, too. A treasure chest of memories. She thought of Hayley and Jenny.

'How could they?' she asked quietly as Tasha carefully put the lid back on the box and slid it under her bed. Natasha didn't need to ask who she meant.

'I don't think they wanted to kill me,' she said, picking at the duvet cover. 'Not that first time anyway. They scared me. Drugged me and left me. But I don't think they meant for me to die.' She paused. 'It all just got out of hand.'

'What do you remember?' Becca asked. Tasha looked so fragile, her hair almost lank over her face, not the glorious queen bee of the hive at all, that Becca took her hand and squeezed it for a moment. Her skin was cold.

'Oh, god, I don't want to talk about it. Feels like I've spent forever repeating it over and over to Bennett for her statement and the CPS and *everyone*.'

'Sorry, I didn't think.'

'It was seeing Hannah like that. The shock. Must have just clicked my brain back into working properly. It was like feeling a tap come on.' She looked at Becca. 'But how are you? She was your friend. She was a nice girl.'

How many people were saying that about Hannah now? High-achieving student, lovely girl, all that stuff, when actually even the teachers had barely noticed she was there.

'I don't think it's really sunk in yet.' Becca felt a tightening of nausea in her stomach. 'I keep seeing the control panel. When I close my eyes, I see myself snapping at her and moving the slide all at once. I don't think I'll ever not see it.'

'It wasn't your fault. You know that. *They* did it.' She pulled back and looked Becca in the eye. 'It wasn't *us*. It's not my fault I wasn't standing there and it wasn't your fault the light fell.' Her shoulders slumped. 'I wish I still had the diary Doctor Harvey made me write. Maybe I'll start a new one. It was cathartic, you know? I didn't think I'd ever do it but it got shit out of my head.'

'Where is it?'

'Police. They took it as soon as I mentioned it.' They both groaned.

'God, I want a smoke,' Becca said. 'You think those photographers can see the window from where they're parked?'

'I'm past caring. I haven't even left the house unless it's to go to the Police Station. I'm hoping after tomorrow they'll fuck off.'

'Maybe some other kid will die and distract them,' Becca muttered, then realised how awful that statement was. It didn't stop them both laughing, though. Black humour. What was left?

'Let's just sit on the floor by the window,' Tasha said,

opening it an inch or two. 'I'll turn the lamp off. Best they'll get is a glowing cigarette end from a distance. Big deal.'

The cold air outside cut through the gap and Becca sat against the wall, knees under her chin, a mirror image of Tasha opposite but with thicker thighs and way less grace. The limited opening wouldn't be enough to stop the room – and probably the whole of the upstairs – stinking of cigarette smoke, but the Howlands weren't going to give them any shit tonight, if ever again. Alison would just pour another glass of wine and wonder at all her failings as a mother without realising that none of this awful crap had anything to do with parenting, good, bad or otherwise. It was about them. *Their* world. And there was fuck all their families could have done about any of it.

'You want to go to the funeral together tomorrow?' Tasha said, after flicking the light off. 'Let the gawkers get it out of their systems? There'll be plenty of them there.'

'Sure,' Becca said. It was a relief. She didn't realise how much of one until her heart thudded heat through her limbs. She didn't want people staring at her alone. And Tasha was the tragic victim here – not as tragic as Hannah, but Hannah was gone. Natasha was the centre of it all. If she was with Tasha then people might not look at her and see such a monster. *The girl who accidentally killed her best friend.* Maybe some of the hive even thought she was in it with the other two. She knew how the hive worked. Why have a story if you couldn't embellish it?

'I'll get my dad to drive here and then we can follow your dad's car?' she said, exhaling a long stream of smoke. It was making her head spin a little and not helping the vaguely sick feeling she was learning to live with. She hadn't eaten much and barely smoked in days. Her mouth tasted dirty, but she inhaled again.

'Cool,' Tasha said. 'I can't wait for it to be done. To be over.'

'Me, too.' Poor Hannah. Even now, her last ever social engagement, where the girl who could barely scrape together five or six friends for a birthday meal would finally have an audience of most of the sixth form, was being wished away. *I'm sorry, Hannah*, Becca thought, tilting her head back to stop the stinging tears that burst up from her inner well of pity and shame. *I'm sorry I was such a bitch.*

'You going back to school on Monday?' Becca asked.

'Yeah. You?'

Becca nodded. 'I kind of wish it was somewhere different, but then I'd just have strangers staring at me rather than kids and teachers I know.'

'Snap. You heard from anyone?'

'No. My phone's been off. I need a new number. Plus I don't really want to talk about it.'

'A couple of teachers have dropped by but I didn't say much to them,' Tasha said. 'Left that to my mum. I looked on Facebook, though. Loads of people writing on our walls if you haven't checked.' She gave a half-smile in the gloom. 'Like we're mini-celebrities or something.'

Becca bet that there were way more people writing on Tasha's than on hers, but still it was kind of nice to hear that people were thinking of them.

'Hayley's and Jenny's pages have gone,' Tasha said quietly. 'Guess the police or their parents took them down. Probably the police.' She paused. 'Hannah's is still up. I wasn't her friend on there, though. I'm quite glad, really. It would feel weird seeing her last posts.' She looked up at Becca. 'Sorry. That was thoughtless. This is way worse for you than it is for me. She was your friend. And you . . . well, you know. That afternoon.'

I tilted the light. Yeah, she did. Intentionally or not, she, Rebecca Crisp, had killed her best friend. It was her lighting plan, she'd let Hayley up the ladder to move it, even with all their suspicions, and without any training. It was all her stupid fault. She'd made it so easy for them.

'There's loads of shit about Mr Garrick on there, too,' Tasha said. 'Even though I remember now, I still find it weird. I mean, of all the teachers, *Mr Garrick*? He's not exactly Mr Jones, is he? Mr Jones I could almost understand. But Mr Garrick?' She shook her head. 'Like, I know Jenny fucked around but I thought she had some standards at least.'

Becca snorted a laugh, if only to clear away the tears of pity and self-pity that kept trying to escape. 'I just can't picture them doing it.' Even as she said it, the image rose up in her mind. Jenny and Mr Garrick on his desk, his trousers down around his thighs, pumping away. 'Oh, crap, now I *am* picturing it.'

'You're not the one who actually *saw* it!' Tasha said.

They laughed again, small sounds which faded quickly. They'd both been through too much and were too tired and contemplative for belly laughs. They were too hollow for them, Becca thought. Everything had been sucked out.

'I liked him,' Becca said, eventually, flicking the glowing butt of her cigarette out through the window. 'He was kind, if you know what I mean.'

'Yeah,' Tasha said. 'I guess I do.'

'And now he's totally fucked his life up. I mean, it's not like he just fucked a sixth former. He's part of all the rest of this shit. What they did to you to protect the secret.' She looked at

Tasha. 'How do you think he's feeling?' She paused. 'How do you think *they're* feeling?'

She didn't need to use their names. *They* was always going to mean the other two Barbies from now on.

Tasha turned her face to the window and stared out. She didn't say anything for a long time. 'Trapped and scared,' she said eventually. 'And sorry.' She paused. 'Very, very sorry.'

'Yeah,' Becca said. 'I guess you're right.'

'Hey.' Tasha got to her feet and put the light on. 'Did you see that girl? Emma? On Facebook? Friend of Aiden's?'

'Who?' Becca's stomach pinched hard but she wasn't sure why. 'I haven't been on.'

'I just saw she'd posted something on his wall about being glad it was all sorted.' Tasha reached out a hand and pulled Becca to her feet. 'So I clicked through to her page and she doesn't have it set private or anything and she'd posted something on Tuesday about having saved a guy from prison. What was all that about? Do you know her?'

Becca felt sick. No, she didn't know her. How could she have saved Aiden? *Becca* had saved Aiden by getting Bennett to search the girls' lockers. Or did Bennett search them because this girl somehow gave Aiden an alibi? He hadn't exactly been forthcoming about the interview, just that they needed to talk over a couple of things. And on top of that, how was Tasha seeing Aiden's Facebook page? Were they friends now? Had he added her?

'Not sure,' she said. 'I might know her. I get confused. He's got lots of music friends.' She hoped she sounded casual but her mind was on fire. He'd been weird with her but she'd presumed it was because of Hannah, not because of something he might have done.

'But he didn't say anything to you about it?' Tasha's eyes were sharp. Becca shook her head. Somehow it made her feel like a failure.

'Maybe I got the wrong end of the stick, then,' Tasha said. 'Who knows what she was talking about? Probably someone else. Or just making a joke.'

'Yeah, it'll be something like that.' Becca suddenly wanted to be on her own where the ants in her brain could run wild without her having to pretend to be listening to anyone. 'Anyway, I should get home. My mum's mental at the moment. She didn't want me to come out at all.'

'I know what you mean. Mine's the same. But you'll come over here first tomorrow? Maybe ten?'

'Defo. I don't want to go on my own. It'll be better with you.'

Tasha enveloped her in hug so tight Becca was sure she could feel the fast beat of her heart pressed against her chest. 'Thanks for everything, Becca. You've been amazing. I don't know how I would have managed without you. I really don't.'

Becca squeezed her back, her head filled with thoughts of Hannah. 'See you tomorrow,' she said. 'Let's get it over with.'

She waved goodbye to Alison Howland, still drinking in the kitchen, and then left. She kept her coat hood up and her head down. The journalists still skulking outside her and Natasha's houses might get a picture, but it wouldn't be a very good one. And so what if they reported that the *two tragic teenagers* met up before the funeral? What did it matter? Becca was finding she cared less and less about the outside world. She just wished they would leave it alone and let them get on with getting over it all.

Her phone buzzed halfway home. It was Aiden, checking

on her and saying he'd come to the funeral the next day if she wanted him there. Jamie was going, too, so he'd catch a lift with him. Three kisses on the end. Her fingers itched. Everything itched, apart from her heart, which was aching. Jamie wanted him to go to the funeral and suddenly he'd decided to be there? Where did she fit into that picture? Why didn't he want to be there for her? He was supposed to *love* her! Her rage surged from her brain to her fingertips and they whizzed across the screen.

Who the fuck is Emma??
How did she save you from
prison?? And when did you
add Tasha to fb?????

A pause. It felt like for ever before his reply came back.

Are u stalking my fb??
Really??

Her rage swallowed her shame.

Answer the questions!!

Tears came now. She'd held them back while thinking of Hannah, but she couldn't any longer. How shit was that? Hannah was dead but it was the thought of Aiden leaving her that made her cry.

I'll see you tomorrow.
No time for this.

She let out a grunt of rage and nearly flung the phone into the bushes. Now she felt hurt *and* stupid. Why did she have to do that? Why couldn't she have just let it ride and waited? But then why couldn't he have just told her? And why was he being so cold about it? After everything that had happened, everything she'd been through – was *still* going through – why couldn't he just be nice? He knew she got a bit mental sometimes, why couldn't he just reassure her? Why was she always the one having to apologise for being a dick?

She strode home in a haze, slamming the door and racing upstairs to the sanctuary of her room before her mum could corner her. She threw herself down on the bed and started to cry. She pretended she was crying for Hannah, but she knew that wasn't true. Pathetic as it was, she was crying for herself.

Forty-Two

The sun shone, bringing Hannah into the spotlight in front of a crowd for the first and last time in her short, unlived life. Becca wondered if it made her feel uncomfortable. If she could feel anything at all. She glanced sideways at Tasha, her face half-hidden behind big Californian-style dark glasses as they came out of the church and milled in the graveyard and car park. She wished she'd thought to wear shades. Instead, her face was blotchy and tear-stained and her discomfort was clear for all to see. And a lot of people had come. The church had been standing-room-only for the short service.

She'd tried to catch Hannah's mum's eyes but either she was lost in her own grief or she was avoiding looking at Becca. It made Becca's stomach squirm. She couldn't see Aiden or Jamie McMahon. She figured they must be somewhere at the back. Hannah's dad said a few words and the vicar did the same, and then they'd announced that there would be a memorial service for their daughter in a few months' time. They needed time to accept her loss first.

'Who will come then?' Tasha had whispered quietly, and although it was a cruel thought, it was a true one. Hannah's celebrity would fade fast.

Becca was glad to escape the church. She hadn't liked looking at the coffin sitting at the front and imagining Hannah, cold and blue, inside it. She kept picturing her eyes opening full of dead anger and wanting revenge. Who would she come for? Hayley or Becca?

'That was horrible,' Becca said, really wanting to light a cigarette. Behind the two girls, their four parents were talking quietly, in that way adults did, as if they understood all of this so much better than the teenagers. As if they had some special magic that gave them insight. It was all bullshit. 'I hated seeing her there, you know? I couldn't help thinking she could hear or something.'

'She's dead,' Tasha said. Becca couldn't see her eyes, but her mouth tightened. 'I've been dead, remember. There's nothing.' She paused. 'Oh, god, here they come.' Becca looked up. A small flurry of femininity was heading their way, hair styled and black outfits just that little bit too tight and that little bit too well thought out for proper grief. *Barbies-in-waiting.* There'd be pictures on Instagram later.

They wafted towards Tasha, clinging to the space around her like cheap perfume. They didn't even glance at Becca but still managed to crowd her out without even noticing as they gushed about Hayley and Jenny and Hannah and how terrible it was but how happy they were that Tasha was okay. All so typical.

Behind her, Becca's mum hadn't noticed her isolation. Her head was tilted slightly as she listened to Alison Howland, one arm around the small of the woman's back. Both were pristine, of course, but Alison slightly took the edge on easy glamour. *Sorry, Mum*, Becca thought, watching them as one listened and one spoke. *You were never a Barbie either, were you?*

'I want those bracelets back,' Alison said, tearfully. 'Natasha chose them herself, you know? Those girls were her best friends. I thought they loved her.'

'I just don't understand it,' Becca's mum answered. 'Why they would go to such lengths? I didn't know Jenny but Hayley, when she used to come round and play, was always such a bright little thing. Pretty, too. Poor Natasha . . .'

Becca zoned them out, just as Vicki Springer carefully elbowed her way past into the sacred circle around Tasha. She barely noticed. Even her own mother felt more sorry for Tasha than for either Becca or poor dead Hannah. She scanned the crowd, looking for Aiden, but instead saw Amanda Alderton. Hannah's mum was at least a stone thinner than when Becca last saw her, and was politely greeting strangers. She looked pale and exhausted. Pain was etched in her every movement, all her bubbly humour gone as if it had been an illusion. Becca felt sick looking at her, but took a deep breath and forced herself forward. She'd liked the Aldertons, she realised. Even when she'd mocked them internally there had been something warm about their company. *Too little, too late, Bex*, she told herself. *As if you liking them makes a difference now. There'll be no more family lunches. No more sandwiches in their kitchen.* That thought made the truth of it all hit home harder than even seeing the coffin had done, and before she'd even reached Hannah's mum the tears had come, almost from nowhere, hot and wet on her cheeks.

She sniffed hard, wiping her nose with the back of her hand, not caring how it looked. 'I'm so sorry,' she said. 'I'm so, so sorry.' She stared up at the woman, her eyes pleading. She needed to know they were okay with her. She needed Hannah's mum to hug her, to tell her it was all going to be okay.

She didn't do either. They stood facing each other for a moment, Becca crying and Amanda all contained grief. Through the blur, Becca couldn't read the woman's expression, but she was aware of others nearby – Mark Pritchard, less cocky than usual, was just alongside them, head down and talking to James Ensor. They both looked up.

'I'm so sorry,' she repeated, more quietly this time, barely more than a whisper.

'We don't blame you, Rebecca,' Hannah's mum said. She didn't touch her, though, and there was little warmth in her voice. *Rebecca.* It was so formal. 'We know Hannah's death wasn't your fault.'

'Thank you,' Becca said. 'I loved her, you know. She was my best friend.' She wiped her eyes, clearing her vision.

'Yes, she was.' Amanda Alderton drew herself up an inch taller. 'She was a good friend to you. It's a pity you were so easily distracted.' She turned her back then, and it was like a slap in the face to Becca. Her mouth fell open. Of course Hannah had talked to her mum about Becca. Hannah talked to her mum about *everything*.

'I wasn't . . .' she mumbled. 'I didn't mean to . . .' But Amanda Alderton was no longer listening. The sunlight, barely cutting through the February cold, was suddenly too bright. Becca didn't want to be there. She didn't want to be anywhere. She wanted to run back into the church and fling herself on Hannah's coffin and beg for her forgiveness.

'She doesn't mean it.'

Becca jumped slightly and then sank into relief. It was Tasha, free of her new acolytes.

'I imagine by the time the memorial comes around she'll want you to do a reading or something.' The cremation, that afternoon, was family only. Becca was doubly relieved she didn't have to watch that after her exchange with Amanda. Natasha nodded at the crowds that were slowly dispersing, getting back to their own lives. 'You can spot the police a mile off. There – by Jamie and Aiden.'

Becca looked up. Aiden was smoking under the trees, Jamie alongside him. Her heart managed to leap and sink simultaneously. She needed to speak to him. To make things better.

'See?' Tasha said. 'By the exit.' Becca dragged her eyes away and clocked the police straight away. Four men by the church gates, wearing suits but not involved, facing out towards the journalists no doubt waiting to get more pictures to fill their morbid pages. Two of the officers pulled their phones out at the same time. Signalled one of the others.

'Something's going on,' Becca muttered, frowning.

'Something's always going on,' Tasha said. 'They're policemen. It's probably nothing to do with us.' She linked her arm through Becca's. 'Come on, let's go and talk to Jamie and Aiden.'

It was what Becca wanted to do . . . but she really didn't want to do it with Tasha in tow. Her mum had made her leave her phone at home as *a mark of respect*, whatever that meant, and no amount of sighing and begging could make her change her mind, so she had no idea if he'd texted her or not. If he had, she didn't want him to think she was being moody with him, and she had no way of knowing if he hadn't so she didn't know if she *should* be moody with him. God, love wasn't meant to be this *hard*, was it?

She inwardly bitched at her mum. It was probably nothing to do with respect, she just didn't want any photos in the paper of Becca playing with her phone during the funeral of the friend she inadvertently murdered. To be fair, neither did Becca. Especially not after that conversation with Amanda Alderton. But that wasn't the point.

'Hi, girls,' Jamie said. 'How are you coping?'

'Just an awful day,' Natasha said. 'It's still surreal. Isn't it, Bex?'

'Yeah. Horrible.'

Aiden looked up at her from under his fringe. Normally she found his long hair pretty hot, but right now it felt like he was using it as a barrier between them. He didn't touch her, or take her hand. 'You okay?'

She nodded. 'I will be.'

'Becca's been amazing,' Tasha gushed. 'I'd have been lost without her.'

'You look well,' Jamie said. 'And I hear your memory's come back?'

Becca let their conversation drone out. Her pulse thumped in her ears. 'Can we talk?' she said, softly, taking Aiden's arm and pulling him slightly away from the other two. 'You know, about last night. I was upset and maybe overreacted and—'

'You always overreact, Bex.' He sounded tired. Worn down. 'Why do you think I don't always tell you everything?'

'What do you mean, you don't always tell me stuff?'

'See? You're doing it again. You really want to do this now?' He was looking at her like she was a child and it stung. Her face burned. Did she want to do this?

'I don't want to fight or anything,' she said, hating how needy she sounded. 'I just wanted to say sorry.' *But I still really want to know who Emma is and how come you're one of Tasha's Facebook friends*. She bit the thought back.

'You always say sorry,' Aiden said. 'And you always mean it at the time. But it never stops all your jealousy and insecurity. It does my head in.'

'I don't mean it, I—' Tears came, hot and hard as he cut her off.

'Emma is just a friend of mine. She works in a bar. After I dropped you off that night I went for a drink and then we went and got stoned by the river and fell asleep in my car. She told the police and they let me go.'

'Why didn't you just tell me?' Becca said. 'I wouldn't have minded.' But even as she said the words she knew it was a lie. She did mind. She thought that was their place. That was where *they* went. And who was this girl that he could be such good friends with her and not ever mention her? Did they have history? *Emma.* Probably cool and older. Not a pathetic teenager like she was.

'That's bullshit and you know it,' he said, lighting another cigarette. His hands were shaking as he offered her one. She took it. She didn't care what her mum might say or whether the photographers saw it.

'I didn't want to do this here,' he said.

'Do what?' *Don't say it, don't say it, don't say it.* 'Don't you love me any more?' There it was. The whiny question.

'Nothing's ever as simple as that.' He couldn't look her in the eye. 'Of course I still care about you.' He shuffled his feet as Becca's world stopped still. He was going to do it. He really was. 'But this has been a shitty couple of weeks. For both of us. I think maybe we need some time on our own. To figure things out. You know.'

She didn't know. She didn't want to know. 'It's Hannah's funeral,' was all she could manage to say.

'I didn't want to do it here.' He sounded so lame. He *was* lame. Suddenly she was filled with rage.

'Why the *fuck* did you even come today?' she asked. Jamie and Tasha looked over, the sharpness in her voice like a knife through the air. 'Why?'

'I thought you might . . .' Suddenly he was the one on the back foot and it felt good to Becca. She cut him off. Whatever he was going to say, it was bullshit.

'You know me. You knew I'd want to talk about it. So if you didn't want to do it here, *why did you come*?'

'I didn't think,' he muttered.

'Hey, you two—' Jamie tried to intervene but Becca flashed him a glare that shut him up. This wasn't his business and he wasn't her dad and he hadn't saved her from drowning. He could shut the fuck up.

'You didn't come here for me. You came for yourself. You wanted to feel better and you know I can't freak out here *at my best friend's funeral*.' She took a deep, shaky breath and wiped away her tears. 'Maybe you should just leave.' She turned and stomped off towards the gates, still clutching her cigarette.

'Becca?' Tasha called after her. Becca didn't pause. She couldn't look back. If she did, Aiden would see how her heart was breaking. She leaned against the wall and inhaled hard, even though the camera lenses in the road glinted at her. She didn't care. Fuck them. Fuck all of them. She let the smoke burn her lungs as her legs shook and her hands trembled.

'*Is there a team on the way? Do you want me to come?*'

She half-listened as one of the policemen talked into his phone, pacing a few feet away. Aiden had really done it. He'd dumped her.

'*Do the press know? A couple of their cars just left here.*'

She wasn't sure what felt more surreal – Hannah dead in a coffin or Aiden not wanting her any more. Maybe Hannah would laugh at that. Maybe she'd think Becca deserved it.

'I'm on my way.'

No, she wouldn't. Hannah wasn't like that. Hannah would get them hot chocolates and cake and listen to Becca as she cried and smoked and wailed about love and she'd say all the right things. Hannah was a good person. She'd been a good person.

The tears came thick and fast after that.

Forty-Three

Extracts from the *Brackston Saturday Herald*, Saturday 6th February

The scandal that has erupted from Brackston Community School took a sombre turn for the worse yesterday. Peter Garrick, the school's 38-year-old English teacher and exams officer, was found dead in his home during the funeral of Hannah Alderton, who was killed during a play rehearsal on the 26th of January. Sources close to the investigation claimed that Mr Garrick had been suspended from the school, although he was not believed to have any involvement in her death. Mr Garrick, a married father of two, is thought to have been alone in the house at the time of his death and police do not think anyone else was involved.

Although police have not confirmed that Mr Garrick was the member of staff facing charges of sexual activity with a minor while in a position of trust, sources confirm the CPS will not be pursuing that case in light of Mr Garrick's death.

Two 16-year-old girls, who for legal reasons cannot be named, remain in custody and have been charged in the matter of Hannah Alderton's murder.

Brackston Community School was closed yesterday to allow students and staff to attend the funeral of murdered sixth former Hannah Alderton. Although the sun was shining, the community's grief was apparent as peers and adults cried and hugged outside the church after the short service. It is believed that Hannah may not have been the intended victim. Although our source will not confirm who the target was, Hannah Alderton attended the same school as Natasha Howland (pictured above left at yesterday's funeral), who was found near-dead in the river in January.

Also attending the funeral was Rebecca Crisp (above right, smoking) who, like Natasha Howland, has not returned to school since Hannah Alderton's death. Both girls have been seen entering and leaving the police station on several occasions but neither is considered a suspect in the case. Both girls were present at the time of Hannah Alderton's death. It is clear that her friend's death has affected Rebecca Crisp greatly.

Although the Head Teacher and governors of the school have issued a statement asking that pupils to be allowed to return to their studies in peace, many parents are concerned by recent events and have called for the police to place a community liaison officer in the school and for the government to launch an inquiry as to how events such as these have been allowed to unfold in such a high-achieving school.

Forty-Four

Extracts from **NATASHA HOWLAND'S STATEMENT TAKEN BY DI CAITLIN BENNETT AND DS MARC APLIN ON TUESDAY 26TH JANUARY. DR ANNABEL HARVEY PRESENT AS APPROPRIATE ADULT.**

Time commenced: 20.15.

It was Thursday after school. Yes, the seven January. The day before I went in the river. So weird how I remember it all now. It's like a box just opened in my head – a jack-in-the-box – and all the memories jumped out and back into their places. Sorry. I'll try and stick to it. Yes, I'm okay. Still shaking a bit. That was so awful. Hannah. God, poor Hannah.

Okay. This is what I remember. I followed them, Thursday after school. Yes, Jenny and Hayley. They'd been so odd with me. More than odd, kind of like they didn't want me around? Yeah, they'd been like that for a while. Maybe a couple of months? It was getting worse. Little bitchy comments sometimes. I'd been trying really hard to find out if I'd done anything wrong but couldn't think of anything. I just wanted my friends back rather than this feeling that they were, at best, pretending to like me.

Anyway, Thursday. They'd been so closed off. Tight. I'd seen them like that before, giggling together. Telling me it was nothing. At lunchtime I asked them if they wanted to go and hang out in Starbucks after school. I had money – Jenny never really has any cash and Hayley's parents are stricter with pocket money than mine, she kind of has to earn it by doing stuff around the house and looking after her little brother, but my parents just give me money when I ask for it – so I figured they'd come if I was paying. Sounds pathetic, doesn't it? Like I was trying to buy them, but it's true, I kind of was. Hayley said she had to go to the indoor track and practise and Jenny said she had to stay behind for extra Maths for her GCSE retake.

I got the feeling they were both lying to me and it really hurt. They'd done it before, too, and this time it made me a bit crazy. I mean, why couldn't they just be honest with me? So – god, I sound like such a loser – I went to the Maths department and checked out the revision group schedule but there was nothing listed. I even spoke to Mr Russell-Woods – he's the Head of Maths – and said Jenny had asked me to check, but he said it wasn't on that night.

So anyway, I pretended I'd left then followed them. I knew they were out at the back of the PE block where Hayley smokes. They'd hidden from me there before. They didn't leave school till after five and now I know why – that's when Mr Garrick left. I had a hoodie on and kept it up but they never looked behind them. They were too busy talking, arms linked, and laughing. It really hurt my feelings. I didn't even want to fight with them, just to see what they were doing that was so interesting they had to lie to me about it.

They walked to the big car park at the back of Asda. You know the one? So you know that bit at the back is never full.

And it's dark there. I don't understand why they made it that big – like everyone in Brackston is going to shop there at exactly the same time? But anyway, that's where they went. By now I thought maybe I'd got it all wrong and they were just going to meet Hayley's dad or something for a ride home . . . but that didn't really make any sense, either. They could have walked or got the bus and been home quicker. I had kind of stopped caring about why they'd shut me out and just wanted to know what made them go there, of all places.

I stayed back, by the wall where all those huge recycling bins are, pressing myself slightly behind the green one. It was pitch-dark by then and getting cold. I could hear them laughing and talking still, but it was quieter.

Then a car pulled in. A dark four-by-four. When the door opened and Jenny got in, I caught a glimpse of a man inside, but I couldn't make out who he was. Hayley waved at him. He said something to her that I couldn't catch and she said she was fine, the cold didn't bother her.

Jenny was in the car on her own with him for maybe half an hour? Forty-five minutes? I was freezing by then. Hayley went to the café and bought a coffee, but she was still standing around for another twenty minutes or so when she got back. She had her Uggs on and a proper thick coat. She was prepared. I was so cold, but I couldn't move without risking being seen. The car windows were steaming up even though the engine wasn't on. I was a bit shocked but not surprised. I mean, we all know Jenny's no virgin and she'd just got into a man's parked car. They weren't going to be playing chess in there, were they?

So, just when I thought I couldn't take much more of the cold, the car engine started up again and pulled over towards

Hayley. The window came down and Jenny, in the front seat, said something – must have been about dropping them nearer home or whatever, and I caught a glimpse of the man behind the wheel. It was Mr Garrick. I was pretty sure of it.

I felt like I'd been punched in the stomach. I mean, Mr Garrick? He seemed so sweet. Awkward, almost. Not like *hot* or anything? How could he be fucking Jenny? All I could think was that she was trying to screw her way to getting the Maths exam paper early or something. I was totally spinning out. By the time I arrived home I wasn't sure if I'd seen him at all. Maybe it was some other man who just looked a bit like him. I only caught a glimpse. I could be totally wrong. I didn't know what to think.

So I got up early on Friday – took my warmest coat this time – and loitered out by the school car park. I made it look like I was waiting for someone and had an excuse ready – my mum bringing in a forgotten book or something. Not that anyone asked. Have you seen teachers in the morning? I think they hate school more than we do until they've topped up their coffee breath in the staff room. Anyway, finally I saw the car. Same number plate – I couldn't remember it all, I'm not a detective or anything, but the first three bits were lodged in my head. And it was him. It was Mr Garrick.

I actually felt sick. Really properly sick. I didn't know what to do. All I knew was that it was wrong and it had to stop. This must have been why they didn't tell me. They *knew* I wouldn't be okay with it. I mean, he's a teacher and married with kids and everything. And he isn't even hot. I didn't understand it. Maybe he was using the exams to get at Jenny? Maybe she wasn't willing at all? My head was buzzing with questions.

I couldn't concentrate and then at break there was the

announcement about the school play auditions and so I texted them and said I'd buy them lunch in the café – that one just past the newsagent's? It's not great but they do good paninis and you can eat what you want without everyone watching to see if you're getting fat. Being us at school isn't always easy. I keep reading things in the papers and stuff about me and how popular we are, but popular is weird. It's got a serrated edge, if you know what I mean? Sometimes I think it would be way better to just be like Bex or poor Hannah.

So, anyway, we go for lunch. We start out talking about the play and it's like I'm waiting for them to say something about *it*, but of course they don't. In the end I can't stay quiet. I come straight out and say that I followed them. I saw what happened. Their faces – I can still see them now, Jenny's mouth half-open and filled with melted cheese and ham sandwich. Hayley staring at me in that way she does – her lack of expression means it's *all* going on inside. She looked at me that way when I kissed Mark Pritchard at his party and I still don't know why I did that, except that maybe on some level a part of me still remembered everything and wanted to hurt her back.

So they stare at me. Jenny is straight away all 'you can't tell anyone' and that kind of thing. She says she needs him for her exams, so she can make sure she passes her Maths resit and then she can get out of this town. Hayley tells me it's none of my business and I shouldn't have followed them. I say that it's wrong and can't continue and I'm going to tell someone unless they stop it. I say he's being a creep, whatever Jenny thinks. You can't go around fucking your students, it's just plain wrong. He's a paedo. I won't let him hurt one of my friends like that, *I won't*. Hayley says that's why they didn't tell me. They knew I wouldn't leave it alone. We argue a bit. I'm surprised Hayley's so cool with it. Jenny's dad fucked her up and now she's basically shagging a dad replacement?

So, I tell them they've got till Monday to sort it out. And by that I don't mean just finish it, I mean they have to report him. If it's not done by then, I'll go to the Head. Hayley tries to claim no one will believe me but she knows that isn't true. And she knows Jenny's not a great liar, either – not under pressure. I tell them I don't want to fight about it, but he was taking advantage of Jenny. It was pretty much abuse – even if she was going to get through her exams because of him – and she was worth more than that. I loved them but it couldn't go on.

Then lunch was over and we had to head out. They said they'd think about it. I started to cry like an idiot because I hated the fighting. Then Jenny started crying, too, and we all hugged. Hayley said I was probably right and maybe it was all a bit of a mess, but even though we went back into school kind of okay I still felt so awful. It was all round shit. I felt like shit. They were my best friends.

Of course, I didn't realise then how much they hated me.

What happened that night?

I couldn't sleep. Just for thinking about it all. I found Jenny after school for a moment – she was in the toilets texting. Using a different phone. Something cheap. Basic. I figured it was the phone she used to text Mr Garrick. I asked her if she was telling him what I'd said. She said no. She was edgy, maybe a bit high, I don't know. It's hard to tell with Jen sometimes. She says she only does shit with me and Hayley, but you've seen her mum, right? Maybe she had vodka or something in her bag, if she didn't have drugs. She definitely gets high more than me. I only started doing Mandy to keep in with them, but you know, it does feel good. Is that going to get me into trouble, saying that? I don't know where she bought it or anything and it was only ever for us and our friends.

I told her maybe she should tell him. She said I had to give her time. It was so weird. It was as if she actually *liked* him. Properly liked him. Anyway, as I said, I couldn't sleep. When the text came in, at first I was confused and thought it was a wrong number. I didn't answer it, it just irritated me. I had too much else in my head. And then, as I was finally dozing off at about two-thirty, it hit me. The *usual place* was what we used to call the clearing in the woods. I figured maybe Jenny was drunk or something and had texted me on that phone I'd seen her with. I didn't text back because I had no clue whether I was actually going to meet them or not. I thought I'd just go and see if they were there. I wasn't sure I really wanted to talk to them. Maybe Mr Garrick was with them? I really didn't want to face him in the middle of the night. Definitely not without an adult or another teacher present.

I didn't take a coat. They were all downstairs and I couldn't risk waking my mum or dad. I just put my joggers on, and a couple of long-sleeved T-shirts under my hoodie. I figured I wouldn't be out long. If I spoke to them at all, I was just going to let them know they wouldn't change my mind.

But then I saw them. I'd used my phone as a light to guide me there, but they had a big torch, like a kind of man-torch, I guess. I think it must have come from Hayley's dad's garage. Like the rope. They go camping sometimes.

They're there in the clearing. Waiting for me. Just the two of them. They look miserable at first, but then they seem so happy to see me. They want to make things better. To apologise. I ask if Jenny has a new phone. I say I almost didn't come, I didn't realise the text was from them. She says it was a phone she uses with Mr Garrick. She says she'd just texted him to say that they needed to talk and then texted me from it by accident. Says she has mine and Hayley's numbers in there, too, in case her iPhone fucks up. Hers is new to her, but it's not new. It freezes loads. I wasn't suspicious at all. I'd never have imagined they both had other phones they used to bitch about *me*.

Anyway, I'm happy because they say they're going to do as I asked. They know I'm right. I was so relieved! I totally relaxed. They had some booze. Not much. Just some cheap wine. And Hayley gives me a Crunchie. She calls it a token of peace.

They . . . they . . . I don't believe they meant to really hurt me. You shouldn't think they intended to. Not then, anyway. In the beginning they just wanted to scare me into shutting up. But then all this other stuff came out. How they really felt about me. They were probably high. At first we were just talking. They were trying to be all friendly again. It made me happy. I drank the wine. I felt woozy and then they started to cool. Little digs at me. Snide comments. I can't remember what, exactly, but about how great I thought I was and how I was nothing but a spoilt brat. Then I felt really woozy and began to freak out. I couldn't stand up properly. Then they started in earnest.

They tie me to the tree. They start shouting at me then. Mean stuff. I don't remember exactly what because my head was spinning. I was really tired but I was so cold and fighting to stay awake, and the bark was pressing into my back and everything ached, and I was so afraid. Afraid of my friends. They looked so wild. They were saying how much they hated me. They hated me before this thing with Mr Garrick. Hated how I always controlled everything. Didn't let them breathe. They felt like I thought I owned them. Hayley's pacing and smoking, venting at me with so much venom. They don't want to be friends with me any more. Something about James Ensor. I dated him a couple of times. Hayley says she liked him and I'd taken him from her. I try to say I didn't know she liked him but my words are slurry. She says I was doing the same with Mark Pritchard. So much stuff I couldn't take in. They said I thought I was better than them. Smarter than them. And sticking my nose in with Mr Garrick proved it. They were drunk now and so angry. I don't know what time they'd met up but they must have been drinking for a while before I got there.

Everything gets hazier after that. I think I fell asleep or passed out for a while. I don't know. The next thing I remember for sure was Hayley waking me up. Cutting me free from the tree. It was so cold. I couldn't feel my fingers. The temperature had dropped. Really dropped hard. I don't know when it started, but snow was falling, too, heavy and white. Although the clearing was pretty protected by the trees I could see an inch or so on the branches already. It must have been coming down hard for a while, and long enough for us to sober up a bit.

I tried to stand up and fell on the ground but they didn't help me. I think I asked what was going on. Jenny had the torch in one hand and a long stick in the other. I couldn't see the wine bottle anywhere. They must have thrown it somewhere out in the trees.

Could I have some more water? Thanks. This is . . . difficult.

*

Hayley crouches beside me and whispers something about me having learned my lesson and not to talk about stuff that wasn't my business. She says that I have to leave them alone or they'd do far worse to me. I almost throw up there on the ground. I was so scared. I was still confused and my head hurt really badly from the wine and whatever they put in it to make me so drowsy. I didn't really know what was going on. I just wanted to go home. I know it sounds shallow, but I didn't care about Mr Garrick any more. Hayley had a stick, too, and she whipped it through the air and hit the ground. I remember the dull whack on the earth, right by my face. I remember Jenny giggling at that.

They tell me to run.

I try.

I think they follow me a bit. I hear some whooping. But I don't know for sure. I was so scared. I remember my lungs burning. I remember my legs were so weak.

I still don't remember how I ended up in the river. I was running through the woods, the branches hitting me. I didn't know if they were behind me or not. I just wanted to get home. To my mum.

I remember hitting the freezing water. I remember seeing snow on the bank by the fields. But I don't remember if they pushed me. I know you want me to remember but I don't. I can't say I do. I'm sorry. I was running through the woods and the next thing I remember is hitting the water. I remember trying to swim to the branches on the other side. And then there's just darkness until I woke up at the hospital.

I'm sorry, that's it. I don't know if I ran into the water or if they pushed me. I just don't.

Forty-Five

Extract from DI CAITLIN BENNETT'S NOTES (UNOFFICIAL RECORD) FOR REPORT TO CROWN PROSECUTION SERVICE – FRIDAY 5TH FEBRUARY

Neither girl has offered a full confession or a complete account of events in regard to the death of Hannah Alderton or the near-fatal incident with Natasha Howland. However, Jennifer Cole, currently undergoing a mental health evaluation, has indicated Hayley Gallagher was the instigator – at least in the death of Hannah Alderton – through her repeated, 'Hayley said she'd think of something.' Whether this will be admissible evidence will depend on the outcome of the evaluation.

Given the nature of the texts they exchanged on the PAYG phones found turned off and hidden in their bedrooms, it's clear both girls intended harm to Natasha even before she discovered Jennifer's relationship with Peter Garrick. The phones appear to have been bought with the express purpose of bitching about her (maybe didn't want her seeing the conversation? Their primary phones would always be out and about – showing each other things on social media sites?) rather than talking about, or to, Garrick. There are no texts to him on either phone. All the texts are about Natasha Howland. There are clear aggressive fantasies and jealousies evident and these increase in number and violence until the night of Howland's accident. Both girls state in texts on several occasions that they wished she was dead. That they didn't want to be her friend any more. They wanted rid of her. They text on Friday 8th January about doing it that night. Activity on both phones ceases after the text that came to Natasha Howland's phone. Presumably they were turned off after the last text was sent from the wrong phone. Jennifer's drug usage as evident in blood tests probably led to this mistake.

Retrieved deleted texts from the phones registered in their own names, which they used day to day, also imply their guilt and show a continued dislike for Natasha. They openly wish that she'd died, and there are references to a 'him' – Peter Garrick, we believe – and there is a lot of concern about whether Natasha will regain her memory. Hayley's insistence that they delete these conversations again implies their guilt. Much is in the subtext, but the story seems clear. They were definitely afraid of what Natasha Howland might have remembered and shared with Rebecca Crisp, who may be lucky not to have been targeted also. There was a sense of urgency between them that something had to be done.

This correlates with events post-accident as recounted by Natasha Howland in the diary of events and feelings she was asked to keep as part of Dr Annabel Harvey's therapy, and those are in turn confirmed by Rebecca Crisp.

Forty-Six

Excerpt of CONSULTATION BETWEEN DR ANNABEL HARVEY AND PATIENT NATASHA HOWLAND, WEDNESDAY 02/03, 18:00

NATASHA: Look, we can keep talking about this for ever, but it won't change anything. I don't want to have any more of these sessions. I think I'm okay. There's nothing that time won't solve anyway. Coming here and talking to you makes me feel like it's still going on. It's not. It's done. My memory's back. Jenny and Hayley and Mr Garrick – well . . . you know all about that.

DR HARVEY: Are you still keeping a diary?

NATASHA: The police took it, even though I told them it was private. It has private thoughts in it. So thanks for that. I haven't bothered since. I was doing it because you asked me to, because my memory was gone, but I don't need to do that now. All the mysteries have been solved. Nearly, anyway.

DR HARVEY: Is that what you think these sessions have been about? Solving the immediate mysteries for the police?

NATASHA: They are, aren't they? You can't tell me Bennett wasn't eager for me to remember what happened that night and wanted you to help me with that. Anyway, I googled you – you work with the police all the time, so it's not just all about my feelings, is it?

(Pause)

Are you seeing Hayley and Jenny, too? I know you've seen Becca at least once.

DR HARVEY: You know I can't discuss other patients. How is school?

NATASHA: I feel like you're trying to put a jigsaw puzzle together from bits of all our brains. See if the pieces lock together into a complete picture. Then you'll know everything about all of us.

(Pause)

School's okay. There are no newspaper guys around any more – I guess there won't be until the trial – so that calmed everyone down. No audience, I suppose. Not that I give a shit. It's nice to be able to walk around the house or garden without worrying about long lenses watching me. They wanted me to do some talk shows – I think they asked Becca, too – but we both said no. Police agreed that was best, anyway. Maybe after the trial is over we should do it, but not now. I miss Hayley and Jen sometimes. I try not to, and it's not like I don't have new friends – Vicki and Jodie were quick to jump into their places – I think Jodie lost half a stone over a weekend just to make me like her.

(Laughs)

How shallow. But then how shallow am I, because she does fit our look better without those thunder-thighs.

DR HARVEY: Are you seeing much of Rebecca? I thought you two had become close.

NATASHA: Not really. That upsets her, I think – has she said something?

(Pause)

Of course, you can't say. Ha. I haven't really seen her. Now this is all over it's too weird. The Hannah thing was so horrible and she's still dealing with that. When I look at her I see all this shit, all the betrayals of friendship, and it might not be her fault but I just don't want to be around her. She texts me sometimes – sounds stupid but we were playing this game of chess and texting each other our moves. She texts about my next move and I always say I haven't had time to look. It's like she's not brave enough to say, *Hey why are you freezing me out?* so she talks about chess instead. That makes me cringe a bit, too. God, I'm such a bitch, but it makes her feel like a bit of a Hannah. No spine. I just want to move on, you know?

DR HARVEY: Why did you ask for me as the appropriate adult present rather than your mother when you gave your statement?

NATASHA: You've met my mother.

DR HARVEY: She seems a very pleasant woman. She obviously loves you a lot.

NATASHA: She suffocates me. Don't you remember what it was like? To be my age? No privacy. Not really. I wanted to talk without her hearing everything. Squeezing my hand and stuff. She'd want to discuss it all afterwards, too. It was easier with you there. No offence, but I don't give a shit what *you* think. You don't live in my house.

DR HARVEY: How do you feel about your refusal to try the hypnosis? Do you wonder if Hannah might still be alive if you'd recovered your memory sooner that way?

NATASHA: Is this a guilt question? I think about it sometimes, of course I do. But I couldn't have done it. Even the way people talk about it – *going under* – it's like drowning. I couldn't do it. I just couldn't.

(Pause)

Are you saying I *should* feel guilty? No one knows I refused hypnosis apart from us and the police. No one knows I said no.

DR HARVEY: No, I don't think you should feel guilty. But that doesn't mean you don't.

NATASHA: (Pause)

Well, I don't. Like I don't feel guilty about not talking to Becca any more.

(Pause)

I talk to her ex-boyfriend a bit though. Aiden? I like him better now he's grown up a bit. We chat on Facebook. Text sometimes. I think he's going to ask me out again.

DR HARVEY: How do you think Rebecca will feel about that?

NATASHA: Stupid question. She won't like it. She'll hate it. But it's not like I broke them up or anything. And you can't go through life worrying about other people's feelings all the time. What about your own feelings? I saw Hannah die. She did it so *easily*. So carelessly. It was like a light being switched off. She was just gone. No more Hannah. She spent all her life worrying about other people. Maybe if she'd been more selfish she'd have had more fun. I was so close to being as dead as her. It could have been my funeral everyone fucking Instagrammed and was so emotional at and forgot the next day.

DR HARVEY: Why are you finding this so agitating, Natasha?

NATASHA: (Pause)

Sorry, I didn't realise I was so heated. I just . . . I just can't get my head around how quickly we're forgotten. I mean, we might as well have some fun, right? That could have been me. Why worry about all this inconsequential stuff? Maybe that includes other people. Maybe they're inconsequential, too? Unless you love them. And maybe even then. Does that make me sound crazy? It's hard to explain what I mean.

DR HARVEY: Are you trying to say you don't care if you hurt Becca by talking to Aiden?

NATASHA: (Laughs)

Yes, I guess that's what I'm saying. Although it makes me sound like such a bitch. Weird, huh? They tried to kill me because they thought I was a controlling, selfish bitch, and now I am one. But he asked me out first. And we're teenagers, it's not like they were going to get married or anything. I'm probably doing her a favour.

(Pause)

Sometimes I think I should stop talking to him, but it's not as if that would make him get back with her, would it? So what would be the point? I can't make him not like me. And I like him. He's not *braggy* like the boys at school. Do you think I'm a terrible person?

DR HARVEY: I don't think there are terrible people. There are only people.

NATASHA: Careful, that was nearly a smile!

(Laugh)

There you go. You look almost human.

DR HARVEY: How are you sleeping now?

NATASHA: (Pause)

Did you do that on purpose? On the shelf?

DR HARVEY: What do you mean?

NATASHA: Those shells. There are thirteen of them. And the books on the window ledge. Thirteen. I don't remember them being there before. So are they a test?

DR HARVEY: You're very observant.

NATASHA: Why didn't you just say, 'Are you still seeing thirteens, Natasha?' in that Siri voice of yours? Why set a trap for me?

DR HARVEY: I didn't see it that way. Have I upset you?

NATASHA: I don't like being tricked.

DR HARVEY: I apologise.

NATASHA: What if I'd seen them and not mentioned them?

DR HARVEY: I was interested in whether you would mention them.

NATASHA: Why?

DR HARVEY: Because mentioning them implies you want help understanding it.

NATASHA: So you can persuade me to keep coming back?

DR HARVEY: I understand why you want to move on, but I also think you could still benefit from continuing our sessions.

NATASHA: You think I'm mental.

DR HARVEY: I think you've been through some extremely distressing events.

(Pause)

NATASHA: I'm sorry.

For snapping about the number thing. It doesn't matter really, does it?

DR HARVEY: How are you sleeping?

NATASHA: On my side mainly.

(Short laugh)

Sorry. I don't know. Just . . . I still have the fear of the darkness. I still have the dream. You know, the voice in the dark.

DR HARVEY: Whose voice is it?

NATASHA: That's the thing – in my dreams I know who it is, but when I wake up, I don't remember. All I know is that someone speaks to me and I'm terrified. I thought when my memory came back it would stop, but it hasn't.

DR HARVEY: It may take some time. Your subconscious is still processing all of this. These dreams may last until you remember exactly how you got into the river.

NATASHA: Great.

DR HARVEY: I know you're reluctant, but hypnosis might help you. Perhaps if we could reach your dream state and—

NATASHA: No. No hypnosis.

DR HARVEY: Well, think about it.

NATASHA: I won't change my mind. I won't change my mind about ending these sessions, either. This is the last one. It's over. Your seashell trick backfired. I don't trust you any more. I don't want to talk to you.

DR HARVEY: I'm sorry you feel that way. I can recommend a different—

NATASHA: No more therapy. I don't need it.

Forty-Seven

She didn't know if the newspaper had been left open at that page on purpose for her to see, or whether it was just accidental. It was hard to tell these days. Spring sunshine streamed through the large windows and it should have lifted Becca's spirits. She loved the approach of summer, the thought of the long holiday ahead, the joy of leaving the house without being nagged to drag on a coat, but now the bright end-of-March warmth barely touched her. Everything was fucked up, everything had been fucked up since Hannah's funeral, which felt like forever ago. A long, drawn-out hell with no imminent pardon. The headline was just the icing on the cake.

Suicide note found in Nicola Munroe case confirms tragic teenager took own life.

Fucking great. Her heart sank with the memory of storming into Jamie McMahon's house like some screaming banshee. All that worry for nothing. Aiden had nothing to do with it after all. She stared at her phone, chewing hard on her bottom lip. She typed fast before she could change her mind.

Saw about Nicola Munroe.

V sad, but must be relief for
it to be over? x

She hit 'send'. She didn't know if it would be a relief or not. She didn't know if the police had interviewed him again. She didn't know much of anything.

In the first few days after he'd broken up with her, she'd done all the things she'd sworn she wouldn't: sent drunk texts begging him to come back, sent angry texts, sent friendly texts, tried calling him. She cringed when she thought of some of the messages she'd left. The only times she'd heard back were replies to one or two of her friendly texts but even those were perfunctory. Like they were strangers. Like she hadn't ridden him in his car or screwed in his bed and told him she'd love him forever.

Forever. That word haunted her. *Best friends forever. I'll love you forever.*

Forever had turned out to be flighty. The only ones who'd found forever endings were Hannah and Mr Garrick. Becca didn't sit in the Science corridor any more, even though it would be preferable to the sixth form common room, where everyone ignored her. She'd tried, but it felt spooky. As if Hannah was lingering there. Waiting for her, filled with reproach. She'd never thought of Hannah as vindictive but it was hard to separate Hannah from all the *Hannah backlash*, as if her ghost had somehow caused it.

She stared at her phone. No answer from Aiden even though she'd put a question mark on the end to prompt a response. She tried not to feel disappointed. She should be used to it by now. She hated herself for even texting. He wasn't her business any more, even if she still woke up every morning and hoped to find a text saying he'd changed his mind, dumping her had been a terrible mistake. That he still loved her.

She stared at the paper but didn't read the story. She should have been in Theatre Tech but she was bunking off. It wasn't like she was going to get in any trouble. It was easier all round if she dropped out of that subject – in fact, she was pretty sure everyone would be happier if she dropped out of school completely.

Tasha didn't speak to her any more, either.

> I'm sorry Bex, I really am, but
> when I look at you all I see is
> poor Hannah and what Hayley
> and Jenny did to me. I know
> it's not your fault, but I really
> need to try and move on.

She'd even stopped answering her texts about their chess game. She had her new *Barbies* in tow as well as the continuing sympathy of the whole school and town. Becca could only imagine how many Facebook friends Tasha had now. Sometimes she was tempted to log back in and see what was going on in that other world, but she'd deactivated her account and deleted her Twitter feed after all the bad shit happened.

It was always going to be this way. Tasha was still the beautiful victim, but haters needed someone to hate and Becca was the ideal candidate. She'd controlled the light, after all. She'd let Hayley go up the ladder. Technically, as she'd overheard in the girls' toilets when she first came back to school, she was as much a killer as Hayley and Jenny.

It also turned out Hannah *did* have other friends. Becca

might have been too self-absorbed to notice them, but they existed. Perhaps Hannah had liked her best, but Becca wasn't her only friend. Apparently, being invisible in school wasn't the same as being friendless. When Becca started hanging around with Tasha again, it wasn't just her mum that Hannah shared her hurt with. That nameless girl Becca had seen Hannah head to Geography with turned out to be called Adele Cotterill, and Hannah had cried on her shoulder *a lot*. The worst part was, according to Adele and all her posts on the *Hannah Alderton Memorial Page* she'd set up, Hannah was never bitchy. Hannah had always seen the best in Becca. It was probably true, as well. But Adele had taken it on herself to tell the world that Rebecca Crisp didn't deserve any sympathy. The Aldertons didn't think so, either, and she agreed with them. There were victims here, but Becca wasn't really one of them. She was just a shallow girl who dumped a good friend and then inadvertently killed her. Adele was careful never to actually blame Becca for Hannah's death. It all just *hung* there, a stagnant cloud covering her webspace that just wouldn't clear.

About an hour went by after the Memorial page went up before Becca saw the first nasty post. She couldn't miss it. Her phone pinged with new notifications of people writing on her wall. None of what they said was good. Other people tweeted her. She'd felt sick. She still felt sick when she remembered it. Worse was Tasha trying to calm people down and stick up for her. Saintly Natasha, who was suddenly everyone's friend. No one cared that Tasha had never given a shit about Hannah. Because at least Tasha had been honest about that. She hadn't been her friend then dumped her. Not like she'd done to Becca back in Year Seven, although that appeared to have been forgotten. But Tasha gave up fighting against the online onslaught after a day or so, and in the end Becca had just closed everything down, Twitter, Facebook, Instagram, all of it. It was easier that way. People weren't so good at being bitchy face to face and she could take being ignored and the snide, half-heard comments in the corridors. But that was enough.

Sometimes she looked at the wreck of her life and thought, *How has this happened? I was only trying to help.* Worse, Natasha was wrong about Hannah being forgotten quickly. Hannah had become a symbol of a kind of quiet purity. Becca, on the other hand, was a pariah. A user. A shallow, selfish, weak girl who only cared about getting back in with the in crowd and had taken advantage of Tasha's accident to make it happen. No one wanted to forget Hannah – even though no one had a clue who she was until she died – because that meant they wouldn't get the fun of hating Becca.

Two girls and a boy came in, glanced her way, then sat in a circle of chairs in the far corner, and Becca took it as her cue to leave. She wanted a cigarette anyway and had one already rolled and ready to go. She'd stopped smoking straights and moved to roll-ups because she was smoking so much now, maybe twenty a day, that she couldn't afford them on her allowance. Even her mum had noticed the increase – Becca could see it in the continually pained expression she wore when she looked at her daughter. Julia Crisp clearly had so much she wanted to say but was no doubt under advice to just let Becca work it out for herself. Julia Crisp had never been very good at that. Becca thought it must be killing her to smile and be sympathetic and nothing more. Still, at least she got to smoke as much as she wanted without being bitched at.

The breeze bit enough to make her shiver but the sun was

warm. Within a month the last of winter would be banished, packed away again until October. Hannah was the one who'd died, but out here, Becca was haunted by Hayley. Or rather by Hayley's *absence*. She could almost see her leaning against the wall, expression so full of disdain, carefully inhaling her Vogue. No harsh, head-spinny roll-ups for her. *I might be in prison*, Hayley's absence said in Becca's head, *but you're not exactly a winner here, are you?*

Before self-pity overwhelmed her, Becca abandoned her half-smoked cigarette and headed back inside. She didn't want to stay in school but she had nowhere else to go. No play rehearsals to look forward to, no Aiden to hook up with, no friends to meet. Maybe *she* was the ghost, aimlessly drifting the corridors.

In the end, she went to the only place where she felt any sense of peace – the Art Rooms. Down in the basement, stuffily warm now that winter was fading but the school heating remained on, it felt like a world outside of school, quieter than the library, students lost in the sleepy calm that came with concentrated creativity, and with plenty of space to set her easel up in a corner and hide behind it. It was easier not to feel ignored in the Art Rooms. People didn't talk much in here, anyway.

It wasn't a coursework piece, but something Dr Harvey had told her to try. Just painting her feelings. It seemed to be working. Becca had thought she'd be left with some kind of vivid postmodern canvas of angry coloured splashes, but somehow what had arrived was woods and snow and an icy river at breaking dawn. It was an image of the calm before the storm. The empty stage before Tasha burst through the trees and was either pushed or fell into the water. It was the beginning. Yes, it was all going on behind the scenes for Tasha, Hayley and Jenny, but this was the grand entrance onto centre stage that swept Becca into the action.

'It's starting to look quite beautifully eerie.' Miss Borders put two mugs of tea down on the nearby table and pulled up a stool. 'I particularly like the hints of red in the sky and the sheen on that corner of ice.'

'Thanks.'

'You've been down here quite a lot.' She waited for Becca to put her paintbrush into the water pot and then handed her a mug. 'I put one sugar in. Hope that's all right.'

The tea was too milky for Becca and also too sweet, but she smiled anyway. 'Thanks again.' She liked Miss Borders but hoped she wasn't going to launch into the well-meaning *Are you all right?* conversation that so many teachers had insisted on having with her. They'd all noticed how she was being shunned, and they'd probably all heard about the Facebook and Internet stuff, and they brought it up but didn't really want to talk about any of it. The students thought all this was happening to just them and that the teachers didn't count, but Becca had seen their strained, upset faces. Mr Garrick must have been quite popular and now he was dead. Shamed and dead.

'It's funny,' Miss Borders said, thoughtful. 'I remember you all in Year Seven. Hayley was quite gangly then, wasn't she?' She didn't look at Becca as she talked, her eyes still studying the painting. Becca figured it didn't take a genius to figure out why she'd picked this landscape. 'She admired you, I always thought. She always glanced your way if she said something funny.'

'I think you got that wrong,' Becca said. She put the tea

down and picked up her paintbrush and palette again, not wanting the pools of acrylic to dry. 'Natasha was our centre. She was probably looking at Tasha.'

'Oh, she looked at Tasha first, but it was a different kind of look.' She paused and sipped her tea. 'I paint portraits of people in my spare time. I understand looks.' She let out a small half-laugh, half-sigh. 'God, it feels like yesterday, but now you're all grown up. I'd only been teaching a couple of years when you started your first at Secondary. All so eager to please. No attitude. How times change.'

Becca didn't know what to say to that. She didn't know what to say to any of it. She was fond of Miss Borders, but what could she possibly understand about them? She probably didn't even remember her friends from when she was at school.

'It's very rare for Year Sevens to fall out the way you did, you know?' This time the teacher did look at Becca, but it wasn't a pitying look. They could have been talking about some TV show rather than the slow destruction of teenage lives. It was just a chat. A thoughtful chat, but that was all. It made Becca feel a bit better. 'There are arguments and tears and they fall out and make up,' Miss Borders continued, 'but Year Sevens are normally still too much in awe of the *big school* to get really bitchy. That stuff kicks in around Year Nine.'

'I must have just been unlucky,' Becca muttered. She leaned forward, concentrating on a small patch where the river met the bank.

'It's odd.' Miss Borders had settled in. She was obviously going to talk for as long as it took to drink her tea. 'How things have turned out. Of the three of you it was only Natasha I didn't like. I shouldn't say that, I know. Unprofessional.'

She winked at Becca. 'But it's true. I still don't, if I'm honest, even after everything she's survived. She always struck me as spoilt. Children shouldn't be allowed to have everything they want. It's not good for the character. And I'm not sure hers was too pleasant to start with.'

'Tasha's parents are pretty nice,' Becca said. Even now, she was still defending her.

'I'm sure they are.'

'But you're right,' Becca conceded. 'She's got them wrapped round her little finger.'

'Not just them.' Miss Borders leaned back slightly on her stool. 'I never understood why you two – and then Jenny – were so in awe of her. She didn't strike me as being all that much to write home about. You and Hayley, well, you were proper kids. And there in the middle was Natasha. So contained.'

'I don't really remember,' Becca said. 'We were just kids.' She didn't look up from her painting but she had a feeling Miss Borders was giving her a *Yeah, right* kind of look.

'She was very pretty, though. So was Jenny, when she turned up. And Hayley had that cool beauty of hers. Long before any of you noticed, it was there bubbling under her skin waiting for her cheekbones to rise to prominence. I would love to do a portrait of Hayley.'

'You probably could now. It's not like her schedule's that busy.'

'Cattiness doesn't suit you, Rebecca.'

'After what she did?'

There were a few moments' silence after that, and at first Becca thought Miss Borders was feeling awkward, but then she realised she was still drifting through her memories, sifting and sorting them.

'Hayley was so upset when you all fell out.'

'Not that upset,' Becca said, and shrugged.

'Oh, she was. It was the only time I saw her stand up to Natasha. No one else ever did.' She looked at Becca, a warm smile on her face. 'Not even you. Everyone just followed her around. But when you fell out and you started sitting in Art on your own, and little Jenny was in your seat, Hayley was upset. She tried to make it better but Natasha wouldn't allow it. I used to listen to them at lunch, Hayley pleading for you. And then one day, I think Hayley just gave up. I saw her crying in the corridor and asked her what was wrong but she wouldn't say. I asked if it was to do with you and tried to talk to her about friendships but she said I didn't understand. After that she became cooler. In all senses of the word. The start of the Hitchcock blonde.'

Becca didn't know what a Hitchcock blonde was, but she knew what Miss Borders meant: the start of the Barbies.

'Brains, beauty and sex, those three together. Quite something to watch them growing up.'

'Yeah,' Becca said. 'I guess.' She was starting to feel disgruntled. Even Miss Borders was infatuated with the Barbies.

'Ah,' the teacher said, picking up on her mood, 'but those traits aside, they are – they *were* – absolutely contrived, while you are your own creation. You're who you're supposed to be. Your style is your own. There's more to admire in that. It's artistry. It's probably why Natasha gravitated back to you when she lost her memory. People need truth.'

Becca listened carefully for some edge of pity or condescension but couldn't find it. These were the kindest words someone who wasn't family had said to her in what felt like forever.

'I've been thinking about them since all this happened. Well, them and you. And through everything – and it's a terrible thing to say – I find myself feeling sorry for Hayley more than Natasha.' She got to her feet. 'I guess I still see that gangly, awkward little girl sobbing her eyes out in the corridor. Funny how these things can affect us for so long.' She paused. 'I think you were actually lucky you got away from them.'

'Well, being dragged back in certainly hasn't done me any good.' Becca tried to smile. Dragged back was an exaggeration and everyone knew it. Becca had launched herself at Tasha, whether she'd admitted it to herself at the time or not.

'She's always been so controlling,' Miss Borders mused, stretching a little. 'Some women are game-players and Natasha Howland was born to it. You were taken off the board and Jenny brought on.'

'Like a new queen in chess,' Becca said.

'Yes, I suppose so.' The Art teacher picked up her cup. 'But I suspect that in Natasha's eyes, everyone else on the board is a pawn. She's replaced her friends quickly enough.' She put her hand on Becca's shoulder. 'It must not feel like it now, but all this will fade.'

And there it was. The adult moment. Becca smiled and then put her paintbrush down.

'I know. You're right.' She didn't know that at all, but it would make Miss Borders feel better if she said so. 'I think maybe I'll clean this up and head out for some fresh air.'

'I'll take care of it. You go. A walk will do you good.'

The smile felt like a grimace on Becca's face but she kept it up, despite wanting to scream, '*No, what would do me good is for my boyfriend to come back and everyone else to realise that none of this was actually my fault!*'

'Thanks, Miss,' she said instead as she grabbed her coat and bag. Suddenly the warmth was claustrophobic and her favourite teacher was irritating her. Adults couldn't put anything right with words, with that smug *when you're older you'll realise* shit they always churned out. Becca sometimes wondered if maybe they'd all forgotten what it was like to really *feel* stuff. This wasn't just a playground spat. People had *died*.

With at least half an hour to go before the final bell, the playground was empty and there were no reluctant teachers doing their duty at the gates. Becca didn't look back as she walked through them, barely around the corner before lighting the leftover half of her earlier cigarette. She had no idea where to go. It was great to be out of school and away from all the bitching, but she didn't want to go home, either. She had some money but no desire to go and sit in Starbucks on her own, and anyway, within an hour people from school would arrive, and she wasn't in the mood to stare them down.

She walked idly, not really paying attention to where her feet were carrying her, her mind mulling over what the Art teacher had said. Becca hadn't realised Miss Borders paid them so much attention when they were small. How weird that she never liked Tasha. Something about that unsettled Becca – shifted the sands of her memories – and she wasn't sure why. She *knew* Tasha could be a bitch. Or could be back then, at least, so no surprises there. Maybe it was hearing how upset Hayley had been all that time ago that made her feel strange.

Maybe.

But something else was wrong. Something more recent that Miss Borders' words had brought almost to the fore of her memory, but which she couldn't quite grasp. Like Tasha clutching at the branches in the river, only in this case whatever was bugging Becca was sucked back down into the depths every time she was close to seizing it.

Maybe it was nothing. Whatever it was, it couldn't be that important. She checked her phone, for the thousandth time, to see if Aiden had texted, but of course he hadn't. A small flare of anger burned inside her. That was just rude, wasn't it? How hard could it be to send a short *thanks* or something? He was probably working, her rational brain tried to tell her, but she shoved it to one side. Aiden was a shit. That was all.

She froze when she saw the three *For Sale* signs standing rigid, wedged together as if jostling for best position, on the front lawn. She hadn't realised she'd walked this far. She'd been looking at her feet and lost in her own thoughts. Why had she come here?

She stood on the pavement and stared at the house. Hayley's house. It looked tired. A faint tint of red marred the white garage double doors, as if some paint had been scrubbed off them. Maybe it had. The recycling box outside was filled with wine and spirit bottles. It wasn't just Jenny's mum who was drinking too much these days, then. The curtains were pulled tightly across all the windows, both upstairs and downstairs. Would it be the same at the back? Were Hayley's family living in darkness, waiting for someone to buy their house and let them get away from here and start again? Judging by the number of estate agents' boards, they weren't having any luck.

Becca was suddenly sad, her body filled with a heavy, weighty ache like first-day period cramps. Maybe Aiden wasn't the only shit. Maybe she was one, too. She hadn't spared a single thought for the fallout Hayley's family faced. Or Jenny's mum. Had she been rehoused by the council? Had she moved from booze to drugs? It's not like she didn't know how to get hold of any. *Like mother, like daughter.* If Hayley's parents were getting through that many bottles in a week then anything could have happened.

She wanted to cry. For the millionth time she wondered how any of it had come to this. Tears blurred her vision and she didn't even notice the front door opening.

'You.'

The word was acid and Becca jumped, wiping her tears away quickly. 'I'm sorry, I was just—'

'Just what? Come to gawp?' Hayley's mum, her body scrawny-thin under her baggy jumper and jeans, threw the black bag into the wheelie bin in the drive. 'Maybe spray some more poison on our house?'

'I haven't . . . I wouldn't . . . I'm sorry—' Becca's face burned. Why had she come here? Why did Hayley's mum hate her? It wasn't her fault. It wasn't. She hadn't done anything. Hayley's mum stormed over until they were face to face and Becca recoiled slightly, her breath coming fast. Was she going to hit her?

'I'm sorry. I—' Not knowing what else to say, she asked, lamely, 'How is Hayley?'

Mrs Gallagher let out a bitter half-laugh. 'Like you care? Or now that you have no other friends, you suddenly want her again?'

Becca stepped back a little, shocked.

'Oh yeah, I hear things. My little girl's not the only one hated on Facebook, is she?' Hayley's mum's eyes were red-rimmed and dark circles hung so heavy from them they were saggy bags sitting on her thin cheeks. 'What's the matter? Cat got your tongue for once, Miss Detective? You think you're so clever, don't you? Well, look at what you did. Jenny's in the mental hospital and my Hayley's broken. She's on drugs, you know? Did you know that?' She pointed a skinny finger at Becca. 'She's broken.' She tapped her chest. 'In here. She barely makes sense any more, just sitting there slurring her words together. She talks about you and Jenny, though. Still cares about you. After all this. And now she won't even see me any more. She says it's no use.' She reached out and gripped Becca's arms, shaking her until her bag slid down from her shoulder. 'Do you know how that feels? Do you know how helpless I feel?'

The fight suddenly went out of her and she started to sob, hard, angry sounds, coming from deep inside her chest. She slid to the ground, a heap on the tarmac, her loose fingers trailing down Becca as she crumpled.

Becca glanced around, helpless. She felt sick and didn't know what to do. In the end, she crouched beside the fragile woman. 'You should go back inside,' she said, as gently as she could. She wanted to put an arm around her but was scared she would lash out. 'Can I help you inside?'

'She says Jenny's right.' She was staring into some private hell, and Becca wondered if she was already drunk. Maybe. 'She says it is all her fault. She shouldn't have thought they could make it okay. And now Hannah and Peter Garrick are dead.' Her words were barely more than a mewl. 'And she won't explain it to me. She just says no one will believe her. She won't see anyone.' The sobs came harder, tearing from a deep well. 'And I'm so afraid she'll die in there.'

'I'm sorry,' Becca said again. She didn't know what else to say. She wasn't sorry about Hayley, not really, but sorry for all this pain. She stayed where she was in her crouch, her legs starting to get pins and needles, until Mrs Gallagher's tears slowed. She let out a long, raggedy breath and wiped her nose with the back of her hand before looking up. She was weary, as if this kind of emotional breakdown was happening too often these days.

'I hated you,' Hayley's mum said, sitting back on her heels. 'I think maybe I still do.'

Tears stung Becca's eyes then. Adults didn't hate teenagers. They weren't supposed to. And Becca hadn't done anything wrong.

'She doesn't, though.' The woman hauled herself to her feet and Becca did the same, until they were facing each other once again. 'She thinks about you more than she thinks about me.'

Becca shook the tears away. 'What do you mean?' Why would Hayley think about her? Was she planning some kind of revenge?

'She won't let me visit any more.' The grief was threatening to overwhelm her again.

'What does she say about me?' Becca pressed.

Hayley's mum started a slow shuffle back to the front door. She paused after a few feet and turned. 'She just says, *She used Becca*, over and over.' They stared at each other, and the woman shrugged before turning away again. 'But maybe it's the drugs,' she said, the words drifting back. 'I don't know what to think any more. But I don't want to think about you.'

Forty-Eight

She half-ran all the way home, her head on fire somewhere between anxiety and hurt. She needed a quiet, private space to think. Seeing Hayley's mum like that had been horrible. She was more damaged than Amanda Alderton was at the funeral and her daughter was actually *dead*.

Hayley. The tree-climber. The ice-cool blonde. The killer. It sounded like she was going into a total meltdown wherever they had her locked up. Was it easy to get drugs in prison? Maybe. But why would Hayley lose it now? Becca remembered her so calmly climbing the ladder to adjust the stage light. No nerves then. Maybe none of it had felt real at that point. She thought of Miss Borders, quietly documenting the death of their friendships, and she felt a sharp pang for the simplicity of those early days at school. What had happened to stop Hayley defending her when Tasha replaced her with Jenny? Why had Hayley been reduced to sobbing in a corridor?

Why do you even care? she asked herself. *It was all a long time ago. You don't need anyone. You're fine on your own. Screw them.* The words were tough, and sometimes she half-believed them, but they were hollow. They were easier to believe when she had Hannah and Aiden, and when being in the cool gang was just a very distant memory. These days were different. She had fresh wounds to nurse. It was like being in Year Seven all over again, but way, way worse. But did she remember their childhood friendships as they really were? Miss Borders said they all just did as Tasha told them – is that how it was? Yes, Tasha had always been the central one, but how had Becca felt about her, really?

Her head started to throb. Her mouth was dry and she needed some water, but she didn't want to risk bumping into her mum downstairs. Instead, she tugged a piece of gum from a crumpled packet in her pocket and chewed on it, then opened the window. In the drawer by her bed were the last of her Marlboro Lights, the straights she now saved for special occasions, and she took one out. The smoke tasted good, not the petrolly head-spin of the filterless roll-ups, just warm and woody. It reminded her of Aiden. She checked her phone again. Still no text.

Bastard.

The delicious cigarette in one hand, she went to her overcrowded and untidy shelves and yanked out her old photo albums, forgotten and almost falling down the back. She hadn't looked at them in ages. But there was still something niggling at her, something half-remembered, and maybe a dip into the past would jolt it free. She turned the cardboard pages, the photos stuck to them behind cellophane. It was good to see proper photos that were hers alone, not shared with the world on Instagram and Facebook.

Grinning childish faces – hers a lot rounder then than it was now, but also a lot happier. Terrible clothes. The three of them together. A day at the beach – *whose parents took them?* – she couldn't recall, but she remembered the ten-penny machines they played and never won on. The gap in Hayley's front teeth while she waited for ever for the new tooth to grow through. Becca's sixth birthday party – not so smiley because she'd been forced to wear a purple dress she hated because her green dress got ruined and—

—and then she froze, her hand still touching the photo. *Her green dress.* How had she forgotten her perfect green dress? *It had got ruined. Natasha had ruined it and she'd blamed Hayley.*

She felt sick and her head swam slightly as she sucked in more smoke. The green dress had been a long time ago. It couldn't have any relevance to Tasha and Hayley now, surely? It was just Tasha being a spoilt child. But still. It was a jagged piece of jade lodged in her mind. It meant something. It wasn't so much what Natasha had done back then, but *how* she had done it.

She looked at the beautiful soapstone chess pieces on the board pushed to the back of her small desk, patiently waiting for the next move in the unfinished game. They'd been evenly matched when Tasha stopped playing. Now their kings were almost forgotten, staring at each other from behind their defences.

Chess.

The itch at the back of her mind came back. The sense that she'd missed something important. Something right under her nose. *Chess.* She looked again at the frozen pieces, the worm of memory wriggling through the mud to reach the surface. The chess set. The funeral.

Suddenly it was there. Clear in her head. What she'd overheard.

Natasha chose them herself, you know? Those girls were her best friends.

Is that really what Mrs Howland said? Or was her memory playing tricks on her? There was only one way to find out.

She checked her watch. If she was fast she could get to the Howland house before Natasha finished school. She lobbed her cigarette through the open window without bothering to stub it out, then rummaged in her cupboard until she found the item she needed: a red cashmere sweater, bought for her by an aunt at Christmas and definitely a size or so too small. Perfect.

She was out through the front door before her mother had time to call her back and set off at a jog. She didn't have a lot of time. Maybe Natasha had plans after school or maybe not. Becca wasn't part of that circle any more.

Only when she'd rounded the corner onto Natasha's street did she slow down. She couldn't go in panting and dripping with sweat. She needed to look normal. Steady. She leaned against the cool brick wall by the front door for a few seconds until her breathing was back to normal, then stood tall and pressed the bell.

'Rebecca!' Always Rebecca, never Bex or Becca.

'Hi, Mrs Howland.'

'Come in, come in. Natasha's not home yet.' Alison Howland was back to her elegantly stylish self, perfectly made-up and colour-coordinated even though it was just an ordinary weekday afternoon and she'd probably only been to the supermarket, if that. Maybe she'd had lunch with friends. Becca imagined Alison Howland lived a perfect, perfumed life. Even the tragedy of Natasha's fall into the river had turned out more tragic for others than for the Howlands.

Fresh magazines were piled up on top of the unused Airbook on the kitchen table but even that didn't make the room untidy – the magazines were too high class for that. Instead it looked *styled*, like in those photoshoots of famous people's homes. Relaxed rather than uptight, but still oozing with chic.

Becca held up the sweater. 'I found this at home and thought it might be Tasha's. It's not mine.'

Alison took it and examined it. 'I don't think so. She doesn't really like cashmere.' She smiled apologetically. 'It's lovely, though.'

'Oh,' Becca said. 'Maybe it was Hayley's or Jenny's.'

Alison's face tightened then, and Becca almost hated herself for the sting of pain she'd clearly caused the woman. Maybe Alison still had wounds to heal after all.

'You may as well burn it, then,' Alison said, bitter. 'They won't be wearing anything other than prison uniforms for a very long time once the trial is done.'

Becca nodded, her hot face flushing again. Alison, who must have seen her awkwardness, squeezed her shoulder. 'Oh, I'm sorry. It's not your fault. I just . . . well, it's been hard for everyone. I know Gary is hurt, too. He was very fond of them. Especially Hayley. And then they . . . they tried to . . . well. I've never seen him so upset and angry. It's the *deception*. The lies.'

'It's such a shock,' Becca muttered. She wanted to get to the subject of the bracelets but didn't know how. Should she just blurt it out? Ask about them? 'They were all so close.'

'And they were so sweet, so helpful afterwards – that's what stings the most. I *cried* with them. They sat at the hospital with her, fetched things from her room for her so we didn't have to leave her bedside. And all the time *they'd* been responsible? I still can't get my head round it sometimes. Even now. Even with it all out there.'

Becca hadn't seen the Howlands since Hannah's funeral,

and although Alison might be less upset now, none of the pain of what the girls had done had faded. She was still living in that moment when everything changed. She needed therapy more than Becca did. How would she have reacted to seeing Hayley's mum weeping on the drive outside her house? Becca hoped she'd be kind, but the icy hate she could see in Alison made her think it wouldn't have been a pretty scene. They damaged her perfect life. That wouldn't be forgiven easily. *Like mother, like daughter.*

'And I want those bracelets back,' Alison hissed. She wasn't looking at Becca any more. 'Natasha *chose* them. I told that policewoman to get them back for me but apparently I can't have them yet.'

And there it was. Becca hadn't even needed to ask. She *had* heard right at the funeral. Her face tingled and her breath caught. Tasha had said her mum chose them, but that wasn't true. Natasha had chosen them. She glanced down at her watch.

'I'd better be going,' she said. 'I've got a meeting with the counsellor in a bit.' She didn't but nor did she want to be hanging around here when Natasha came home. She'd look so *needy*. And she wanted to think.

It was only a small lie, after all. Maybe Tasha had just said her mum chose the bracelets because she didn't want Becca to feel left out. But what other small lies might she have told?

'Of course.' Alison gave her a sudden, surprising hug, which Becca returned, too shocked to do anything different. 'You were always the best of them, Rebecca. I was so sad when you all drifted apart.'

Becca said nothing, just muttered a goodbye and let herself out. She was feeling shaky. Alison Howland obviously had no idea they'd drifted apart all over again, or seen all the shit about Becca on the Internet. But then she didn't go online, according to Tasha. Never used her brand-new computer. Becca herself was reaching the conclusion that it was the best way.

'Bex?'

She looked up. *Oh, shit.*

'What are you doing here?' Tasha squinted in the low afternoon sun. It was hard to tell if she was annoyed or just struggling to see, but her tone was definitely displeased.

'I brought this.' She half-held up the jumper. 'Found it and thought it might be yours.'

'Really?' Tasha raised an eyebrow. 'That?'

Becca gritted her teeth. Tasha the bitch was back then. She had a point, though. There was a reason other than the size why Becca had never worn it. There was something middle-aged about it.

'Yeah, I should have known. I guess I . . .' She shuffled her feet and rounded her shoulders. 'I just wanted to see you. Been ages since we've talked. Wanted to check you're okay about everything.' It was the best she could come up with. And wasn't entirely untrue. It hurt that they weren't friends any more. It hurt a lot.

'I'm fine.' Tasha softened. 'I'm sorry about all that stuff on the Internet. Must be tough to have to delete all your shit.'

'I don't really care about that,' she said, although she did. Despite being free of the trolling, it was like she'd cut an arm off. Much longer and she'd be setting up fake accounts just to feel like she wasn't in an entirely different universe from the rest of the school. 'I miss hanging out, that's all. It was good being friends again.'

Tasha looked awkward, her eyes darting past Becca to her front door, seeking escape.

'I just don't feel ready, you know?'

'Sure,' Becca said. For the first time since all this started, Tasha looked insincere. 'Sure, I get it.'

'Thanks, Bex. Don't think I don't love you. I do. Without you, well, who knows how everything would be now?'

And how would that be? Becca thought. *What exactly did I do for you, Tasha? Why does Hayley think you used me?*

She shrugged. 'I'd better go.'

'Cool,' Tasha said, relieved. 'I'd better get in as well.'

Becca took about four steps away from her before turning back. 'Tash,' she called out.

'What?' The other girl was nearly at her door, moving fast.

'Why did you tell me your mum picked those bracelets you gave Hayley and Jenny?'

'What?' It was clear irritation now. She wanted Becca gone.

Well, fuck you, Miss Perfect, Becca thought, heading back towards her. *I'm still here.* 'Those friendship bracelets. When you got me the chess set. You told me your mum chose them, but she said *you* did.'

'Does it matter?' Tasha said. She put her key in the lock, looking at Becca over her shoulder. 'What difference does it make now? I don't actually remember. Did I say that? Maybe I meant we chose them together.'

'Yeah, maybe,' Becca said. She wasn't convinced. She could remember it clearly. They were in the theatre. She remembered because she'd felt so fucking special that Tasha had chosen her present and not theirs. Heat fizzed at her insides. 'You're right,' she said. 'It's nothing.'

She turned and walked away, waiting to hear the sound of

Tasha's front door shutting. It didn't come for several seconds. Tasha had watched her go.

She lied, Becca thought, and in that instant she knew it for a certainty. *She lied to me.* But why? Hayley's words, in her mum's tearful voice, echoed in her head. *She used Becca.* And then of course there was the memory of the green dress. The world trembled with possibilities Becca didn't want to examine. She didn't want to think that way. She couldn't. But this was starting to feel like the green dress all over again. Maybe they hadn't changed so much since then after all. Natasha had fooled her then. Had she fooled her all over again now?

*

That night, she smoked the last of her Marlboros out of the window and thought about Natasha's lie and Hayley's words and the green dress until her brain felt like it was being pushed through her mum's juicer. Why had Tasha lied? It wasn't a big lie. It might not mean anything. People lie all the time to save other people's feelings. Maybe she'd been feeling bad about Becca's present being less personal. It could be that. It *could*. But it didn't feel like that. And Tasha's memory might have gone but she'd not had a personality transplant. She wasn't the kind of girl to lie simply to make someone else feel better. She could still have won Becca's friendship back without it. So why would she lie?

She leaned out through the window and let the cool air tease her face. Was Hayley lying awake in her cell right now? Was she off her face on prison smack or something? Or locked up in some hospital ward to get her off it?

The bracelets. The green dress. *She used Becca, too.*

The green dress was like a tendril of weed, wrapping around

her legs and dragging her down towards the darkness where the past and the present collided.

Tasha was always the core of the group. It was true. They all had danced to Tasha's tune, as if they knew even as small children that she was the special one and their place in the world would depend on her favour. Even after the incident with the green dress, how deceptive and mean she'd been, it had remained the same. Natasha could always charm you back. Becca breathed smoke into the night air and her eyes ran over the dark shapes of the garden: the black hulk of shadow that was her dad's shed; the two-seater swing lurking by the fence; the plants rising out of the black earth. It all looked alien, sinister and unclear without daylight. A murky world.

Tasha lied. That thought wouldn't fade. And now Tasha knew that Becca knew she'd lied. Tasha, the straight A* student, the girl who breezed through her GCSEs top of the class, the chess player who did nothing without a *reason*, would not be fooled by Becca's shrugging it away. She picked up her phone and scrolled to Tasha's number. It was no longer near the top of her most recents. Ditched again. Funny that.

> Suddenly remembered
> my green dress. Crazy
> huh? All those years ago
> and I think about it now.
> Wonder why.

She typed the words fast and then pressed 'send'. She flicked the cigarette butt through the window, closed it and lay on her bed, her heart racing.

When her phone buzzed back so fast, she jumped.

Sorry, was working. Yeah, it's
a relief. Thanks.

Not Tasha but Aiden. She stared at the words. They were cold and distant. No kiss. It wasn't like her Aiden at all. But then, as it had turned out, he'd never really been hers at all. How could he be when he'd kept so much from her? She hated herself for having texted him in the first place. Why was she so weak? Why was she such an idiot? She flicked off the light and raged and burned into the night, fighting the urge to reactivate her Facebook page just to see what was going on in his world. In the end she turned her phone off and put it on the other side of the room on top of her wardrobe so she couldn't get to it easily. She felt sick. Why was heartache so hard to get rid of?

Forty-Nine

The next day she missed the morning at school to go and navel-gaze with the well-meaning but monotonous Dr Harvey. She didn't talk about seeing Hayley's mum or Tasha's. She didn't talk about the green dress. She didn't talk much at all, and in the end pleaded a headache to cut the session short. The afternoon passed in a haze of English, the ghost of Mr Garrick still hovering over the class, and especially over the shoulder of the nervous and twitchy supply teacher who had taken his place. She was good enough as a teacher, Becca figured, but she didn't have any history with them, and the ghoulish look on her face whenever her eyes rested on Becca told them all that she'd studied the newspapers avidly for every detail of the morbid saga that had affected so many of the class.

Becca kept her head down and let the lesson drift over her. Tasha hadn't got back to her. She couldn't decide if that was weird, or if she was now so low down in the hive's social structure that she didn't even warrant an *I have no idea what you're talking about* text. Maybe Tasha didn't remember. Becca hadn't until she'd seen the photo. But surely she'd have remembered as soon as Becca mentioned it? After all, Tasha had got in proper trouble with her mum over it. One of the rare times her parents ever really told her off. Maybe she was still figuring out how to respond. Maybe it was all just craziness in Becca's head.

When the bell went, she ambled to her locker to dump her books and spotted the new Barbies, Jodie and Vicki, up ahead. She groaned internally. It wasn't that they were bitchy to her – she didn't merit enough attention for that – but she was well aware of their disdain. If anything, these two were worse than Hayley and Jenny. They knew they were the second choice and had no intention of losing their new prestige, or missing a moment to revel in it.

They glanced her way and then giggled together, gossiping. Becca opened her locker door to block them out but their words still drifted her way.

She's meeting him in Starbucks – like NOW.

I can't believe she fancies him but she says he's been really sweet.

I know! Mark Pritchard's going to be so fucked off when he hears.

Mark's way better-looking.

Yeah, but guitarists must be good with their fingers.

God, you're disgusting!

Becca's stomach churned. *She. She. She.* There was only one *She* who could dominate their conversation like that. Only one *She* Mark Pritchard had mooned around after. Natasha.

Guitarists' fingers.

Unsure if she was going to throw up or not, she slammed her locker shut and hurried outside. She needed fresh air and a cigarette. Aiden. They were talking about Aiden. Aiden and Natasha. Her palms burst into a nervous sweat. It couldn't be true. They couldn't be going on a date, could they? He wouldn't, would he?

Starbucks. That's what the bitches had said. She was meeting him in Starbucks *right now*. Had they meant her to overhear it? To stick a little knife in her already broken heart and twist it? She bet they had. It wasn't enough to cut her out, they needed to cut her down, too.

Aiden wouldn't do that to her. Her feet pounded the pavement hard, sticking just the walking side of a jog, not wanting to look too desperate. He wouldn't. He'd know how much it would hurt her, and she might have been a bit mental sometimes but he had no reason to want to hurt her any more than he had by breaking her heart. Surely he wouldn't have asked Tasha out. Surely he wouldn't?

But he had.

That became very clear when she stared through the glass. His back was to the window, but it was Aiden's black leather jacket and Aiden's beautiful dark hair. His elbows were on the table, and as she watched, Tasha leaned forward and took his hands, her perfect head tilted sideways, blonde hair tumbling down one side of her face. She was smiling, and then she laughed at something he'd said, and Becca could almost hear it, flirtatious and oh so confident. So not-Becca.

Becca wanted to storm inside and pull that blonde hair out by its dark roots. She wanted to scream in rage and hurt and anger. She wanted to kill them both. She got out her phone and jabbed a text to Aiden.

Really? Really? Tasha?? I knew
you fancied her. I KNEW IT.
Can't believe you'd do this.
I can't believe you'd hurt me

like this. You're a shit. You're
both shits!

Her fingers trembled as she punched 'send'. Her nose was running with the shock. Through the glass, she saw Aiden glance at his phone. In that instant, Becca's eyes met Tasha's. They stared at each other, the winner and the loser, the way it had always been. Tasha smiled. A knowing smile. It was like a slap in the face.

Becca turned and ran.

She didn't even know she was crying until she got home. She didn't want to stop running. She wanted to run and run until she was on the other side of the world from Brackston and all its poison. How could he do this to her? How could he? Her phone buzzed. Aiden.

What is the matter with
you???? It's COFFEE. No biggie.
Jesus fuck Becca. What is it with
you??? You're fucking mental.
Are you stalking me?

She cried afresh then. There wasn't even hatred in his text. It was irritation and that was worse. She was *annoying* him. That was all. There wasn't even enough emotion there to make him hate her. She'd made herself look stupid *again* and this time Tasha knew about it. They were together. No way he'd got that text and not showed her.

God, she just wanted to die. She stormed up to her bedroom and slammed the door, not caring if it was childish. She flopped face down on her bed and sobbed until her pillow was a damp mess of tears and snot. She didn't care about Tasha's lie, she didn't care about Hayley's words, she didn't care about that stupid green dress. None of it mattered and it didn't make sense anyway. This, though, *this* was all real. If her life had been over before, it was doubly over now. Tasha would tell Vicki and Jodie about it, and they'd tell the rest of the school. It was probably all over the Internet already. Everyone would be laughing at her. Jealous, mental Becca Crisp.

She missed Hannah. Suddenly. Sharply. Hannah would have been able to calm her down. If Hannah hadn't died then none of this shit would even be happening. Maybe she and Aiden would still be together. She took a deep breath before her overwhelming self-pity started to make this all Hannah's fault. It was *her own* fault. Her fault for being mental. And Aiden's for being a lying bastard. And Tasha's for being the sort of girl who always got what she wanted so easily.

She hated them all. She hated herself. No more overthinking it.

She dragged herself down for dinner, pretending to eat and avoiding conversation, and when her mum asked what was the matter, she just shrugged and said she missed Hannah. It was the easiest way to get them to stop talking to her. Her parents were as shit at talking about their emotions as she was. The last thing she wanted was to tell them Aiden and Tasha had been on a date. She could manage without *their* pity.

Later that night she got a text from Casey saying she should know she was getting trashed again on Twitter. Vicki and Jodie's feeds were full of stuff saying she'd gone properly mental over Aiden. Facebook, too. She buried her head in the pillow and hated herself all over again. Why would Casey tell her that? Admittedly, Casey was almost the only person who was still civil to Becca – probably because she'd been through that whole *Is Casey Morrison a dyke?* stuff back in Year Ten so knew how it felt. But still: why tell Becca that shit was going on? Maybe Casey thought Becca should man up about it. Get back online and face it.

She stared at her phone. She didn't care what people were saying about her, not so much, anyway, but her curiosity about Tasha and Aiden was overwhelming. Would their Facebooks say *in a relationship*? Did she want to see? Maybe they'd see she was online again and immediately unfriend her. Would that be such a bad thing? The thought of Aiden ditching her on Facebook made her stomach flip again. She'd look quickly and then deactivate again. *Two minutes*, she promised herself. *Just to know.*

So she took a deep breath and logged in.

Fifty

'So, do you fancy doing it again?' Jamie said as they strolled up the gravel path to the house. Although their evening had been good, the tension easing after the first glass of wine, he felt like a teenager now, awkward and stumbling. He'd just suggested a drink and maybe some food, a vague request that didn't have to be seen as a date, but asking her a second time stripped that pretence away. He was way too out of practice at all this. But at least they had the law in common, even if she'd been more interested in his music, which was a pleasant surprise.

'Sure,' Caitlin Bennett said, and smiled at him. 'Why not?'

He grinned. 'Great. I could do this weekend?'

She was about to answer when the arguing from inside his house distracted them both.

'You got visitors?' she said quietly. Her demeanour had changed, a tension in her stance that made her suddenly a policewoman again.

'Aiden's staying for a while, but that's it.'

'Girl trouble?'

'Sounds like it.'

They were nearly at the front door when it opened and Aiden almost shoved Becca out through it. She was sobbing, and under the security light Jamie could see that her face was blotchy.

'You are all over her on Facebook!' she shouted. 'Liking everything. You added her even before we'd broken up! I knew you still liked her! I *knew* it!'

'She added me,' Aiden sounded weary. 'But you're not listening. I didn't *still* like her. But at least she's not mental. She gives me some space.'

'You guys okay?' Jamie said. It was a stupid question. Okay was something they clearly weren't. Aiden had told him they'd split up and that Natasha had been messaging him, but apparently Becca was still really hurt.

'I'm going,' Becca said. She saw Caitlin and in her surprise almost said something, then stopped herself. Their arrival had taken the wind out of her anger, though, and she turned to leave, nearly tripping over Biscuit, who was hovering by her ankles, unhappy at her upset. She crouched and fussed him for a second, hiding her face, before storming past them all. Biscuit whined, watching her go. *Yeah*, Jamie wanted to say, *I wish we could make it better with a face-lick and a waggy tail. But life's not quite like that.*

He was glad he wasn't a teenager. He might be out of practice at the dating thing, but at least both he and Caitlin were old enough and cynical enough to know that sometimes things work and sometimes shit gets in the way. There were no promises of love forever after, not really.

'Sorry,' Aiden mumbled as Caitlin said goodnight and left them to it. She'd only drunk one glass of wine and her car was still here. What had started as a routine follow-up visit had turned into a great evening, and part of him had hoped maybe she'd come in for coffee and they wouldn't have to say goodbye quite yet, but Becca's histrionics had put paid to that. Still, she'd said yes to another date, so it wasn't all bad.

'What happened?'

'Just Becca being Becca.'

'She still getting all that hassle on the Internet?' Jamie felt a bit sorry for her – she'd had a rough ride and now somehow she'd become almost as vilified as the two girls who were guilty, and that was crazy.

'A bit. She's not on there much, though. I don't know why she went on tonight. She's just going to make herself feel worse by looking at it.' He lit the butt of a joint and inhaled.

'And what about you and Natasha?' He felt like a parent more than a friend, carefully navigating the minefield of teenagers' lives to see what was going on. 'Is that turning into a thing?'

Aiden shrugged. 'She's hot and everything, but I don't know. It's not a thing. But she's different. Confident. And she totally came after me; I didn't chase her, whatever Becca thinks.' He paused, then the shadows clouding his face cleared and he looked at Jamie through the smoke. 'What about you and the detective, then? Where have you two been till this time of night?'

Jamie laughed at the sudden role reversal. 'It was just a friendly dinner.'

'Yeah, right,' Aiden said. He looked like he was about to say more when his phone buzzed.

'Becca?' Jamie asked. Aiden shook his head.

'Tasha.'

'I'll leave you to it, Casanova,' Jamie said and headed with Biscuit to the sitting room. He should probably send Caitlin a text himself. Just a *Thanks for a great night*. Something like that. Something casual. Something that hopefully didn't make him sound like too much of an idiot. He smiled to himself. Maybe he should ask Aiden's advice.

Fifty-One

Anyway, I'm sorry. Feel like it's my fault. I'm totally going to kill Jodie and Vix tomorrow. They shouldn't stir shit up online. It's so year six. X

I press send and wait. I'm sitting on my bed in the dark, but the curtains are open and the moon is full and low, throwing a fractured pool of light onto the carpet, splintered into white streaks by the thick branches of the tree outside.

11.45

Aiden

Not your fault! U've done nothing wrong. She's mental. Just unlucky she saw us. Forget it. X

11.46

Tasha

As long as you're OK. X

11.49
Aiden
Yeah just embarrassed she was so mad in front of Jamie and that policewoman. At least she left then. X

11.49
Tasha
Bennett was there? X

I'm surprised by this. What did she want? Why is she still hanging around here?

11.50
Aiden
Think they were on a date. Pretty sure Jamie's hot for her.

11.51
Tasha
Gross!;-)

I smile, relieved. It is pretty gross. Caitlin Bennett probably doesn't even shave her legs. But it's also kind of perfect. Bennett seeing Becca's hysterics – that's a lucky bonus.

11.51
Aiden
Yeah!

I bite my bottom lip and my fingers fly over the keyboard.

11.52
Tasha
If you want to do coffee and
whatever again, just let me know.
Really enjoyed it;-)xx

11.55
Aiden
Me too xx

Like he has to tell me he enjoyed it. Of course he did. I know this already. Like everyone else, he's so predictable.

11.57
Tasha
Night;-)

11.58
Aiden
Night xx

I think about how I kissed Aiden this afternoon after Becca saw us in Starbucks. He drove me home and I leaned across in the car that smelled of leather and sweet weed and tobacco, and then his lips were on mine. It was easy. And it wasn't as bad as I'd expected. He didn't try and force his tongue down my throat like Mark Pritchard had. Maybe he was just surprised, but he was gentle. I don't know quite what to make of it. Perhaps I shouldn't think about it at all.

I should go to sleep, or at least try to. I need more than the three or four hours a night I'm getting and it's wearing me down. I'm sure Dr Harvey would have plenty to say about it if I went back to her, but I have no intention of doing that. I look over at the chessboard, the white and black pieces neatly lined up and ready for battle again. Becca doesn't know it but I finished the game against her a while ago – me against me. I tried to think like her for her pieces. My side still won. Now that game is over. Done.

Becca has unsettled me, though. That question about the bracelets first. I could see she was upset but that's no big deal. It doesn't really mean anything – we're not friends now, anyway. But the green dress? I'd forgotten about that. Why bring it up? Why suddenly remember something I did all those years ago? If she misses hanging out with me so much, why bring *that* up? Hardly our happiest friendship memory. What did she *want* from that text? What did she expect me to say in reply? Was it a warning shot?

I stare at the neatly organised chequered board. In my head I make my opening gambit, thinking through all the eventualities, my mind always at least three moves ahead, constantly studying the board, deciding which pieces to sacrifice and which to save. It's second nature to me. I almost text Becca, but I don't. Silence is golden. If this is a fresh game we're playing, then I'm already winning.

My eyes itch with tiredness and I lie back and stare up at the ceiling. Moonlight slashes across the paintwork. I count the shards of light. Thirteen. Of course. Everything I count always comes to thirteen. I force my eyes to stay open. The darkness is waiting for me in my sleep, whispering to me, and I won't go there. I won't. I count to thirteen again and wonder why I'm so afraid.

Fifty-Two

After drifting off in a pool of shameful tears for an hour or so when she finally got home and into bed, Becca barely slept. In her restless dreams she relived that moment over and over – seeing Aiden and Tasha together through the Starbucks window. The hand-touching. That look from Tasha. In her dreams she was filled with rage, beating her anger against the glass until her fists bled. The glass held. She was kept from them and her frustration made her murderous. She wanted to kill them. She burned to.

She woke in a sweat, confused and disorientated in the dark, but her brain was fizzing. A moment of clarity amidst all the stupidity – *her* stupidity. That look on Tasha's face when she saw Becca. That small smile.

As if she'd been expecting her.

She opened the window and rolled a cigarette and lit it with shaking hands. She needed to think clearly. Maybe she was getting paranoid or actually going crazy or something, but her mind was knotted and needed untangling. What had Aiden said to her last night? When she was screaming and shouting at him, trying to punch him, before Jamie and Bennett came back? She ignored the instinct to cringe at her own behaviour and focused on his words instead.

Natasha had added Aiden to Facebook.

Natasha had asked him to go for coffee.

She'd started liking his photos first.

Maybe he was lying. Maybe. But Becca kept thinking about that look on Tasha's face through the glass. A quiet self-congratulation. A triumph. What had Miss Borders said?

I suspect that in Natasha's eyes, everyone else on the board is a pawn.

Wide awake now, Becca flicked her bedside light on and grabbed some paper and a pen. She needed to try and put her thoughts in some order.

We're all pawns was the first thing she wrote.

Aiden, Me.

Hayley? Jenny???

Hannah??

She lied about the bracelets. Why? To make me her friend.

Hayley says, 'She used Becca.' Maybe not talking about Tasha but who else could it be?

After catching the bracelet lie, I texted about the green dress incident. No answer.

BUT then she has coffee with Aiden. I saw them.

She paused, dragging hard on the tobacco until she heard the paper crackle as it burned. The big *Why?* kept itching at her but she ignored it. This wasn't about reasoning or figuring anything out. This was about putting events in order. Looking behind the scenes of those events. Behind the scenes was her skill.

But not by chance. I heard Vicki and Jodie talking about it. Exact details of where. Enough so I know it's Aiden.

Guitarists' fingers. Did she tell them to do that? Make sure I heard? Maybe slagged me off? Everyone hates me anyway.

But they'd do it just to please her.

WHY???

She leaned back against her pillows. Always the whys. The big whys and the little ones – all her suppositions led to nothing without an answer. Maybe she was just seeing things that weren't there. Making crazy connections between coincidences. Maybe it was crazy—

She froze and her eyes widened slightly, a chill creeping across her skin as pieces of the puzzle locked into place in her mind. *Holy shit. Holy fucking shit.* Becca gripped the pen tightly as she scribbled, her words all haste and sharp angles.

Tasha <u>knew</u> I'd go mental when I heard about Aiden.

I call her out about the bracelet lie. She feels threatened. I send her the text about the green dress. She thinks I'm making a point/threat? <u>She's worried I know something.</u>

So she makes her move: she plans me catching her with Aiden. She gets her new Barbies to make sure I know they're at Starbucks and will go there to see for myself. (BITCHES.) Then they stir all that shit up on the Internet about my freak-out.

She knows I'll hear about the shit-storm online. That I'll look like a crazy jealous ex-girlfriend. That no one will believe a word I say.

IS THAT THE POINT?

She doesn't know what I know (what does she think I know??) so she's made me look totally mental.
It's like a game of chess. All her pieces in place in case of attack.
Pawns. We're all pawns to her.
So what is it she's afraid I know?

Satisfied, the jumbled thoughts out of her head and on the paper, she let the pen drop. To anyone else it would look crazy. She knew that. But she also knew Natasha. The *real* Natasha, not just the charismatic veneer. She'd forgotten her for a while, for a long while, in her envy and desperate need to be back in the pack. And Natasha had hidden that part of herself away. But Becca *knew* her. Maybe that's what Natasha was afraid of?

She thought of Aiden for the first time without wanting to spit nails in his eyes. Poor bastard. He was just another pawn like the rest of them.

She finished her cigarette but didn't roll a fresh one. She left the window open, though, enjoying the cold breeze. The curtains fluttered and the bright moon shone in streaks across the ceiling. She stared at them, her mind both calm and whirring as she ran over and over events. She thought of Jenny in the psychiatric ward, or wherever they'd taken her. Hayley, broken and afraid and refusing to see her mother. No one listening to a word they said. Natasha, queen of the hive again with new Barbies in tow. Becca discarded, her purpose served.

It didn't make sense yet – she knew that. And she knew she should go to sleep. She should at least try. But her heart was racing with adrenaline, her body willing morning to come around faster so she could move forward with these clues, so instead she just lay there, staring into the murky darkness and waiting for everything to become clear.

Fifty-Three

The dawn had brought clarity, and by six a.m. Becca was up and dressed and sitting at her computer, the house silent around her. She didn't check her social media – Aiden and Natasha had both unfriended her on Facebook, and there was nothing else of any use. She'd seen all she needed to see – was maybe *meant* to see – anyway. And the rest of the hive could go and jump off a cliff like the lemmings they were for all she cared. She'd make her peace with Hannah her own way.

Her notes from the night before were on the desk beside her as she searched the Internet. She knew what she was looking for: newspaper articles relating to the case. More importantly, some hint of Hayley's version of events. Everyone knew Tasha's – Becca had heard it from the horse's mouth – but in the whirl of Hannah's death and Mr Garrick's suicide, anything else had been drowned out. Maybe the papers weren't even allowed to publish Hayley's and Jenny's versions of events? Maybe their lawyers had told them not to say anything? Maybe, in light of what happened with Hannah – and that was a massive sticking point for Becca, Hayley sabotaging the light – it was all considered pretty much a done deal.

Perhaps it was as simple as: no one cared about their side of things. It could wait until their trial.

Still, Becca scoured and trawled through the myriad local and national items. Some were short, just a paragraph, others longer. She hadn't looked at the papers in the aftermath of it all. Her mum wouldn't have them in the house, and as far as Becca was concerned, she'd lived through it – why would she want to read about it? It was strange to see her own tearful face staring back at her, captured by some press man outside Hannah's funeral. Loads of photos of Tasha. None of Hayley or Jenny. Not even their names were mentioned. She scrolled and scrolled until the articles began to blur into one. The best she could find was a statement from a lawyer saying that the two teenagers charged would not be pleading guilty to either the murder or the attempted murder charges and neither had made a full confession.

She was about to give up entirely when, finally, it landed in her lap. She stared at the article from some local rag, written a few days after the arrests. Before Hannah's funeral.

. . . the mother of one of the teenage killers accused of the murder of Hannah Alderton and attempted murder of Natasha Howland, who for legal reasons cannot be named, posted the following status on Facebook (subsequently deleted) after her daughter's arrest.

'[Name redacted]'s version of events is very different and the truth will out and then you'll be sorry. Yes they went to the woods but it wasn't the way everyone's saying. There was a film. It was blackmail. My little girl didn't kill anyone and right or wrong she loved him. Screw all of you for believing that bitch. My baby is the real victim here.'

It is believed that the 16-year-old's mother developed

issues with alcohol after the breakdown of her marriage, in which a local source claims both the accused and her mother were subjected to abuse. It is unknown whether this will form part of her defence. The girl, who also cannot be named for legal reasons, is currently being evaluated to ascertain if she is mentally fit to stand trial. A police source told this reporter that no film of a relevant nature was found in Natasha Howland's possession.

Becca read it over and over until the article was burned into her mind and then she jotted down key phrases in her notes.

A film.
Blackmail.
It wasn't the way everyone says.

She stared at that for a long time. Blackmail. A film. If events that night hadn't gone as Natasha said, maybe that's why Hayley and Jenny kept quiet. This film. Did Natasha have something on them? But what? And why didn't the police find it? What could have happened during the time Natasha didn't remember? She thought back to Hayley and Jenny in the hospital. Were they upset or nervous? She hadn't spent long with them, and then they'd gone to collect some stuff for Tasha. Her mind whirred. *They went to Tasha's house alone.* Had they really been looking for this film rather than wanting to fetch music and books?

She gathered up her stuff and put the computer to sleep, her head pounding. As the shower kicked on in her parents' en suite, she ran downstairs yelling a goodbye and headed out into the fresh air to make her way towards school.

It still didn't make any sense, though. How else could it have played out, if not the way Natasha claimed? How did Hannah fit in? It had so clearly been a second attempt to kill Natasha, after they'd convinced Jenny and Hayley that Tasha's memory was coming back. They'd tried a second time because they were afraid she'd remember what they'd done to her, surely? It must have played out as Tasha said. It *must* have. They'd taunted her, drugged her, tied her up and then she'd nearly died. It was bullying gone badly wrong.

The pieces floated around her mind like a jigsaw, nothing slotting together properly. But if everything was exactly as Tasha said, why would Tasha worry about what Becca was thinking? Why set her up to go crazy after seeing her and Aiden together? And why couldn't Becca stop thinking about that ruined green dress? When she got to school, she didn't go to the sixth form room or whatever lesson she was supposed to be in, but went to the theatre instead.

She hadn't been near the place since Hannah's death and as she walked down the cool corridor she felt sick, her mouth drying and head spinning a little. She almost turned around and ran at one point, but she needed to see where it happened. She needed to remember clearly what happened to Hannah. If she couldn't make sense of it then the bracelet lie and the green-dress memory and the *She used Becca, too* all meant jack shit. They were just leftover pieces of a puzzle she couldn't quite put together and she'd be stuck forever with the feeling that everything was very, very wrong.

She took a deep breath and pushed open the door. The space was empty. Mr Jones was teaching in a different room and with the play cancelled the theatre had the air of a place forgotten. People avoided booking it for anything, and events were being held in the Sports Hall instead. No one wanted to be reminded that a girl died in here. For a while it had been locked up while the police inspected the lights and the whole rig got a new safety check, and then to keep the ghoulish Year Sevens away, but kids' interests moved on fast and, at some point, the Head must have decided the facility should be available for students and teachers to use. But of course they didn't.

The ghosts of the past flickered like an old film in front of her as she stood in the doorway. The memories came in and out of focus.

Snapping at Hannah and then storming to the control box.

Natasha feeling sick. Hannah taking her place.

The light falling.

She could almost see her own face through the viewing glass of the control box, horror and shock registering as Hannah crumpled.

The shades of their past selves shifted backwards, to that lunchtime. Jenny snapping. Becca and Tasha locked in their pact to try and unnerve their two former friends. The light needing to be moved. Hayley shimmying up the ladder. Jenny, high and edgy, snapping at Hannah. The fight that ensued. Jenny telling Hannah that Becca had been at Tasha's. Everything was exactly as she remembered it. There were no secrets to be revealed here. She turned to leave, half-afraid that Hannah's ghost would materialise and beg her to stay because she was lonely, and then paused. It came to her then. Clear as day.

She hadn't taken the caretaker's ladder and tools back.

Natasha had.

They'd all gone to lessons – everyone but Tasha. She'd

hugged Becca and thanked her for being such a good friend and said she'd take the tools back.

She'd left Tasha alone with the light, and the ladder, and everything she'd need to loosen the bolts and take the safety chain off.

The only reason Hannah had been standing there was because Tasha said she felt sick and dizzy. Had Tasha *made sure* she wasn't standing there? And then Hannah, sweet, eager-to-please Hannah stepped in. Maybe Tasha had wanted it to look like Hayley and Jenny had tried to hurt her – she hadn't suggested leaving the scene for another day – but then Hannah put herself under the light and suddenly, just like that, it became much more serious.

It was only supposed to fall, Becca thought, her legs trembling. *It was only supposed to look like they tried to hurt Tasha.*

But why?

She turned and let the heavy door slam shut behind her before leaning against it. *Why would Tasha frame them like that?* Tasha had lost her memory. At that point she didn't remember about Jenny and Mr Garrick. She couldn't remember anything from Thursday lunchtime onwards. And she *had* been pulled out of the freezing river, dead to all intents and purposes, and so lucky that Jamie McMahon had been there and found her.

Becca felt sick. Accidentally or not, she was convinced that Natasha had caused Hannah's death. More pieces of this strange puzzle that didn't fit. If they were pieces at all. Becca had no proof that Tasha moved the light. Maybe she didn't. But that look on Tasha's face through the Starbucks window kept coming back to her. As if Becca had done exactly what

Tasha expected her to. For a moment, the veil slipped and someone else shone through. But that was hardly evidence. And evidence of what? What was Becca missing? What game was being played?

The bigger question was had *she* been played? Right from the start.

And then another question struck Becca, one that made her head spin some more.

When *had* it started?

The bell rang and she pushed her way through the sudden rush of students towards her English class. Emily didn't sit with her any more, and as she walked into the small room, she could feel them all sniggering at her.

'You need to get yourself a bit of pride,' Emily said, voicing what everyone else was no doubt muttering. 'What's happened to you? Who does crazy stuff like stalking their exes? Get over it!' A few giggles at that, but Emily wasn't laughing. 'You're going to turn into one of those women who cuts her husband's dick off.'

'Oh, just fuck off,' Becca muttered as the supply teacher, Miss Rudkin, came in. It wasn't witty or clever, but it was the best she could do with a head full of much more serious things.

She slid into her seat and got out her folder of notes and the book of poems, but she also pulled out her brainstorm of recent ideas. As the class got started, she let herself drift into her own thinking. Miss Rudkin never asked her any questions anyway. She looked at her thoughts laid out before her, then picked up her pen to add to them.

There were two ways to look at this situation, Becca decided. Everything pointed to Natasha's version of events being true. *Everything* fitted her version of events. Everything fitted really neatly, the evidence slotting together and pointing to Hayley and Jenny. They were pretty much wrapped up with a bow and handed to Bennett. Mainly by Becca herself. She groaned internally at that.

Because what if you flipped it over?

What if Hayley and Jenny were telling the truth and *Natasha* was lying? How much fitted together then?

She thought about the two mobile phones which held so much incriminating evidence. The CCTV of Jenny in the shop. DI Bennett playing that game with the coat in the Head's office. Jenny's expression on seeing it there. She'd looked genuinely surprised. Not guilty. Surprised. What had Hayley said? Something about Jenny's coat having a burn on its sleeve? A blonde girl in a Primark coat bought those phones. CCTV didn't catch her face. It could have been any blonde girl.

When did Tasha dye her hair blonde???

It was a good month or so before Christmas, that was for sure. Half term in the Autumn? October? It must have been around then. She scribbled as the thoughts came to her in a jumbled surge.

What if Tasha found out about Jenny and Mr Garrick's affair <u>before</u> that Thursday? A long time before.

What if she waited? And planned?

There was a long pause before her pen moved again.

What if Natasha never lost her memory at all?

Fifty-Four

I answer Aiden's text saying I have a headache and will call later. It's a delaying tactic and I'm annoyed at myself for not just playing along. I know I should, but I just want a few minutes' peace. Jodie and Vicki are irritating me. Aiden is irritating me. They're all so fucking needy. I don't like the sound of the swear word in my head. It's like a momentary lapse of control.

I need to get a grip. I do not make mistakes. I am meticulous and always have been. I am a planner. Even in that stupid – but admittedly useful – diary I admitted that. People so often try and make themselves look *good* when they lie. That, however, should never be the point. The point should be to distract from the truth. Whether you look good or not is irrelevant. All that matters is that you sound believable.

I always knew Bennett would ask for the notebook – Dr Harvey was bound to tell her about it, and if she hadn't, I'd have slipped it into our conversation and then done exactly what I did – made a big fuss about not wanting to hand it over, but then handing it over all the same. *Voilà.*

There's a lot of honesty in that notebook DI Bennett took away with her. My thoughts on my family, sex and my fear of sleeping – that's all true. As are all the conversations I wrote down. It's easy to lie when you've created the situation to begin with, and the best lies are half-truths anyway.

*

I can hear my mother calling me for dinner and her voice reminds me that no one likes a perfect person anyway. They're either too uptight – like my mother – or too sweet. Sweet girls have no friends. Look at Hannah. I try not to think about Hannah. She wasn't part of the plan. She inserted herself into my plan. To be fair to me, the light was an improvisation. I plotted everything else out meticulously, but the light just presented itself and I couldn't resist.

And now there really *is* a murder charge. Poor Hayley. Poor Jenny. That wasn't supposed to happen. I'd been angry with them, but I only wanted to teach them a lesson. Have them publicly shamed; excluded, maybe. A couple of years of counselling for a bullying incident that got out of hand. I wasn't supposed to die. That instantly made it all more serious, but I could have kept that under control. Blamed myself.

Hannah, however, has changed things. And this irritates me, too, but I can't do anything about that now and perhaps it's better this way. I doubt Hayley, Jenny and I could be friends again, nice as the thought is, whether I'd taught them a two-year lesson or a lifetime one. It's all their fault, anyway. If they hadn't been planning to discard me as if I was some nobody like Hannah Alderton instead of the one who *made* them, then I wouldn't have needed to do anything. They were prepared to humiliate me. Everyone wants to be my friend. *Everyone.* They always have. How dare they think they were better than that? They started all this by thinking they didn't need me any more. And as for Hannah, well, it's not like I forced her to stand under that light. And she was never going to be anything more than a candle waiting for snuffing. I never see the point in people like Hannah.

Becca. I wonder what is going on in Becca's crazy jealous little head. Becca is the cause of my strange mood, I know it. I just want to get back to normal, but along comes Bex with her mentions of green dresses and lies and then this afternoon, when we were leaving school, she comes right up to me and asks when I'm dying my hair brown again.

It's not like you need to be blonde any more, is it?

That's what she said. There was a challenge in her eyes, I'm sure of it. Was she expecting me to react? To give something away? If so, then she's as stupid as her tobacco-stinking needy ex-boyfriend.

Or was it something else? Was she trying to let me know something? But what? How much can she know? The green-dress situation is similar – even if the outcome this time has been somewhat more dramatic. I set Hayley up to take the blame then, too. Becca remembers that. But even if she's got suspicions she can't prove anything. Can she? I'm not sure if my uncertainty about her intentions is disturbing me or entertaining me. It's not like she can harm me. Not now. It's done. The game is over. And she's still doing exactly what is expected of her. Her jealous rage was perfect. No one will believe a word she says even if she does know something. Her reaction was so predictable.

Everyone is so predictable.

My mum calls again. 'In a minute!' I shout back. She's mouse-like now. I see worry in her eyes all the time and I wonder how she could have given birth to me, raised me, and still not *see me* at all.

But I guess she does have some cause for concern. I was technically dead for thirteen minutes and, precise as I had been in my planning, that was unexpected.

Thirteen minutes. Maybe that's why I see the thirteens everywhere. A reminder of how close everything came to ending. To the joke being on me. It wasn't even my fault. I guess it goes to show – the best laid plans of mice and men . . .

I still get angry thinking about those extra five minutes I spent in the water. If I could get away with it, I think I'd kill that dog. I remember that class hamster in Year One. The one that bit me and made my finger bleed. The one Hannah Alderton loved so much. How I broke its neck, even as it squealed and wriggled in my hands. I would like to do that to the dog. I still might, one day, when all of this is forgotten.

All my careful planning. All those early-morning runs through the woods and the park, watching who was out regularly, who walks dogs, or walks to work, or is just some insomniac who can't sleep. I had it all timed to the minute and Jamie McMahon and that mongrel dog were like clockwork. I watched them from behind the trees across the river, saw where the dog likes to nosey down by the banks. McMahon sometimes on his phone – which was perfect. I'd need him to have a working phone. Every day the same time. Apart from that day. *My* day. The day I needed them there. The dog hid his collar *that* day. When I went to give gushing thanks with Mum and had to pet it, I wanted to snap its scruffy neck.

Still, even if it did suddenly raise the stakes for Hayley and Jenny, I didn't die for good and it was far more effective than just feigning unconsciousness for a moment. No one questioned my amnesia. I still stuck to my plan. Even when

Dr Harvey suggested hypnosis, I had an answer for that. *Too much like drowning.*

I'm quite proud of the way I continued so calmly, even though I don't really feel proud of things I've achieved in the way that other people do. I am sometimes *satisfied*, but that's different. I did die, though, and I still woke up and got on with having everything unravel as planned, so I think a little bit of pride is allowed. I planned it all and even with the odd glitch it's unfolded perfectly.

I wonder if I should do something about Becca. Something final. The thought feels less extreme after what happened with Hannah. In for a penny, in for a pound, after all. But I decide against it. Not yet, anyway. I've made Becca a joke. No one takes her seriously. And I'm not sure what her intentions are yet – she may not know anything at all. And if I'm honest, I'm quite enjoying her occasional unpredictability.

I go to the bathroom and put some drops in my eyes before heading down for dinner. It doesn't ease their tired burn. I need to stop being afraid to sleep. I need to stop being afraid of whatever is waiting for me in the darkness. Being afraid was never part of my plan. Being afraid is not who I am.

Fifty-Five

This time Becca left the house before her mum was even awake. It was just gone seven a.m. but she'd been up, pacing and thinking, for hours. She'd sent Aiden one text at about two in the morning – *Be careful* – but didn't hear back. He might have told Tasha about it, and fine by her if he did. This was no longer about Aiden, and she found that her anger and hurt were melting away to nothing. She just felt a bit sorry for him. He was being used exactly like she had been.

She needed to do two things before school. The first was the hardest, but she had to do it if she was going to understand what happened with those two mobile phones.

'What do you want?'

Hayley's mum was up but she looked like death.

'Who is it?' Hayley's dad loomed large in the background before coming into view. 'Oh. You.'

Becca's heart thumped hard and her face burned, but she forced herself to speak. 'I'm sorry, I just need to ask you something. It's important. It might help Hayley.'

'You've done a great job so far.' His voice held so much disdain for her – he couldn't even muster hate. She must look pathetic. Some little puppy dog of Natasha's who'd helped put their daughter in prison. And they were right.

'Did Natasha ever come here?' She pushed on, not wanting to give them time to slam the door in her face before she asked her question. 'After she was found in the river. On her own?'

They stared at her for a moment, and then Hayley's mum sighed. 'No. No, she didn't. She didn't even come here with Hayley. She was *your* friend by then. She hadn't been here for a while *before* her accident. Only Jenny.'

Becca felt a surge of disappointment. If Tasha hadn't come here, then it was stalemate, and maybe she *was* just on some major paranoia jag.

'You're sure?' she asked.

'Yes, I'm sure,' Hayley's mum repeated. 'Now fuck off.' The words, tired and loaded with grief, were like a heavyweight punch in the solar plexus and Becca instantly took two steps back. You didn't hear those words from someone's mum. Not in Becca's nice middle-class life.

'I'm sorry. I was just trying to help. I'm sorry.'

'Leave us alone,' Hayley's dad grumbled, and he leaned across his wife to close the door. 'You've done enough damage already.'

'Wait.'

The word was barely more than a breath.

'Wait,' Hayley's mum said again. She looked at Becca; a fragile, fluttering broken bird.

'There was one time. When she brought the bracelet. Hayley was still at school and I was here on my own.'

Becca's heart leapt; a dog tugging at a leash with excitement. 'Did she give it to you?'

'No.' The woman's eyes crinkled as she remembered. 'No, I stayed downstairs. She went up to Hayley's bedroom and left the gift box on her pillow. I remember thinking how sweet it was.'

Becca grinned. She couldn't help it. She must have looked crazy, standing there in the face of all their heartache smiling like a loon. 'Thank you,' she said. 'Thank you.' She turned and left them staring after her, hurrying down the street. It wasn't a stalemate at all. In fact, the pieces were nearly in place for the endgame.

'Why does it matter?' Mrs Gallagher shouted after her. 'What difference does it make?' Becca didn't answer. Maybe they'd figure it out for themselves. First she needed to *prove* it.

*

DI Bennett was no use. Becca got a bus into town and was at the Police Station by eight a.m., and waited fifteen minutes before Bennett arrived. She came in clutching a take-away coffee and looking like she hadn't slept much.

'Rebecca? What are you doing here?'

'I need to talk to you. About the CCTV footage.'

The detective frowned, confused. 'Why? I'm working on another case now. Everything has gone to the prosecution services.'

'Did you just look at cameras in the phone shop? Did you follow the girl out? Or check Primark's cameras?'

'Rebecca, is this because Natasha is seeing Aiden now? I know it hurts, but—'

'It's got nothing to do with that!' Becca wanted to thump her and her faux sympathy just to get her to *listen*. 'It's about the coat. You said it yourself: it was a cheap coat. There were hundreds of them. How can you be absolutely sure it was Jenny wearing it? How do you know someone else didn't buy it in Primark and wear it to look like Jenny? Hayley, Jenny and Natasha are *all* blondes. Could you tell them apart from a distance? In a grainy camera shot? Honestly?'

'Look, the case is closed,' Bennett said. 'And with no small thanks to you. Let it go. Get on with your life.'

'Hayley might not have been the last person to touch the light that killed Hannah,' Becca said, defiant. 'We had lessons but Natasha had a free. She said she'd take the tools back, so we left her there. We left Natasha by the light with the tools and the ladder.'

Bennett stared at her in shocked disbelief. 'Are you trying to tell me you think Natasha bought the phones, and that Natasha killed Hannah?'

'That's exactly what I think.'

They stared at each other for a long moment in the hubbub of the desk sergeant's reception area. Bennett hadn't even invited her inside to talk. She clearly saw Becca as a nuisance.

'When is your next appointment with Doctor Harvey?' the policewoman said, eventually, and Becca burst into frustrated laughter.

'I know what you think. You think this is because of Aiden. That I'm angry and jealous and crazy, and maybe I am all of those things, a little bit. I know I've made myself look really stupid. But this . . . it isn't that.'

'Go to school, Rebecca.' Bennett was getting impatient. 'Don't make things worse for yourself.'

Becca smiled at her bitterly and shrugged, starting to walk away. She hadn't really expected anything different. 'Doesn't it bother you?' she said over her shoulder before the woman could disappear through the main doors and into the hub of the building.

'What?'

'How neat it all was? The receipt in the locker? The phones in their bedrooms, still with all those texts on them? The evidence might as well have been wrapped up in a bow and given as a gift. It basically was. And I delivered it. And don't you find those texts odd? I bet they stopped immediately after the night Natasha went in the river. Nothing more after that? Don't you think that's weird?' She stared at the policewoman but got no reaction.

Bennett said nothing for a long moment and then repeated, 'Go to school, Becca,' and let the door close. Becca stood outside in the sunshine and rolled a cigarette.

So that hadn't worked. It was time for Plan B.

The evidence Bennett didn't have.

The film Jenny's mum talked about in that deleted status update.

That was the key.

They said the police hadn't found it, and for a while Becca had thought Tasha must have got rid of it somehow. But then she remembered the box of mementos under Tasha's bed, full of stuff from years gone by. Natasha *kept* things. She would have kept that film somewhere, whatever it was. Kept it for insurance against Hayley and Jenny speaking up if nothing else. And having spent the whole night lying awake thinking about it, Becca was pretty sure she knew where it was hidden.

She smiled. She was excited, she couldn't help it. In some ways, she was glad Bennett hadn't taken her seriously. That would have been the sensible route. But this way, she'd be able to play her own game. *Time to get even, Tasha*, she thought. *This time it's definitely my move.*

She checked her watch. She had a lot to do today.

Fifty-Six

Excerpt of CONSULTATION BETWEEN DR ANNABEL HARVEY AND PATIENT REBECCA CRISP, MONDAY 04/04, 15.30

DR HARVEY: And what feelings do these Facebook and social media postings bring up in you? Do they make you angry?

REBECCA: They did. A bit. I haven't really thought about it much these past few days.

I've been distracted.

DR HARVEY: What by?

REBECCA: (Pause)

What's the difference between a psychopath and a sociopath?

DR HARVEY: What makes you ask that?

REBECCA: I've been thinking about motivations. Why people do things to each other.

DR HARVEY: Is this about Hayley and Jenny?

REBECCA: What's the difference between the two?

DR HARVEY: The simplest way I can put it is: a psychopath has no morals or ethics. A sociopath has morals, but their moral compass is very definitely skewed. They are both manipulators. Both can be charming.

REBECCA: Do you think you could spot one?

DR HARVEY: Which one?

REBECCA: Either.

DR HARVEY: Perhaps. Not always.

REBECCA: Why do they hurt people?

DR HARVEY: They don't always.

REBECCA: But the ones that do?

DR HARVEY: I don't believe that either Hayley or Jenny suffers from either of those disorders.

REBECCA: You assumed I was talking about them – I didn't say that. I'm just curious.

DR HARVEY: A psychopath might not need a reason. It may be just for a sense of power. The enjoyment of another's pain. A sociopath would have a reason, albeit perhaps not one that would make someone without the disorder go to such an extreme. Something that might just irritate or annoy you or me could make them want to harm a person. Each case is unique, though.

(Long pause)

Have you deleted your Facebook again? Are you feeling angry towards your peers, perhaps?

REBECCA: (Laughter)

Don't worry, I'm not planning to go all Carrie on my school. I'm just trying to figure out how someone like that would think.

DR HARVEY: Both psychopaths and sociopaths are, by the nature of their condition, essentially entirely selfish. Only selfish motivations make sense to them.

REBECCA: I see.

DR HARVEY: I'm not sure this is a healthy interest for you at the moment. Have you thought any more about trying some physical outdoor pursuits? I can recommend several residential camps for young people with PTSD.

REBECCA: I really don't have that.

DR HARVEY: It's my assessment that you do.

REBECCA: (Pause)

To be honest, Doctor Harvey, I haven't got that much faith in your assessments right now. But thank you – this time you *have* been helpful.

(Rustling)

DR HARVEY: We still have twenty-five minutes left of the session.

REBECCA: I'm going to take your advice and get some fresh air.

Fifty-Seven

I found myself keeping an eye out for Becca at school today. I half-expected her to appear around a corner and look at me knowingly, like in one of those old police detective shows my mum watches on Sunday afternoons. I didn't see her, though. I went for coffee with my new Barbies after school and they asked me about Aiden, so I flirted with him a bit by text to keep them happy. They think I'm going to fuck him soon. They don't know me at all. He's hot for it, though.

I get home, throw my bag on the floor and grab some juice out of the fridge. Coffee makes me dry and feel a bit sick. I don't even know why I drink it. I drain a glass of orange juice and pour a second to take upstairs with me. The house is quiet. For once, mum's out rather than waiting for me to get in so she can cluck around me.

I think about how easy it is with boys. To get them hot. It doesn't take much, does it? I told Aiden I'd thought about him putting his fingers inside me. Vicki screeched with laughter at that – and I've told her she'll have to do something about that laugh if she wants to stay – and I blushed and smiled knowingly, rolling my eyes at her as if it was something I'd let so many boys do.

I have no intention of letting Aiden put his fingers inside me.

The thought makes me squeeze my thighs together hard. Even though his kiss wasn't so terrible, that's as far as I'm willing to go in this charade. I wonder if maybe I should feign concern for Becca and end it before it's really begun. It's served its purpose now. Becca looks crazier than ever and sounds bitter and angry at everything.

Still, even if it has served its purpose, Becca's recent behaviour makes me want to punish her.

I count as I walk up the stairs, happy when the number of steps I take rises above thirteen, and then go and flop on my bed. It's only just half-five but I'm tired. I'm also bored. Whatever else, these past few months have been interesting. Even if only to me. Now I feel a bit disappointed. It was so very easy, all things considered. And now, well, it's just *ordinary* again. There isn't even the play to look forward to. If Hannah hadn't been such a simpering idiot and stood under the light, at least it would probably have been recast and gone ahead.

I hear a buzz and look at my phone. Nothing. I sit up. After a few seconds, the buzz comes again. Definitely the sound of a text message. I rummage in my bag and there, at the bottom, snarled up with a lip gloss and some tissues, is a mobile phone. *Another* mobile phone.

I stare at it. It's cheap and basic and it's not mine. My heart races. I'm not sure if it's fear or excitement, but life has suddenly got interesting again. I click on the text icon. The handset is a dinosaur but I know my way around it. It's been carefully chosen. It's exactly like the two I bought from the One Cell Shop.

Look at all the saved messages, the text tells me, black words against a green screen. Beyond retro. I scroll through the options and click again. I look at the incoming and then the outgoing messages. There is a whole conversation here, between this phone and the one sending the instructions. Nothing out of the ordinary, just chatter. I have a long sip of my juice as I take it in. I almost smile, although not quite. My heart thumps and another text arrives.

Easy to do, isn't it?

And then another.

Guess where the receipt is?

I still don't answer.

It's in your locker. Amazing
how thin receipt paper is.
How easily it slides through
the gap around the hinges.

Becca's little brain has been working overtime. Did her memory of the green dress spark all this? Or was it the lie? I guess it's both. She enjoys puzzles, Becca. We're similar like that.

I'm quite impressed. Gold star for fat little Rebecca Crisp. But it's nothing real. She can hypothesise all she wants about phones and receipts. I'll let her make her moves and then decide what to do. She's always been an aggressive opener, but the game is won or lost in the closing moves. Time to reply:

You always did have an
overactive imagination

There's no point pretending I don't know who it is, even though there is nothing being admitted. I feel like we're watching each other over a chessboard.

:-)

I look at the old-school smiley and for the first time I feel a nub of irritation.

What's so funny?

A pause. I'm about to throw the phone into my bag in disgust when it buzzes again.

My imagination didn't invent
this film I'm watching.

I stare at it. My skin chills. She couldn't have it.

Anything missing from
home? ;-)

My breath is coming fast now with the shock and I race down to the kitchen. She can't have it. That bitch couldn't have found it. She couldn't.

Fifty-Eight

Becca stared at the sleek Airbook with the New York sticker on the front and waited, her palms almost sweating with nerves, for the next text to arrive. She had no idea if the film was on the computer or not – her attempts to crack the password had locked her out – but it was the only place she could think of where Tasha might safely save it: her mum's forgotten, unused laptop, sitting on the kitchen table.

Getting it had been relatively easy. She'd taken the keys from Tasha's bag in the Barbie corner of the common room and then sneaked in when Alison Howland went out. She'd only had to wait for half an hour or so. Then she'd dropped the keys and the pay-as-you-go phone into Tasha's bag during last lesson. It was Drama and she knew the Barbies didn't lug everything down to the studio for that. Tasha didn't, at any rate. Not when there was always an eager-to-please new Barbie's bag she could stash her mobile and purse in.

And that was it. Done. Of course, now she'd find out if it was worth it. She waited, the seconds ticking away in the silence.

You're not watching it.

Her heart dropped. Shit. Had she got it wrong?

> You couldn't break that password. I changed it. It's completely random.

Becca grinned. The game was on. She typed back.

> Okay, I fess up. I'm not watching it. But it's still on here. You know it. I know it.

She waited.

> It's perfectly explainable. Fragile memory. Maybe I filmed it that night and forgot.

Tasha was so arrogant. She was clever, but she'd never been quite as clever as she thought she was.

Possible but unlikely, Becca responded. How was Tasha feeling now? Sweaty? Irritated? Not so nice when you were the one being played.

> Probable and likely.

She was always so confident. Becca wished she could see Tasha's face when she realised how one small detail on the film could unravel her whole version of events. It all came down to

Hayley's accident. Her damaged wrist. The timings. Natasha was a planner. And the first part of her plan would have been to create something concrete she could keep and use. The film. She'd have made that before she dyed her hair and bought the phones. Which meant if Hayley was in it then her wrist was injured. Her cast didn't come off until right before Christmas. She'd be wearing it in the film.

Becca sent another smiley face, sure it would wind her ex-best friend up. Then after a moment, she added:

Rethink that. If you
haven't figured it out in
five minutes then you're
not as bright as I
imagined.

She put that phone down and picked up her iPhone. She went to Aiden's number.

Thought u should know,
Tasha will be dumping u
within the hour.

She pressed 'send' and then tossed the phone down. She didn't bother checking for a reply. Aiden wasn't important any more.

Fifty-Nine

I take four deep breaths and I hate that each of them is shaky and my hands tremble. I sit on my bed and stare at the phone. I'm missing something. Becca is never this confident. What does she know that I don't? What could she possibly be so sure about *without* seeing the film?

I run through it all in my head as I pace, needing to get rid of the nervous energy in my legs. I want to head to the woods for a run, but I can't. *Be calm*, I tell myself. This is still just a game. A dangerous one, but a game all the same. More than that, it's *my* game. And at least I'm not bored any more. I try to smile but I catch sight of myself in the mirror and I look slightly deranged. What could she know?

I took the film in the Asda car park. Same car, same man, same girls. I didn't upload it to mum's laptop until that Friday night, so it could easily be a glitch in my memory that I forgot about it. It wouldn't be great, but I can cover it.

So what is it? Oh, Becca, Becca, Becca, little fat Rebecca who still carries all those wounds around with her as if the flab still sticks, what have you thought of that I've missed?

I imagine her sitting at home, smug, waiting for me to answer. I hate being behind someone else. I'm *always* two steps ahead. I refuse to ask.

Was it something in the weather? No, both were clear, dark evenings. Nothing was different. Nothing!

And then everything stops for a moment. Even my heart. I know what it is. I know why Becca is all smiley-face-smug and patient.

Hayley's wrist.

If I'd taken the film on Thursday night, when I said I'd found out about Jenny fucking Mr Garrick, the night before I went in the river, then Hayley's wrist would be fine. But I took the film way earlier, when I *really* found out. And back then Hayley's wrist had that hard support on it.

I stare at the phone and want to stab Becca in the eyes through the crappy screen. This is enough to ruin me. It's proof and Becca knows it. If Bennett finds out that I knew about Jenny and Mr Garrick for *months* before I went into the river then everything changes. It might not explain why, but it sure as shit proves that I lied about my memory loss. And lied a lot. It's a thread that could unravel everything. It turns the tables.

A cool calm washes over me as I think about the bigger picture. Becca *hasn't* taken this to Bennett. She's come to me instead. Why?

Because locking me up can't be what Becca wants.

I stare at the chessboard in the corner, the pieces raring to go, and then send back a text.

Congratulations. Well
thought out. What's that,
a bishop you've taken?

This is still my game.

Oh come on! It's defo your queen! ;-)

I grit my teeth. My tolerance of the smileys is starting to wear thin.

So what do you want?

I wait

To start with, I want
you to dump Aiden.

I almost laugh aloud at that. Really? Surely this is worth more than *that*?

You still want him???

The answer came back fast.

No. But I think he's better
off the board. He's served
his purpose, hasn't he?

I feel something close to impressed. Perhaps I've underestimated Becca. She's right, too. It would be good to be free of him. I grab my normal phone and type out the text, almost cringing as I do so. Feel sorry for Becca, this is too soon, blah blah sweetness and light. I press 'send'. Then I text Becca on the other phone.

Done.

I almost want to thank her for freeing me from him and his potential fingering but I'm not sure she's ready for that yet. She was fond of him, after all.

What else?

A pause. She's doing it for dramatic effect which is irritatingly obvious but I let her have her moment. This game is far from played out.

I want my life back.

Before I have time to read it, the phone buzzes again. And then again.

My better life.
I want to be your
best friend.

I smile, sink back against my pillows and look at the tree outside my window. Of course. This is all Becca has ever wanted. This is manageable.

Let's talk.

Becca's made her point with the phones. She's clever. She's figured me out. Now we need to get rid of them and the film. God, in some ways she's so ingenious and in others so predictable. It will take some doing, this demand of hers, if I decide to play along. Restoring her to popularity. Maybe I should for a while. It might be more interesting than the current dullness, but there are other directions I could take this game. Whichever way it goes, I intend to win.

At least now I know her aim. My other phone buzzes but I ignore it. It'll be Aiden and he's already forgotten as far as I'm concerned.

It's good to have something to mull over. To plan.

I grin harder when I realise I haven't tried to count any thirteens since Becca's first text. She's better therapy than Dr Harvey ever was.

Sixty

Jamie opened the red wine and let it breathe. It was past eleven but he'd prepared a late supper of cheese and biscuits and cold meat for when Caitlin arrived. One thing this budding relationship had in its favour was that neither of them kept normal hours. Other people in Brackston might be thinking of going to bed now, but Jamie was still wide awake and had only just stopped working in time to shower and make himself look as presentable as he could manage.

He heard the car pull up on the gravel and his heart sped up a little. He hated himself for feeling so nervous but it was a while since he'd been on a date, and although they hadn't planned for her to sleep over tonight, there was a sense that it was implied. She lived on the other side of town and was coming straight from work, and there was no way she'd drink and drive.

'Hi,' he said. She looked good. She always wore trouser suits when working, dark and serious, how she liked to present herself, but now she was wearing jeans and a red blouse with matching lipstick. Her hair was down, too, falling glossy around her shoulders. He took a deep breath. It was definitely a date.

'Can I come in?' She was hesitant on the doorstep, reaching

down to pat an eager Biscuit and then holding up a bottle. 'Just in case you've run out.'

'No danger of that.'

He stepped aside to let her in and took her coat. As they headed – both a little nervous, he decided – to the sitting room, Aiden came down the stairs. He immediately tucked the joint he was carrying into his pocket, but Jamie doubted Caitlin had missed it.

'I thought you had plans tonight?' Jamie asked.

'Sorry, they were cancelled. I'll stay out of your way, though – just grabbing a drink.' He looked despondent, and Jamie poured them all a glass of wine. It was good having Aiden there for a moment – he broke the tension and gave the two awkward adults a focal point. Jamie couldn't help but wonder how long it was since Bennett had been on a date. It became harder to meet people as you got older, and it was easier just to live on your own.

'You look miserable,' he said. 'Everything okay?'

Aiden shrugged, the half-energy move that usually meant so much more. 'Tasha dumped me.'

'Sorry to hear that.' And he was, although Aiden could probably use some of the single-man time Jamie had experienced too much of. 'Bit sudden, isn't it?'

'Yeah.' Aiden paused. 'I think Becca had something to do with it.'

'How?'

'It's weird. She texted that Tasha was going to dump me – not a raging crazy text, just said that Tasha would dump me within the hour, and then next thing I know I get a text from Tasha doing just that.' He sipped his wine. 'I'm not bothered or anything, not really, but it came out of the blue. She'd been texting me earlier and everything looked pretty good.'

'Maybe Becca and Tasha have made up,' Jamie said. 'You know what girls are like.'

'Yeah, maybe.' Aiden turned back to the hallway. 'Anyway, I'll leave you to it. Going to watch some TV in my room.' He nodded at Caitlin. 'Have a nice evening.'

Given how stooped Aiden's shoulders were as he left, Jamie thought maybe Aiden was finding it more painful than he was letting on. He was learning the hard lesson that women were not so easy to understand after all.

'I don't think they've made up,' Caitlin said, pulling a grape free from the cheese board and popping it into her mouth before sitting down on the sofa. 'Becca and Tasha.'

'Why do you say that?'

She took her shoes off and curled her legs up, and suddenly Jamie felt more relaxed. It felt natural somehow, that she should be here, relaxing in his home. He sat beside her.

'Becca came to the station. She basically said she thought Natasha had done it all herself. The fall in the river. Hannah's death. She thinks Tasha orchestrated the whole thing.'

'Natasha? That's crazy. I mean, I know Becca was upset and everything, but what would even make her come up with that?'

'She was talking about the CCTV footage of Jenny buying the phones. Wanted to know if we'd watched where she went after. Said Natasha was the last one in the theatre the day Hannah Alderton died.' Caitlin looked up. She was thoughtful. 'She said it had all been wrapped up too neatly, and she'd delivered it to me.'

'Crazy talk. Poor girl. She needs more therapy, I think.'

'Maybe.' Caitlin leaned back, catlike, against the sofa,

looking into her wine glass. 'But she did make a few valid points. We'd not looked at where Jenny went after the phone shop. I've had someone digging the CCTV footage out this afternoon. Poor Marc is still at work.'

'You don't believe her, though?'

'No.' She shook her head. 'But we do need to dot our i's and cross our t's before the court case.'

Jamie watched her. She was with him but not entirely with him. 'Is something bugging you about it?' he asked.

'Only about the phones. Because Becca had a point. Why did Jenny and Hayley stop using them after that night? Why did they keep them, with all that incriminating evidence on them?'

Jamie leaned back beside her, their arms touching. 'Teenage girls, I guess. Maybe they just never thought they'd get caught.'

'Yeah, you're right. That's what I figure.' She looked over at him and smiled. 'Enough about work. How's your and Biscuit's day been?'

Sixty-One

Usual place? Midnight?

Becca sent the text at ten and then sat there, in her room, weighing up all the ways it could play out until her parents turned the lights off downstairs and went to bed.

By the time she'd sneaked out of the house, backpack on, she was wondering for the thousandth time if she was being ridiculous. Or stupid. It could all be over now. *She* might not be able to get into the computer but the police could. But that would mean convincing Bennett to try to unlock it rather than just arrest Becca for theft, and the pay-as-you-go text conversation didn't make a strong enough case. Bennett thought she was crazy as it was. She could easily argue Becca was sending both sets of texts herself and dismiss it. Which was all too ironic since it was exactly what Tasha had done in the first place.

The woods were dark and she turned the torch on to find her way. She tried to ignore her nerves. She wasn't alone in the woods. Tasha would be at the clearing – *the usual place* – already. She'd probably been there for ages. She'd want to be sure Becca hadn't set traps of any sort, or maybe she was setting traps of her own. And Tasha wouldn't be afraid in the woods alone at night. Most people worried about monsters or psychos. Tasha *was* the psycho.

Becca tried to stay confident as trees started to crowd around the narrow path and dark branches jagged on her clothes and scratched at her face. The torch was a weak David against the Goliath of the night and her stomach jittered. She should have just gone to the police. She should have, she knew that. But this wasn't only about justice. This was about finding out *why* Tasha had done all this, and she was never going to share that with Bennett. She might come up with some reason, something plausible, but it wouldn't be the truth. Perhaps tonight, with just the two of them, Becca had a chance of getting it out of her. She owed it to Hannah. She owed it to Hayley and Jenny. She owed it to *herself*. This wasn't about Bennett. This was about all of them.

There were four torches in the clearing, one in each corner, creating a lit stage around Natasha, who was sitting on the fallen log, a bottle of wine open by her feet. As the last trees parted, Becca flicked her own light off. It was redundant.

'Slight overkill, don't you think?' she said.

'I don't like the dark.' Tasha got to her feet and raised her plastic cup. 'Here's to you and your clever brain, Bex.' She sipped and then sat back down to pour one for Becca. 'Come and sit with me.'

It was all strangely calm as Becca took off her rucksack and Tasha held her out a drink. She looked at her ex-best-friend for a long moment until Tasha laughed, and then took a sip from both and gave Becca the choice.

'Don't worry, it's not poisoned.'

Becca took a cup, drank, and bubbles fizzed in her nose. 'Is this champagne?'

'I thought we'd earned it.'

We. Suddenly it was we. As if Becca was part of all this madness. Becca lit a cigarette – she'd splurged the last of her cash on ten Marlboro Lights for the occasion – and they sat in quiet for a while as she smoked.

'So you agree?' she said. 'We're best friends again?'

Tasha's blonde hair was spun gold in the light. Even now, with everything Becca knew, she still looked perfectly beautiful. A breeze rustled the trees. It was as if they were the last people alive.

'Yes,' Tasha said. 'Yes, I think we are. To be honest, it'll be a relief. The others are dull. Like bad photocopies of Hayley and Jen.'

'And you didn't exactly like them.'

Her head whipped around to face Becca. 'That's not true! There were moments when they pissed me off, for sure, but I loved them. They were my best friends.' She paused. 'They just didn't behave.' She sipped her drink and grew thoughtful as she focused on the immediate situation. 'But we'll have to manage it carefully so it doesn't look too odd. I'll stage an argument with Vicki and Jodie. And I'll make up some shit about you on Facebook that's good. People love me. Right now they all love me more than they ever have before. They'll accept it.'

Still reeling slightly, Becca wondered just how Natasha's mind worked. Did she realise how crazy she sounded? There wasn't even a hint of self-awareness when she said she'd loved Hayley and Jenny. After everything she'd done framing them for murder and attempted murder and destroying their lives, she could still say that with a straight face?

Tread carefully, Becca thought. *Tread very carefully on this dangerous ground.*

'The green dress,' Natasha said, with a rueful smile. 'I'd forgotten all about it. I loved that dress. I hated that you had it.'

'I'd forgotten about it, too, until I saw a picture and it all came back to me. I nearly killed Hayley when that nail varnish was spilled all over it just before my birthday.' She paused, remembering. 'All that set-up you did. Telling me how jealous Hayley was of my dress. Planting the nail varnish bottle in her room days before so I'd see it there. I think you created the biggest fight me and Hayley ever had.'

'And that's why you got suspicious this time.'

'Yep, that and the lie about the bracelets. You weren't quite so clever about it back then.'

'We were only little,' Tasha said. 'If my stupid mother had kept her mouth shut it would have been fine. She was so *appalled*. Mothers of friends should never be allowed to be friends. Still, if it were now, I'd have bought the nail polish myself and kept it secret instead of my mum *knowing* it was mine because she'd paid for it, Then she'd never have been able to say it must have been me who sneaked into your room and poured it on your dress. Everyone would have just believed it was Hayley.'

'I think you've gone a little bit further this time,' Becca said dryly. She'd been too nervous for dinner and the fizz was going to her head. 'Two people are dead.'

'Yes, it's safe to say that things have become a little more serious than I'd planned,' Tasha said.

'No shit.' Her snort of laughter came out of nowhere, but once she'd started, Becca couldn't stop despite how shocked she was. It was ridiculous, them sitting here talking about everything that had happened as if it were just a little argument that had got out of hand. Becca thought of Amanda Alderton's face at the funeral and somehow that made her laugh even harder. It was laugh or cry. It was hysteria, maybe. Whatever it was, Tasha stared at her for a moment and then they were both laughing, unable to stop, setting each other off into fresh fits of giggles each time one of them started to get themselves under control.

It's like the old days, Becca thought with a pang as her sides began to ache and her eyes watered. *The old, old days, when we were small.*

Finally, both girls having worn themselves out, the laughter faded to the occasional burp of a giggle and then sighs, before silence.

'We're like the girls from *The Crucible*,' Tasha said when she had the breath to speak. 'Out in the woods, laughing and casting our dark spells.'

'I'm not getting naked, though. Not with these thighs.'

'Ha.' Tasha smiled at her, genuine warmth in it. 'You were always the funniest.' She squeezed Becca's arm affectionately before looking away. 'You know I need the laptop back.'

Becca unzipped her backpack and pulled out the slim silver Airbook. 'Here. It needs charging.'

Her heart thumped as Tasha took it. She saw her eyes fall on the New York sticker on the corner of the lid, and then she grinned again.

'Thanks, Bex.' Tasha got up. 'My legs are stiff. I've been sitting here for ages. Shall we go for a walk?' She held up the computer. 'I might just lob this into the river. My mum never uses it anyway.'

Becca stood and Tasha linked arms with her. 'Maybe this is

how it was always meant to be, Bex,' she said. 'You and me. Best friends forever. And if you figured all this out on your own, just imagine what we could do together. Sort out Jamie McMahon's dog, for one thing. Get even with Aiden for being such a creep?'

'We'll have plenty of time for all of that,' Becca said.

They walked for a while before Becca spoke again. But in the end she just had to ask. They were in a bubble tonight, a private space of their own. If Natasha was ever going to open up, it would be now.

'It must have taken so much planning,' she said. 'And then faking the amnesia. You even *died* for a bit.'

'That shouldn't have happened. That was Jamie McMahon and his wretched dog's fault for being late on their walk.'

'But *why* did you do it, Tasha? Was it over Mr Garrick? Please tell me you didn't fancy him, too.'

'Don't be gross!' Tasha laughed. 'Of course I didn't.'

'So why?' Becca asked again.

Tasha took a deep breath. 'It's really not all that complicated,' she began.

Sixty-Two

They were stretched out on the sofa, Caitlin's head on his chest, watching an action film when her phone began to buzz. Thus far it had been a very chaste evening, but with Aiden upstairs Jamie didn't really feel like taking it to the next stage, and it felt good just to be relaxing with her. It felt natural.

'Oh god, what now?' she muttered, reluctantly reaching to the table to pick it up. They'd moved on to the second bottle of red and both had a pleasant, hazy buzz going. *Marc Aplin* showed on the screen and she sat up, answering it.

'This had better be important.' She looked at Jamie apologetically as she answered the phone. He wondered if this was why she was single. How did men take coming second to her job? He couldn't imagine it bothering him. It would be hypocritical, after all. If anyone loved his job, it was him. Her back stiffened.

'Are you sure?' she said. 'Can you send it over to me?' She signalled to Jamie for her coat and he went and got it before clearing some of their buffet debris away in case she needed the table space. She rummaged in the wide pockets for her iPad mini and once she'd found it, kicked her coat to one side.

Jamie sat beside her again as she rolled the cover back to make a small stand and turned the tablet on. He felt slightly awkward, like he was intruding on a personal call or something, but he was also curious. Was this a new case she hadn't mentioned? Or was it still something to do with the girls? She said Becca had come to see her and they were still investigating – was this some fresh evidence?

'I've got it,' she said, and clicked on a link.

It took Jamie a moment to figure out what he was watching, the images pixelated and jerky until the iPad settled down and started playing it properly. It was the shopping centre. Near the exit.

'I see her,' Bennett muttered into the phone, her eyes focused on the screen where a girl in a coat was walking towards the rear exit doors and the car park. 'Nothing unexpected yet.' The clip changed to the exterior and the cinema loomed in the distance on the other side of the banks of cars. The girl stopped and undid the coat, pulling it off fast. She looked around her for a second and then stuffed it into a bin.

'Have you got a close-up?'

Jamie was still staring at the small figure in the film when Caitlin shut it down and went back to her inbox. She clicked a second link. A still made large.

'That's not Jenny,' Jamie said, softly. 'That's Natasha.'

Caitlin was on her feet, the phone still pressed to her ear. 'So she bought the coat in Primark, put it on and then ditched it after buying the phones. Have you got footage from Primark?' A pause. 'It doesn't matter anyway, this is enough. I want her brought to the station. And Rebecca Crisp, too. Rebecca had figured this out. Call me when you've picked them up. I'm going to need a—' She stopped as Aiden appeared in the doorway. 'You had more than one glass of wine?' she barked at him. He shook his head.

'It's all right,' she finished, 'I can get a lift in. Find those girls and then call me back.'

'What's going on?' Aiden asked. 'I just came down for a Coke.'

He looked mildly stoned, which irritated Jamie as they had a detective in the house, but he figured she wasn't going to give much of a shit right now.

'It's Becca and Tasha,' Jamie said. 'I think you might have got your mentals the wrong way round.'

Aiden stared at him. 'What are you talking about?'

Caitlin's phone rang and both men turned to hear what was said.

'Bennett.' She was pacing, a small, tense figure, and Biscuit was matching her steps at her heel. She stopped suddenly, the dog almost barrelling into her calves.

'What do you mean they're not at home?' She looked at Jamie as she talked to her sergeant. 'But it's gone midnight. If they're not at home then *where the hell are they*?'

Sixty-Three

'You were all *my* friends,' Natasha said. 'Don't you see?' They'd walked a little and then paused, Becca smoking some more.

'It was up to *me* to decide who stayed and who went. Like when you started getting all that puppy fat, and when Jenny arrived at school, I knew I had to swap you out. You didn't fit with what I wanted. How I wanted to be seen. Hayley said it didn't matter but it did. I had to threaten to tell everyone she'd pissed herself in my dad's car that summer to get her to stop whining. Jenny fitted better. There wasn't space for you, too.' She looked sideways at Becca. 'You understand, don't you?'

'Sure,' Becca said, glad of the night around them, hiding her face. Tasha made her craziness sound so reasonable. But then she believed Becca was willing to let all of this go, just to be her best friend again. She must think Becca was as crazy as her. Becca was glad her voice at least was calm. 'I mean, I *didn't* get it, not at first, but I do now. But I still don't understand why all *this*? And why involve me?'

'I knew Jenny and Hayley wouldn't say anything,' Natasha replied, after a long pause. 'You know, *afterwards*. When I woke up and my memory was supposedly gone. They'd want to find the film first, and obviously they didn't know about my little trail of evidence leading to them. I *had* met them in the woods. We'd arranged it at lunch, not by text, though. As far as they knew I'd only found out about Jenny and Garrick the night before, just like in the statement I gave to the police. But obviously I wasn't quite as *goody-two-shoes* about it with them. When we met that night – and it wasn't at three a.m., it was earlier – I told them I'd followed and filmed them in the car park with Mr Garrick. I told them I hadn't decided what to do about it, or what I wanted in exchange for it.'

She pushed away from the tree she'd been leaning on and took Becca's arm, and they started to stroll again, slow and easy, as if it was a summer afternoon, not the middle of the night.

'It was fun watching them squirm and beg, pleading with me not to do anything. I told them I'd think about it and we all left. Later on, I came back and ran through the woods, planted the rope and the capsule cases and all that stuff, got myself scratched up and then jumped into the river. I knew it would be cold – it'd been snowing for a while by then – but I thought I'd only be in there for a few minutes. I'd planned to swim to the other side and crawl out in time to pretend I was unconscious, ready for Jamie McMahon and his dog to find me on the bank. But I hadn't realised *just how cold* it would be in the water. That I couldn't make it. That Jamie and Biscuit would be late.' She shivered, trapped for a moment in the memory. 'He found me eventually and I was okay, I guess. And it was better for the amnesia story. No one doubted it after I died.'

'But why fake the amnesia? Why not just say they pushed you in the river after you confronted them about Jenny and Peter Garrick?'

Tasha stared at her for a moment as if the question was stupid.

'Where would the fun be in that? It was about *punishing* them. For keeping secrets from me. For lying to me for months. They needed to think I didn't remember any of it. I knew they'd suck up to me. I knew they'd find an excuse to go to my room and try to find the film. They must have searched when they went and got my iPod and stuff and brought it to the hospital. They must have been desperate by then. They knew it wouldn't look good for them if they said we'd met in the woods that night, especially as I'd accidentally died. It would look like they had something to do with it. It was easier for them to keep quiet and bide their time, hoping I never remembered. Which of course made them look even more guilty when everything I'd planted incriminating them came to light.'

'Are we all so predictable?' Becca asked. The path was widening as they neared the river. They had been pieces on a chessboard, that was for sure, but there was no opposition. Just Tasha moving them around as it pleased her.

'We've all been friends for a long time,' Tasha said. 'And Jenny *loved* Mr Garrick, disgusting as that is. She wanted to protect him. You're proving more interesting, though. More like me. Under the skin.'

'I guess so. But you still played me. You knew I'd come to the hospital.'

'I wasn't planning to be in the hospital for so long. But I had planned to befriend you again. I figured it wouldn't be so hard. You were only hanging around with Hannah, after all. I mean, god, Bex, there's stooping low and then there's *low*.'

Becca ignored the comment. She'd done enough disservice

to Hannah while she was alive. She wasn't going to slag her off now that she was dead.

'You needed someone you trusted to get suspicious of them,' she said. 'You needed me to pass evidence and suspicions on to the police while you sat back and prodded me in the right direction and played the victim. You wanted it to look like it all came from me and that you were still scared of them.'

'Pretty brilliant, wasn't it? The set-up at the clearing was the first test. To see if you'd buy it. And you did. Hook, line and sinker. After that, I knew you'd see anything they did or said from that angle. *My* angle. And why not, when everything fitted?'

It was brilliant. Becca had to give her that. 'And Hannah?'

'Oh, be fair. That was as much you as me. If you hadn't wanted that light moved and got Hayley to do it, the idea would never have occurred to me. I improvised, but you set it up so well. I thought it would be perfect for keeping the pressure on Hayley and Jenny, and give me a wonderfully dramatic moment to "remember". It wasn't meant to fall on Hannah. It was meant to look like they'd tried to drop it on me. I mean, to be honest, Hannah messed everything up a bit. She got in the way. Trust her to die so easily. I didn't want Hayley and Jenny to go away *forever*. Just for a while. Just to learn their lesson. To remember that I'm the one who made them and without me they're nothing. I mean, we're still pretty much best friends. They need to remember that.'

An owl hooted and Becca nearly jumped. Tasha was talking so casually. So clinically. As if Hayley and Jenny would ever be her friends now. How badly wired *was* her head? Sociopath, not psychopath. Maybe both.

'It feels good to talk about it all,' Tasha said. They were

nearly at the river. 'It's been a lot to hold inside.' Her voice quietened. 'Maybe now I've shared everything, the dreams will let me go.'

'And of course,' Becca said, wanting to get everything clear, 'once Hannah died, that was the perfect time to get your memory back.'

'When I saw Hannah drop and Bennett walked in, it was sublime. Everything fell against them at once. No one was going to question that evidence. Not with my statement to back it up and that notebook I was keeping. Why do people always believe diaries? They're just words.'

They had reached the river and Becca's heart thumped hard as they turned to walk along the uneven bank. Had Tasha turned right on purpose, so that Becca would be closest to the water? Easier to shove?

'Why didn't you say they pushed you? In your statement.'

'I thought about it, but I didn't need to. Far more convincing to say I didn't remember how I fell in, don't you think? Spelling it out would have been too much. It's like in that diary – I wasn't perfect in it, but I was believable.' She smiled, broad and happy. 'Believable is all that matters. See?'

She's enjoying this, Becca realised. Tasha was loving showing off how clever she'd been. How far ahead of everyone. How meticulous.

'But *why*, Tasha? Why do any of it in the first place? *Why* were you punishing them? Surely not just for keeping Mr Garrick a secret.' Now that she had the full confession, she needed to understand why. And sociopath or not, it must be more than just that.

Tasha stopped walking. Close up, Becca could see something like hurt in her face. Hurt and maybe anger. A lot of anger. For a fraction of a second, Tasha looked truly ugly. Moonlight cut pale across her face, highlighting the dips in her cheeks, and her eyes shone from deep black circles. Her mouth was a tight slit as she seethed with memory. Even her hair, now so golden-blonde, appeared tar-streaked in the night. She looked like a dead girl from a horror film to Becca. And emotionally maybe that's what she was. Finally Becca was seeing the *real* Tasha. The one on the inside. The fucked-up crazy one.

'They didn't want to be my friends any more,' Tasha said, eventually. She was staring at a point somewhere beyond Becca. 'I knew it. They started going off together just the two of them. Not inviting me. Making excuses to not include me. I couldn't believe it. Their *arrogance*.' She spat out the last word. 'One night, Jenny got high and said I was too controlling. Too judgemental.' She shook her head a little. 'How dare she? *I'm* the Barbies. *Of course* I controlled them. I made them the most popular girls in school. I *shaped* them. How could *I* be dumped by *them*? I have always been the most popular girl, Becca, you know that. Ever since primary school. Now, with only sixth form left, they wanted to take that from me? How would everyone view me if they left me? I'd be a loser. I don't lose, Bex, you know that. I tried to make it better for a while, but then I overheard them talking about me. Calling me cold. Psycho. Control freak. They thought I was a bitch to them. They said there was something wrong with me in my head.'

No shit, Becca thought. She wondered if there had been other incidents like the green dress over the years. How many times had Natasha played Jenny and Hayley off each other until they got wise and decided they'd had enough?

'So when I found out about Mr Garrick, I knew what I had to do. I had to show them. To teach them a lesson. They needed to see what I was capable of. There were less than two years left of school and I would *not* be shamed. I would *not* be threatened. Not by *them*.' Tasha looked at Becca. '*I* decide who stays or goes, not them.'

'So this had nothing to do with Mr Garrick at all?'

'Of course not.' Tasha barked out a harsh, unpleasant laugh. 'Like I care who Jenny's fucking? If she'd told me about it I might actually have helped her – made it work far more in her favour. But they didn't trust me with *that* little secret. Oh no, they wanted to keep that for themselves. As if they could. As if they could ever keep anything from me. They thought I'd do something horrible to him. That's what Hayley said. And they didn't want that. It made me laugh. Like they've ever really known what was best for them. That's why they've always had me. They thought I was going to put that film on YouTube and make them a laughing stock. And I could have. But that would have been too obvious, wouldn't it? That's what someone ordinary would have done. That would have just been spiteful. What I did, well, I wanted them to *learn* from it. What I did had a point. Things just got slightly out of hand.'

You're crazy, Becca wanted to say. *Proper batshit crazy*. Instead, she shrugged. 'They kind of deserved it.'

'Exactly!' Tasha said. 'They don't get to dump me.' She turned and stared out over the dark water. 'They don't even get to dare think that way. They should have been grateful to me. They *belonged* to me.'

Although the weather had been warmer, now that it was the dead of night and they were riverside, the breeze was cold as it lifted Becca's hair and she shivered. She was ready to go home now. She was just about done here.

'You going to throw that in or what?' she asked, nodding at the laptop. Tasha looked down at it for a long second and then spun it like a Frisbee, out to the middle of the river. There was a flash of silver and then a splash. They both stared after it.

'Well, that's that, then,' Becca said.

'That's that.'

Becca had taken a small step back from the bank, her heart racing, willing her feet to stick like glue to the earth beneath. This was Natasha. There was no way of knowing where she would take this next.

'Don't worry,' Tasha said, still looking out over the water. 'I'm not going to push you in.' She looked over her shoulder. 'I admit I thought about it. I mean, it wouldn't even be suspicious. You committing suicide where I'd nearly died. It would have so much pathos, wouldn't it? Like you actually wanted to *be* me.'

'Everyone wants to be you, Tasha.' For a moment Becca thought she might have overplayed it. She was never *that* directly complimentary. Tasha just kept talking, though.

'And all that stuff on Facebook and me dating Aiden would be enough to push you over the edge.' She giggled. 'Literally.'

'How come you changed your mind?' Becca said.

'I don't know. Affection for you, I guess. You've been so clever to figure it all out. It would be a waste of a brain to drown you. I think we can have some fun. For a while, at least.'

Becca wondered how long Tasha would allow her to play before she changed her mind. A week? A month? Becca would always be looking over her shoulder, waiting for the axe to fall.

'Best friends forever,' she said softly.

Natasha turned around and, unexpectedly, pulled Becca into a tight hug. 'Best friends forever,' she agreed, her warm breath in Becca's ear.

Her father's old Dictaphone in Becca's pocket suddenly beeped loudly and the girls jumped apart, startled. Becca's heart raced as Tasha's eyes widened and then darkened with rage.

'What?' Becca said, trying to sound casual. Normal. Relaxed. She took a step backwards and almost fell over a clump of earth. *Shit, shit, shit*, she thought. The tape had ended. *Shit shit shit.*

'What was that?' Tasha said through suddenly thinned lips. 'Were you recording this? Recording *me*?' Her voice turned into a snarl, and as her shoulders hunched and she coiled to strike, Becca saw her like an animal, a predator of the night, a wolf or a fox, all teeth and hunger.

'No . . .' Becca started, lamely, knowing how pathetic and scared she sounded. 'No, it must just have been my phone running out of battery.' It hadn't been her phone and Tasha knew it.

'Give it to me!' Tasha shrieked, lunging forward and grabbing at Becca's pockets.

'Stop it, Tasha!'

Becca tried to push her backwards, but Tasha was all sinewy strength, clawing and hissing at her.

'You fucking *bitch*, Becca,' Tasha spat into her face as they struggled. 'You fucking nobody bitch! I was going to make you *special! Give me that tape!*'

'Fuck off, Tasha!' Becca said, finally finding her own rage. 'Just *fuck off*!' She grabbed the other girl's arms and shoved. Tasha held on. The world spun as both girls lost their footing.

Oh shit, Becca thought as her eyes met Tasha's and saw her shock and fear reflected there. *Oh shit, oh shit. We're going in.*

Sixty-Four

Sirens wailed in the night. They were getting closer, but they didn't sound close enough for Jamie's liking. His legs burned as he ran, his breath ragged from his chest. He could hear Caitlin behind him, swearing as she stumbled, tripping over in the dark, the torch she carried a crazy jagged spotlight that couldn't cover enough ground to make it worthwhile.

The clearing where Natasha said the girls had tied her up. It came to him in a flash, barely ten minutes before, as Caitlin was sending officers to check the school and the graveyard where Hannah was buried. Julie Crisp, Becca's mum, had called them back in near hysterics. While searching the house for clues to where her daughter might be, she'd found an Airbook, not her husband's, with a mark on it where a sticker had been peeled off. It had been on his desk with a note from Becca:

If I don't come back, I love you, and give this to the police. There's a film on it they need to see. I don't have the password.

Abruptly it became clear to Jamie: they'd have met in the woods. They must have. His house was on the wrong side of the river, but there was a narrow bridge maybe five or ten minutes up from where he'd found Natasha. They could cross there, he'd told Bennett. They could probably make it before her men in their cars.

She was at the door before he'd finished the sentence, and now here they were, any wine buzz vanished, running and stumbling as fast as they could. Biscuit had raced past them both and he didn't waste any breath calling the dog back.

'Where's the bridge?' Caitlin panted, catching him up.

'That way – to your right.'

They both turned, and then Jamie grabbed her arm.

'Stop! Wait!'

'What?' she snapped.

'Listen!'

Biscuit was barking. Back the other way. A sharp, high bark. A bark that demanded attention.

One more frenzied bark, a shriek, and then just a loud splash.

'That way!'

Not waiting to see if Caitlin was with him, Jamie turned and ran through the dark in the direction of his dog.

Sixty-Five

They were screaming at each other when they hit the cold water, and the muddy taste filled Becca's nose and lungs. She couldn't breathe, but still they wrestled as the currents pulled them down into that cold, dark, alien world. The night sky taunted her, moonlight dancing on the surface as she finally broke free, her arms bruised and aching. She struggled upwards, desperate for air, and then hands grabbed her again. Tasha was not giving up. *Tasha*, Becca realised, suddenly terrified that she was going to die here, *would never give up*. She twisted in the water to face her one-time best friend.

Natasha looked like a banshee, hair wild around her head in the water, eyes still filled with rage as her pale hands, almost ghostlike, clung to Becca's coat. She was screaming something, bubbles of air escaping her lips with the words, their meaning muted and muffled by the water that was squeezing the life out of them both.

Becca kicked out, struggling, but as her lungs burned with lack of air, her blow had no impact. Weeds grasped at her feet as the water dragged them, and she pulled her heavy legs up and away as she desperately wriggled out of her jacket. She didn't care about the tape. It would be ruined now anyway. Tasha gripped the fabric, twisting and tugging it, making

Becca squirm harder to free herself. Why was Tasha still fighting her? Why couldn't they both just get out? How crazy was she? One arm free, Becca turned away and tore her other arm out, kicking upwards with the last of her energy now the weight of the coat was gone. She glanced back towards Tasha, sure she'd be reaching for her, determined to drown her and then make her escape. Tasha wasn't human. She was a monster.

Tasha *was* trying to follow her, her arms outstretched, grasping. She too kicked upwards, with more strength than Becca had left, and for a moment she was coming up fast, but then suddenly she stopped, halted by something that pulled her slightly downwards. Becca saw the surprise register as Tasha let go of the coat and looked down. Becca saw it then, too.

Tendrils from the depths, dancing in the currents. Dark weeds, octopus-like, wrapping around Tasha's legs. As she struggled, desperate to pull free, their hold was only growing tighter.

Help me.

It was the last Becca saw of Tasha. That sudden panic. The shock. The fear. The mouthed words from lips that looked dark against the eerie white of her face.

Help me.

And then she was breaking the surface and sucking in a long lungful of sweet, beautiful, terrible air. Becca coughed and spluttered and took sharp, raw breaths. Oh, it tasted so good. She sobbed, tears she had no energy for coming anyway. She tried to swim but her limbs wouldn't work, tired and numbing in the cold. Her Converse were heavy, pulling her feet down, wanting to sink her. The bank looked a long way off.

I can't help you, Tash, she thought as her head dipped below the surface again, into that dark and deathly silence. *I don't think I can help myself.*

And then there was fur, and scratching claws, and a hot mouth at her neck. Teeth sank into her hoodie and dragged. She heard the pants and grunts as a dog scrabbled and paddled, dragging her to the bank, and with the last ounce of her will to live she forced her feet to kick.

Sixty-Six

I watch them up there on the surface. So far away. A different world from this quiet endless darkness. I watch and rage. Paws paddling. Becca's feet wearily kicking towards shore. I want to scream at the unfairness of it all. Stars blur the edge of my vision and, eventually, I release the last of the air from my lungs and let the cold, filthy water in.

The river sighs, satisfied. It's been waiting for me. The river and the darkness from my dreams. Maybe I never really coughed all of it back out. I can't believe I'm here again. One minute, we were on the bank. The next, I'm dying in the water. *Dying.* Like Hannah. All over in an instant. I can't believe it. I won't. Someone will save me. Someone will come.

And then I hear it. The voice from my dreams. The one I never remember. The one that terrifies me.

You thought you could leave me here, the voice says to me.

It's my voice. Of course it is.

The part of us that died. I've had to wait alone in the cold and dark. All this time.

My hands struggle again to touch the surface that I can no longer see, *Let me go.* My thoughts sound like I'm begging. I hate that. *I was never meant to die here. We were never meant to die here. I am not meant to die here.*

She's holding my ankles, this dead crazy me. I kick at her, I rage against her, I hate her. I can stop this. I can make it end. She has to release me. I need to live, to put all of this behind me. Even if I have to go to jail, I can survive. I'm young and it won't be for long. *I don't lose*, I tell myself over and over. *I never lose.* I think of the chessboard at home. The pieces waiting patiently for me. *Let me go*, I plead again, squeezing my eyes shut.

When I open them, the other me, the dead me, hair wild and eyes filled with glee, still has her pale hand clawed tightly around my foot. Even in the cold of the river her fingers are bony ice. Cold glass. She will never let go. I can't see her lower body. It's lost in the endless quicksand void beyond. She smiles. I hear her in my head, just like in my dreams. A whisper. Dead. Vicious.

I don't lose, she says. *You don't get to dump me and move on. You're staying with me. This is the endgame, Tasha.*

I want to cry and wail and scream against it all. I'm the one who plans, I'm the one who wins. My vision is darkening. I can't see properly. But I can still see her. The me who isn't me, who can't be me.

I want to play with you.

I let out a moan, my last word, my last sound, one of horror, sucked away by the water.

Be my best friend, she whispers with such cold longing as she pulls me into the terrible blackness. *Be my best friend forever.*

Acknowledgements

Big thanks go to the whole team at Gollancz, but especially Sophie Calder and Jen McMenemy, not just for work on this book but for their hard work pimping Gollancz authors throughout the year while remaining so smiley. Of course, big thanks to my editor, Gillian Redfearn and my agent Veronique Baxter. And a final special thanks to Gillian's brother who helped out with the technicalities of theatre lighting rigs!

Turn the page for an excerpt of
Sarah Pinborough's haunting novel

The Death House

'Moving and totally involving. I couldn't put it down'
Stephen King

AVAILABLE NOW

One

'They say it makes your eyes bleed. Almost pop out of your head and then bleed.'

'Who says?'

'People. I just heard it.'

'You made it up.'

'No, I didn't,' Will says. 'Why would I make that up? I heard it somewhere. You go mad first and then your eyes bleed. I think maybe your whole skin bleeds.'

'That is such a heap of shit.'

'Shut up and go to sleep.' I roll over. The rough blanket scratches me on the outside and my irritation at Will's over-active imagination scratches me from the inside. I let out a hot breath against the wool. My irritation is irritating me. It comes fast these days, flares from the ball of a black sun that's been growing quietly in the pit of my stomach. The two boys fall satisfyingly silent. I'm the eldest. I'm the top dog, the boss, the daddy. Of Dorm 4, at least. My word goes.

I yank the starched sheet up until it covers the edge of the old blanket. The dorm isn't cold so much as cool – the kind of chill ingrained in the bricks and mortar of centuries-old buildings, a ghostly, melancholy chill of things that once-were, now part-lost. We suit the house, I think, and that makes the ball contract in my gut. I shiver and pull my legs up under my chin. My bladder twinges. Great.

'I can't sleep,' Will says plaintively. 'Not with that going on.' He yawns then and I can see him in the gloom, sitting up cross-legged on his bed, fiddling with the metal bars at the foot of it. He's the youngest in our room, and is small for his age. He acts younger, too.

The constant whispering comes from the bed opposite Will's on the other side of the room. The cuckoo in our nest, Ashley, is on his knees beside it, praying. He does this every night at lights-out. Religiously.

'I don't think God is listening,' I mutter. 'You know, given the situation.'

'God's always listening.' The prim voice floats in the frigid air – a stretched reed with a breeze cutting across it. 'He's everywhere.'

My bladder twitches again and I give in and push back the covers. The floorboards are cold – fuck knows how Ashley's knees must feel – but I ignore my slippers. I'm not a granddad.

'Then your praying makes no sense,' Louis says, matter-of-fact. His bed is closest to the door and he's staring up at the ceiling, his hair here and there and everywhere. He still gesticulates as he speaks, even though he's lying down. 'Because if your God *is* everywhere then he's also inside you and therefore you could speak to him from the quiet privacy of your own mind and talk all night if you wanted without making a sound and he would still hear you. Of course, there is absolutely no scientific proof that any form of deity exists, or that we are more than a collection of cells and water, so your God is just a figment of someone's imagination that you've bought into. Basically, you're wasting your time.'

The whispering gets louder.

'Maybe he's having a wank under the bed and trying to cover the noise,' I say as I reach the door. '*Fwap fwap fwap*.' I grin as I make the hand gesture.

Louis snorts a laugh.

Will giggles.

My irritation lifts. I like Will and Louis. I wish I didn't, but I can't help it. I glance back as I close the door. They look small in the large room. There are too many beds for just the four of us – six against each wall. It's like everyone else has gone home and somehow we were forgotten. The door clicks shut and I creep along the corridor. It's a long way to the bathroom and even though I have bigger things to frighten me than the shadows and emptiness of the tired manor house, I still move quickly. The last rounds haven't been done yet.

I hurry down the wide wooden stairs, clinging to the banister in the dark as if it were the railing on a ship wearily cutting through the night ocean. The whole house is silent apart from the gentle creaks and moans of the old building itself. I think of the others sleeping in the dorms spread throughout the draughty wings, and the nurses and teachers in their quarters, and then my mind can't help but imagine the top floor. The one where only the lift goes. Where the kids who get sick disappear to in the night, efficiently removed while the house sleeps. Swallowed by the lift and taken to the sanatorium. We don't talk about the sanatorium. Not any more. No one ever leaves the house, and no one ever comes back from the sanatorium. We all know that. Just like we know we'll each make a trip there. One day I'll be the kid who vanishes in the night.

I pee without closing the door or turning on the light, enjoying the relief even though the liquid stream on ceramic is loud. I don't flush – Mum's rule of no flushing at night still sticks – and then I yawn into the mirror without washing my hands. That rule has changed. Germs are not our biggest problem here. Not that, to be honest, I ever remembered much *before* anyway.

They say it makes your eyes bleed.

I lean in closer and stare at my eyes. They're normally bright blue but look drowned grey in the grimy night. I pull down one lower lid and can make out the streaks of tiny veins running away to my insides. No blood there, though. It probably isn't even true. Just Will's stupid imagination making shit up. I'm fine. We're all fine. For now.

'You should be in bed.'

The voice is soft but it makes me jump. Matron stands in the corridor by the window, the moonlight through the glass making her white uniform shine bright. Her bland face is barely visible.

'Aren't you tired?'

'I needed to pee.'

'Wash your hands and go back to bed.'

I blast cold water onto my palms and then scurry past her, taking the stairs two at a time. It's the most she's said to me since I arrived here. I don't want her to speak to me. I don't want her to notice me at all, as if somehow that will make a difference.

'Matron's coming,' I whisper, back in my own room.

'They're asleep,' Louis says. The words blur together. I'm not surprised. It's about the right time.

'I don't understand why they give us vitamins before bed,' Louis slurs. 'I don't understand why they give us vitamins at all.'

I half-smile at this from under my rough blankets and too-crisp sheets. Louis – with his six A levels by the age of thirteen, and who'd been racing through university stupidly early before this stopped him – might be some sort of genius, but just like the others, he's missed the obvious. I don't point it out. They're not vitamins; they're sleeping pills. Matron and the nurses like the house silent at night.

I wait, tense, for another ten minutes or so before I hear the door handle turn and the soft shuffle of soles as she checks each bed. The last round before morning. Only after she's gone do I open my eyes and breathe easily.

It was a Friday when they came. It was hot, hotter than normal, and he'd taken his time on the way back from school. He'd bought a Coke from the shop on the corner but the fridge wasn't working so it was warm and sticky. He drank it anyway, belching loudly after draining it and kicking the can across the street. His mind was drifting through the landscape of the day. Mr Settle droning on about the continuing global climate instability as they all baked and dozed, bored in the classroom. The History essay he owed. The fight with Billy. That was going to come back on him at some point. He didn't even know why he'd started it other than Julie McKendrick had been watching, and it felt like Julie had been watching him for a few days now, even though he couldn't quite believe it. Tomorrow night was the party. Tomorrow night, everything could change.

Julie McKendrick was always there in some part of his brain. It was too hot to work. Too hot for school. But it wasn't too hot to think about Julie McKendrick and the fact that she might actually like him. He was so lost in his own world he didn't notice how quiet the street was, how all the little kids were inside, not sitting out on the pavements or racing around on their bikes as usual. Billy and the essay had faded and he was mainly wondering if what he felt for Julie really was love or just that she was the fittest girl in the school and he might actually get to kiss her. Maybe even put his hands inside her bra. Just thinking about it made his mouth dry and his heart race. He wondered how it would feel. He wondered if he'd actually find out the next day at the party. Even when he saw the van outside his house, where his dad's car would be parked later when he got home from work, he still didn't put two and two together. Not until he heard his mum crying. By then it was too late. And it was too hot to run.

Two

'My money's on one of the twins,' Louis says, and glances at me. 'You still taking bets, Toby?'

We're at breakfast, the gong having summoned us down to the wood-panelled space that might once have been an oversized drawing room but is now our dining room. The ornate stone fireplace remains unlit and the only evidence of a previous existence is a tired purple velvet chaise longue pushed up against a wall, and brighter patches on the faded yellow paint where pictures must once have hung. The sun breaks momentarily through the gathering clouds outside and light streams through the vast windows, sending dust-motes dancing curious in the air. The warmth feels good on my face and as I finish my tea, I wonder if maybe Matron and the nurses put something in our breakfast drinks, too, like I heard they used to give men in prison to stop them wanting to fuck or fight.

Louis is trying to eat a fried-egg sandwich made with toast that's not quite done enough and an egg that's too runny. Most of it's going down his T-shirt but he doesn't seem to care. We're on a table of our own – our table ever since we arrived. New habits form quickly. There are sixteen tables but only eight are used, one for each of the occupied dorms. We don't talk to the boys from the other dorms much any more, even though there's only twenty-five of us left. The girls, Harriet and Eleanor, sit at a table at the back. I'm not sure how old they are, but Eleanor's still young and Harriet might be older but there's nothing hot about her. She's bookish and dumpy and her mouth is nearly always turned down in an unpleasant pout. They have always excluded themselves, and mainly I forget they're even here.

'Yep,' I say. 'Which one?'

'Either. I can't tell them apart. The one who's trying not to look like he's sniffing. Is that Ellory or Joe? Whichever, he's been getting sick and trying to hide it for days.'

The twins are in Dorm 7. Dorm 7, like our own, is still complete. It's become a matter of unspoken rivalry between us – which dorm will keep a clean survival sheet the longest. Of all the dorms, only Dorm 7 really counts to me. I stare at the table opposite and realise Louis is right. One of the two identical lanky, spotty boys sneakily wipes his nose with the back of his hand. He doesn't reach for a tissue even though there are paper napkins on the tables. I watch him. It's really hard to tell. The symptoms can be so different.

'I'll take your bet. Two washing-up duties?'

'Done.' Louis smiles. 'I call double or quits. If he goes, the other one goes next.'

'Why?' Will sits down with a second bowl of cereal. Will may be tiny but he eats more than anyone I've ever known. 'Cos they know each other?'

'No, because of science. They're identical. When it goes in one of them, it's logical it'll go in the other soon after. It's genetic, after all.'

'Oh,' Will says. 'Right.'

'But that reminds me.' Louis gets up, egg still dripping from his chin, and before I realise what he's doing, he's over at the Dorm 7 table, smiling at Jake.

'Oh, shit,' I mutter.

'Jake,' Louis starts, 'I was just wondering if you could help me with something. I'm doing a kind of study of where we've all come from and roughly how long it took us to travel here. Firstly it was to find out where exactly we are, but we've sort of figured that out now, so I . . .'

'Oh, this isn't going to end well,' Will says, peering over his glasses.

I groan inside. Louis and his stupid information-gathering. No one in the house comes from the same part of the country. We know that. So why does Louis need to know the details? What is it with him and his precision in everything? Over the past week, Louis has become obsessed with trying to collate as much data on the inmates, as he calls us, as he can. This in the main has not gone well. For a start, he's failed to factor in that people lie. I've lied. I'm sure the rest have, too. No one wants to talk about their private history from *before* anymore and definitely not to someone from another dorm. The nervous friendliness we'd shared at the start is gone. The dorms have become packs and we stay within our own.

'What the fuck has it got to do with you?' Jake slowly gets

to his feet. He's speaking quietly – there are nurses by the food station – but the threat is palpable in the air. Cutlery goes down. Heads turn.

'I thought it would be interesting to—' Louis, the genius, the prodigy, is oblivious to the tension.

'Why don't you just fuck off?'

Jake's the same age as me, but the stories about him spread on day one, in nods and whispers. He's been in reform school. He's stolen cars. I don't believe a lot of the wild tales of *before* that I've heard in the house, but Jake is different. Jake's knuckles are scarred and when we first arrived, the back of his head had a gang symbol shaved into it. If you look closely you can still see the shape of it in the new hair. I have no intention of messing with Jake. Jake is no Billy in Year 13.

'Is Jake going to punch him?' Will looks at me and, worse, so does Ashley. I've got no choice, not if I want to keep whatever respect they have for me.

'I'll talk to him.' If there is some kind of drug in the tea, I'm not feeling it now. My nerves jangle as I walk over to them. Not for what might happen now – the nurses don't tend to interfere, although I doubt they'll stand idly by in a fight – but for what might happen later. I never got my beating from Billy. Maybe I'll get it from Jake instead.

'Sorry, Jake,' I say, trying to sound casual. 'Louis wasn't thinking.' I look at the wild-haired boy between us. 'Go and wipe that egg of your face. You look like a dick.'

'He looks like he's been sucking a dick,' Jake says. His

table-mates snigger. They're gazing up at Jake like he's a god.

I force a smile.

'Yeah, I guess he does.' The worst thing is, now I look at Louis, Jake's right. A strand of not-quite-cooked-enough egg white is glued to Louis' chin.

Louis crumples a little, looking hurt, and wipes his mouth. 'It's egg,' he says.

'Just shut up and sit down, Louis,' I snarl at him, and Louis, shaken by my tone, drops his head and shuffles back to where Will and Ashley are waiting, finally aware that all the eyes in the room are on him. I look at Jake, not sure where to take this next. 'Like I said, sorry.' I turn and walk away.

'Fucking retards,' Jake says to my back.

Not retards, Jake, fucking Defectives. We're all Defectives here.

I don't say it, though. I just sit down and sip my tea and hope that's it done. Nobody speaks as we watch Dorm 7 gather up their plates – the youngest, Daniel, a chubby boy of about eleven, clears Jake's away – and then head out in a line behind their leader, each of them sneering as they go by, as if they think they could all take me on, not just Jake. I ignore them. Only when they've gone does Louis look up.

'You didn't have to agree with him.' He's smarting.

'Yes he did,' Ashley says. He's nibbling a piece of carefully buttered toast. 'Just because you're clever, you think you know everything. You don't. Sometimes you're plain stupid.' He sounds smug, no doubt still annoyed with Louis for taking the piss out of his praying last night.

'Let's just forget about it.' I want breakfast over. I wish I could be friends with Jake – not that I like him, but at least we're the same age. If we were friends I wouldn't feel as if I'm such a fucking *nanny* so much of the time.

'Maybe we'll get letters today,' Will says. 'They said our parents could write to us. They must have written by now. We've been here weeks. Maybe they'll even be able to visit.'

'Do you still want to learn to play chess?' Louis says. 'I'll teach you, if you like.'

Will smiles, the letters momentarily forgotten. I might be the boss of the dorm, but Will is most fascinated by Louis, and although their minds are miles apart, it's clear Louis likes Will, too. I wonder what Louis' life was like before this – all that brilliance but always several years younger than his classmates. No real friends. Always treated like a bit of a freak. I suspect Louis mentioned the chess on purpose to distract Will. There weren't going to be any letters, and definitely no visits. That had all been clear on my mother's face as she screamed my name when they put me in the van. This way no one has to know when it happens. It's *cleaner*.

For our families, at least.

More from Sarah Pinborough . . .

• • •

THE DEATH HOUSE

This is an exceptional, contemporary heart-breaking novel

Toby's life was perfectly normal . . . until it was unravelled by something as simple as a blood test.

Taken from his family, Toby now lives in the Death House, an out-of-time existence far from the modern world, where he, and the others who live there, are studied by Matron and her team of nurses. They're looking for any sign of sickness. Any sign of their charges changing. Any sign that it's time to take them to the sanatorium.

No one returns from the sanatorium.

Withdrawn from his house-mates, and living in his memories of the past, Toby spends his days fighting his fear and wondering how much time he has left. But then a new arrival in the house shatters the fragile peace, and everything changes.

Because everybody dies.
It's how you choose to live that counts.

• • •

'Moving and totally involving. I couldn't put it down'
Stephen King

'Shocking and gripping, albeit ultimately hopeful and utterly moving, and it's Sarah Pinborough's finest novel to date' *Sci-Fi Now*

'Compelling, heart breaking, yet sinister this novel is beautifully written and thought-provoking'
Telegraph and Argus

THE DOG-FACED GODS TRILOGY

A world in recession, a shadowy secret organisation, terrorist attacks . . . and one DI who must unravel it all

Recession has gripped the world, leaving it deep in debt to The Bank, a secretive company run by the world's wealthiest men. Pulling the strings in the background, they answer to no-one and do as they please.

Meanwhile the sinister Man of Flies, spreader of a lethal virus, has come to London and it's up to DI Cass Jones to catch him. But he is already burdened by visions of his dead brother, and a personal investigation to save his nephew . . . and has no idea he is heading into conflict with The Bank . . .

• • •

'Those who like their fantasy dark should grab Sarah Pinborough's *A Matter of Blood*' *The Times*

'Pinborough's fiction moves at a breakneck pace. Once you start you can't stop . . . she understands how people tick. I always trust the ride, because I know I'll wind up some place good' Sarah Lagan

'A pitch black thriller with a fierce emotional payload – gritty, authentic and compelling' Michael Marshall

'A gnarly, involving and atmospheric mystery that explores some very dark territory. Uncomfortable timely, exceptionally well-written' *SFX*

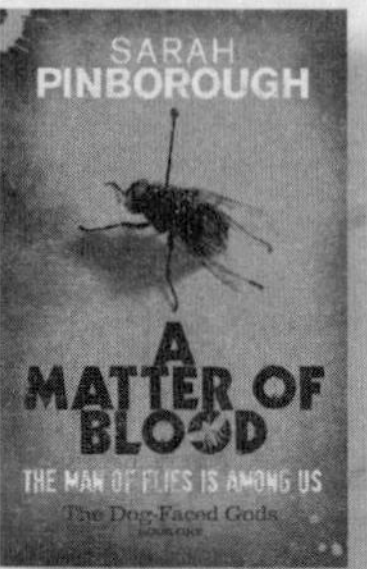

SARAH PINBOROUGH was born in 1972 in Buckinghamshire, and now lives just a few miles away after a childhood spent travelling all over the world (her father, now retired, was a diplomat). When she was eight she packed her trunk and left the Middle East for a ten-year stretch in boarding school. The memories provide her with much material for her horror and supernatural thrillers . . .

• • •

Find out more by following @SarahPinborough on Twitter.

ABOUT GOLLANCZ

Gollancz is the oldest SF publishing imprint in the world. Since being founded in 1927 Gollancz has continued to publish a focused selection of bestselling and award-winning authors. The front-list includes **Ben Aaronovitch**, **Joe Abercrombie**, **Charlaine Harris**, **Joanne Harris**, **Joe Hill**, **Alastair Reynolds**, **Patrick Rothfuss**, **Nalini Singh** and **Brandon Sanderson**.

As one of the largest Science Fiction and Fantasy imprints in the UK it is no surprise we have one of the most extensive backlists in the world. Find high quality SF on Gateway written by such authors as **Philip K. Dick**, **Ursula Le Guin**, **Connie Willis**, **Sir Arthur C. Clarke**, **Pat Cadigan**, **Michael Moorcock** and **George R.R. Martin**.

We also have a strand of publishing in translation, which includes French, Polish and Russian authors. Gollancz is home to more award-winning authors than any other imprint, with names including **Aliette de Bodard**, **M. John Harrison**, **Paul McAuley**, **Sarah Pinborough**, **Pierre Pevel**, **Justina Robson** and many more.

The SF Gateway

More than 3,000 classic, rare and previously out-of-print SF novels at your fingertips.

www.sfgateway.com

The Gollancz Blog

Bringing you news from our worlds to yours. Stories, interviews, articles and exclusive extracts just for you!

www.gollancz.co.uk

GOLLANCZ
LONDON